W9-BWI-364

Sandman, Sleep

Also by Herbert Lieberman

Novels

The Adventures of Dolphin Green
Crawlspace
The Eighth Square
Brilliant Kids
City of the Dead
The Climate of Hell
Nightcall from a Distant Time Zone
Nightbloom
The Green Train
Shadow Dancers

Plays

Matty and the Moron and Madonna
Tigers in Red Weather
Goodnight Grace Kelly Wherever You Are

Sandman, Sleep

Herbert Lieberman

A·THOMAS·DUNNE BOOK

St. Martin's Press
New York

SANDMAN, SLEEP. Copyright © 1993 by Herbert Lieberman. All rights reserved. Printed in the United States of America. No part of this book may be used or reproduced in any manner whatsoever without written permission except in the case of brief quotations embodied in critical articles or reviews. For information, address St. Martin's Press, 175 Fifth Avenue, New York, N.Y. 10010.

DESIGN BY DAWN NILES

Library of Congress Cataloging-in-Publication Data

Lieberman, Herbert H.
     Sandman, sleep / Herbert Lieberman.
          p.   cm.
     "A Thomas Dunne book."
     ISBN 0-312-08886-8
     1. Father and child—Fiction.   I. Title.
PS3562.I4S26   1993
813'.54—dc20   92-44024
                                     CIP

First Edition: April 1993
10 9 8 7 6 5 4 3 2 1

"Mr. Sandman, send me a dream . . ."

—"Mr. Sandman," words and music, Pat Ballard

A time in the
not-too-distant future

Prologue

Today Jones is to come. If not today, then tomorrow; if not then, by no later than the next day. As usual we won't see him. But as usual we'll know he's here. His presence will be felt as it always is, whether he's here or many miles distant. It makes little difference. As always, he's with us. Always and forever.

In preparation for his arrival, a great stir fills the house. My sisters and brothers are already aflutter, for when Jones is about, there's a certain air of something—a shock of excitement. Call it festive, call it scary. It's a bit of both, and while you can't exactly characterize these visits as pleasant, they're far from boring.

There'll be gifts and games, surprises. Oh yes, many surprises—Jones loves a good surprise.

All this is not to suggest that in the absence of Jones our lot here in the castle is gloomy. Quite the contrary. Our typical days are quite lively. The demanding discipline required to hone both mind and body goes on with unflagging zeal. We study and write, play music and exercise in the various gymnasia throughout the castle. Our curriculum hews closely to that of the standard medieval university system. Here, the quadrivium and trivium are a way of life. Mornings: arithmetic, music, geometry, astronomy; afternoons: grammar, rhetoric, logic.

Yet in the end, I confess, life is simply not as challenging as when Jones is about. He keeps you on edge; on your toes, so to speak. When he's gone, gone too are the banquets and balls, the masquerades and mummers' shows the great man so admires.

Jones's visits are annual. He comes once a year, for holidays, mostly. But sometimes for no apparent reason at all he'll simply drop in unannounced, and those are the most unsettling times—times of testing which implies uncertainty, a strong hint of radical change to come in one's life, not necessarily for the better.

Now is one of those unannounced times. No one has had time to adequately prepare. Even Signor Parelli has been taken by surprise. He scurries about, drilling us in our lessons, exhorting us to mastery of the calculus and our fifth Latin noun declensions. At such times he's remorseless, driven by the same scourge as we are, but I'm not certain that he knows it.

Letitia, my sister, practices the flute with a kind of fervent despair on the slim chance she may be asked to play something for Jones. Right now, at this very moment, she's practicing that small Purcell elegy on Matthew Locke—a perfectly simple piece a ninny could play. She goes at it with a frenzy that is near hieratic. And all because she believes that it will please Jones. What folly. But who am I to say? I've done more than my own share of trying to please in my time, all in the same futile hope. Fool, I say. No one will be spared.

With Jones's arrival possible at any moment, my brother Ogden finds it wise to be at work over his microscope. Just today I saw him squinting through the lens cap at some rare species of hymenoptera one of the gardeners brought him from the field. This passion of his to collect and classify things in dusty albums has grown into a form of madness. Periodically, Ogden takes his albums down from the shelves and thumbs through them with that air of solemn self-absorption that is supposed to suggest genius. He is at his most peaceful when skewering with a pin some squirming, pitiful little thing, shortly to be mounted with great care under glass, where it then takes its place amid rows and columns of desiccated insect husks. And all this because he's gotten it into his head that Jones has a keen respect for collecting and cataloguing. Poor fool.

But Ogden's no different from the rest of us—Sofi, Letitia, Cassie, Leander, Cornie—well, perhaps not Cornie, poor fellow—he's a different matter entirely. But the rest of us, all off in some dark, distant corner of the castle busily cultivating some trivial accomplishment on the vague, mostly misguided, notion that it will please Jones. And if you will please him, he'll do you no harm.

Fruitless. All fruitless. I used to think as my brothers and sisters do. Propitiate him and everything will be fine. Pursue some foolish, arcane, thoroughly useless body of knowledge— the charting of stars, the penning of bad verse, the solving of mind-numbing conundrums. Pretend you're having a wonderful time. I was more zealous than all of them, and better at pretending. But the years and repeated disappointment have brought me to my senses. I no longer try.

They think of me now, my brothers and sisters, as an apostate—fallen away. They shun me out of fear that association with me may harm their chances with Jones and thus greatly foreshorten their tenure here.

I understand this and hold nothing against them. If they can save their skins, more power to them. My quarrel's not with them. It's with Jones. He and I have a score to settle. One day my father and I shall finally meet up and have a go. I know I will lose the game but it shall do my heart good for having played it.

Part 1

Durance Vile

"And I the monarch of each race
Had power to kill, yet strange to tell
In quiet we had learned to dwell
My very chains and I grew friends,
So much a long communion tends
To make us what we are . . . even I
Regained my freedom with a sigh."

—George Gordon, Lord Byron, "Prisoner of Chillon"

1

"Feint. Parry."

"Feint. Parry."

"Lunge. Extend."

"Feint. Parry."

"Excellent. Splendid *froissement*. And back and back and—
Watch your line, Jonathan. Your heel's way out. See where it is?
And back and back. Extend. *Fleché* . . ."

"Asshole."

"Toady."

"Fart breath."

Grunts and hisses. Spatterings of saliva. Ogden and I were
on the strip. Slashing at each other as we had for the last hour or
so. We lunged and flailed up and down the fourteen-meter *piste*
upon which we carried out this daily idiocy. Jones says it teaches
not merely grace but self-confidence, poise and inner peace. If
so, not for me. I come away from the exercise twitching. Jumping
at my own shadow.

We wear uniforms consisting of white nankeen jackets and
trousers. Beneath my jacket I wear a sweatshirt, an inner plastron
called a *cuirrisade*, a cup jock that chafes my privates, a mask

with a visor that nearly suffocates me, and heavy shoes that make me feel I'm glued to the earth.

I was hot and miserable; Ogden no less so, the only difference being that he lives for all this ceremony and combat. I despise it. He plays the game as though his life depended upon it, just as he does everything else. With him, it's all keeping score.

"Palms up, Jonathan. Supination," Signor Parelli brayed. "Up, up. Blades up."

"Slimy puke."

"Fag nuts."

Ogden lunged, then *flechéd*, coming in hard over my pommel.

"Your mother was a camp follower," he snarled at me through his visor.

"Yours was the wife of three camel drivers."

"What's all the gabbing?" Signor Parelli fumed. "*Remise. Remise.*"

Ogden slashed forward again, coming like a pile driver. "Die, for Christ sake, pus-head."

"I try, but I can't," I muttered to myself. I stepped back and he hurtled past me, almost toppling in the act.

Enraged, he came roaring back, left leg cocked high, kicking like a pony. "I'll squash you for that."

"Worm," I spat at him through my visor.

"Quit the chatter," Parelli warned. "We're not here for small talk. Stay on the *piste*. Dammit, Jonathan. Can't you see where your feet are? Nice *coulé*, Ogden. Lovely *croise*. Good. Very good. *Balestra* and again. Lunge. Extend. Lunge. And back, and back and parry. . . ."

All the praise was, of course, for Ogden, the comely, who does all things well. Ogden's perfection. I'm a clod. Ogden deserves praise. He works hard. I'm a sloth. He's remorseless and unyielding. If he loses, he grows surly and falls into a funk. Your consummate competitor, he does whatever he's told. Leaps through all the hoops. Wags his tail whenever they raise the post another notch. Takes it all very seriously. I take nothing seriously, least of all myself. But that's my way. I cannot change and so I don't complain. I've dug my own grave here.

This morning we've forsaken our foils. In preparation for Jones's visit, we've gone instead to the épée. Of all three weapons—foil, saber and épée—Jones most admires the épée. It is by far the heaviest and most destructive. It has the stiffest blade and, when driven at top speed as in a *fleché*, can do horrendous damage.

Hence the plastron inside our triple-layered jackets to prevent wounds of the chest.

Ogden suddenly drove forward, howls and spit flying from beneath his visor.

"Perfect *balestra*." Parelli laughed his appreciation.

I parried with a high line *quarte*, then a counter *quarte*, deflecting him neatly with timed thrusts.

"Neat maneuver," I congratulated myself when Parelli's commendation as usual failed to come.

Momentarily we disengaged. Ogden was glaring, his teeth gleaming behind the bars of his visor. "What's the score?" he snarled at Parelli.

"Four-four. Sudden death."

Our blades clashed. Sparks showered down on us from the impact.

"*En garde*." Ogden slashed forward, the muffled thud of each blow ricocheting off the padded walls. Feinting, I side-stepped neatly. He fell short, gliding past but already lunging back into his *reprise*.

I heard the whimper of rage as he charged.

If he could have willed me dead then, he would have. This time his recovery was clumsy and I sensed him tiring. When he *flechéd* again, he nearly tripped. I grabbed his blade with my gloved hand. We locked arms and I felt the quiver of his straining muscles. Infuriated, he tried to yank his blade free. When he found he couldn't, he threw a leg behind mine and tried to trip me.

"Foul. Foul." Parelli pranced forward on his bandy, leotarded legs, more like a dance master than a fencing master. He tried to prise us apart but by that time Ogden and I were fused in fatal embrace.

I flung my blade to the side of the room. Tearing off my mask, I seized Ogden in a headlock, whirling him in circles about the room all the while he kicked and thrashed at me.

"Stop. Stop." Signor Parelli tried to wedge himself between us, tripped instead and went down on his back and shoulders.

Ogden started to kick at me. "Snot rag."

"Ass-licking sniveler," I shot back. He tried to knee my groin. I laughed out loud and rode him like a bucking horse.

"Let go, Jonathan," Parelli gasped, arms about my waist, trying to pry me loose.

"Get him off me." Ogden's panicky shriek rose from beneath my armpit. "Get him off, for God's sake. He's going to kill me."

"Let him go, Jonathan." Parelli's warm breath came at me on waves of cognac and garlic. "Damn you—let him go."

All three of us coiled together, grunting and writhing about the *salle*. In the scuffle, Ogden's mask flew off, clattering to the floor. It went bumping off into a corner. Next thing I knew his teeth had sunk into my hand. I roared with pain. Again, his leg shot behind mine. This time I went over, slamming my back down hard on the *piste*. I felt all the air rush out of me. Stars flashed in my eyes as he ground a heel into my chest, then slapped the blade of his épée hard against my thigh, making a sharp splattering sound.

"You're dead, scumbag," he shrieked triumphantly. "*La belle. La belle.* I win. Five to four. I win." His slashing blade made wooshing circles in the air as he stomped a maniacal little dance all about the *salle*.

2

". . . and so comets are described as the lawless members of the solar system. Comets obey no celestial regulations. They come and go as they please. A comet moving from its perihelion distance to the sun and earth may disappear for periods ranging from a few years up to many thousands of years. That's why the reappearance of the comet we study today, Zabrini-Mechner, is of such moment."

"Oh, spit!" Cassie slouched in her seat. "I, Cassandra Jones, do will thee dead." She beamed her serpent's gaze at Madam Lobkova. She couldn't care less about Zabrini-Mechner and its impending visit, but there she was, trapped like all the rest, in the stuffy domed room that served as an observatory at the top of one of the castle's six drum towers.

"Cassandra?"

She looked up, startled. "Ma'am?"

"Zabrini-Mechner?" Madam Lobkova looked miffed. "Its periodicity. You did hear the question, didn't you?"

Squinting thoughtfully, Cassie played for time. "That would be three hundred years, ma'am. First observed in 2 A.D. by the

Phoenicians. It came in 302 A.D., 602, 902, 1202, 1502, 1802, 2102. . . ."

"That will do." Madam Lobkova, ready to move on to red stars, cut her short. It was time to peer through the great reflector poking skyward out of the retractable dome of the tower.

The reflector at Fraze was one of the largest telescopes in the world. The main mirror, cut from quartz, was nearly two hundred inches in diameter. The mirror had been designed and cut in Switzerland to Jones's specifications.

He's coming today, Cassie thought. At any time he could be here. Possibly even timing his arrival to coincide with Zabrini-Mechner. What a cunning touch. That would be him, to a tee, she thought viciously. Pure Jones.

"Hydra—twenty-four million light years. Pegasus—twenty-four million light years. Bootes—two hundred and forty million . . ." Letitia's voice quavered as she did her presentation. Her voice always quavered when it came to presentations. She sweated heavily during classes and sometimes a bad smell came from her. Taking a gulp of air to steady herself, she went on listing distances of galaxy clusters.

Cassie's eyes pursued Madam Lobkova's brass loop earrings. She grew drowsy watching them swing back and forth, dying sunlight glinting from the fleshy lobes. With the turban she almost always wore because her hair was thinning, Lobkova looked more like a palm reader in a storefront parlor than a teacher of astronomy and music.

"The event is quite rare." Madam Lobkova's voice droned on through the mote-filled air of late afternoon. "Zabrini-Mechner is scheduled to arrive between 8:05 and 9:00 P.M. It will remain visible for only forty minutes, then fly off again."

I can feel Jones moving toward us through the sky, Cassie thought. She wished the lesson were over now and that she and Leander could sneak off to the old tower at the north end, where they could hide together forever in one of those ancient musty bins. She'd be content to die there if only Leander were there too, by her side.

She thought to herself—Spit! What is Zabrini-Mechner to me, or me to Zabrini-Mechner that I should give it a toss? Damned if I'll come back here after supper and look for it.

3

In a bare, uncarpeted room with high mullioned windows, both sisters lay side by side. Each on a leather-padded medical examination table, they lay under blankets to keep warm. Both were attached to hemodialysis machines by means of a pair of thin yellow tubes. One ran from a leg artery, the other through an adjacent vein. Despite the fact that both sisters had perfectly healthy kidneys, they had to be dialyzed twice a month. At the Institute, bimonthly hemodialysis was part of the regimen, standard operating procedure for all of Jones's offspring.

Dressed in a short silk chemise, Sofi had the rumpled, languorous look of someone just waking from sleep. She stretched, curling her toes sensuously beneath the covers. "Don't you love the feel of a man's hands on you, Lettie?" She turned to grin wickedly at her sister.

Letitia made an odd face, a pass at disinterest that failed.

"How is it best for you?"

"Best?"

"You know. What sort of person and all . . ."

Letitia sighed, resigning herself to interrogation. "Well, naturally, someone whose hands are good and who's patient."

15

Her legs pedaled nervously beneath the covers. "Must we keep discussing this?"

Turning to gaze at her sister, Sofi grew very quiet. The teasing, mocking glint had left her eyes. The two kidney machines gurgled softly, dials oscillating left to right in the gathering shadows. After a while she spoke: "Sometimes, I do wonder what it would be like with someone new."

"New?"

"Perhaps with a stranger you'd enjoy it more," Sofi prodded gently.

Letitia considered a moment, then clamped her mouth shut, trying to smother her embarrassment. At last she could bear it no longer. "Why do you say things like that, Sofi? Is it supposed to shock me? Is it your idea of a joke? You know you wouldn't dream of carrying on like that."

"Like what?"

"With a stranger."

Sofi winked at her older sister. She arched her back, then poked her brightly painted toes out from beneath the covers.

"Why wouldn't I? What would happen?" Sofi half rose from the table, the long graceful arc of her torso straining beneath the silk chemise. "Nothing's happened to you, has it?" She examined her outstretched toes again, deliberately avoiding her sister's astonished stare.

"What exactly is that supposed to mean?" Letitia shot back.

"All I meant, dear, is that I hope Uncle Toby doesn't find out about you and you know who." Hearing the quick gasp beside her, she turned and winked coyly at her sister. "Don't worry, Lettie. My lips are sealed."

"How did you know?"

"I'd have to be blind not to see it. And I'm not blind. Just don't be so damned obvious about it. Or that will be the end of your dear friend and probably you, too."

Letitia's finger fidgeted at the border of the blanket.

The lilt of Sofi's voice had taken on a hard edge. "Nothing's going to happen. Not if you're clever. And, as I say, I don't know a thing."

A low stricken wail rose from somewhere deep within Letitia. "You don't think Uncle Toby . . . ."

Sofi pondered a moment, then shot an arch glance her sister's way. "Leave Uncle Toby to me. You just make sure the naughty Umberto behaves himself—"

Letitia's handwringing stopped in midair. "What do you mean, behaves himself?"

"Now come, Lettie. Let's be adult. Parelli's no Boy Scout. He's tried one or two things with me, I don't mind telling you. I sent him packing."

Letitia kept her eyes on the ceiling, as though not listening.

"And he's played fast and loose with some of the upstairs maids as well," Sofi chattered on heartlessly. "One in particular— Felicia, Alicia, some such thing. Her husband almost strangled him. Uncle Toby had to get rid of the man."

Letitia swallowed audibly.

"Grow up, Lettie. Parelli's a big boy. Surely you don't think you're the first."

"Of course not— No, I never . . ."

"Nor will you be the last," Sofi rattled on, enjoying the glamorous role of woman of the world. "Chambermaids are one thing, however," she chattered on. "You're quite another. You're family. One of Jones's own. With you, he's playing with fire."

Her final word sounded like the clap of doom to Letitia. "Oh, God. Oh, dear God." A burst of sobbing followed.

Her grieving had caught the attention of a white-smocked technician passing by. He poked his head in.

"Get out," Sofi railed at him. "I'll let you know when you're needed."

Speechless, the poor man scurried off as Letitia's sobbing rose in volume.

"Oh, for God's sake, Lettie," Sofi snapped. "Stop it. Get hold of yourself. I can't stand it when you whine."

"Oh, God. Oh my God. And Jones due here any min—" Letitia yawned unaccountably, in mid-sentence. "I'm so sleepy, Sofi. So cold."

"Don't worry, dear. It's only the medication starting to take hold."

4

"Greystoke, Nigel: Appointed for a study of an analysis of herpes zoster genes in yeast selection systems. Ninety-two thousand dollars.

"Geha, Raif Salim: Appointed for studies in molecular immunology. Three hundred twenty-six thousand and five hundred dollars.

"Van der Rohe, Wilhelm Fritz: Appointed for studies in chemical vapor deposition. Three hundred twelve thousand and four hundred dollars. Vapor comes high these days, wouldn't you say?"

"Keep going." Toby Jones wagged a hand impatiently. Signor Parelli caught the drift of his mood and quickly resumed entering the names of newly appointed Fellows into the Foundation ledgers. Tabulating the sums awarded each project, he read the names of the scholars aloud.

Umberto Parelli's position at Fraze was something of an enigma. While he bore the title of Administrative Assistant to the Director and was a full rabbi or instructor at the Institute, his authority in the castle was sharply curtailed. By birth a Corsican, he didn't admit to that. Through a variety of ploys, he liked to put it about that he descended from a long line of Tuscan counts with extensive holdings in the hillsides around Siena.

He was what the fashionable journals usually describe as "dashing." Tall, whip-thin, with dark unparted hair swept straight back from the forehead, he had the slightly oily look of a film idol in the days of silent cinema. To heighten that impression, he affected jodhpurs and Russian cavalry boots and had a fatal weakness for foulards knotted raffishly about the neck.

No one was quite certain how he first came to the Institute. One story has it that Jones came across him working as a bar waiter on the waterfront in Ajaccio and was immediately struck with the young man. True, he had a classical education, but from a somewhat minor university. And, of course, the tale of a cultivated young nobleman fallen upon hard times appealed greatly to Jones, whose philanthropy had far more to do with whim than good common sense.

For Parelli the career as tutor to the Jones progeny was a coup. He'd never lived so well and scarcely ever dreamed he would. There were disadvantages, to be sure. For one thing, the prospect of spending the rest of one's working life under the heavy thumb of Mr. Tobias Jones could not have been a happy one. For another, the money was good but there was nothing to spend it on. For a social creature like Parelli, the isolation at Fraze was unbearable. Then, too, there was a scarcity of available women, the most attractive by far being Mr. Jones's daughters, with whom he was expressly forbidden all but pedagogical contact. Were he to push his luck in that direction, he could be back in his waiter's apron on the quay at Ajaccio overnight. So he behaved himself (for the most part) with admirable restraint, but took this exclusion as an affront. Yet, regardless of how much it rankled, he kept silent. And since the other women at Fraze, chiefly household staff, were for the most part baggy sexless drudges, Signor Parelli went about with a great deal of pent-up steam. It made for a very short fuse.

"Well," Toby fumed. "What's the damage?"

Signor Parelli's manicured fingers danced over the keys of a desktop computer, sending a blur of green numerals squirting across the console screen before him. When they came to rest, he adjusted his eyeglasses and read aloud: "Thirty-four million, six hundred and twelve thousand."

"Thirty-four mill . . ." Toby Jones's jaw dropped. "And that's just the Foundation. We have yet to do the Institute grants. And then there are the universities and hospitals, not to mention the out-and-out freeloaders."

By then he was verging on apoplexy. He waved more crumpled paper in the air. "No doubt you've seen these requisitions for new laboratory equipment?"

Parelli nodded warily.

"Two and a half million, at the very least. Absolutely criminal. They must burn equipment over there. Fabian's no better than a common thief. Knows he can fleece us and no one there to say a word."

Toby pushed his chair from the desk, rose and raked a hand through his thatch of salt-and-pepper hair. "Spite work. Sheer venom. That's what I call it. All this squandering, so that by the time he gets ready to kick off, the larder will be bare, and all these scavenger scholars, these big-league charity panhandlers with their fleets of chauffeur-driven limos will have trundled off with all the boodle." Toby hefted a solid onyx paperweight, carved in the shape of a baboon flashing fearsome teeth. For a moment, Parelli was certain he was about to fling it. But he didn't. Instead, he merely held it aloft, quivering, poised between gravity and thwarted desire. "When he dies," Toby went on with an ominous quiet, "and that's only a matter of time, I intend to leave here, and I don't intend to go as a pauper."

Parelli watched the numerals afloat on the indigo screen and wondered where in that troubled equation he himself figured. But he was too frightened to ask. Instead he said: "When is he due?"

"Within the next twenty-four hours."

"Has he made his selection yet?"

"No, but the metabolic tests back from Geneva are fairly conclusive. Fabian has graded our first choice superior. Class A. Preferred. Even up to and including gene strand twenty-four."

For the first time that afternoon their eyes met in silent understanding.

"And what about the Bessarabian?" Parelli inquired.

"She gets nothing."

"She'll scream like a stuck pig."

"Leave her to me."

"I'd like nothing better." Parelli gave a look of extreme

20

distaste, adjusted his eyeglasses on the bridge of his beakish nose and proceeded to read aloud once more from the Fellowship roster: "Kubota, Shigeko: Appointed for studies in Malay shamanism. Five hundred and three thousand dollars . . ."

Mr. Tobias Jones stared straight ahead, scarcely hearing.

5

I do not worry.
I do not regret.
I do not envy.
I do not waste my time or the time of others.
I do not covet earthly goods.
I do not seek admiration.
I do not seek personal advantage over others.
I honor my Father.
I honor my Uncle and my Masters.
I honor my brothers and sisters.
I honor the past.
I relish the present.
The future is forever.

Nine voices trailed off in a ragged listless drone. Some had raced ahead to completion while others lagged behind. No two people finished at the same time.

It was the dinner hour. We gathered in the great oblong dining hall around a long refectory table scuffed and scored by centuries of wear. The last of the sun slanting through the stained lancet windows washed the stone floors in hues of red and cerulean.

Every meal at Fraze, without exception, began with this recitation, Jones's version of grace, a kind of secular catechism composed by the Founder and committed to memory by his many offspring.

The ritual completed, servants passed around plates and we fell upon our dinners. The menus always varied but the food was unsatisfyingly similar—vegetables and fruit, one slice of un-salted whole-grain bread, plain tea with no sugar. For dessert there was a gelatinous substance, a different color each night, sprinkled with a scurf of dry sweetish crumbs over the top. Total caloric intake, 600 calories. Never more, never less.

This regimen was intended to keep the body temperature low—91 degrees Fahrenheit. Several drugs were taken in con-junction to ensure that result. That day we'd also had our bimonthly hemodialysis and our transfusions of TRX5-SODS— sodium oxide dismutase, which leaves the taste of scallions in your mouth for days after. In the morning one of Dr. Fabian's assistants would conduct the quarterly physical examinations. The low body temperature made us drowsy and cold and mostly disagreeable.

Cornie (my brother Cornelius) sat smiling blankly, staring into the depths of his empty saucer. In the flickering half-light of two crystal girandoles, the red port wine birthmark spattered across the side of his face seemed more disfiguring than ever. Spatulate in shape, it ran from the right temple to a place directly beneath the right cheek, where it ended in a series of inverted jagged peaks. It marked the place where at the moment of birth, Cornie's capillaries had burst. Despite his otherwise strikingly handsome features, most people found him grotesque.

Taller in stature than the rest of us, he was also the oldest. His age, however, like all of ours, was unknown and impossible to guess. There was something aloof and simian about him. His walk was a mixture of shambles and lurches. Enormously powerful, he could crack two-by-fours with the edge of his palm and carry crates of several hundred pounds on his shoulders. Yet his touch upon you was light as a cat's paw.

Though he's the eldest of our clan, in mental age he's little more than five or six. Uncle Toby says he's simpleminded. "Tetched" is Cassie's blunt but not intentionally unkind descrip-tion.

23

Cornie makes a low cooing sound like a pigeon when he eats. We're under strict instruction to take no notice of him as he forks his food, or to call attention to the mess he makes of his clothing and the place at the table around where he sits.

Because of his disability Cornie is excused from tutorials and confrontation seminars. Nor is he required to perform in the awful masque and mummers shows that pass for diversion around here. Because he eats fast , wolfing his food down, he is permitted to leave the table before the rest of us.

Tonight, most of the talk at table is about Jones's imminent arrival. My sisters and brothers are clearly uneasy.

6

Directly after dinner Uncle Toby clapped his hands and announced that there'd be a magic show that evening.

Once a year, usually at holidays and always when Jones is in residence, Toby would treat us to one of his gala magic shows. Magic is a passion of his, and once you've seen him perform, you'd understand why. For one thing, he's a superb magician and illusionist. Watching him, you feel yourself in the presence of some powerful force of mystery, something quite otherworldly, while at the same time nagged by an uneasy sense of fakery. Viewing these performances, I always find my eye seeking some hint, some clue by which to unmask the deception. I know it's there, yet I confess I've never once been able to uncover it.

At nine o'clock sharp we found ourselves seated in the ballroom—a wide space crammed with bridge chairs, walls lined with statuary, caryatids prized from ancient temples, suits of armor worn by crusaders.

A small proscenium stage had been set up for the occasion and the only illumination came from a single powerful klieg light mounted on a tripod at the rear of the room. Equipped with a number of gels, it cast powerful beams of multicolored lights onto the action taking place on stage. One of the kitchen staff operated the light.

Organ music was piped in softly from somewhere behind a makeshift arras suspended behind the stage. It lent to the proceedings a faintly sepulchral air, as though you were in some mortuary establishment, attending a memorial service.

For starters, Uncle Toby ran through a number of the standard repertoire, things we'd all seen dozens of times but, done with such skill, they all seemed fresh and new. As magic, they were distinctly lightweight, designed primarily as a warm-up. He executed a number of clever things with eggs and coins, bottles and crepe paper. At one point, brightly colored silk ribands wafting in midair were severed with scissors. Like decapitated serpents they wriggled through the klieg beams, drifting slowly downward to the floor, where they reassembled themselves before your eyes.

Then, attired in a swami's turban, a lapis lazuli the size of a quail's egg implanted in its folds, Uncle Toby shinnied up a slowly swaying rope winding its way to the lofty ceiling. When he reached the top, he slid back down, collapsed into a somersault and landed deftly on both feet. We burst into applause.

The juggling sequence was breathtaking. Starting simply with apples and oranges, it quickly escalated into Indian clubs climaxed by lethally sharp Malaysian kris. The coup de grace of the evening occurred when the klieg light was switched off and we were plunged into total darkness. The organ wheezed a mournful dirge and I suddenly became aware of a blast of cold air at the back of my neck, as though something had rushed past my ear. Suddenly the room was alit with twelve flickering candles in a gold candelabrum mounted on a lectern on the stage.

Uncle Toby began by spinning one of the lighted candles between his fingers like a twirling baton. You'd think that the motion itself would have been enough to extinguish the candle but, no, it glowed even more brightly as he increased its speed. To this he added one, then two, then three candles, all of which he tossed into the air, moving them so rapidly that shortly they became trailing comets inscribing a flashing calligraphy across the darkened ceiling.

The object, of course, was to get all twelve candles flying in the air simultaneously. But not simply that. That would be too easy. It was rather to get them all airborne at one time so that they created a dazzling light show and, of course, without extinguishing a single candle.

By the time Uncle Toby had six in midair, it was doubtful he could launch another. Yet he did, and with even greater ease than the candle that had preceded it.

We gasped and applauded and stamped our feet. Across from me Letitia and Sofi sat cross-legged on large pillows on the floor, their skirts hiked up about their thighs, oblivious to how provocative they could be. Leander and Cassie sat on bridge chairs beside me, their mouths open in pure childish wonder. Madam Lobkova sat off to the side, a rapt, vaguely annoyed expression in her eyes. Head tilted back, she watched the circle of tapers whirl dizzily overhead, spinning and looping above us like a large wheel. What kept them aloft? I wondered. What kept them from falling?

At one point during the performance I glanced up, startled to find Ogden's dark, unforgiving gaze fastened on me. Still smarting from the morning's combat, he was planning his revenge. I had no idea what form it would take, but I had little doubt it would come. In matters of revenge, brother Ogden can be relied upon.

By then Toby had launched ten lighted candles above the ballroom. They soared around us in a loop of fire. They rose and dipped and hung upon the air like some large bird. The organ swelled to a crescendo. Uncle Toby reached for the twelfth and final candle and flung it carelessly upward, where it took its place with the others. They wheeled above us in perfect design, like some grand and distant constellation.

There were gasps and cheers as the candles spun above our heads. With a series of strange twisting movements of his body, Toby played them like a lariat. At times he brought the candles down so close you could feel the heat of them brush past your ears.

But that was by no means the end of the show. With some dazzling bit of legerdemain, the candles returned to Uncle Toby like a flock of circling starlings that all in a single motion alight in one place. As each effortlessly took its place in the candelabrum, Toby extinguished it with a quick puff from his lips.

The light went up and we'd scarcely recovered our composure when it dimmed once more. From behind the arras the rattle of a snare drum sounded. Toby brought his palms together with a single explosive clap. The organ skirled. From off to the side a

27

grating noise was heard. It was like the sound of stone being dragged over stone. Shortly, four burly porters appeared. They shuffled forward onto the stage, rolling between them a long rectangular box. On closer inspection it turned out to be a coffin or, more accurately, a sarcophagus.

Fashioned out of richly veined Carrara, it rattled along on tiny wheels. It was clearly very old, anodyzed with a greenish yellow patina. The lid, however, was a chased bronze out of which the supine figure of a man had been struck. From where I sat I had the impression of a tall, lank shape. The legs and rib cage gave an impression of emaciation. The face was that of a sleeping man with closed eyes. He wore a neatly trimmed mustache and goatee. The sunken cheeks and cavernous eyes conveyed a quality of saintlike repose. The overall sense I had was that of a holy man whose entire life had been given over to prayer and self-denial.

From the moment the sarcophagus rattled to a halt and was lifted off of its wheels onto a pair of sawhorses mounted on the stage, a pall descended over the room. The boisterous playfulness of moments before gave way to something rather somber and foreboding.

Uncle Toby's costume for the performance—a black dinner jacket, white gloves, homburg, and a boutonniere at his lapel— had given him the gay appearance of a kind of 1920s boulevardier; now, in the reddish glare of the overhead klieg that same costume seemed suddenly lurid. In some way I cannot quite express, I felt light-headed, strangely out of breath. I had a strong desire to leave. To get out quickly. And yet I couldn't bring myself to move.

Cornie made a series of low, cooing sounds and I could feel Cassie stiffen beside me. Madam Lobkova's breathing quickened. The organ music had stopped and now there was only an unnerving silence.

Uncle Toby stood off to the side, the fingers of his right hand trembling at his temple, his eyes closed as though he were deep in concentration.

No sooner had the porters left the stage when the legs of the sawhorses appeared to tremble. In the next moment, the sarcophagus, standing unattended, appeared to vibrate, then to rise slowly. It rose several inches, then nearly a foot, and seemed to float freely between the sawhorses.

On the other side of me Leander cringed. Signor Parelli,

28

standing off to the side, stared transfixed at the coffin. Following the line of his gaze, I was startled to see its bronze lid move.

Ogden leaned forward, the rapt, sullen gaze in his eyes narrowed to begrudging curiosity.

The air of expectancy hovering above the room was almost palpable. Our eyes fastened on Uncle Toby, waiting to see what he would do next. But he did nothing.

My eyes returned to the bronze figure on the coffin lid. For a fleeting moment I was certain I'd seen the rib cage rise and fall as though the figure were breathing.

There was nothing visible between those two sawhorses, nothing that could lift a box of that size and weight from below. I looked in vain for any trace of something—piano wire, perhaps— by which the casket might be raised up from the ceiling. There was nothing. When I looked across at Uncle Toby, he was still standing off to the side. Leaning slightly off-center, head up, eyes closed, lips sealed, he appeared to be asleep on his feet.

What followed is hard to describe and remains unclear to me to this day. The box, which had hung perfectly still in midair for several minutes, swayed slightly, then started to descend. When it reached a point roughly an inch above the crossbars of the sawhorses, it stopped momentarily, then resumed its descent. In the next moment the sawhorse legs creaked audibly and ap- peared to sag beneath the settling weight. There was a scraping sound. The casket seemed to shift and, for an awful moment, it teetered. I remember Madam Lobkova starting from her chair and Parelli almost lunging toward it.

But that was unnecessary. The casket then settled squarely between the sawhorses. What followed was a grating sound. The lid, which was heavy, jiggled visibly, then started to rise.

It rose two, three inches, then four, stopped at a point from which a hand, attached to a thin bony wrist raising the lid from within, became clearly visible.

From somewhere behind me, I heard a gasp.

Leander sat with his face turned away from the frightening scene. I knew it was all just a trick, yet my scalp tingled.

In the next moment something—a small dark shape— appeared to spring from the box and jerk back and forth wildly. Several of us jumped. Someone laughed as the grotesque little Pulcinello puppet nodded obscenely on its stick.

Suddenly Uncle Toby slumped. Legs buckling beneath him,

29

he crumpled in a heap on the floor. Signor Parelli rushed forward, crouching above him, trying to revive him.

As the lid of the sarcophagus slammed shut with a heavy thud, the light came back up. Again the snare drum rattled.

"Jones," Madam Lobkova whispered beneath her breath. "He's here."

7

Later that night Cassie came to my bed. She usually did when frightened or upset. It was always the same: the timid rattle of the doorknob, and the door creaking open. The frail silhouette framed against the dim light of the hallway stood there barefoot, wraithlike, shawled in a blanket, waiting to be invited in.

This time it was on the pretense that her room was cold. Often she complained that Letitia's snoring next door woke her, or that the cries of some animal outside in the forest kept her from falling asleep. Under no circumstances would she admit to fear.

"Can I stay with you tonight, Johnnie? My room is . . ."

"Cold. I know. Sure. Hop in."

I lifted the edge of the quilt and she slipped in beside me, snuggling under my arm with a grateful little sigh. My arm fell across her narrow bladelike shoulders like a protective wing.

"Go to sleep," I said, turning on my side and boring into my pillow. She lay still a while, then sought some safer, more clinging position against my side. Shortly, her small moist palms slipped 'round my waist and hugged me to her chest.

"So that's it." I sighed and turned over, raising her nightshirt up beneath her stripling arms. Cassie's breasts are little girl's breasts—shallow, hard cones with tiny pink caps that remind me of the peppermints Madam Lobkova used to bring us before bedtime when we were children. "Sweet dreams," Madam used to say as she popped one into your mouth.

I kissed my little sister's breasts and when I took them into my mouth, she moaned slightly.

We rubbed against each other, precisely the way Uncle Toby and Madam Lobkova had always instructed us to from the onset of puberty—deemed by Jones to be the optimum age for humans to commence their sexual lives. Cohabit only with closest family—those whom you know to be free of disease. Feel joy, Uncle Toby would preach. Not lust. Lust is demeaning.

The hot liquid itch of release came with a rush. Cassie moaned softly, then flung herself off me. "He's here now, isn't he?" Cassie whispered. "You saw tonight. It's my turn this time. I know it."

"Don't be silly."

"It could be. Even you said so."

"Well, it won't be. You're too young and that's that."

"What about that other girl? That Serena? She was my age."

"She was older. At least three years older. Anyway, that was a mistake. It should never have happened."

"But it did. It did. *Poof*, she was gone."

She grew sullen and quiet, crushing herself harder up against me, as though she intended to push through and past me. "What if it is my time?"

"Then you'll go. And that will be that."

She made a high keening sound and I clapped my hand over her mouth.

"Shut up, for God's sake. You'll have the whole house up."

"What happens to me then?" Her teeth chattered and she'd started to shiver.

I rolled to the far side of the bed, ignoring her.

"What happens?"

"You'll take up Jones's ministry and travel with him. You'll be assigned to one of the other residences."

She eyed me warily. "Which one? Where?"

"Once I heard Uncle Toby speak of some place in the Antarctic. Polar meadows and ice floes. Glaciers as far as the eye can see. Penguins and sea lions. You'd like that, wouldn't you,

Cassie? And the house is an ice castle. Turrets and moats and towers. Just like Ivanhoe."

The thought of that appeared to calm her and she fell back sleepily onto the pillows, tension draining from her body as exhaustion overtook her.

I rubbed her back in a slow circular motion, lulling her to sleep.

Her head rolled sleepily to the side. "Be careful, Jonathan," she mumbled into her pillow. "They're out to get you."

"Who says so?"

"Ogden says . . ."

"Bugger Ogden. Who cares what Ogden says?"

"You will if . . ."

"If what?"

She folded her arms, clamped her eyes shut and pursed her lips. "If they turn you over to the Woodsmen," she shot back, then buried her face in the pillow.

Startled at the thought, the next instant I was laughing. It was a harsh, cheerless laugh, even as the awful reality of the possibility came over me. They could well do that. Chuck me out. Turn me over to the Woodsmen. I've given them provocation enough. I'm certainly no testimonial for the "great experiment." Why I do what I do, I can't say. It would be so easy to do like the others. Be docile and grateful. Jump through the hoops. But I can't. Sometimes I can hear myself saying, "Fool. Comply. Comply." But I can't.

"I hope they do." I glared down at Cassie, but she was fast asleep, her thumb stuck squarely in the center of her pink cupid lips. A tiny bubble of saliva pulsed there. "I hope they do chuck me out to the Woodsmen," I muttered into the clammy shadows.

It's all Jones's fault. All of this. I blame it on him. Just for once I'd like to stand in the company of my father—with none of the masks or concealment or the curtain of dark he insists upon during these awful audiences, and tell him what I think of him. If I might just speak with him, free of all constraints. Look into his eyes. Just once. Imagine, his actually having to set eyes on his son. Perhaps I'm unsightly. No doubt I am. But he's my father. Who knows, I might even resemble him. Would that please or infuriate him? I'd be satisfied just to talk with him once. Perhaps I might then, at last, find some peace.

Cassie stirred, and half rising mumbled something in her sleep.

"What?" I said, not certain I'd heard her right. But in the next instant she'd flopped back down onto her pillow and was fast asleep.

Letitia lay sleepless beneath the rumpled sheets, her fingers fretting ceaselessly at their silk borders. Beside her she could feel the smooth naked flanks of Sofi radiating healthy animal heat. She slept deeply. Sleep came easily to Sofi as did most things. Nothing came easily to Letitia.

Lying on her side, she watched the steep slope of her sister's breasts rise and fall in a beam of moonlight. It made her conscious of the flat, shapeless dugs lying cold against her own chest.

It seemed unfair that nothing, not even that simple physical endowment, could have worked out well for her. Whereas with Sofi, it was always a windfall. Sofi need never lift a finger and still all things would come to her. Letitia, regardless of how hard she strove, barely hobbled through.

A shaft of pale, silvery moonlight fell across Sofi's face, momentarily illuminating the profile and heightening its sense of deep repose. It was that mindless serenity, that perfect animal contentment that so infuriated Letitia. How could Sofi sleep, knowing that Jones was right there, in the castle? That the next few days would be nightmarish. That fates hung in the balance. The mere thought of it made Letitia's palms tingle. Yet Sofi still slept. Hadn't she seen the hand, the lid of the coffin rising, the gray scrawny wrist visible just beneath it? And that hideous little doll.

The great man's idea of a prank, no doubt. So macabre. So perverse. So typical. Jonathan as much as said it, too. Right then, at that very moment, Jones was there, concealed somewhere in an unidentified room, its whereabouts unknown to all except one or, perhaps, two entrusted cohorts, and just waiting for the morning.

Like her brothers and sisters, Letitia had never seen her father. Her only contact with him had been in darkened rooms, behind a screen under strictly controlled conditions, where at best you might see only a shadowy silhouette. Peculiar behavior for a father, but Jones was not just any father. And it was his way. Such was his power. Who was to question it?

As a child she liked to go to bed imagining him. She used to picture herself finally meeting him, face to face, and yet the

34

prospect of such an encounter made her physically ill. Just as she was now, always that same frightened little child. Her palms tingling. Always expecting chastisement.

Outside the door she heard a soft, whooshing sound, like a slippered foot, gliding up the uncarpeted hallway. When the footsteps paused on the other side of the door, her heart slugged in her chest and she could barely breathe. The doorknob jiggled, made an impatient rattling noise, then turned.

In the next moment, a square of light flooded the room. It swept across the ceiling and down the opposite wall, then vanished as the door swung closed. In that brief instant, someone had crossed the threshold and entered the room. Across from where she lay, she could barely make out a robed figure standing against the door. She heard its breathing. It appeared to be peering through the darkness at the two occupants of the bed.

There was a scuffing noise as the figure took several quick steps forward into the room. Then it was standing beside the bed, the sweet, malty smell of recently quaffed whiskey rising in warm waves all about it.

"Lettie."

She swallowed deeply. "Yes, Uncle Toby."

He gave a sharp tug to the comforter. "Move over, I'm coming in."

Obediently, she moved aside. Toby Jones shed his robe and tossed it behind him at a nearby chair, then slipped into bed between his two nieces.

In a cupboard off the main kitchen, sprawled atop a butcher block, a butler and a scullery maid coupled heatedly. Trousers down about his ankles, hips scissored between her thick muscled thighs, the two moved in unison as pieces of crockery suspended from little hooks above them rattled gently against each other in the close, soap-scented shadows.

35

Part 2

Jones

Whenever a god dies, look for him to rise in another place.

—Anonymous

8

It's time now to tell about Jones. There's much to say and one can't be certain where best to begin. Certainly I don't know all of it, though I keep trying to find out. In any case, Jones is our father. I have said as much, but the truth is we know little of the man. All we know is what Uncle Toby and Madam Lobkova have chosen to tell us. Their occasional divulgences are grudging and, even then, carefully edited.

Jones is said to be an old man but still vigorous. He leads an active and productive life in the outside world. A man of considerable celebrity, he is much written about. Still, few people actually know him, much less have met him. Most of those who claim an acquaintance are liars.

If you're one of those given to thumbing almanacs or directories to the titled and famous, you've no doubt come across the name with lengthy entries following it. Depending upon the source you're using, he may be found under the general headings of Humanitarian, Philanthropist, Educator, Financier, Philosopher, Inventor, Scientist, and so forth. He is all of these things.

The truth is most people's lives have been, in one way or another, affected by Jones, yet few know anything about the man or in what way he has touched them. What is put out in the reference works is mostly bogus, planted by Jones's agents, who know well their master's passion for obfuscation and secrecy. Certainly we, his own children, bespeak volumes of just how unforthcoming he can be with the facts of his personal biography.

We are told that he is shy to the point of reclusiveness. Few people have ever seen him and there are only two or three photographs of the man known to be authentic. These are kept in bank vaults, in acetate envelopes the seals of which are not to be broken for a period of five hundred and fifty-five years following his death.

A Japanese photographer of somewhat dubious credentials claims to have snapshots of Jones changing planes at a small air terminal in some undeveloped tropic land. He's offered to sell them to any magazine or syndicate for an exorbitant sum. No one has taken up the offer. For one thing, the quality of the photography is poor, and for another, Jones is not known to travel commercial airliners—at least not under his own name. Therefore, improbable as it seems, even we his own offspring have little idea what the man looks like.

The best and only clue we have to Jones's physical appearance is that he's said to strongly resemble his younger brother, our Uncle Toby. This we have from Madam Lobkova. While as a clue this is admittedly scant, nonetheless, it can be taken as authoritative. Lobkova is one of the few of that crowd who can be trusted.

Regarding Jones, here's what is known in broadest outline. The second child of notably unremarkable parents; as near as can be determined, they operated a dry-cleaning establishment in the city of Baltimore—a place, I believe, that lies somewhere on the mainland—far to the south of here.

He had very little formal schooling. In his early teens he demonstrated a modest talent for invention, turning the basement of his parents' home into a kind of laboratory-workshop—a room littered with wires and dry cell batteries, magnetos, the salvaged innards of broken clocks and old Ford motorcars. His greatest pleasure was to dismantle motors plucked from the wrecks of rusty furnaces and discarded old household appliances, then reassemble them into something entirely new. Out of all of this seeming rubbish and an insatiable curiosity came such clever innovations as the battery-operated can opener, the plastic zip-lock food storer, an electric staple gun and a waterproof instant-drying mucilage for the back of postage stamps, to name but a few. Even today, years after its introduction, the government continues to pay Jones millions in the form of royalties for the exclusive privilege of using his mucilage on the back of their postage stamps. For Jones, this is mere pocket money.

His estate still controls the patents for all these clever devices which yielded him the first millions upon which his fortune was built. Only a candy manufacturer on the mainland, a man who concocted a synthetic chocolate bar made from wood fiber and artificial flavorings, to be sold for a quarter, is said to be worth more. But by far, the lion's share of Jones's fortune was made in steel, railroads, shipping and petrochemicals.

It was the sort of success people dream about. A purely American success in that it was so vast and grew out of such inauspicious beginnings. Of course there were the critics and detractors. With that sort of success, this is virtually a given. But if just half of what is attributed to him is true . . . his accomplishments are monumental and carry with them the most enormous implications for the future of mankind. It goes straight to the heart of the question of how humans shall live on this planet, if indeed they are to continue to live here at all.

Shortly after the so-called Good War, which Jones spent in Washington (he served as chief of a highly secret unit of Naval Intelligence, detailed specifically for the job of decrypting message intercepts coming out of the Reich's Chancellory in Berlin and beamed at German embassies as far-flung as Tokyo, Buenos Aires and Melbourne), he underwent his momentous "sea change."

All of this came about before he was thirty. Then something happened—a transfiguring episode. I gather it was something painful. An accident of some sort, something to do with a fire. Quite awful and disfiguring. We don't know the exact details. In any event, shortly after, he sold everything to devote himself entirely to scientific research of some unspecified nature, and philanthropy—the two dominant passions of Jones's life.

With his formal withdrawal from the world of commerce, he began to read philosophy and religion. Shortly, trusts and endowments became his bywords. University chairs, wings of large museums and hospitals were founded in his name. Astronomical sums were channeled into foundations which worked as a kind of talent agency to locate people possessing the sort of

41

special scientific aptitudes Jones was seeking at the moment. Then, leaving the management of his financial affairs to his brother, Toby, he pitched himself headlong into his own work. He referred to it as "the System."

The System is an ongoing life study embodying the evolution of Jones's philosophical development. Its principle teachings are propounded in *De Juventute*, his seminal work on the subject. *De Juventute* is the bible of the System, and also contains the core blueprint for Jones's theory of child rearing.

A cardinal principle of the System is that infants are to be separated from their natural parents at birth and reared by a cadre of highly and specially trained professionals, called masters or rabbis. As a result, my brothers and sisters and I have never seen our father face to face. Nor do we know the identity of our various mothers. No two of us have had the same mother. Instead, we have a surrogate mother, Madam Lobkova. She is Jones's handpicked mother to us all—the *magna-mater*, his only concession to the notion that some element of the feminine principle, no matter how scant, may be desirable during the crucial formative years of child rearing.

One of the highlights of Jones's annual visits to the castle is the one-on-one interview he conducts alone with each of his children. These interviews are generally of about an hour's duration. There is no specific agenda. The floor is thrown open and one is invited to say what one pleases. While we are perfectly free to voice our dissatisfaction on a wide variety of subjects relating to household, academic, domestic, emotional, medical and even interpersonal problems, one must take care never to introduce matters that may entail in any way questions concerning our past or future. For instance, Where did we come from? Who was our mother? When, if ever, shall we meet her? Where do we go from here?

Jones considers these annual talks inviolate. In Chapter 8 of *De Juventute*, they are described as "encounters" and he will brook no interruption once they've begun. At the start of the talk a phosphorescent green light above the desk goes on and does not go off until the last grain of sand in an illuminated hourglass drops to the bottom cup.

Surrounding these talks is a strained air of geniality, commingled with an undercurrent of dread—a dread born of the knowledge that, contingent upon what you say, the whole course of your life might change within a fleeting instant.

42

One further detail must be added. These yearly audiences are conducted in a small, bare room. The curtains are drawn so that the area is plunged in a kind of gray, subaqueous light. The only visible feature of the interviewer is the dark outline of his silhouette to mark where he is seated behind a nearly opaque screen—this to conform with the requirements of the System that demand strict parental estrangement.

After five or six days of a typical visit, one can sense Jones beginning to withdraw. His characteristic enthusiasm for revels and pranks starts to pall and thus begins the process of his disengagement from all familial contact. You know then that his days among us are numbered. Without prior announcement, he'll take his leave in the early morning before dawn, when all of the castle still lies asleep. In your waking dreams you turn and hear the concussive beat of helicopter blades pummeling the air. As the copter circles and dips low over the six drum towers, you can feel the vibrations of it inside your stomach. Shortly, the noise subsides and fades into the distance and Jones is gone for another year.

At that point you take it for granted that the matter you raised during your audience is to all intents and purposes closed.

Thus you learn that in matters that count, that pertain directly to one's well-being, even one's very survival, you have absolutely nothing to say.

One additional point. At the conclusion of these annual visits, shortly after Jones's departure, one of my brothers or sisters will quietly vanish from the castle. That person's sudden disappearance is never noted or remarked upon. In several weeks, letters will reach us from distant shores, bubbling with enthusiasm, telling of wonders, of the marvels to be seen on the outside abroad with Jones. In time, the letters will cease and we know, though it is not discussed, we shall never see that brother or sister again.

9

And so to Fraze.

The house we call home is not, strictly speaking, a house. It lies in the center of a forest on an island about a hundred miles from civilization. I can't be more specific other than to say that it's situated at nearly the most northerly point of the North American continent. Its exact whereabouts have always been kept strictly secret.

According to those who know such things, the house is actually a chateau. In terms of sheer size, however, it comes closer to a castle with spires and towers and battlements. I, for one, prefer to think of it as a castle. Like my sisters and brothers, I've never actually been outside the castle and therefore have never seen it. Whatever sense I have of the exterior structure has been extrapolated from my knowledge of the interior.

The castle is virtually inaccessible—no nearby rivers or waterways by which a boat could approach; a landing strip on the castle's wide sweeping lawn just large enough for a helicopter; no roads in or out except the footpaths through the forest now largely effaced by time, and virtually impassable in all but the most clement weather. Some say the Indians made these

44

paths, their moccasined feet having crisscrossed and grooved the forest floor over the course of centuries. But there has been no trace of Indians here for years. They, like so much else in the place, have simply vanished. Only the Woodsmen remain. But that's another story and I'll get to them shortly.

The grounds about the castle are large and, except for the surrounding lawn, uncultivated—so as to discourage approach. You cannot see beyond the ring of trees on the perimeter of the property. It wouldn't matter if you could, since nothing lies beyond them but more trees—miles and miles of deep, untracked and inhospitable forest. Uncle Toby and Madam Lobkova have warned us about the forest. Moreover, they've actually been out there, to the outside—the only members of the household who've ventured beyond the castle walls. Signor Parelli, who has never been there, likes to describe the forest as a fearful place.

The castle is unimaginably large—hundreds of rooms, salons and parlors, bedrooms and sitting rooms, sculleries and storage areas. Separate wings spread in every which direction. There are three floors in all. The first is composed of service areas—kitchens and work spaces; the second is living quarters for the immediate family; the top story is where the servants and professional staff are domiciled. Up there, too, are the laboratories in which the scientific program of the Humanus Institute—Jones's research center—is pursued.

At the very bottom, the sublevel, there are the cellars. These are an intricate, mazelike network of caverns. The part that is finished houses the maintenance machinery for the castle—furnaces, water pumps, generators, ducts and air conditioners, as well as a huge wine cellar. The rest of it is unfinished, deliberately so as to discourage any dangerous trafficking there. Several servants (up to no good, insists Uncle Toby) have disappeared in those mazes, never to be heard from again.

We—my brothers and sisters and I—are strictly confined to the second story of the castle. Under no circumstances are we to visit the lower or upper stories. To be caught doing so is to become immediately subject to expulsion or some otherwise fearful but unspecified chastisement.

The castle dates back to twelfth-century France in the time of Henry II and yet it has sat on this land, five thousand miles away from its native soil, for the better part of ten decades.

While traveling in the Loire shortly after the war, Jones came across it. Known as the Chateau de Fraze in Eure-de-Loire, it had

45

everything that would appeal to his fanciful sensibility. It had steeples with oriel windows. There were six drum towers, a portcullis and battlements upon which one could walk and see the surrounding countryside for miles. There was even a dungeon.

A fine keel-shaped roof built of chestnut and slate shingle surmounts the whole. There are several extraordinary examples of rose windows with radiating tracery. When the sun reflects off them at a certain time of day, they give the impression of lace. The masonry blocks of the building are of tufa hewn from the red soil of Anjou. In the dying sunlight of a summer afternoon, a rose hue shimmers from the walls, suffusing the sky above us with an unearthly pink glow.

From the moment Jones laid eyes on this fairy-tale construction, he determined he would have it. But there was a problem. First, he had to convince the French government that it was to their benefit to permit an architectural treasure, a crown jewel of the national birthright, to be purchased by a foreigner.

Jones started by offering an astronomical sum of money, far in excess of anything the government could ever hope to realize from the sale of a chateau that had fallen into spectacular disrepair. Sensing that it had a large fish on the line, the government reacted precisely as Jones knew it would. It termed his offer derisory, carried on as though it had been insulted, and broke off all negotiations.

Jones's game had never been haggling. He wanted what he wanted when he wanted it. And so he simply made an offer that made a mockery of all the government's lofty pretensions. National pride and dedication to the preservation of historical birthrights quickly crumbled in the face of what is generally called the profit motive.

The deal was made. Papers were signed and monies exchanged. Jones was immediately besieged by historians and archivists, architects and various craftsmen all eager to provide him with ambitious plans for upgrading and modernizing. But Jones hadn't bargained a fortune for an upgraded twelfth-century chateau in which Plantagenet ghosts were rumored to still prowl only to transform it into some modular glass nightmare. He wanted the original just as it was, but on his own land. He hadn't told the government that. When they finally heard, they screamed foul, but by then they'd already cashed the check.

So, the Chateau de Fraze was dismantled and carried stone

by stone across the Atlantic. Packed in crates and stored in the holds of nearly a hundred freighters, it required whole argosies to bear the kingdom across the sea, where it would then be reassembled at staggering cost far up in the frozen fastnesses of the northern wilderness.

For all of its beauty, the castle has peculiarities. First and foremost is the fact that it has few doors to the outside. This was in keeping with Jones's wish that all natural means of entrance and egress be limited to the strictly necessary.

There are points of entry to be sure, portals through which supplies may be taken and wastes carried off. Such points of egress are controlled and secret, their exact whereabouts unknown. Only Jones and Uncle Toby have in their possession up-to-date charts which pinpoint the exact sites of these exits and entryways.

This may strike the casual observer as odd, but it conforms perfectly with Jones's principle of "isolation" as propounded in the System. He specifically designed his living space as a complete and self-contained world so as to obviate ever having to leave it.

While there are no visible doors in the castle, there are innumerable windows—hundreds of them. The windows are made of unshatterable glass and cannot be opened or closed. We may gaze out over 360 degrees to the sweeping vistas of sky and forest. You can see straight out to the horizon where great flotillas of fleecy clouds droop motionless like daubs of paint. As if in a dream, they give the impression of having hung in precisely that fashion for thousands of years.

Just as we have few doors through which to come and go, we have no calendars. This is because Jones hates time and refuses to be tyrannized by it.

But by far the oddest of Fraze's eccentricities is its total absence of mirrors. Jones abhors mirrors. In the third chapter of *Juventute*, he maintains that mirrors are an evil that encourages self-preoccupation and self-love.

By banishing mirrors, indeed all reflective surfaces, Jones asserts that the castle's occupants will never be tempted to dwell morbidly upon themselves. Instead, they will come naturally to look outward and seek ways in which they might serve the good of others.

There have been times, usually at dusk, when the lights go on in the castle, that I've caught a vague reflection of someone staring back at me from the window glass. Under the best of circumstances, all I'm able to see there is a blurry outline—an eyeless face beneath a thatch of dark, spiky hair. Hardly a portrait, I'd say. More an indistinct oval in which the facial features are a series of small smudges afloat on a sea of gray—not unlike a charcoal portrait that has been much erased.

I once asked my sister Sofi to tell me what I look like. She never answered the question. Instead, she averted her eyes and laughed, by which I inferred that my appearance was either laughable or, possibly, so unfortunate that she couldn't bring herself to remark upon it.

I've never asked the question of anyone since. Nor do I go past the windows at dusk. Once the sun falls, I avoid all windows like the plague.

Thus, without mirrors or calendars, all we have to measure the passage of time is the picture we have of each other in the present, contrasted with the memory of one another we carry from the past. Accordingly, there is little sense of place or time or self here. No one knows their birth date, nor is much fuss made over the matter. As to my own age, I think I am fifteen or perhaps twenty-seven, or possibly one hundred and nine.

So it is that our lives go on from day to day. By no means unpleasant, most would characterize our situation as idyllic. There are, of course, the daily squabbles with one's siblings; the long bouts of ennui. When classes are over for the day and books and games and music will not suffice, you have all you can do to keep from bashing your head against the long expanses of unshatterable glass.

After dark, when all the lights in the castle are extinguished, each of us retires to a separate room. Then come the noises, the restless tread of footsteps in the hallway, the cry of an infant from somewhere above, and someone lulling it to sleep with a sad song. I know neither the infant nor the singer. I couldn't say if the singer was a woman or a man, or whether the song being sung is in English or some foreign tongue.

Shortly comes the giddy laughter and scuffling sounds. Doors opening and closing, the stifled noise of urgent couplings. Finally a cough, the flush of a toilet down the corridor and at last silence as the castle settles down for the night.

In *Juventute*, Jones teaches that the cardinal sin, the sin of all sins, is fear. He abhors fear and has gone to great lengths to excise it from our lives. Indeed, most, if not all, of those things that ordinary people fear in this life—sickness, hunger, destitution—have been eradicated at Fraze. But still there is one thing left for us to fear—the one thing that even Jones has not been able to banish from our lives. That is the Woodsmen, and I've left them for next.

10

We have often seen the Woodsmen, the aboriginal settlers of this land. They come out of the forest and stand at the edge of the property, seldom approaching the house. Standing perfectly still just before the trees, looking up at us, it is almost impossible to know they're there unless the fact is pointed out to you. Undoubtedly, they are a principal reason we're forbidden to leave the house. In the recent past, several of the gardeners working out of doors, surprised by the sudden appearance of the Woodsmen, have been carried off and never heard from again.

Mostly we see them in the morning just after sunrise, or at dusk when they're hunting. During the daytime they retire to their camps far back in the woods. You glimpse them from the windows, a slight flashing movement at the edge of the forest. Small of stature, the tallest of them seldom exceeds forty inches. These elfish figures are stocky and powerfully built, with heads overlarge in proportion to the rest of their bodies.

Broad-shouldered, pigeon-chested fellows with short heavy arms and stumpy legs, they convey a sense of great strength. They do not walk so much as pitch and roll. Their typical attire is a waist-length jacket of goatskin with a brightly colored jerkin worn beneath, and knickerlike trousers, also of goatskin. In the forest, they're shod in a sort of puttee boot laced up to the knee with thongs and into which the bottom of the knickers has been tucked. At home in their encampment, they favor buskins.

They are almost always seen with a clay pipe planted squarely in the center of their mouths and something resembling a kind of sharp-pointed crushed Tyrolean worn atop their heads. Typically, they appear in groups of five or six, seldom more, and never singly. Groups exceeding that number are unusual and always imply trouble—sickness, some incursion of their land or some grievance they seek to redress—as a rule not peacefully. At such times the household is placed on full alert. No one is permitted out except Uncle Toby, whose task it is to negotiate a settlement.

Around their pot bellies the Woodsmen wear wide garrison belts from which dangle an ax or an adz—sometimes both. These tools are fashioned by hand out of stout branches cut into manageable lengths onto which highly polished ground stones have been attached by means of the same goatskin thongs used to lace their boots. Due to the Woodsmen's shortness of stature, oftentimes the handles of these tools bump and scrape along the ground. It is important to note that while these tools may seem crude and of Stone Age quality, the "goat people," as they're also called, wield them with astonishing skill.

At the safe vantage point from which we view them, the impression given by the Woodsmen is that of something elfin and jolly, totally benign. That's an impression, however, you'd do well to eschew. Looking more closely at them, there's something decidedly disturbing in the silent, watchful manner with which they stare up at us from the forest's edge—as though weighing some course of action regarding us here in the castle and merely awaiting the propitious moment to put their plan into play.

Uncle Toby claims that the Woodsmen have evolved a language all their own—one he insists bears no recognizable resemblance to any of the standard systems of Indo-European tongues. The vocabulary comprises a series of shrill, yawping sounds that can be made to convey different meanings by merely inflecting the tonal range at the moment of utterance. By this means, they are able to expand a few basic sounds into a language of fairly extensive vocabulary.

Of all of us here in the castle, only Madam Lobkova has

achieved sufficient command of the Woodsmen's language to understand and be understood. For some reason, unknown even to Uncle Toby, the Woodsmen regard her with special awe. Perhaps it is the fact that she has unlocked the mystery of their tongue which makes them both respect and fear her.

In the winter and late fall when the leaves are down, we can see the Woodsmen's fires at night, far back in the woods. One particularly bitter winter, sickness had struck their camp and they were unable to go about their normal rounds. We heard that several of them had died. They sent a message up to the house and Uncle Toby and Madam Lobkova, along with a small well-armed force of household militia, went back to their camp with medicine and supplies.

Toby had been back there once or twice before with Jones, both as young men when they'd first embarked on the "auspicious" little project that was eventually to evolve into the Institute. What they saw before them was scarcely imaginable. They found the Woodsmen living in a warren of pens and crude hatches amid squalling infants and innumerable goats, all living in a state of unimaginable squalor. Thriving and numerous, they were living at the level of some sort of pre-Cambrian life, atavisms rutting about at the dawn of time. Human and animal waste littered the dirt floors. Mounds of offal and the bones of animals half consumed lay moldering all about, sending up a stench that hovered like a palpable haze above the encampment. Of that visit there were aspects of which both Uncle Toby and Wanda decline to speak, even today, apparently so unsettling were they.

The Woodsmen's diet is composed chiefly of the milk and flesh of goats, supplemented with a variety of roots and rhizomes harvested from the forest floor. In addition, they eat apples and berries, mushrooms and wild artichokes all growing free and in profusion above the earth. They are much given to an alcoholic beverage brewed from a mash of barley and wild rice which they call Jum. This is sometimes combined with a ciderlike substance called Og, distilled from apples but far darker and harsher than the innocuous version of it we drink.

On those late autumn nights just after the solstice, when the Woodsmen are full of their Jum, they're apt to become raucous and overly playful. You can hear them hooting and baying back in the trees at their camp. It is on those nights that we double the guard and take every precaution to secure the castle.

At present the Woodsmen's number is upwards of several hundred. For purely security reasons, Uncle Toby conducts an informal census at the close of each year. The figure is, at best, a rough estimate and, of necessity, measured from afar. But if it is anywhere close and if the Woodsmen are as fierce as we have come to believe, then it's a puzzle to me why they've never attempted to seize the castle. Certainly, they outnumber us by nearly six to one. If they truly wished to overrun us, they could do so with little effort. Although we have guns, no one here is much skilled in their use. Jones abhors violence. He has always discouraged firearms on moral grounds, while not actually forbidding their presence on the premises. Though very much a visionary and a believer in the perfectability of man, Jones is by no means naive. Several weapons are always kept on the battlements in clear sight of the Woodsmen. Sometimes they are discharged harmlessly into the air just so the unpredictable little folk know we are not at their mercy.

At dusk I look toward the windows to see if the Woodsmen have gathered out there at the forest's edge. We have been repeatedly instructed that if for any reason whatever they were to come out of the forest and approach the house with menacing intent, we are to go directly to the cellar and conceal ourselves in a special chamber built there by Jones. It is a kind of crypt, I'm told, with reinforced steel doors, adequately ventilated and amply provisioned with a larder of canned foods and fresh water readily at hand from an underground spring. Safe inside, we'd be unassailable and could sustain a siege of up to three weeks. If the siege were to last beyond that, each of us is to be provided with a gray-blue capsule. Uncle Toby says it's a tranquilizer but I believe it is cyanide.

Part 3

Let the Games Begin

The prince had provided all the appliances of pleasure. There were buffoons, there were improvisatori, there were ballet dancers, there were musicians, there was Beauty, there was wine. All these and security were within. Without was the "Red Death."

—Edgar Allan Poe, *The Masque of the Red Death*

11

In the days following there were games and revels and musicales; there were matches and feats of skill, demonstrations of wit enough to make one sick to one's stomach; my brothers and sisters all behaving like performing seals. The stench of fear was sickening. All of this amid the constant talk of Jones—where he was, where he might be, what surprises he might have in store. And then, of course, there was the question of the personal audiences. When would they start? Who would be summoned first? Was the order in which one was called significant?

One night Uncle Toby had a casino set up in one of the banquet halls. There were roulette wheels and baccarat tables and dealers of bezique. We were permitted to wager lavish sums, but with a kind of paper scrip—nonredeemable house money. Uncle Toby got up in tails and a top hat, wore rouged cheeks and painted lips and spun a huge Catherine wheel. We laughed a great deal, but I don't recall that it was much fun.

The following night we gave a staged reading of *The Jew of Malta*, and the night after, we put on our tired old *Iolanthe*, one of Jones's favorites. Still, we didn't know if Jones was present at any of these events. No one ever told us, of course, and that, too, was unnerving. There was little doubt, however, that he was somewhere in the castle.

The following day the audiences began. It was Sofi first. I was there when she was summoned. We were all there, finishing breakfast, when Signor Parelli appeared.

We all knew what he was there for. It was the way he entered, standing in the doorway, gleaming 'round at us with his icy smile. His eyes swept past the rest of us and settled on Sofi. "Ah, so you're here."

"Where else would I be?" Sofi shot back, her smile matching his for sheer brass.

You had to admire Sofi. Whatever other negative traits she might possess, cravenness isn't one of them.

"Come along," Parelli said, staring her up and down, checking her appearance. "He'll see you now."

As she rose to follow him out, you thought you were watching a decathlon runner striding forward to take her place in the winner's circle. She was that self-assured.

Emerging from her meeting with Jones an hour later, she was incandescent, a sign we all took to be auspicious. Jones was in one of his benevolent phases—at least for the moment.

Letitia fixed her sister with a queasy stare. "Well—what did he say?"

"Obviously nothing too dire." Ogden smirked. "Not from the looks of her."

Sofi spun lightly on her feet as though she were dancing, then, squealing with pleasure, let herself fall back onto the divan.

"How was it?" I asked. "What did he want to know?"

"What he told me, you'll know soon enough."

Her devilish green eyes mocked me. The answer was pure Sofi. She knew how to turn simple questions into taunting enigmas so as to let your imagination wreak havoc with your peace of mind. Before I could say something equally nasty, she turned her back to me and addressed Letitia. "Jones would like to see you next."

The sickeningly grateful lapdog awe faded from Letitia's face. Her chin sank to her chest. Rising to her feet, she tottered momentarily. A soft whisper of footsteps sounded just outside the door where someone, not yet visible, had arrived to escort her to the place where Jones awaited her.

58

12

That week the audiences persisted with heartless irregularity. Interviews were set up, only to be canceled for undisclosed reasons, then rescheduled, then canceled again. It had all the earmarks of spite and deliberate perversity.

Throughout this period Uncle Toby and Signor Parelli were mostly invisible. They were in residence all the time but usually behind closed doors, where meetings of a secret nature were being conducted.

Nor did they appear at dinner. They ate, presumably with Jones, in some remote part of the castle, their discussions continuing without pause far into the night.

On those infrequent occasions when they did appear, it was only for the briefest periods. They were, it seemed, always between one meeting or just on their way to another. They seldom addressed us and their faces wore a look of anxious preoccupation.

Within the next few days the revels and games ceased. An uneasy silence had fallen over the house; anxiety hung like a suffocating haze above the living quarters where we came and went in a frazzled state.

Then, on the seventh day of Jones's visit, Ogden was called. Visibly shaken, he gave the impression of a pot about to boil over, its lid dancing madly on the rim. He expressed it in the only way he knew. He swaggered and grew physical with everyone around him.

His meeting with Jones, when at last it came, endured for an unprecedented hour and three-quarters—far longer than any of the other audiences heretofore. When at last he emerged from the ordeal, he appeared shaken, his face the color of parchment.

"How did it go?" I asked.

He looked around edgily. "It went fine. We had lots to cover. Talked about his travels. Then we discussed the future. Talked about me. My plans. Said he'd been up to see my specimens. The frittalaries and the hymenoptera. Very impressed, he said. Wanted me to continue with my studies, but work harder. He . . ." His voice trailed off and despite the effort he was making, some of the buoyancy began to sag. "Listen." His eyes gleamed and his hand clutched my sleeve. "He said something about a problem."

"A problem?"

"With one of my brothers or sisters. He didn't specify which."

"What sort of problem?"

"He said one of you is going about saying things about me."

"Things?"

"Something about one of you passing information about me to Parelli. Damaging information. I swear, Jonathan . . . if you've been . . ."

"Don't be ridiculous. What have I to say to Parelli? He wouldn't believe me, anyway."

The thought of my poor relations with Parelli appeared to pacify him. When I made a move to go, he called after me. "You'd better not be lying to me, Johnnie."

13

Dear Leander,

Today we visited the great open air bazaar in the market-
place at Dar Es Salaam. Tomorrow we go to Zanzibar to tour the
leprosarium facility at Kisha. This should be excellent preparation for our three-day overland drive into the interior to view for
ourselves the tragic devastation inflicted on the Bantu from the
recent six-month drought. We are told to prepare for the worst.
Jones says we must be strong and compassionate in the face of
such suffering. I can only hope that I'm up to the job—and what
a job it is—a once hearty, thriving people reduced to stick
figures, mere skin and bones, schistosomiasis, trichina, malnour-
ished children with the swollen bellies of Kwashacant, infants
rummaging in the baked earth for animal droppings out of which
they hope to pluck a kernel of corn. It is too heartbreaking to
contemplate.

Every time I think of such things and view such suffering, I
thank my lucky stars that I grew up with a father like Jones, who
taught us the value of meaningful work and gave purpose to our
existence. I only hope that some day all of you may feel the

61

exhilaration I feel today, having been fortunate enough to have earned my place in the Service.

With deepest love to all of my brothers and sisters at the Institute.

Your brother, Caradoc

Leander looked up at me, his reedy voice trailing off in the chill, motionless air. The hand holding the letter fell to his side. "Wonderful, isn't it? Great for old Caradoc. I hope the same happens for me," he said, his voice fervent with emotion.

"Don't hope too hard. You may get your wish."

Anger flashed in his eye, then quickly boiled off. "You don't believe in anything, do you, Johnnie?"

"I can't see that it matters one way or the other."

"It matters to me."

"In that case, I'd forget about Caradoc. There is no Caradoc. When he left here, he ceased to be."

Leander flushed, then flapped the letter up at me. "If there is no Caradoc, what do you call this?"

I looked down at the letter and smiled. What a strange thrill of pleasure I'd felt, tearing my poor brother's hopes to tatters. I have a trunk full of such letters. They're commonplace around here. They arrive regularly from all four corners of the globe, from brothers and sisters who've passed through here, now out in the Service, ecstatic with their work and its many rewards.

But there's a funny thing about these letters. They all seem very much of one tone and all appear to share a common vocabulary (certain words and phrasings, repeated with striking frequency). And they all look as if they'd been drafted on one typewriter, all characters having the identical typeface, although we're told they're the work of dozens of different people, writing from literally all over the world.

"He asked about you."

"About me? Why would he ask about me?"

"How should I know? I'm just telling you he asked."

"What did he want to know?"

"All kinds of things."

"Like what?"

"How should I know?" Cassie sat cross-legged on the bed,

picking at a scab on her knee. "Why keep asking me all these questions?"

"Because you were there. You spent close to an hour with him."

"And Leander." She sat bolt upright. "He wanted to know about Leander. If that old fool touches Leander . . ."

"He won't take him, if that's what you're thinking." I pulled her hand from the scab, which had started to ooze blood.

"I don't think I could live another minute if they took Leander—" She stopped short, suddenly recalling something. "He told me how much he loved me. Spit! I wanted to laugh out loud."

She bounced up and began to stalk about the room. "I don't care if he is my father. I hate him." Her voice rose louder. "I really do hate him. That smarmy talk and that old-man smell. Mothballs and dirty dentures. I could smell it from behind the screen."

"Cassie . . ."

"Oh, quit your whining, Jonathan. You're always whining about things and you never do anything about them."

"What do you expect me to do?"

"Kill him. Kill him for me. Or for yourself. Or, for pity's sake, just shut up."

Her rage had spent itself, only to lapse into dejection. Once again cross-legged on the bed, she began digging at the scab on her knee. Several times I pushed her hand away from it. But each time it snapped right back, gouging and scraping away. "If you keep picking like that, you'll make yourself bleed," I said again.

When I looked down at her I was startled. Something had transformed her. There was no longer anything left of that pink, scrubbed, beaming little girl I knew so well. What I saw there now was more than just a little frightening.

63

14

Jones had by then been in residence nine days and gotten through four interviews. The only two remaining to be done were Leander and myself. Leander had been scheduled three times and canceled three times. By then he was near collapse. He hadn't slept in days. He had little appetite, and what he ate, he could barely keep down.

Still uncalled, I felt as shaken as Leander. But I was older and more practiced at masking fear. In those last awful days I skulked about, all bluster and pose, daring my masters to take action against me and terrified they would.

Then came the tenth day and Leander was summoned. When Parelli entered the game room, Leander jumped to his feet, anticipating that fateful moment for so long that when it finally came, his response was practically automatic.

Before he left he went about the room, pumping hands as though certain he wouldn't be returning. It all had something of the sadness of a farewell about it. He kissed Cassie on the cheek and it seemed to me she was close to tears. When he came to me he stopped and looked up into my face with that look of sweet, unshakable trust. The effect of it made me cringe. I could feel myself shrivel before him. And that smile, full of genuine goodness, never once faltered.

In the next moment, he turned, and I watched the slight, wraithlike figure move off stiffly down the hall. Toes pointed slightly inward, he half stumbled, half walked, the effort at lighthearted bravery taking its toll. I stood watching from behind, the figure receding into the distance, growing ever smaller. Then the resounding thump of a heavy wooden door closing echoed from the end of the corridor, and he was gone.

I didn't hear a word of it until hours later. Anticipating the worst, I'd expected to hear it secondhand from one of the others. But, as it turned out, the outcome of the audience came directly from Leander. He refused to give details of what had transpired between Jones and himself, but the quiet, almost radiant, smile seemed to suggest that what had gone on was far from what had been expected.

"It's the first time I felt I knew him. He was there and I was really with him. It didn't matter that I couldn't see him. You know what I mean, Johnnie? We talked. The two of us," Leander reeled on giddily. "Just as I'm talking to you now. Just as easy as that."

His eyes glowed with a feverish radiance. Sweat had soaked through his shirt. His voice choked with the satisfaction and pride he felt at having had a genuine talk with his father. His face, rapt in wonder, had an almost beatific expression and when he put his arm about me in a brief, shy hug, he felt hot. I could feel the dampness of his shirt and the slight wiry frame still trembling from his recent encounter.

The more he spoke, the more a heavy weight of desolation descended on me. So far everyone who'd been called appeared to have gotten through unscathed. After ten days in which Jones had been in residence at Fraze, I remained the only one who had yet to be summoned. And thought I still felt I would be called, nevertheless, I was to be the last, and that, in itself, struck me as ominous.

I waited now somewhat more anxiously for my turn with Jones. Days passed and still I waited, full of that sense of onrushing catastrophe. I could feel it in my chest like a fist closing over my heart. I waited to hear Signor Parelli's quick nervous tread clicking down the hall. When that failed to come, I waited for Madam Lobkova, or to be summoned by Uncle Toby

65

himself. I waited for some word, some hint, anything. Nothing came, and for all of my barely concealed contempt for the System, its elaborate customs and rites, its grand airs of elitism, which I despised, I desperately wanted to be called to an audience. I waited and waited. The silence was deafening.

Instead of a summons from Jones, we received a request for a command performance of *The Tales of Hoffmann*, one of Jones's favorites. He couldn't bear to go off for another year without seeing it.

Playing Olympia, the robot mechanical doll, Letitia whirled with fierce despair about the small, makeshift stage. Knowledge that Jones himself might at that very moment be present in the darkened hall, witnessing her performance, drove her to near frenzy.

Sofi, with her sultry pre-Raphaelite looks and decent enough mezzo-soprano, sang Nicklausse. Tarted up to a fare-thee-well in rouge and mascara, she wore a gown of puce organza with a décolletage approaching indecency.

Ogden, of course, was Spalanzani. He played the part with the same air of grand disdain he brought to everyday life.

Off to the side in a tiny orchestra pit, Cassie pounded an out-of-tune piano, her short legs pedaling madly to keep up. Swaying and dipping above her, Madam Lobkova fiddled her violin, pleats of ruddy flesh sagging like wattles beneath her bare arms.

I, of course, was the odious Coppelius. In all of these ghastly home-grown productions, whenever someone grotesque is required, I am your man—your Coppelius, your Lindorf, your Dapertutto, your Dr. Miracle, your Rigoletto. I am your Iago, your humpbacked Quasimodo, your wen-nosed troll of the night, your toadish unctuous sycophant. Something to be hissed and jeered at during the Punch and Judy, and wildly cheered when a rude paddle slaps my face.

I was dressed all in black, just as you would imagine the evil Coppelius. Black shirt, black stovepipe trousers, topped off with a black skullcap worn at a jaunty angle, giving me a slightly rakish look. Skulking and dipping and bumping about the stage on my crutch, I looked like a battered old storm-tossed crow with an injured wing. But it was poor Leander who bore the brunt of our inept little theatrical. Attired in a slouch hat and a badly frayed set of Uncle Toby's black tie and tails, Leander played Hoffmann. Onstage virtually every minute, he had to sing the lion's share of that awful score. Together, he and Letitia slid and tripped and swanned about like a pair of drunken tango dancers. As the mechanical doll animated by the springs and sprockets Spalanzani had put inside her, Letitia careened forward, swirling and lurching like some infernal machine possessed by demons.

Ever faster she spun until, achieving a dizzy fervor, she spun out through a rear door at the back of the stage. Hoffmann staggered to his feet. Bruised and sweating, he limped off behind her, while still singing in his strained, sweet soprano:

> "Tu me fuis? . . . qu'ai-je fait? . . .
> Tu ne me reponds dis?
> Parle . . . t'ai-je irrites? . . . Ah . . .
> Je suivrai tes pas."

The rest of us stood frozen on the stage waiting for the lights to fade us out. In that moment a clap was heard, neither applause nor appreciation, but rather a single sharp crack of the palms followed by another and another at somewhat lagging intervals. It had come from somewhere at the darkened rear of the ballroom. Someplace behind Uncle Toby and Signor Parelli. Nothing was there but darkness. Yet the ghostly echo of those three handclaps still rang on the darkened air.

Backstage, just behind Letitia, Leander banged through the swinging doors into a cupboard off the scullery that served as a changing room for the cast. From outside the pantry, Cassie and Madam Lobkova sawed away at some semblance of a reprise. Shortly, Madam Lobkova appeared. "Costumes, everyone. Second act in five minutes."

"Has anyone seen my spats?" Ogden lunged past. "I left them right here on the drainboard."

Letitia lit on Sofi. "You heard him, didn't you? He was right out front. Those three claps. That was him. You heard, Sofi."

Eyes narrowing, Sofi began to unzip her costume. "I'm not sure what I heard."

Madam Lobkova went about fussing over each of us, straightening a tie, pinning a hem, flattening a lapel. Within the tiny space, she maneuvered around, her great girth using up air and generating body heat. She kept clapping her hands and barking instructions. Outside, the opening strains of the Barcarole had started up. "Better get changed, Lettie. You've got two minutes."

Across the back of the stage, Cornie glided noiseless as a phantom, shifting a divan on his back.

Sofi buttoned herself into the svelte clinging velvet of Giulietta's gown, hurrying forward toward the parterre where Ogden now stood screwing a monocle into his eye. He had made his transformation into Crespil, ready to follow Sofi out for the Barcarole.

A shy tug at the tail of my jacket brought me around. I looked down to see the frail, pallid figure of Leander staring up at me. Beads of sweat glistened on his forehead. He was trembling. "There is someone out there, isn't there, Johnnie?"

I turned to go, but he tugged me back. "Lettie's right," he said. "It's him. It's Jones."

I turned from him and hauled on my Dapertutto cloak.

"I saw a face . . ." Leander followed after me. "There was a light around it. A kind of weird glow. It was in the back."

"In the back? Why didn't I see it?"

"I don't know. That's what scares me. No one else seems to have seen it."

Deathly pale, Leander seemed about to tell me something, but before he could, Madam Lobkova reappeared, spun him about and herded him toward the parterre.

From outside in the ballroom, the first harsh boom of Ogden's baritone sounded.

Madam Lobkova seized each of Leander's narrow shoulders, gripping him hard. "All right, Hoffmann. You're on."

In the next moment she pushed the small, stiff, slightly resisting figure through the curtains, then trundled out behind him to take up her position in the pit. Letitia and I were left alone in the pantry, twenty feet of roiled, overheated air crackling between us.

She didn't look at me but kept glaring out at the audience through a crack in the curtain. "I don't care what Uncle Toby says," she hissed. "I'm not going with him. I'll kill myself first."

How we got through the final act, the Antonia act, I don't know. By the time we reached intermission, and changed costumes for the Antonia sequence, everyone, including Madam Lobkova, was showing signs of extreme stress.

Sofi was to sing the Antonia role. Ogden would sing Crespil. I, as usual, was the evil Dr. Miracle. Leander continued as

68

Hoffmann, now with a kind of strange exaltation that alarmed me.

The scene was set in Munich at the home of Crespil. The room was stiff and austere. There was a couch and an armchair. Several violins hung on the walls. At the rear of the stage were two doors. In the foreground, at the left, were two French windows opening out onto a balcony. It was sunset. Between the two doors a large portrait of a woman hung on the wall. This was Antonia's mother, the ghost the evil Dr. Miracle had summoned up.

In the final moments of the scene, Antonia, knowing full well that she has consumption and that the strain of singing will result in her death, has sung her heart out and is rapidly expiring.

Ogden's Crespil then flowed in as the broken-hearted father:

"My child . . . speak.
Come, speak. Execrable death."

Leander, as Hoffmann, rushed onstage:

"Why these cries?"

I, as Dr. Miracle, hobbled out into the lights with my slurred, lurching gait. Then, just as Hoffmann flew to Antonia, Crespil, seizing a knife from the table, attacked Hoffmann.

Playing Nicklausse, Letitia rushed in and stayed Crespil's dagger:

"Oh unhappy man."

I watched Leander turn to Letitia. "Quick. Give the alarm," his quavery tenor rang out, but I had the distinct impression he was not singing—no longer playacting. Something leapt in his eye. "A doctor," Leander gasped. "A doctor."

The lines were precisely those Hoffmann was supposed to sing but at that moment, there was no doubt in my mind that his cries for help were real.

Moving far more quickly than was seemly for creaky old Miracle, I approached Antonia and felt her pulse.

"Dead," I sang, staring wide-eyed at Leander, who was blue and struggling for breath.

Just then another of those sharp hand claps rang out from the rear of the ballroom. Our heads turned toward it, seeing nothing but a vacant darkness. And in that spot Leander stood stricken, gaping up at me, eyes pleading for help, like someone caught in a tide being swept out to sea. In the next moment there was a loud concussive sound followed by a great puff of smoke.

I recall falling back, shielding my eyes against the heat and billowing smoke. Within the sudden blinding glare I saw the black silhouettes of Sofi, Ogden and Letitia strewn sideways like chips of wood flying off of a buzz saw. I had a vague impression of Cassie and Madam Lobkova ducking their heads in the orchestra pit. The next few seconds are a blur, comprised of total confusion.

Shortly, the smoke started to clear. It rose languidly upward, curling into wisps corkscrewing through the beam of an over-head klieg light. In the place where Leander had stood, there was nothing. He was gone. Vanished, as though a wand had been waved. Only that battered old slouch hat of Hoffmann's he'd worn all throughout the performance still remained. It lay on stage at the precise point where he'd stood, tilted on its side, the brim of it spattered with a dusting of fine ash. There was something awful about it.

That night at dinner it was as though Leander had never existed. His name went not only unmentioned, it was pointedly avoided. His place at table had been removed, the area vacant as if no mortal had ever occupied it. My brothers and sisters worked hard at averting their eyes from the spot, whereas mine kept drifting back there, seeing his face—that laughing, shy, generous spirit, floating above the china and crystal and linen napery placed at the setting he'd occupied for so many years. Madam Lobkova was the first to excuse herself, pleading fatigue and retiring to her room.

Later, upstairs, I tried to go to bed early. When I couldn't sleep, I lit my lamp and tried to read. It was Hakluyt, I think. One of those quaint old geographies of the ancient world with maps and morbid chronicles of lost and vanished races.

As much as I tried to concentrate on topography, scales and azimuths, I could think only of Leander. His face, pallid and harried, hovering above me, the eyes staring, full of terror, pleading for help just as he had those last awful moments on the stage.

"Where are you now, Leander?" I whispered at one point into the chill shadows of my room. "What have they done with you?"

A deathly stillness had fallen over the house. Even the unseen individual who sang lullabies upstairs each night was silent. Exhausted, I flicked the lamp off and made a concerted effort to sleep. But it was useless. The face of Leander, his voice and doomed eyes, haunted the darkened room.

15

They were like a pair of startled rats scuffling over crumbs. Parelli saw me first, standing on the threshold peering through at them.

"There's a door, Jonathan," Uncle Toby said crossly. "You're supposed to knock."

Parelli walked off, leaving me standing there. I waited to be invited in. When I wasn't, I pushed the door open and stepped into the room. "Where's Leander?"

I watched the dark frown slide across the edge of Uncle Toby's jaw. Something alert and wary had come into Parelli's eyes. The two of them stared at me, I thought uneasily.

"Jones has appointed him to the Service," Toby announced without looking up from his papers.

"I don't believe that. I think he's still right here in the castle."

Toby's gaze never rose from the desk. Parelli hovered there like a sentinel above him, his chest swelling with importance.

"I want to know where my brother is," I persisted.

"You puzzle me, Johnnie." Toby sighed and shook his head. "I can't say I recall your ever showing much interest in Leander. Why all of a sudden now?"

My cheeks flared as the sting of that rebuke struck home.

Toby pressed on. "Is it possible that our Jonathan is upset because he has yet to be called for an audience with Jones, or that, as more likely, he may not be called at all?"

"That would suit me just fine," I snapped back.

The long, dark column of Parelli's shape rustled in the shadows.

"Perhaps that's your trouble, Jonathan," Toby replied quietly. "Perhaps you've outgrown us here. Perhaps you should be moving on."

"Perhaps I should," I shot right back. "No matter where, it's got to be better than this."

He regarded me a moment, then shrugged. His eyes returned to the desk top with all of its impressive mounds of documents and correspondence.

I wondered if I'd been dismissed, but then suddenly Toby's head rose. "I believe we have nothing further to discuss, Jonathan."

I rose stiffly from my chair. "I would like to see my father as soon as possible."

"Whatever for?" he asked.

"I'd like to ask him several questions that have been bothering me for some time. First I'd demand to know what he's done with Leander. Then I'd kill him," I said without batting an eye. I had the pleasure of seeing Uncle Toby blanch.

There was a lengthy pause and Parelli coughed nervously in the shadows. Uncle Toby was about to reply. But before he could I was on my way out. All I heard was the sound of the door slamming behind me.

"Why come to me?"

"You were fond of Leander."

"I was." Madam Lobkova seemed nervous at having to concede it. "But I can do nothing for him."

"You have influence with them. You might prevail on Jones. . . ."

She moved away from me in that heavy, waddling gait of hers. "I have no influence whatever. In matters such as this, once a decision is made . . ."

"But he's so young. . . ."

"There were many younger."

In a step or two she was before me, pressing both my hands

73

between her own. They were hot as an oven. "But I assure you, Jonathan, everything that happens here in Fraze, though it may seem heartless and arbitrary, has a point." Her hands gripped mine. "Some day you will understand. Take my word for it. But this is not the time."

"When, if ever, will it be the time?"

She gazed down at the floor, shifting her great weight from one foot to the other, unable to look me in the eye. "Give it up, Jonathan," she urged. "Accept or come to grief."

"I'll come to that either way. We all will," I said, "won't we?"

16

Closeness was never a desirable feature of relationships at Fraze, but I'd been closer to Leander than to any of my other brothers and sisters. Call it his loyalty, his generosity, his compassion, or merely simple goodness of heart. None of us had such traits to the degree he did. Not particularly loyal or generous myself, I was at a loss to explain my inability to turn my back on Leander and simply walk away.

Outside in the corridor I blundered forward down the passageway, scarcely caring where I was going, moving just out of a sheer need for physical motion.

At one point I passed a shadowy corner when a hand took me from behind. My fist shot up and I wheeled around. Instead of an assailant, I found myself peering into the grave, startled face of Cornie. Along with a series of grunts and whinnying sounds, he waved his hand frantically in my face, urging me to be still.

"What is it, Cornie? What's up?"

He gave a quick glance over his shoulder, then drew me deeper into the shadows of the hallway. From his pocket he withdrew something and thrust it toward me. I could see little in that light, so he pulled me down the corridor to a nearby window and, standing in that pale illumination, he opened his cupped fist and pushed it at me. Cushioned at the center of that large, callused palm was a brass button, a shred of torn fabric clinging to its back.

"Leander." The name rushed from me like pent-up air. "That button's from Leander's cutaway. He was wearing it yesterday when he vanished."

Cornie nodded eagerly. His grin caused the splash of purple on the side of his face to inch higher up his cheek.

"Where did you find it? Show me, Cornie. It's important."

The great head bobbed up and down, followed by a burst of wet stutterings that nearly choked in his throat. He flailed his arms in frustration, then simply grabbed my sleeve and started to haul me up the passageway.

Cornie's legs were a good deal longer than mine and I had to struggle to keep up. He was, of course, older than the rest of us. He'd been around much longer and knew many of the secrets of the old castle. Down corridors and through dank, unoccupied passageways we plunged headlong as though pursued by demons. Just when I thought I could go no farther, we made an abrupt turn through a pair of heavy oak doors set into an arch and entered a stone chapel.

Nine hundred years earlier, when the castle had stood on the banks of the Loire, the old French count who'd built Fraze as a residence and retreat for himself had built a chapel there as well. As was the custom then, such chapels were used for daily services and ceremonial functions—baptisms, weddings, funerals and the like. Cruciform in shape, the place was a miniature basilica. It had its own nave and transept, an altar and presbytery. There were painted narthex doors at the entry.

In its present incarnation it had been stripped of every last vestige of formal religion. Years ago the original crosses, icons, reliquaries and mosaics depicting scenes from the Scriptures had been taken down and replaced with decor of a less sectarian nature. A niche where once an effigy of the Holy Virgin had resided now contained a vase of dead brown flowers. Only a faded outline of the figure was still visible where it had been pried from the wall and the wall had been plastered over.

Under its present ownership the tiny chapel had fallen into disuse. In the past it had always been presented to us as a sort of museum of the Dark Ages, where absurd and outmoded practices took place and people were taught to cannibalize their gods. Shadows and silence clung about the coigns and arches and fragrant wood. Once inside, one tended to speak in whispers and even feel the presence of spirits that had passed through there in transit to some other world. In the minds of the Jones children, it was a place to be shunned.

"Show me where you found the button, Cornie."

Holding it before him and making small, excited sounds, he dragged me up to the altar. Stained-glass lancet windows depicting biblical scenes curved sweepingly around the apse. They told the story of Abraham preparing to sacrifice Isaac.

Tugged forward, up the stairs to the choir, I stumbled into the chancel rail and nearly tripped. The dusty, cushioned silence of the place seemed almost a reproach, as if our presence there was a desecration.

"Is this where you found it, Cornie?"

He made a gargling sound and stamped his foot on the floor. In the next moment he took the brass button and lay it against the foot of the altar.

"Like that? You found it there lying on its side?"

His head bobbed eagerly. Then, with a single sweeping motion, he yanked off the tapestry cover, revealing the stone altar beneath it. Suddenly stooping, he leaned his shoulder hard up against the granite block and pushed.

Shortly I heard a low, scraping sound as the altar, turning on a hinge, slowly grated its way over the stone floor. I leaped to Cornie's side and, throwing my weight in with his, we pushed together.

When we'd succeeded in swinging the altar nearly a full ninety degrees on its axis, we found ourselves looking up into a black winding tunnel. It was the entrance to a narrow unlit stairway that climbed somewhere high into the castle battlements.

We stood there a while, slightly breathless, peering upward into the damp, narrow stairwell. A low, moaning wind soughed from somewhere above. There was no illumination and you could see no more than four or five steps ahead. But it was obvious from the curvature of the inner walls that the stairway was located in the center of one of the drum towers.

I heard a grunt, then felt a rude push at my back. It was Cornie urging me up, his great arms flailing out in sort of a swimming motion behind me, as though propelling us both forward.

The next I knew we were bounding up the stairs, taking the steps, despite the inky darkness, two at a time. Tripping and stumbling, we climbed until I thought my heart would burst. It seemed as though we would climb forever, but at last a crack of gray showed on the wall up ahead where morning light poured through a window.

Five, six, seven steps more and suddenly we emerged on level ground in a square stone room. A small oriel window looked out over the soaring tops of trees. The windows were barred and anchored to each wall was an iron ring from which hung heavy restraining chains. The place had been a dungeon of some sort built in the olden days to confine prisoners.

Not far from me, where one of the chains dangled from the sweating walls, a small pile of something lay heaped in a mound on the floor. Something about the light there and the position in which the mound lay on the bare, sweating floor made my heart sink.

It took me a while before I could get myself to approach it. When at last I did, I came at it warily with the same caution you use to approach a trapped creature, sick and cornered and about to charge. At first I thought it was alive, a large water rat, perhaps, not at all uncommon in these old stone structures. But on closer inspection, the frightening little mound turned out to be clothing—trousers, shirt, shoes, socks, underwear and a worn, shiny jacket, the cutaway Leander had worn the day before as Hoffmann. No doubt of it, right down to the loose threads and ragged hole where recently a single brass button had been torn from the fabric.

A cry of triumph caught in my throat, but when I turned to share my discovery with Cornie, he was gone. Except for myself the little dungeon was empty. I rushed to the head of the stairway and called down after him. There was no reply, only the hollow sound of my own voice echoing back at me, ricocheting off the cold stones up through the empty stairwell.

Poor Leander. How he must have suffered—stripped naked, sitting on the cold stone floor for hours, chained to a wall. Why had they found it necessary to treat him so harshly? What purpose could such cruelty have served? Unless he'd tried to resist. But knowing Leander, that seemed improbable. He was the most gentle and compliant of creatures. Whatever it was, whatever had transpired here the night before, I shuddered to think. Could Leander still be here in the castle? Common sense argued no. Madam Lobkova had as much as confirmed that.

Going back down the stairs, I moved as though in a walking sleep, numb, devoid of feeling, my eyes open but seeing nothing. I was scarcely aware of reaching the little stone chapel until I'd passed through it on my way to the bottom of the tower.

When I looked up again, I found myself on level ground, before another of those barred oriel windows. Just to the right of it was a heavy arched door. To my amazement, it stood open. Light and fresh air poured through it, bringing with it the sharp, resinous scent of piney northern daylight. Doors never stood open at Fraze. It simply didn't happen.

For the first time in my life, freedom lay a foot or two away. But instead of moving directly for it, I stood paralyzed in my tracks, too terrified to move. I don't know how long I stood there, clinging to the safety of the walls, like a chained dog straining on its leash. I waited, breathing rapidly, trying to catch my breath.

At last, like a bather dipping his toes into an icy surf, I stepped gingerly out into the sunshine. The day was beautiful. Sparkling and clear. Birds darted in the branches above me. I filled my lungs with cold northern air. I gulped it. I chewed it. I was dizzy with the heady sensation of it.

In all the excitement, I'd forgotten about Leander and it wasn't until I'd taken several steps from the castle that his plight came roaring back at me with terrible immediacy. Speared on a lower branch of a nearby spruce, I saw what appeared to be a ragged swatch of cloth. On closer inspection, it turned out to be a wad of goatskin. I had little doubt as to what it was and none whatsoever about where it had come from. If there'd been any doubt in my mind as to where Leander had been taken, those doubts were at last put finally to rest. This then was what my Uncle Toby meant when he spoke of the great honor of being selected for the Service.

17

That evening (the last, we were told, of Jones's visit for the present year), Uncle Toby threw a gala ball. It was attended not only by the immediate family but by most of the household staff and the Institute technical personnel as well.

It took place in the grand ballroom beneath crystal chandeliers. We wore costumes and masks and danced on parqueted floors. Some came as musketeers and Minotaurs, others as dryads and harlequins. A sizable number came turned out as characters in fairy tales.

I had little heart for it, but one was expected to attend, and penalties were exacted if you failed to. I came as Caliban, all tricked out in tattered rags and a fright wig. Streamers of confetti and balloons rained down from the ceiling, festooning the furniture and tangling in the glittering chandeliers. A number of the Institute staff served as fiddlers. We danced *bourrées* and *chaconnes* by the hour and much wine was consumed.

I danced and drank hard and tried to blot from my mind the image of that ragged wad of goatskin on the footpath outside the castle that day. The brass button Cornie had shown me I carried in my pocket, reaching down to feel it there from time to time.

At first there was no trouble recognizing the person behind each domino mask. But as the night wore on and more wine was consumed, one masked face looked pretty much like any other. At one point I thought I was dancing with Letitia, attired as Mother Goose. I was bursting to say something about my discovery in the tower that day, but for some reason I didn't. Instead, I rattled on, overloud, my tongue loosened by wine, not realizing that my dancing partner was quiet—unnaturally quiet even for Letitia, until it occurred to me that it wasn't Letitia I was dancing with at all. It was one of the third-floor chambermaids.

As the night wore on, the music became frenetic. Out of the corner of my eye I caught a glimpse of Uncle Toby got up as a corsair, complete with tricorn hat, knee-length boots and an eyepatch. He was dancing a drunken gavotte with an houri in silk orange harem pants, whom I guessed to be Sofi.

Parelli, attired as a grenadier, kept doffing his hat to the ladies and swanning about from one partner to the next. Ogden, done up like Reynard the Fox, wore a rubber nose with an obscene red knob glowing at the tip. But even that couldn't conceal the leer of disdain he showed for the whole proceeding.

Madam Lobkova was the easiest to pick out. Her girth alone was sufficient tip-off, but if there was any doubt at all, the fortune-teller's costume of scarves and layers of voluminous skirts, surmounted by a turban, put the question quickly to rest.

At one point Cassie whirled past, partnered by someone dressed as a Pan. Half man, half goat, he had sharp little horns thrusting outward from his forehead. I could hear the cloven hoofs clicking on the parquet as they spun by. He was not much taller than Cassie, and I assumed him to be one of the young boys who serve as wine bearers in the dining room.

An hour later, the ball had grown unruly. I was dancing with someone, I'm not sure who, when Cassie whirled past again. Still dancing with her Pan, she drew alongside me. In the next moment I felt a wad of crumpled paper crammed into my hand. When she'd spun past, I opened it and read the words "The Monk" scrawled across it. That—and nothing more. When I looked around for her, she and her Pan were gone.

Earlier that evening I had seen a figure dressed in a coarse brown cassock with a hood drawn up over his head. I'd noticed that whoever it was didn't dance or mingle with the revelers, but merely stood alone off to the side, leaning up against a colonnade observing the proceedings.

I didn't know what to make of the message. By then the party had deteriorated into noise and drunkenness. Several of the revelers banged timbrels and tambourines and sang bawdy songs. Fights broke out and the brawlers had to be removed from the ballroom, kicking and punching as they were dragged off by the house security guards to their rooms. A number of others, lolling on divans, clothing in disarray, coupled amorously. Others stretched out beside them, mumbling, drowsing and past caring.

I recall dancing with someone. I don't know who. The room reeled about me. The innumerable tiny crystals of the chandeliers had all run together into one blinding ball of light. I'd become entangled in streamers and swung at them wildly.

The lady I danced with had large painted puce lips. She laughed a lot and showed a good deal of gold in her mouth. Each time she laughed she ground her hips hard up against mine and sprayed me with saliva.

At a certain point I felt my head spinning. Trying to regain my balance, I half turned from her. When I turned again she was gone but there was the hooded figure. This time he was standing at the side of the room, in a crowd of revelers, yet strangely alone. The cowl of his hood swept up around his neck and dropped down low over the forehead. A dark expanse of gauze mask showed beneath the hood and, though he was by no means nearby, I could feel the strong pull of his gaze from behind it.

It was Cassie's monk. The subject of her scribbled note. But why had she found it necessary to point him out to me? And then with a gradual dawning in my drunken head, it occurred to me that what she meant, of course, was that the monk was Jones.

Given his well-known penchant for secrecy and disguise, it wouldn't be unlike Jones to come concealed in this fashion. By then, pretty much far gone in wine, my anger rising, I lurched toward him.

The rest is all a blur. I have a recollection of rough hands seizing me before I could reach him, of being lifted and carried up a flight of stairs. With a great deal of sniggering, I was hauled into my room, stripped of my Caliban costume and tossed unceremoniously into bed.

Yet I didn't sleep. Instead, I lay awake for some time,

wondering if that was actually Jones I'd seen at the ball. I thought about Leander and Uncle Toby and my brothers and sisters, and what course of action, if any, I should take.

Several hours later I was awakened and informed that Jones, my father, was dead.

Part 4

The Investigation

"Well, this is the point, the essential thing: When you were going upstairs . . . I think you said you were there between seven and eight?"

—Inspector Porphyry, in Fyodor Dostoevsky's *Crime and Punishment*

18

The night Jones died went something like this:

I was awakened at approximately 4:15 A.M. by Signor Parelli. He was dressed in his pajamas with a suit jacket thrown over his shoulders. He wore street shoes on his feet and no socks. Informal attire and hastily put together, I'd say, for a man who makes a religion of grooming.

I'd been dreaming of something. I can't recall what. I felt two sharp jabs about my upper arms, and then heard the gruff voice of Signor Parelli talking to me in excited whispers. "Jonathan . . . get up . . . Jonathan."

"What? What is it?" My eyes struggled to focus.

Parelli snatched up the robe at the foot of my bed and tossed it at me. "Put that on and come with me."

"What's going on?"

"Never mind. Just come along."

Though it was four in the morning, most of the lights in the castle were ablaze. Chandeliers glared from every salon; dozens of wall sconces blazed a path of blinding light before us.

Parelli moved along the corridors at a swift, angry pace. The soles of his shoes fairly rang on the stone floor.

Our way took us through a network of hallways and bisecting passages, up a flight of stairs and into a wing of the forbidden third story. When we reached there the place was abuzz with nervous activity. People swarmed in droves through every room, some of them still attired in their party costumes. Most of them I'd never seen before. I was astounded at the sheer number of them. Passing these people now in the upstairs corridors, the impression they gave was that something had happened—something momentous and certainly untimely enough to have gotten the entire household up at that hour of the morning.

We were in a long, narrow corridor, vaulted over by high groined ceilings. Marble busts, suits of mailed armor, portraits of figures long dead, lined the hallways. Most of the doors opening onto the corridors were closed. But at the end of one, a single door stood open. A plane of light from within slanted across the hall, casting an eerie white rectangle on the wall opposite.

A small crowd of people had gathered just outside the open door. They spoke in low voices to each other. When we approached, their talk broke off. As though an order had been given, they parted before us and we entered.

We found ourselves in a small anteroom giving on to a large chamber just beyond. More people milled about inside and a low buzz of conversation wafted outwards through the open door leading to the larger room. Inside, more people appeared to move about, solemn and unspeaking, each seemingly intent on his own special task.

Just as Parelli and I entered, Ogden was leaving. Clad like me in pajamas and a robe, he looked badly shaken. When we stood aside to let him pass, his eyes stared straight ahead, scarcely noting us.

"Come along," Parelli whispered in my ear. He took me beneath the arm and half pushed, half nudged me forward. I followed numbly, feeling a bit breathy and stiff, as though I were moving on rubber legs. I still had no idea what had happened. Parelli, for some unaccountable reason, had not bothered to tell me.

The room we now found ourselves standing in was lit by an immense chandelier hung directly above the center of a salon. Countless tiny lights shimmered through the hundreds of pendant teardrop crystals bathing the ceilings with shards of jagged light.

The room was furnished with an array of French period

pieces. Above it all, a large rose window dominated the head of the room. There was about the place an air of solemn grandeur and when you entered, your voice dropped automatically to a whisper.

Across the room I spotted Madam Lobkova. Dressed in a bulky quilted robe, her abundant hair confined in a sort of bedtime snood, she came over and without a word kissed me. I could see she'd been crying. "Oh, Jonathan," was all she could manage, over and over again, wringing her hands and patting my arm.

Uncle Toby beckoned us from a distant corner of the room. He'd been talking to a man who turned and observed us as we approached. Toby looked ashen and badly shaken. Glancing at Signor Parelli, he asked: "Have you told him anything?"

"He knows nothing."

Toby turned back to me. "Jonathan, we've suffered a terrible loss tonight. I'm afraid Jones is dead."

"Jones," I muttered, and lapsed into dumb silence, scarcely comprehending a word of anything that was being said around me. They all seemed to be watching me, expecting me to say something or break into sobs. But, of course, I felt nothing. How could I?

"And this, Jonathan," Uncle Toby was talking again in that grave, grandly sympathetic manner I believe he was affecting for the benefit of the stranger beside him, "is Colonel Porphyry, Chief of District Security. He's been good enough to fly out from the mainland on fairly short notice."

I turned to meet the gaze of a small, paunchy man with a thick neck whose bulky frame radiated an air of quiet force. There was a formality about his dress—dark suit, a white shirt and a tie—but the manner in which he wore it, or perhaps his bearing, suggested someone more accustomed to wearing a uniform.

I presumed he was a policeman or a detective. I'd read about such people in books and imagined that they'd be a fairly coarse lot. This man was scarcely what I'd expected.

Intelligent, slightly impertinent eyes assessed me quickly. "I'm sorry we meet under such sad circumstances," he remarked, poking a pudgy hand toward me.

I looked into a mournful, slightly equine face, the head disproportionately large in relation to the medium-statured frame. His voice was husky and just compassionate enough to

89

make you wary. There was about it some sort of vague accent I was unable to place.

I thanked him and stammered something idiotic about being sorry, too, then looked around, not knowing what else to do with my eyes. He watched me, waiting for some sort of emotional outburst. When in fact none came, I believe he was embarrassed. We stood aside for a moment to permit two uniformed functionaries, associates of the Colonel (he had brought about ten with him), to unwind a steel spool of measuring tape and lay it on the floor between us. While they went about their work we continued to converse.

"When did all this . . ." I started to inquire.

"Sometime early this morning," Colonel Porphyry replied. "The exact time is what we're trying now to determine."

"What about the others?" I asked. "Have they been told?"

"Ogden was just here," Uncle Toby said. "Letitia and Sofi have been told, but they haven't been asked up yet."

"Cassie?"

"No reason to wake the child. She'll be told in the morning."

"And Cornie?"

Uncle Toby nodded in the direction of the bedchamber. "Cornelius is in there with him now."

Toby had indicated the small room off to the side to be Jones's bedchamber. All the while we spoke in hushed whispers, a number of uniformed men filed in and out of the room with open pads and various paraphernalia. They worked with the silent, fixed intent of worker bees, each going about his appointed task in the hive.

"May I see him?"

"Now, Jonathan . . ." Toby started forward. I was aware of Colonel Porphyry studying me throughout this exchange. This time when he spoke, those wet sibilants began to smack slightly of the Balkans. "Mr. Jones, I regret I must tell you . . . your father's death was not due to natural causes."

Several moments passed before the import of that registered. "Are you sure?"

"There seems little doubt." His eyes swept past me, moving on into the small room off to the side. "He's in there now. These people you see here going in and out are my staff." The short stubby fingers inscribed a wide arc. "They're attempting to gather whatever pertinent data may still be about."

90

"Yes, I see. But I still fail to understand why I can't see my father."

"Of course you can see him." The Colonel gave a smile of surprise. "That's certainly within your right. We were simply concerned that . . ."

"Jonathan," Uncle Toby blustered, "it's not a pleasant sight."

Madam Lobkova's hand groped my sleeve again, tugging me gently toward the door. "Come away, Johnnie. You really don't want to go in there."

I shrugged her hand off. "I want to see my father," I said again, this time more forcefully.

"And so you shall," the Colonel said.

Uncle Toby and Parelli glanced at each other. Madam Lobkova's fingers fluttered at the piping on her robe. She regarded me with a fretful gaze. I watched the great dome of Colonel Porphyry's head signal ever so slightly to a tallish, hulking figure who stood just inside the entrance to the bed-chamber, looking out at us.

In the next moment, as if by pre-arranged plan, they all stepped back and suddenly I was standing alone, facing the narrow doorway through which my father, whom I'd never seen in life, now awaited me in death.

He was smaller than I'd imagined. Before I had only seen his outline behind a screen. Now my view of him was clear and unobstructed. He wore a nightshirt with his calves, hairless, milky white, knobby veined, sticking out from below its hem. His feet seemed unnaturally small and the legs themselves reached only halfway to the end of the bed, heightening the impression of smallness. An image I shall never forget was the sight of a tiny pair of carpet slippers, old and shabby, the stitching at their soles unraveling. They sat neatly on the floor beside his bed. Not at all the slippers of the second richest man in the world, I thought. The room seemed quite small, too. Surprisingly so. One would have imagined something far grander for Jones—something vast with arched ceilings and wainscotted walls. This was almost monastic in its austerity.

The single concession to luxury was the bed—immense and canopied with a silk embroidered tester. Beside that was a small table upon which a tumbler of water stood. A set of full dentures sat at the bottom of the glass grinning outwards. To the pink acrylic resin base upon which the plate was mounted, a cluster

91

of tiny bubbles had formed and attached themselves. The water in the glass had turned a pale, cloudy yellow. A monk's robe had been tossed over the backrest of a chair beside the bed.

I'd been prepared to see something ghastly. At least that's what I'd expected from all the hemming and hawing that had accompanied my request to see my father. But, with the exception of the comforter—which was in disarray, spilling half off the bed—and a small, oddly delicate spattering of blood on the white duvet, everything else appeared to be remarkably intact.

It occurred to me that I could make no logical connection between myself and this person—this stranger lying there in bed who was supposed to be my father. Was this actually Jones— philanthropist, humanitarian, the inventor of the zip-lock bag and waterproof mucilage, the architect of the world-renowned Jones System, the patriarch of a tribe said to be legion, and my father? Somehow, he didn't look old enough for all of that.

He lay on his side, eyes open, staring at the wall. He showed no sign of fright or of his having suffered pain. It was as if the deed were done while he slept. Done cleanly and painlessly. Only the skin drawn tight over delicate facial bones had taken on the waxy sheen of recent death.

It was not until I drew close that I saw the feathers standing upright just beneath his chin and then realized that what I was looking at was the end of a dart, the point of which was sticking through his throat. It was steel, with white feathered fletching, the sort of thing we used to chuck at the wall in the game room when we had nothing better to do. This particular dart was six inches long. It had entered deep into Jones's throat and gave the impression of having impaled him on his pillow. The shaft had entered cleanly, and, given the point of entry, the carotid artery, there was remarkably little blood. The hemorrhaging must have been almost entirely internal.

Three other people were in the room when I entered. One was the tall hulking guard I've already referred to; another was a swarthy Levantine woman in the white uniform of a nurse. She said nothing as I drew close to the bed and never once acknowledged my presence there but watched me out of the corner of an eye. Though she busied herself folding odds and ends of clothing, she never lost track of my movements, all the while muttering words in what sounded like a Semitic tongue. It was only after I'd been there several minutes that I realized it was some sort of prayer or incantation she was reciting. The clothes

I presume had been Jones's, for she kept sprinkling them with disinfectant, then packed them into a carton. The room smelled heavily of asafoetida.

The third person in the room was Cornie. He sat on a chair beside the bed and held the hand of his father, as if waiting for him to awake. He appeared to be staring into Jones's open eyes, attempting to decipher some riddle there. There was something unspeakably sad about it. That big, overgrown, witless man with his five-year-old mind and the spiky purple smear that dripped down the side of his face, making him look as if a pot of jam had been tipped over on his head.

Approaching the bed, I stood beside him. It struck me that he was aware of my presence but wouldn't acknowledge it. Clearly, he was grieving. If Cornie had limitations, the ability to feel loss was not one of them.

An endless procession of people came and went. Mostly they were uniformed men, Colonel Porphyry's forensic staff. They didn't bother us but went about their work—taking measurements, dusting for prints, gathering with tweezers odd bits of tiny things to be quick-sealed in plasticene envelopes. All very impersonal and professional.

I don't know what occupied my thoughts. I'm certain it wasn't Jones. It might have been Leander. In the two days since his disappearance, I felt more strongly his presence there in that room at that moment than at any time before.

I became aware of Madam Lobkova beside me, her pudgy childlike hand trembling at my elbow.

"You're much like him, you know," she said, staring grief-stricken over my shoulder at the diminutive waxen figure on the bed. "Of all of them, you come closest to the man in character and spirit."

The grip on my elbow tightened. "Come along now. Let's go back out. They'll be wondering about us."

I nodded toward Cornie. He was still holding Jones's hand, his lips moving in silent communion. "What about him?"

Madam Lobkova glanced his way, then shrugged. "Leave him for now. He'll be fine."

We turned and went back out.

Parelli and Uncle Toby had left by then. Colonel Porphyry stood alone, absorbed in a sheaf of reports and dispatches which he lip-read to himself. He seemed oblivious to the small army of technicians swarming about him.

"Will there be anything else?" Madam Lobkova inquired as we came up to him.

He glanced up from his reading and gazed at us through yellow-tinted spectacles, a vague expression in his eyes as though he couldn't quite recall who we were. Then a gleam of recognition animated his sallow features.

"Ah yes, of course. Forgive me. I get a bit lost in my paperwork." He gave a self-deprecating little laugh and fluttered the sheaf of dispatches at us. "No reason to keep you." He nodded at Madam Lobkova. "I'd appreciate a moment or two with young Mr. Jones, however."

Wanda glanced at me uneasily.

"Will that be all right?" he asked me.

"Of course."

"In that case, I'll be on my way." Wanda returned the Colonel's nod brusquely and with some misgivings turned and moved out.

"It's nice to get over here from time to time," he said when she'd left. "Although I can't say the bouncing of helicopters agrees with me." The Colonel patted his round, slightly bulging stomach by way of emphasis. "It's years since I've been off the mainland. Of course, when the District Magistrate asked me to come over, I leapt at the chance. Who wouldn't?" He laughed, then grew immediately solemn again. "However, it's all too tragic about your father. Very great man. It's like the end of an era. A great oak has fallen in the forest."

He looked to me for some small acknowledgment of his eloquence. The best I could manage was a nod and I could see at once he thought my response not up to the occasion. Unruffled, he went right on.

"Still, I must say I do enjoy the wilderness isles. A great relief from the stress of the mainland. I am forever fascinated by the fact that you people here are in a special time zone. I confess, as often as it's explained to me, it remains beyond my comprehension that you can be cheek-by-jowl with us on the mainland and yet be nearly a full day ahead of us in time."

Again he waited for me to respond. This time I didn't even try. By then he'd gotten the message. "Perhaps we can talk outside. It will be more private."

He took my arm and led me over to one of the small divans placed about the little anteroom and, as we sank in a single motion, the big overstuffed cushions sighed beneath us. Every-

94

one seemed to have gone except for one of the upstairs porters sweeping the hallway just outside the door. For a brief while we listened to the sad, slow whisk of his broom scraping over the stone.

"It is strange, isn't it?" Colonel Porphyry resumed. He must have seen the confusion in my eyes. "I mean your father. This sort of thing and all. Hardly expected, wouldn't you say?"

"Hardly." I shook my head in agreement.

"I presume you can think of no reason why anyone here . . ."

"None whatsoever."

"To be sure. And why should you? There's no earthly reason." He appeared to regret having asked. "You're a close family, of course."

I have no great gift of guile and clearly he must have seen the annoyed look on my face.

"Believe me, Mr. Jones. I am fully aware of the rather special arrangements under which you all live here." His voice lingered over the word *special*. "Still, if I may. Is the man lying in there, impaled on a dart, really your father?"

At first I was stunned, then merely irritated. "Of course he is."

"How can you be so sure?"

The question took me aback. "I'm not sure I under-stand. . . ."

"My information is that before the tragic events of this morning, you and your brothers and sisters had never actually seen him face to face."

"That's true," I replied.

"You see my point then." He smiled sympathetically. "You really can't be certain the man you saw in that room with a dart in his throat is your father, can you?"

"Well, he is," I blustered. "It's him. That's all there is to it. I have no doubt. Ask my uncle or Madam Lobkova. They'll tell you."

"They already have. But still . . ." He gave me a long, slow, inquiring glance, as if suggesting things I was too obtuse to grasp. "I have no medical or dental records, no fingerprints, not even a photograph of the man with which I could corroborate that." He smiled again, studying me intently. "You do see my problem?"

"Well, you can take my word for it," I snapped.

"Can I?" The smile grew impertinent. I could see he was

95

doubtful, but he passed quickly over the matter in search of more fertile fields.

"Fascinating man, your father. Visionary. Miles ahead of his time. And this Institute. Out here in the middle of the wilderness. Incredible. At headquarters on the mainland, we keep a whole file on Fraze. Articles, news clippings. But still so little is actually known; so much of the work done here is cloaked in such secrecy."

"That secrecy may pose some problems for your investigation," I suggested.

"Undoubtedly. But with the murder of a man of your father's unique celebrity, the CID has brought great pressure to bear on the Institute to open its files to me."

"And my uncle agreed?"

"He was none too happy about it." The Colonel spoke in low, confiding tones. "But he's just as eager as we are to nab the responsible party. Now then, you assure me you have no reason to suspect that any of your sisters or brothers . . ."

"None whatsoever."

The Colonel gave me a small, polite smile. He'd been fingering a slim silver box from which he now withdrew a pastel-papered cigarillo. "Do you mind?"

"Not in the least."

"Care for one?"

"Thank you, no."

"Filthy habit," he said, tapping the tip of the cigarillo several times against the silver lid of the box. "I keep threatening to stop. No discipline, I'm afraid. I had the pleasure just now of speaking to your brother . . . excuse me . . . his name again?"

"Ogden."

"Yes, of course, Ogden. We spoke shortly before you came in. I don't suppose it would surprise you to learn—"

"Nothing about my brother surprises me."

"—that he feels you had a profound dislike for your father."

"That's true. I did."

"Would you care to comment?"

"No, I wouldn't." The antagonism in my voice seemed to vibrate across the still air.

Colonel Porphyry flicked his lighter and a bluish butane flame leaped from the cylinder. He touched it to the tip of his cigarillo and a swirl of black smoke corkscrewed slowly ceilingward, leaving in its wake the acrid, slightly dunglike scent of

96

good Latakia. He inhaled deeply, two dark pillars of smoke streaming from his nostrils, then laughed lightly. "I didn't think you would."

"It's not that I'm trying to conceal anything."

"Good heavens, certainly not. Why would you?" The Colonel looked hurt. "It may simply mean that you take your brother's opinions with a grain of salt. Not worthy of comment."

"No doubt Ogden also told you that he and I are not overly fond of each other either?"

"Considering the relish with which he tried to implicate you, I must say I'm not surprised."

His eyes narrowing, he bore down harder. "On the other hand, what your uncle told me about you *did* surprise me."

For a moment I was puzzled, then I understood perfectly. "You mean when I told him that if I found my father, I'd kill him?"

"Yes. Is that true?"

"Yes. I did say that."

"What did you mean by it?"

"Just that." A great numbness had set in, along with a sort of reckless indifference. "I meant simply that I would kill him."

"No. Not that." Porphyry's pudgy hands swatted at the smoky air as though he were brushing crumbs from his lapels. "All sons wish at one time or another to kill their fathers. That's normal. I meant the other thing."

"The other thing?" I cast about, at a complete loss for his meaning. "Oh, I see. You mean the business about if I could find him."

"Precisely."

"Well, you understand," I started to explain with a growing sense of how absurd this must all sound to him. "For reasons that have never been made clear to any of us, the place where Jones . . . where my father sleeps . . . slept . . . when he happened to be in residence, has always been kept a very strict secret."

His eyes closed and he pondered that a while. "What I mean is . . . was anyone here beneath this roof privy to his sleeping arrangements?"

"I'm sure Uncle Toby was. No doubt Signor Parelli, too."

"And Madam . . . ?"

"Lobkova? Yes, possibly."

"And until a short time ago you yourself had never set foot

97

in that room there?" He indicated the small bedchamber off to the side where Jones still lay.

"We're not supposed to come up on this floor. It's expressly forbidden."

"That's not what I asked you." He fixed me with his owlish stare. "Let me ask you once more. Have you ever been up here before?"

"In that room, never."

"And on this floor?"

"On one or two occasions," I wearily conceded.

His eyebrow cocked and he shot me a glance of amused surprise. "What sort of game are we playing here, Mr. Jonathan?"

"I'm being as candid as I possibly can."

"While at the same time drawing suspicion to yourself."

"I thought I was doing just the opposite by being candid."

Porphyry's head reared back. He peered at me above the rims of his eyeglasses. "And your brothers and sisters? Are they too forbidden up here?"

"Yes."

"You feel you're in a position to testify to their daily habits and whereabouts?"

"Within reasonable limits."

"Reasonable limits? What exactly does that mean?"

"Well, if it will help matters, I'm certain to the extent that one can be certain about such things."

By that time he was grinning broadly. "And to what extent exactly is that?"

"Inexactly exact." By then I was playing the game as well as he.

He slapped his knee and stood up. "Very good, Mr. Jones. Touché. All right then. That will be all for the time being. Later this morning I shall chat with your sisters."

"Letitia and Sofi?"

He nodded. "There's a third, too, is there not?"

"Cassie . . ."

"Who?" He cocked an ear at me.

"Cassandra. But she's just a child."

"May I remind you, Mr. Jones. Darts are a favorite game of childhood. I myself, as a youth, was devoted to the sport. That particular dart, for instance, sticking so indelicately through your father's throat, comes from a dart board I found in the playroom on the lower floor."

98

"Yes—but surely, you don't . . ."

Colonel Porphyry's stubby finger gave me a cautionary wag. "In a lifetime of dealing with violent crime, Mr. Jonathan, I have seen everything, and I exclude nothing."

The owl eyes hardened. "Let me put my question another way. Is there any reason why you should have wanted to kill your father?"

"I can give you several."

It wasn't the answer he'd expected and for a moment I'd stymied him. But then his eyes twinkled, his head fell backward and he was laughing at the ceiling once more. "I see, Mr. Jones." He nodded appreciatively. "We shall get on famously."

Part 5

The Woodsmen

"Three Rings for the Elven-kings under the sky,
Seven for the Dwarf-lords in their halls of stone,
Nine for Mortal Men doomed to die
One for the Dark Lord on his dark throne."

—J. R. R. Tolkien, *The Fellowship of the Ring*

19

The news spread quickly, because the Woodsmen came early the next morning. They were there at the crack of dawn. How they'd heard, who had informed them, no one could say. All we knew was that several hours after Jones's body had been discovered in his bed, the goat people arrived, more of them than I'd ever seen together at one time. Far more than we'd ever imagined there were.

Cassie woke me, bursting into my room, to inform me of developments. As she leapt all over my bed, I could scarcely make sense of the barrage of breathless half sentences that spilled in a torrent from her lips.

After a minute or so I stumbled up and went to the window. Outside, at the bottom of the garden, I had my first glimpse of them—a silent and watchful phalanx of elfin people, standing so still they might have been painted into the landscape. You had to look closely to see them, since their goatskin dress blended in quite naturally with the backdrop of the forest. But when at last my eyes focused and I could see them massing out there, it took my breath away. The sheer number of them was frightening. And they were not merely at the bottom of the garden, as I discovered when I looked closer, but had fanned out in a large circle ringing the castle's perimeter.

"Everyone's up on the battlements," Cassie said, a little out of breath behind me. "Uncle Toby. Parelli. That funny little man—the Colonel, and a bunch of his people." She rattled on something about rifles and short arms being issued to key people. Her words then came crashing to a halt as she stared out through the window. "What do you suppose it all means?"

"Something to do with Jones, of course."

"You mean his dying and all?"

"Sure. What else could it be?"

I kept staring down to the edge of the forest where the Woodsmen had gathered. By then, a line two or three deep stood motionless, something disturbingly ominous in their silence.

"How do you s'pose they found out?"

"How should I know?" I undressed and started to fling on some clothes.

"What do you think's going to happen?" Cassie followed me around the room while I finished dressing.

"I figure they'll have to bury him, won't they?"

"That means going outside." Her eyes bloomed like huge peonies. "We can't do that. Not with all of that going on out there."

"Not now, anyway. But eventually they'll have to get him up to the old burial grounds. You can't keep him around here. He'll start to stink."

She watched me lace my shoes.

"I saw that Colonel Por . . ."

"Porphyry."

"Right. Porphyry. Whatever. He talked to me this morning. What an odd little man."

"He's a policeman. What do you expect? Come on," I said, gently propelling her out the door. "Let's see what this is all about."

The Great Hall where we gathered was still cold from the night. The sun was barely up an hour and had not yet had a chance to poke its warming rays through the stained-glass windows.

Crowds had already jammed into the ancient auditorium when Cassie and I arrived. More kept straggling in behind us. Aside from the immediate family, there must have been at least fifty of the domestic staff, certainly more people than I'd ever imagined were in residence at the Institute. In addition to valets and chambermaids, cooks and butlers, there were a number of people in the long white smocks worn by the laboratory personnel. Aloof and apart from all others, they behaved like a holy caste—august and unapproachable—made all the more so by the donning of their smocks.

Uncle Toby was on the dais along with Signor Parelli and Colonel Porphyry, who had just begun to address a clearly nervous crowd. "For those of you who have not already met me," he began, "my name is Colonel Porphyry, Chief Detective Inspector of the mainland constabulary. I arrived here early this morning in response to an urgent call from Mr. Tobias Jones informing me of the death of Mr. Orville Jones."

A low, fluttery gasp resonated through the huge hall. Toby on the dais sat plunged in gloom, all the while Signor Parelli hovered glowering above him.

"In the days ahead," Colonel Porphyry went on, "you will doubtless see me or members of my staff about the castle. Please take no notice. Go on with your work. There will be some of you I may wish to chat with. Those whom I need to see will be informed shortly and told where to report.

"As to the slight disturbance outside this morning, I feel certain after my recent inspection of the premises that there's no immediate cause for alarm. These woods people are an aboriginal group, they've been here on the territory for centuries. They've had a long and mostly benign relationship with the government, although I confess there have been occasional reports of unpleasant incidents. By and large, however, they are a pacific people with whom the Institute has enjoyed good relations down through the years. I fear news of Mr. Jones's untimely death has somehow gotten out to them and they are no doubt as much shaken by it as we are.

"Their presence here this morning, far from being ominous, is, I am certain, merely a gesture of respect—a condolence call, if you please—to the immediate family, nothing more sinister. In the absence of more concrete information, however, we intend to be vigilant until we can determine their reasons for turning out in such unusual numbers. The next several hours should tell. If there's any indication of a worsening of the situation, we are in touch by telephone with the mainland and can have reinforcements here in a matter of a few hours. As you've already been

105

advised, my men, supported by the household staff, have taken every precaution to secure the castle.

"In the meantime, may I again urge you to go about your daily tasks just as though we weren't here. We, for our part, will do our utmost to keep out of your way."

At the completion of the Colonel's talk, the sense of unease which had gripped the crowd moments before seemed to have lifted. Smiling, Colonel Porphyry gazed out over his audience with an air of quiet benevolence.

For the moment at least, the situation appeared to have been contained.

20

The day was spent very much as Colonel Porphyry had prescribed. People went dutifully about their normal daily routine. If anyone thought about the situation going on outside the walls of the castle, the matter was never discussed. That morning I went, as usual, to my fencing and astronomy classes. From rooms not distant, I could hear the tortured skirlings of Letitia's flute and Madam Lobkova's sharp, stentorian bark as her ballet protégés did their warm-ups at the bar.

Still, no one referred to Leander's disappearance or to the Woodsmen and the matter of their unexplained presence in growing numbers all about the property. For the time being, at least, both appeared to have been forgotten.

But not by Cassie or me. We spent hours dashing from room to room, glued to the windows, peering down to the edge of the forest. In the time that had transpired between our first glimpse of the goat people and now, the sky had lowered. A system of dark, towering thunderheads, hundreds of feet tall, had come swirling up out of the south. Big pear-shaped raindrops began to spatter the windows, making sharp cracking sounds as they impacted on the glass.

It seemed to me (though I said nothing to Cassie), that since our first glimpse of the Woodsmen shortly after dawn that morning, their numbers had increased. The circle they'd formed then was no more than two or three deep. Now the depth of it stood at four or five. More disquieting, as we watched through the windows, it seemed we could see them wherever we looked. There was no doubt by then that they'd completely ringed the castle.

At one point the rain drilled down with such force that the soil spat up where the drops had struck, leaving the earth pitted and cratered from the constant pelting. Gusts of gnashing wind sent the tops of trees whipping back and forth.

The Woodsmen seemed unfazed by that. They never moved. They never once sought shelter but stood stationary for hours at a stretch in the drenching downpour, just staring up at the castle.

At one point Cassie and I attempted a head count. Moving counterclockwise from room to room with a pair of binoculars, we peered out the windows at the soaked, almost comical little potbellied figures, literally counting them head for head. We gave up somewhere about four hundred, having covered just a fraction over half the circle.

At one point we saw Colonel Porphyry in a wide-brimmed storm hat up on the rain-swept battlements. He was with a number of his people, looking glum and a bit ridiculous garbed in an outsized yellow slicker. He too had been following developments at the bottom of the garden.

Dinner that evening was a gloomy affair. A pall thick as mist hung over the table. No one had felt much like eating except, possibly, Colonel Porphyry, who ate with great zest. Out of deference to our guest, the typical 600-calorie diet was dispensed with in favor of heartier fare. Uncle Toby had gotten it into his head that we *should* eat, that some kind of moral duty attended our eating, simply because Jones would have wanted it that way. "No deviation in normal routine," he announced with brisk cheer.

Though the situation had altered drastically, far from being dead, Jones seemed more alive than ever. His presence hovered above the table and clearly dominated our every thought.

On the other hand, Leander, whose fate was still uncertain, seemed to have been gone forever. No one had yet bothered or, should I say, dared to tell the police inspector about his disap-

pearance, Uncle Toby insisting that the matter be kept to ourselves, strictly a family affair.

Colonel Porphyry now sat unknowingly in Leander's place
at table, eating heartily and carrying on nonstop about life on the
mainland and how it had changed since the days when he was a
boy, growing up there a half century ago.

If there was any awkwardness, the Colonel seemed scarcely
aware of it. He went on, breezily recounting tales of his youth,
going to sea with his father, who was a fisherman, and winning
a scholarship to university, the first in his family to attend an
institution of higher learning.

Periodically, throughout dinner, one or another of the Colonel's people would enter the dining hall, approach the table with
great deference, and whisper something in his ear. His head
tipped slightly to the side, he would listen to the message; all the
while his blank doughy features gave no hint of what it was he
might be hearing.

The storm, if anything, had intensified. The wind moaned.
Lightning and great claps of thunder rent the sky overhead.
Sheets of water boomed like a cataract, sluicing down off the roof
pantiles, splattering with loud cracks onto the flagged terrace
below.

Several times the big chandeliers over the dinner table
dimmed and threatened to go out. Candles and flambeaux were
lit all about the castle in preparation for an expected power
failure. Indeed, several times one of the two chandeliers actually
did go out. We stared up at it, willing it to come back on. When
it did, only a moment or so later, the sense of relief was palpable.

Outside, the Woodsmen's pitch-pine-soaked rag torches
made an eerie fireworks display against the rain-streaked windows of the dining hall.

"This should break by tomorrow," Toby remarked with little
conviction.

"It had better," Madam Lobkova said, nodding. "There's the
funeral. It's already been postponed a day."

"Even if the rain were to stop now," Parelli ventured, "it
would be extremely unwise to try and get up to the cemetery in
the morning. Not with all of those trolls out there." He pursed his
lips as though something had made a bad taste in his mouth.

Computing in his head the decomposition rate of dead
bodies in climates of the present temperature and humidity,
Porphyry stroked his chin. "You have no—"

109

"There's refrigeration, of course," Uncle Toby explained. "But lockers of the size necessary for that sort of storage are only in the kitchen."

"Yes, of course. Completely unsuitable," Porphyry conceded. He looked around. "If I may ask, where is the . . ."

"In the chapel. In a casket. We'd planned a small ceremony. But if the storm should continue . . ."

The Colonel touched one of his small pastel cigarettes to the guttering flame of a table candle, then inhaled deeply several times till it caught. "The storm will eventually stop, of course. The woods folk, however . . ."

"You still think they intend no harm?" I asked.

The Colonel shrugged noncommittally.

"One can't be too sure of anything, but I'm hopeful."

A shade more self-doubt had crept into his voice since the morning.

"One way or the other," Uncle Toby said, "we'll have to make a move in the next twenty-four hours. Even if we have to carry him up to the burial grounds under armed guard."

"Guns," Letitia murmured as though evil gods had been invoked.

Sofi smiled with the placid air of one for whom all problems have a quick solution, "If worse comes to worst, we'll simply phone the mainland."

The Colonel made another of those slightly embarrassed smiles. "I should hope that won't be necessary." He raised his port glass to the light. It filtered through the dark liquid and emerged as a patch of garnet on his forehead. "In any event," Porphyry was quick to add, "my men are armed and posted at every point of entry to the castle. If they come, we shall be ready for them. In the meantime, I should inform you that my Chief of Pathology has just completed his preliminary report. Nothing conclusive yet. He won't be able to provide the cause of death until he has results from additional tests." The Colonel gazed around at us with an air of benevolence. "However, he informs me that Mr. Jones was in remarkably good health for a man of his age. He had the vascular system of a twenty-year-old. The Chief says he'd never seen anything like it before."

Dinner over, uneaten sherbets melting in their goblets, we were about to leave the table when Cassie reached over to Cornie's place and plucked up something left behind beside his plate.

"What's this?" she cried, holding up a small square of paper. She studied it a moment, then shrugged and handed it to Porphyry.

Bemused, the Colonel took it, studied it a moment, then lay it down on the table, pressing its curling edges flat before him. A hushed quiet fell over the room as we tried to read the shifting expressions on his face.

Seated opposite him, in the dim glow of candlelight, I had a faint view of a picture. The best I could make of it was a crude pencil sketch of some sort.

Parelli rose and eased forward to the head of the table to see the sketch for himself.

"Well, what is it?" Sofi demanded.

"Just one of Cornelius's drawings," Parelli announced. "He's always scribbling."

"More a diagram, I'd say," Madam Lobkova suggested.

"Yes—but a diagram of what?" Porphyry asked.

Uncle Toby turned the drawing around and around before him.

"It's a figure lying on a bed," Cassie said.

"With another figure standing above it," I said.

"It's a woman," Letitia suggested timidly.

Porphyry's brow arched. "Which one? The one lying down or the one standing?"

"The one standing," Cassie snapped. "She's wearing a dress. Can't you see that?"

"Ah, so," the Colonel conceded. "A dress or, possibly, a smock."

"Why couldn't it just as well be a man in a robe of some sort?" Sofi demanded. "Cassie—you said you saw someone at the masked ball dressed as a monk."

"She did." I nodded. "I saw him too."

"Perhaps, Mr. Cornelius . . ." The Colonel turned back to where Cornie had been seated and was surprised not to find him there. The place he'd occupied at dinner was now vacant. Finishing his supper before the rest of us, it was Cornie's custom to slip off early from the table, his going scarcely noticed by anyone.

Coffee was served a short time later in the library. I found myself seated on a small settee beside Colonel Porphyry.

"Mr. Jonathan," he said, stirring his coffee lightly. "About this monk you saw last night."

"Cassie pointed him out to me. I'm certain she thought it was my father."

The Colonel's spoon swirled through his cup, making a light tinkling sound. "If this little drawing by Mr. Cornelius is correct, the figure lying down is Mr. Jones. The figure in the monk's robe is another individual entirely."

"It would seem so. But only if you assume the one lying on the bed is Jones."

"Isn't that the most obvious interpretation? Who, then, would be lying in Mr. Jones's bed?"

I thought about it a moment, anticipating his next question. "I don't know," I said. "But I suppose that if Cornie drew this picture, it follows that he witnessed it or something like it. But that's not to say he killed Jones."

"Tell me something, Mr. Jonathan. Your brother, Cornelius—he is . . ." Porphyry tapped the side of his head with his finger.

"He's not crazy," I said. "Only retarded—a bit childlike. Certainly not dangerous."

"Certainly not," Porphyry agreed. The Colonel's eyes closed and he tilted his head back at the ceiling. "It's quite possible someone else dressed in that monk's robe could have gotten up there, driven the dart into Mr. Jones's throat, then fled, leaving the robe behind."

"Possible," I said, then pondered a moment the implications of that. "But why would this person leave his costume behind?"

"Possibly to return to the ball in another costume entirely."

"But why?"

"To provide an alibi." Porphyry sipped his coffee. "After all, didn't both you and Miss Cassie assume that the robed figure was your father? Failing that, if we take Mr. Cornelius's little stick figure drawing at face value, then the figure in the monk's robe is clearly implicated in your father's death."

Everything was happening too fast. The Colonel watched me as I struggled to absorb all he had just said.

"One thing I can tell you," I went on, "the figure I saw lying in my father's bed early this morning was quite small. The figure I saw at the ball dressed as a monk was a far bigger person."

Just then Sofi complained that the room was cold, whereupon Uncle Toby ordered Parelli to start a fire at once.

112

"More coffee would be welcome, too," Colonel Porphyry called after him, hopefully.

"I've already sent for some," Parelli replied, without looking back. "It should be up momentarily."

"Well, then." The Colonel rubbed his hands, settling into an overstuffed chair. "If you'll all bear with me, I have just a few more questions."

Cassie rose suddenly from her chair. "There's no need for more questions. I killed Jones."

There was a long stunned silence.

"Well, why wouldn't I?" Cassie looked around at us scornfully. "None of you would."

"This is very bad of you, Cassandra." Uncle Toby frowned. "This is no time for joking."

He started to whisk her out of the room but before he could, the Colonel had thrust himself between them.

"One moment, Mr. Jones. If I may pursue this just a bit further."

Letitia knelt by her sister's side. "No more, darling. Say no more. You don't have to."

"Let her speak." Porphyry tried to be heard above everyone else all suddenly talking at once.

"Not a word," Uncle Toby thundered. "I forbid it. The child is in shock. She doesn't know what she's saying."

"Oh, but she does." I heard my voice slightly tremulous coming at me over vast distances. "She knows exactly what she's saying."

My words brought all the bickering to a halt. Colonel Porphyry gave me a long, quizzical look.

"I grant you it's confusing," I hurried on. "But if you give me a moment I can explain. You see, I was a witness . . ."

"Witness to what?"

"I was there when Cassie plunged the dart into Jones's throat."

"You're lying," Cassie shrieked. "You were not there."

"You didn't know, Cassie. You didn't see me. But, believe me, I was there."

"Jonathan," Uncle Toby boomed, "if this is your idea of being clever . . ."

"Ladies and gentlemen." Colonel Porphyry was on his feet, clapping his hands to bring us to order. "Will you all kindly resume your seats."

113

It hadn't been the words so much as the manner. Not hectoring, not autocratic. Just a simple firmness fortified by a sense of quiet authority. It worked. When some semblance of order had been restored, the Colonel gazed around at us reproachfully. "Now then, I trust we'll have no more outbursts," he said. "There'll be plenty of time later, Mr. Jonathan, to discuss more fully what you witnessed. But for now I should like to have Miss Cassandra tell me why she believes she killed her father."

The great library clock bonged the hour. Rain pelted the long lancet windows and outside, rags of mist curled like serpents around the towers and battlements.

Cassie, standing alone in the middle of the room, looked oddly small. Hands on hips, head cocked to one side, she glared around at us defiantly. "Well, spit. Don't look at me that way," she began. "Why do you all look so funny? Lettie, you look like you're about to be sick all over yourself. You all knew I'd do it. Sooner or later. One day or the next. What's so awful? We all talked about it. What did we lose? Certainly not a father. He was never that." She folded her arms and stamped a foot. "He may have been a great inventor and a famous man, but he was a rotten father and I'm glad I did what I did before he could do it to me."

It had poured from her in wave after wave of astonishing venom. The sense of anger and hurt in one so young was startling.

"You want to hear how I did it?" She turned with a fury on the Colonel. "You want to know how I got up to the upper floor? No mystery. I walked up there. It was easy. No problem. The doors weren't locked. Someone had very kindly left them open and no one even tried to stop me. And, finding Jones's room—that was easy, too.

"He was there last night at the ball. You saw him, Johnnie. I pointed him out to you. I even wrote you a message. 'The monk.' Remember? He didn't fool me for a minute. It was so easy to find the right room. Maybe too easy. All those closed doors, except for that one open door at the end of the corridor with a big white square of light spilling out from inside. It was almost as if someone had marked the place out for me. 'Here he is,' it said. 'Go get him.' Downstairs in the ballroom, I could hear music; people singing and laughing. One lady was laughing louder than all the rest. I decided to wait until the whole house was asleep. Then I'd return.

"I went back to my room, got into pajamas, set the alarm for

114

two o'clock and tried to sleep. But I couldn't. So I just lay there—maybe two hours. The minute the alarm went off, I was up and moving.

"It was a few minutes past two A.M. when I got back up there. The door at the end of the corridor was still open and there was that same big white square of light on the wall opposite. I remember turning there and walking in. The first thing I saw was a big chandelier hanging from the ceiling in the center of the main room. It had hundreds of tiny bulbs all shimmering through little beads of crystal and I remember thinking what a pretty pattern it made on the ceiling. Then I was walking in out of the dark corridor and the brightness of the light hurt my eyes. My feet felt airy, as if I were floating, and there was a funny hum in my head that made my ears ring.

"I kept thinking I was about to do something. Something big. Something important. And still I wasn't sure what it was exactly I was about to do. There was this dart. I'd had it in my pocket from the game room for days. I don't know why I'd been carrying it around so long, and once or twice I reached in and felt it. I didn't want to see it, didn't want to look at it. So I kept it in my pocket, just feeling it. Squeezing it. Rolling it around in my hand.

"Then I saw the bedroom. It was this funny little space off to the right. It had a low ceiling and something like a night lamp that cast a dim light. I remember thinking how small the room was. And there was no furniture in it except the bed and this little night table beside it. And I remember thinking how strange that a man as rich and powerful as Jones would sleep in something so . . . so mingy and kind of bare. Just the bed and the table and on the table the night lamp and a glass of water and in the water . . ." Cassie's head fell back. Her eyes closed and I thought she was about to cry. But instead she laughed in a loud unnatural way. It didn't sound like her laugh at all. It sounded like someone else laughing inside her. "Teeth," she giggled. "A full set with these funny pink gums grinning at me from out of the glass.

"The bed was big, " she went on, growing more serious. "And there was this sort of funny lace canvas draped on the bedposts over the top of it so it looked a little like a tent he was sleeping in. I remember walking slowly over to where he lay in the bed. It was all topsy-turvy, like whoever was in there had been restless and kicked the sheets and blankets around.

"There were lots of pillows too—maybe five or six or so, just

115

sort of scattered up against the headboard. And beneath all of those blankets and pillows I could make out a shape. It lay to one side of the bed—the side nearest me. The outline of it seemed too small for a bed of that size. And then I saw the toe. It was sticking out from the bottom of the blanket, like something that wasn't attached to anything else. It was white—a kind of sickly white and pointing toward me and the toenail was black—black the way a fingernail gets when you've caught it in the door.

"I knew I wasn't supposed to see him. To dare to even look at him. I knew it was forbidden. Against the rules of the System. But I didn't care. Nothing could have stopped me then. For the first time in a long time I felt happy. And then I noticed that the dart was no longer in my pocket and that I was holding it in my hand, and it was cold and damp to the touch.

"I remember watching my hand raising the pillow, and thinking to myself that the hand I saw wasn't really my hand but someone else's. And I waited there, watching, wondering what the hand would do next.

I watched the hand lift the corner of the pillow between the two fingers, very delicatelike, the way you pick up something squiggly—a worm or something like that. Then I lifted the pillow off of his head.

"Then I looked down at my father for the first time. I don't know what I expected to see. I thought I should feel something. I wanted to feel something but I wasn't sure what. I thought I'd see a little bald old man with a ring of thin white hair like a halo 'round his head. But this person didn't look old at all. Not old like a father's supposed to look. Instead I saw just an ordinary sort of person, kind of nice and dignified and all. The face was looking away from me, pointing to the wall so I saw only one side of it. All I had to do was walk 'round the other side of the bed to see his full face. But for some reason I didn't want to see it anymore. And I remember thinking, Could it be? Was this plain, just-any-old-person really my father? And for a minute, I thought I was going to be sick.

"His neck stretched beneath the pillow and a blue vein stood out in his throat. I watched it and thought I could see it rise and fall—that rubbery, stringy blue cord, so ugly I couldn't take my eyes from it.

"The next thing I knew the dart wasn't in my hand anymore. I recall looking down at my empty palm, wondering where the dart had gone. I thought for a minute I'd dropped it somewhere

116

in the bed and I thought, Oh spit! Now I'd have to go searching for it in all the topsy-turvy mess, and I didn't want to touch the person lying there, or the sheets or anything.

"Then, out of the corner of my eye, I was looking at that blue stringy cord again and thinking that it looked different. There was something different about it. Something funny. And then I saw the feather at his throat. It looked wet and it glistened with something and I thought how pretty it looked, blue with that splash of red, like a flower that had just bloomed there and all."

21

"Ridiculous."

"She doesn't know what she's saying."

Toby was on his feet, moving swiftly around the desk. "Take her out of here. She has no business here."

Instantly, Parelli was at her side, taking her by the shoulder, attempting to march her out.

In a nimble step or two Porphyry had swept around behind Cassie and with his forearm encircled her shoulders, clasping her back against his chest.

"If you don't mind, Signor, Miss Cassie will remain with us a bit longer."

"She doesn't know what she's saying," Toby said. "She's overwrought."

"She well may be," the Colonel agreed. "But now that she's spoken, she's earned the right to hear the rest."

"The rest?" Uncle Toby's jaw dropped. "There is no rest. None of this is true."

The Colonel nodded wearily. "Your nephew claims to be a witness to these acts. It would be useful for us all to now hear his version of the events."

"Both versions are totally false," Toby thundered.

"The child's always been something of a storyteller," Parelli said, rushing to his master's support.

"But this time her story's absolutely true," I said again, louder, more forcefully. "I can say that because I was present. . . ."

"He wasn't," Cassie snapped. "That's a lie."

The Colonel gazed across at Uncle Toby. He shook his head despairingly. "You see, Mr. Jones? Two different versions of the same event."

Sofi's head fell backward and she laughed liltingly upward, greatly amused. "Don't take anything Jonathan says too seriously, Colonel. He's also a bit of a fibber."

Disregarding her, Porphyry scribbled something onto a little pad, then glanced at Uncle Toby. "It's my understanding that the young people of the house are forbidden access to the upper floor. Is that true?"

"Absolutely," Uncle Toby bristled. "It's off-limits."

"Under no circumstances?"

"Without exception."

"Yet last night some of them appear to have wandered up and down at will."

A wicked smile flickered at the corners of Sofi's mouth. "What's forbidden is always so much more alluring."

"Yes, yes." Porphyry waved the remark aside. "I've raised four of my own. I'm well versed in the wiles of youthful behavior." His brow cocked and he looked around at us. "So I may fairly conclude that some of you, or possibly all of you, have visited the top floor at one time or another?"

His gaze moved past each of us, as each in turn nodded a grudging assent.

"Once? Twice?" he inquired. "Miss Sofi?"

Sofi gnawed her lower lip bewitchingly. "Let's just say on more than one occasion."

Uncle Toby had begun to fume.

"I see," Porphyry acknowledged. "And Miss Letitia?"

Lettie had been silent throughout the course of the proceedings. Suddenly addressed by the Colonel, the color drained from her face.

"More than once," she answered beneath her breath as though confessing to some shocking crime.

"Any special reason?"

"Reason?"

119

"Yes, yes. Why do you go up there?"

The tall, lanky figure of Signor Parelli stirred in the shadows.

"Sometimes . . ." Letitia made an effort to reply but only managed to garble her words.

"I'm sorry. I didn't quite catch . . ."

Lettie stared at the floor, her face florid. "Sometimes . . . just to get away from down here."

Colonel Porphyry gazed at her. About to pursue the point, he then thought better of it, turning instead to Ogden. "And you?"

Ogden stiffened with self-righteousness. "I follow the rules of the house. I obey even if others don't."

A series of lines furrowed the Colonel's brow. Then at last his gaze fell on me. "And you, Mr. Jonathan, I know about. You've already told me."

"Yes—I've been up there before."

"More than once?"

"More than once," I confirmed.

Porphyry frowned.

"Look"—Uncle Toby fixed the Colonel with his gaze—"I think you can safely discount everything you've heard here tonight."

Porphyry smiled somewhat ambiguously. "Perhaps the matter is somewhat more problematic than you make it out, Mr. Jones. Your niece Cassie claims to have punched a dart into your brother's throat. And now your nephew Jonathan confirms this."

"You don't seriously believe any of that?" Uncle Toby said.

"What I believe," Porphyry said, "is not important for the moment. I would like, however, to get back to Mr. Jonathan." He pressed me back down into the chair. "You also managed to reach your father's room."

"I already said I did."

The Colonel flicked back several pages in his pad. "And that was at approximately . . ."

"One-twenty A.M. I know because I checked my watch."

"And then Miss Cassie appeared. For the second time, she says, shortly after two."

"Two-ten," Cassie snapped peevishly.

Colonel Porphyry scribbled something on his pad, then looked up. "Which means, Mr. Jonathan, that you were upstairs for slightly over fifty minutes before your sister appeared. What did you do in all that time?"

120

"Most of it I spent hunting for the room."

"And you found it?"

"After some trial and error," I replied. "I went up and down two or three corridors and got hopelessly lost."

Porphyry nodded. "And then at last you did find the room."

"Yes. Just as Cassie described it. The door was wide open and the lights were blazing in the big outer room. In the bedroom, when I entered there was a small dim night light on the table beside the bed where he slept."

Porphyry's tongue darted across his lower lip, giving him for the moment the look of a thirsty lizard in a parched desert. "Then, if I may ask, what did you do with the time between locating your father's room and the arrival of your sister?"

A deadly silence descended. I could sense them all hanging on my every word. "Most of the time I just stood beside his bed," I said at last. "I know that sounds odd."

"How long was that?"

"Perhaps fifteen minutes."

"And what was he doing, your father, at this time?"

"He was sleeping. Or so I thought."

"You mean you're not certain?"

"It looked to me as though he was sleeping."

"What was his physical position at the time? Do you recall?"

"On his side," I said. "The covers drawn up to his chin."

Porphyry brooded. "Which side?"

"The left side."

"And you simply stood beside the bed all that time?"

"Yes."

"You didn't go 'round to the other side?"

"No. After all that time wondering about my father—who he was—I was afraid to look at him. At least directly." The words tumbled bitterly from me.

Porphyry's eyes closed in that way that seemed to suggest he was reaching for something of which he himself was not quite certain. "What was going through your mind at the time? Can you recall?"

"I was thinking that now that I'd found him I could do to him what I'd dreamed of doing for so long."

"You mean kill him?"

"Yes—and I did."

"Good God," Toby said, glaring.

Madam Lobkova made a soft moaning sound.

121

"That will be quite enough." Toby was on his feet. "I almost regret having summoned you here, Colonel."

"Nevertheless, I'm afraid you did." The Colonel smiled at him indulgently. "And at some point the police would have had to be informed in any event."

Uncle Toby appeared to swell inside his clothing. "We'll answer no further questions, Colonel, until we've had recourse to counsel."

"That is, of course, your right." Porphyry turned back to me and without missing a beat said, "You heard your uncle, Mr. Jonathan. You need not, if you wish, answer any further questions without benefit of counsel."

"But I want to answer questions," I protested. "I have every intention—"

A pulse throbbed at Toby's jaw. Stymied, he was uncertain what to do next.

"Where were we, Colonel?" I asked, eager to go on, to finish it before I lost my nerve.

Porphyry glanced at his notepad. "You were saying that you observed your sister from a hidden vantage point outside the bedroom."

"That's right. When I heard her approaching, I stepped into the big wardrobe just outside the room. Leaving the door open a crack, I saw her walk toward the bed."

"And that's how you came to see her kill your father?"

The shift of attention drew back to me with an almost palpable tug. "I didn't actually say that," I replied after a moment. "I said only that she did exactly what she told you she did a few minutes ago."

Porphyry's head bobbled slightly on his thickish neck. "Then what you're saying is . . ."

"Exactly. Cassie thought she killed him. But by that time, Jones was already dead."

"I did kill him," Cassie shrieked. "I did. I know I did."

Porphyry ignored her, his gaze fixed on me. "Let me see if I follow. What you're now telling me is that in the brief time between your arrival at your father's bedside and the time when Miss Cassie arrived there, it was you who killed your father?"

"Not at all."

The Colonel's head snapped back smartly.

"I said that I fully intended to kill my father at that moment. And I certainly went through all the motions of doing just that.

But what I'm confessing to is only having made the same mistake that Cassie had."

"You mean, I take it, that you, too, had killed someone who was already dead?"

"Exactly."

Ogden was snorting, glaring at me, pawing the carpet like a bull about to charge. "Oh, you're clever, you are. So damned clever."

Porphyry shot him an annoyed glance, then turned back to me. "Well, then, if you will be so kind, Mr. Jonathan, please tell us how you went about this business of . . . of . . . thinking you killed your father."

"It's not that complicated." I smiled at his confusion. "I smothered him with a pillow."

"And by then, you say, he was already dead."

"Yes. But I didn't realize that he was until I held the pillow over his face. . . ."

"How long? Do you recall?"

"Several minutes."

"Could you be more precise? It's important."

"Two, possibly three, minutes until . . ."

"Yes, yes." Porphyry nodded eagerly. "Say it. Until you realized . . ."

"Until it occurred to me that he didn't struggle at all. He hadn't once resisted. Hadn't even woken. And his body was stiff."

"Then what did you do?" the Colonel persisted.

"I lifted the pillow from his face."

"And you saw . . ."

"His face was still pointing to the wall. It hadn't moved. It was slightly bluish and the mouth hung open."

Porphyry was looking down, scribbling into his pad. "Yes, yes. Go on."

"Then I noticed the angle at which his head lay on the pillow. It hung at an odd angle. A sickening angle."

"As though the neck were broken. And who do you think broke it?" he asked.

"Me." Ogden came close to a howl. "Shortly, he's going to suggest to you that I did it."

"I'm unaware that he's been suggesting any such thing," Porphyry protested.

123

"Besides, Oggie," I added, "you wouldn't have had character enough."

"Why don't we end this now?" Madam Lobkova bustled forward.

"We'll be finishing up soon enough, madam," Porphyry assured her. "I have just one or two more questions." He turned and looked hard at me. "And it was then, I take it, your sister Cassandra arrived?"

"Yes—a moment or two later."

The big grandfather clock in the dusty corner struck midnight.

Colonel Porphyry slapped both his knees and rose to his feet. "So then, it appears we now have two people who've confessed to the murder of a man who was apparently already dead. Murdered, no doubt, by a third."

A sly little smile sent Porphyry's mouth momentarily askew. He looked around at us, almost affectionately. "Before we retire for the evening, do we have anyone else who wishes to vie for the honor of murdering Mr. Jones?"

Letitia rose and stumbled forward in that distracted, slightly frantic way of hers.

"Oh, Lettie dear. Not you now." Sofi groaned and flopped back down in her chair.

"Tobias—you're not going to permit this," Madam Lobkova pleaded. "She's always confessing to something."

"Please," Letitia cried above the din, "I want to tell you . . . I have to tell someone what I did." Winding and unwinding a handkerchief in her hands, Letitia made a low, keening sound. "I killed him . . . I mean, that is, I wanted him dead."

"That's quite another matter," Porphyry said.

"Let me finish. Please—" Lettie pleaded. Her head drooped into her outstretched palms and her shoulders shook fitfully. "The other day"—her voice rose muffled from behind her hands—"I was summoned to my audience with Jones, and he started to tell me how well I was doing, how pretty I looked, what dramatic strides I'd made in my work over the past year. Then he did something very odd. Almost unheard of. He touched me."

"Touched you?" The Colonel's puzzlement deepened.

"Yes. Here," Lettie said. "On the cheek. Very tenderly. Right there. I knew I was slated for something horrible."

Porphyry cocked a brow at her. "Horrible?"

124

"That's the way it is when they're about to terminate you," Sofi explained. "They become very kind."

The Colonel made an odd expression. "What do you mean, terminate you?"

Uncle Toby half rose from his chair. Parelli moved out of the shadows.

From somewhere deep within Letitia, a low wail began to rise. "When they send you away."

"Send you away where?"

"She means leaving the Institute to join Mr. Jones in the Service," Parelli hastened to explain. "It's a great honor."

Letitia's stricken eyes darted back and forth from the Colonel to Signor Parelli.

Porphyry considered all that had just transpired. Standing there gazing from one of us to the other, he frowned. His body appeared to tremble slightly. But then, in the next moment, he shrugged and gave an odd little laugh. "So. Very well then. I see how things are here. No doubt we are in for some interesting times together."

Later that night I lay in bed mulling over the strange course of events that had brought us to this juncture. Indeed, everything that had happened over the past several days seemed to have come swiftly on the heels of Leander's disappearance—Jones's death, and the appearance of the Woodsmen. Those events appeared directly connected, all related in some manner not yet clear to me. Between us and the mainland lay nearly a hundred miles of untracked wilderness. Except for the helicopter landing strip on the big surrounding lawn, we were completely cut off from civilization.

It was clear that our position, particularly while the storm raged, was extremely vulnerable. And if this was clear to me, surely it was to the Woodsmen. Why, I asked myself, after so many years of relatively peaceful coexistence, had they chosen this time to become threatening? True, in the past their behavior had always been unpredictable, but well within the limits of manageability. Something had happened now to change all that. That *something* seemed clearly connected with the death of Jones.

And what of Leander? If all the others appeared to have forgotten him, Cassie and I, at least, had not. In fact, his whereabouts had become something of an obsession with me. Try as I

125

might, I couldn't forget that sad little mound of clothing in the tower dungeon. Was he still here in the castle? If not, where was he? More important, was he still alive?

Several times over the past forty-eight hours I'd taken out the button Cornie had given me and the piece of goatskin I'd found at the door of the tower. Turning each over in my hand, I rubbed them between my fingers as though they were talismans and I could conjure from them answers no one else seemed ready or able to provide.

Then, too, there was this odd little policeman from the mainland, Colonel Porphyry, with his sometimes merry, sometimes unsettling gaze. It had been roughly seven hours since we'd heard his reassuring words about the Woodsmen and the doubtless benign nature of their visit. After all this time, however, I could see little sign, as the Colonel had suggested, that their presence here in ever-growing numbers was merely the kindly gesture of a simple people expressing their grief. It seemed to me, and by then, I'm sure, to the others, that the Woodsmen had something else in mind. Something quite different. Perhaps the Colonel was not being as forthright with us as he pretended to be. Or perhaps he didn't know the goat people as well as we.

Lying in bed that night, I listened to the storm raging outside. The rain hammered at my window. It coursed in jagged streaks down the panes through which the lurid light of pitch pine torches danced in ever-shifting patterns on the wall. It seemed like hours I lay there sleepless, praying, hoping against hope for some sign that my brother Leander was still alive—still hidden, but safe somewhere in the castle. But, when sleep finally came, I'd still had no assurances.

22

Colonel Porphyry sat in a tiny, windowless cubicle adjoining the rear of Uncle Toby's study. The heat had been turned down for the night and so he sat buttoned up in his yellow slicker, a long wool scarf coiled about his throat, sifting through a mountain of papers.

For a man with a reputation as a particularly keen criminal investigator, the Colonel was by temperament surprisingly unsuspicious. He preferred to let things reveal themselves within the normal course of an investigation. Accordingly, he came with no preconceived notions about how certain events might have transpired.

So it was now. He'd subpoenaed the Institute's administrative and financial files in the usual pro forma way, without having the hint of an idea what they might contain. These files dated back to the organization's earliest days and alone comprised thousands of pieces of paper.

In addition to the Institute's files, Foundation records had been requested, including budgets, payroll data, as well as a roster of Jones's annual philanthropic outlays—information that Uncle Toby would have preferred to keep private.

127

But there was no graceful way of declining. It was all quite official and refusal to throw open these books would have raised even greater suspicion. Accordingly, Toby Jones swallowed his ire and assured the Colonel that he had his full cooperation.

All throughout the day crates of documents were trundled into the study and parked in neat, numbered rows just outside of the cubicle assigned to Colonel Porphyry for the duration of his visit. To read through all of these documents would have taken years and the expertise of a half dozen trained investigators who knew precisely what they were looking for. Under such circumstances, Porphyry was flying by night without instrumentation. But, oddly enough, that's precisely how the Colonel preferred to travel.

His ordeal began just a little after midnight, when all the others broke for the evening. An incurable insomniac, Porphyry was not the least bit tired, even after a heavy meal. Actually, he was rather elated, his mind still crackling from all the after-dinner fireworks in Mr. Toby's study.

After a short while, however, his enthusiasm for reading began to pall. It was dry, official stuff for the most part. An hour of it had bored him. By the second hour he was decidedly cross and by the third, he was struggling to keep awake.

Starting with the Foundation files, he'd found a great deal of scientific material—proposals for grants to study esoteric subjects in faraway places, hundreds of pages of correspondence between Tobias Jones and importunate scholars anxious to escape drab jobs for a year or so and "make a significant contribution to the march of civilization."

Following the Foundation files Porphyry, eyes drooping, dipped into the administrative records. He went at this more selectively than he had the Foundation files, fearing that his eyes would give out before making even a dent in the sheer volume of paper.

A blizzard of vouchers and manifolds, inventory records and bills swam past his glazed stare. He found himself checking order blanks for a variety of technical equipment—spectroscopes, X-ray machines, autoclaves, magnetic resonance equipment, chemical compounds of all sorts, along with a huge pharmacopoeia of drugs.

That was the least of it. What followed was an extensive payroll carefully designating the salary categories of household personnel—everyone from cooks and gardeners on up to the increasingly esoteric vocations of the laboratory staff.

The sort of salaries he saw stipulated for these individuals struck him as princely, if not foolishly extravagant. He made a note to himself to begin interrogating the "white smock crowd" as soon as he'd finished up with the immediate family.

Between midnight and three A.M., having flung the administrative records aside in disgust, Porphyry went on to the Institute's files. These opened with a rather fulsome history of the organization drafted in a spidery hand on foolscap yellowed with age. The authorship and the hand, the Colonel felt certain, were the work of the late Mr. Orville Jones himself.

Entitled *De Rerum Institutio*, the document was mottled with watermarks and crumbling at the edges from old age. It was written in a highblown, somewhat affected language. Porphyry had to read the opening paragraph several times until he felt he had the gist of it. Gradually, he caught on to the stylistic idiosyncracies. Peppered with schoolboy-level Latin phrases and an antique syntax, at first it seemed quaint, then later merely irritating. Eventually, things went easier.

Convinced he would find nothing of use in *De Rerum*, he happened to gaze upon the date of the document, written at the top of the title page. It was July 27, 1991.

It wasn't the date on the document that had caught the Colonel's eye, however, but the fact that it appeared to have been only recently inscribed there. Moreover, the white area directly beneath the date was a tone or two lighter than the surrounding parchment, giving the impression that an ink eradicator had been applied to the spot. Both the eradication and the writing at this particular point were clearly new. Set down in an ink that was darker than that of the original manuscript, the hand that had drafted the date had also made a clumsy attempt to forge the original.

At that hour this observation inspired in Porphyry no more than a mild curiosity. But then, on a whim, he flicked through the records filed in chronological order that followed just behind the history.

In document after document, without exception, an identical adjustment had been made to conform with that on the title page. Invariably, at points where one date had formerly appeared on the original, there was now a slightly bleached-out look, strongly hinting that an ink eradicator had been used and a new date inserted over it.

These changes applied roughly to the first third of the file, involving dates occurring mostly within the final decades of the twentieth century. The last two-thirds of the file showed no signs of alteration.

The point suggested by these changes seemed scarcely dramatic enough in itself to arouse the Colonel's curiosity. Still, it was enough to send him thumbing back to the administrative files.

This time he started not at the beginning in chronological order, as he had in his first go-round, but randomly, back to front. Within the last two thirds of the first drawer of administrative files, he could find no sign of recent tampering. But in the first third of the file, he found an abundance of changes. Just as in the case of the Institute files, dates had been entered on vouchers and invoices, manifests, bills and canceled checks, all drawn in the last two decades of the prior century.

The changes here, like the others, were all recent, and written in a crude counterfeit of the same crimped spidery hand that had drafted the original history of the Institute. The reason that Colonel Porphyry had failed to detect the changes the first time through was that the eradicator used on the bills and vouchers didn't discolor the paper as obviously as it had on the parchment. There the ink used to write over the eradicated spots tended to get runny and plug up, calling attention to itself.

On the desk where the Colonel worked, hunched over mounds of paper, was an electric pencil sharpener. Just below the small hole into which pencils to be sharpened are inserted was a small drawer for catching the wood and lead shavings that accumulated after each sharpening.

From this tiny receptacle he now poured a small quantity of shavings onto the reverse side of one of the doctored records. With a circular motion of his forefinger, he lightly rubbed them over the spot that had been altered.

It took perhaps a moment or two before what he sought finally appeared. Emerging in small raised characters where the lead shavings had fallen away from the ridges left by the pressure of a penpoint, were the letters and numerals of the original date that had been effaced. The date Colonel Porphyry now saw there before him in faint, but nonetheless legible characters was September 9, 1947. The date that appeared on the reverse side, recently entered and quite obviously written directly over the original, was September 9, 1997.

It was at that moment he glanced up, thinking he'd heard the cry of an infant from somewhere above. He listened again, but hearing no further sound, he put it down to his imagination.

It was just before dawn but still dark when Colonel Porphyry appeared, bleary-eyed, on the tower. Dressed in his outsized yellow slicker with a floppy brimmed foul weather hat pulled down low over his brow, he looked slightly drunk.

While the rain had abated somewhat, the wind still howled. Leaning slightly forward into the gusts, the Colonel approached several of his men standing watch on the battlements. The effort gave him a wobbly rolling gait, like that of a sailor moving on a pitching deck.

"Well, lads," he said to the group huddling there, "how goes it?"

They moved aside to make room for him. One of the men, a tall, commanding figure called Magnus, descended from Nordic mariners, pointed to the bottom of the garden. With rain lashing his face, Porphyry squinted off in that direction where the pitch pine torches guttered in the graying dawn.

"The torches seem somewhat fewer," the Colonel remarked hopefully.

"Yes sir," Magnus replied. "Some of the little fellows, they've gone. We watched them march off into the forest. A bit over an hour ago."

Porphyry nodded although he felt no reason to be hopeful. The fact that some of them had abandoned their vigil did not necessarily mean they wouldn't be back in several hours, fed and in dry clothing, ready to resume their increasingly worrisome watch.

"You think they'll come back, Colonel?" Magnus asked.

Porphyry peered down to where several torches danced wildly in the wind. It struck him that he was more nervous about the Woodsmen he couldn't see than those he could. From everything he'd read about them in the research library at the home office, he knew they were skilled trackers and fearless tacticians. It would be typical of them to lull their enemies into a false sense of security, then strike.

Porphyry leaned his elbows on the battlement walls, his head drooping wearily. "I think you can depend on it," he replied, then thrust his jaw into the howling gale, as if to defy it.

131

Part 6

Cornie

One Day in much good Company, I was asked by a Person of Quality, whether I had seen any of their *Struldbrugs* or *Immortals*. I said I had not; and desired he would explain to me what he meant by such an Appelation, applyed to a mortal Creature. He told me, that sometimes, although very rarely, a Child happened to be born in a Family with a red circular Spot in the Forehead, directly over the left Eyebrow, which was an infallible Mark that it should never dye.

—Jonathan Swift, *Gulliver's Travels, Third Voyage*

23

It was near midnight now of that same day that Jones had been discovered dead. Cornelius Jones moved swiftly through the complicated network of tunnels and catacombs winding their way beneath the castle. His motion was swift and catlike, as though he had some specific destination and meant to get there fast.

His way took him through limestone grottoes with low, dripping ceilings beneath which the crown of his head barely passed. Something drove him, all of his actions impelled by a sharp singleness of purpose.

Suddenly, he was running, hurtling headlong through the tunnels, eager to reach his destination before dawn. In another moment Cornie had stepped into a shallow alcove off one of the smaller feeder tunnels. The place was little more than a narrow indentation, possibly four feet wide and recessed two or three feet into a limestone wall. It was a bit like entering an upright rectangular box. Pressing his chest hard up against the rear of the alcove, his cheek grazing the cool, damp stone, he let his right hand slide up and down its inner wall.

At last he found what he was seeking. Almost at once a deep

rumbling noise rose from somewhere beneath his feet. It was the sound of an immense weight moving—the grating sound of stone passing over stone.

The wall directly in front of him appeared to shudder, then buckle slightly inward. A groaning and creaking followed as the wall began to lift. Suddenly, at the point where his knees were, there was no longer any wall.

Still the wall rose, reaching his waist; then above his chest. Once above his head, he watched the bottom of it slide into a pocket in the limestone ceiling, where it vanished completely.

Before him stood open space. There was a sweetness to the air. A whiff of grass and muddy earth filled his head, along with the sharp, resinous scent of alpine forests. The darkness throbbed with cricket rattling and when he stepped into the whirring air, fireflies flashed like streaking meteors before his eyes.

Once outside, Cornie plunged off headlong across the wide slope of lawn gently descending to the edge of the forest some hundred yards away. He'd taken this path often before. Moments later he reached a point at the bottom of the slope where a narrow, nearly invisible wedge had been sliced into a wall of seemingly impenetrable bush. Glancing quickly over his shoulder, he glimpsed the dark towering silhouette of the castle painted against the night sky. Then, with a low, fierce, strangely exultant cry, he slipped into the forest.

Cornie loved the forest. He seemed born to it, particularly at night when the sun had set and the air was ten degrees cooler than in the open field that stood just beside it. He liked the canopy of trees above him and the feeling of the underbrush gradually encircling him. He felt an easy affinity with all the prowling things he knew to be about. With the first hoot of an owl and the pale disc of moon still visible in the predawn sky, he was at peace.

The path he took was an extension of the same one he'd entered at the margin of the trees. It was narrow, only wide enough for a single person to pass, but clearly marked and obviously well maintained. You could see where new brush and saplings that had tried to take hold there had been cruelly uprooted.

Circling an area of large boulders, the path turned downward, moving around a wide dark tarn with the evening stars reflected on its black rippling surface.

The path continued to drop for several hundred feet into a steep declivity, strewn with small boulders which punished the feet of those imprudent enough to attempt a passage without tough, thick-soled shoes. Halfway down the slope, the earth seemed to open. The undergrowth and trees grew sparse. Much of the first-growth trees had been felled; those that remained were spindly and denuded, as though struck by blight.

In the air all about was the smell of something burned, and then of something putrid, like marsh gas; something that hinted of brackish water and rotting vegetation. The ground there grew soft underfoot. Shortly it became spongy and made sucking noises at the soles of his shoes.

Seeing the fires of the encampment up ahead, Cornie moved faster. Approaching, he could see the cramped huddle of pens and, just beyond, the faint outline of low, squat dwellings made of mud and bullrush. Sparks showered upward from the stumpy clay pipe chimneys stuck in the topmost part of each.

It was a strange sight to come on suddenly like that in the forest. It rose along a shallow hill like a toy village. And above it hung a thickish haze, a choking stench of roasting flesh and sewerage leeching out from the edges of the encampment. At the entrance of the village stood a series of rough wood pikes, each surmounted with what appeared to be some form of animal skull.

Cornie's pace quickened. He felt a rush of excitement as, once again, he entered the camp of the Woodsmen.

24

Shortly after dawn the rain stopped. The wind dropped and off to the east where the sun was rising, the skies were brushed with pink.

More encouraging was the fact that the Woodsmen had gone. Where only hours before they had stood three and four deep around the castle, the only movements at the forest's edge now were the faint puffs of dying wind nudging the vacant brush.

Uncle Toby had been up before any of the others. He appeared in the kitchen, bustling and energetic. Freshly shaven, attired in a formal dark suit, he went about barking orders at the staff.

With the first sign of clearing in the eastern sky, he'd woken Signor Parelli and had him issue a command to proceed with the funeral. Several sharp raps on each bedroom door roused us. A voice on the other side instructed us to have breakfast quickly and prepare for the long trek up to the old Indian burial grounds.

It was at a point just behind the scullery we gathered. Already, a dozen burly porters had assembled there. They wore dark suits with white gloves. In addition, ten pallbearers drawn from the house security staff had taken up their places beside the casket.

The mourning party was comprised of my brothers and sisters, Signor Parelli, Madam Lobkova and Uncle Toby, who I noticed carried a holstered revolver barely concealed under his suit jacket. Both the pallbearers and the porters had been issued sidearms. Colonel Porphyry and his own people were to come along as additional protection.

Through the iron grillwork of an immense portcullis, we viewed the world beyond awaiting us. I can't begin to describe the surge of conflicting emotions I felt during those last few moments. Several days before, and for the first time in my life, I'd ventured outside, and then for only a scant few feet. The occasion was so brief it could scarcely qualify as a genuine foray to the outside. This was, for me and my brothers and sisters, our first actual venture beyond the castle walls.

Letitia, gazing wide-eyed through the portcullis, was clearly terrified. Cassie hovered beside me, her small damp hand hanging limp in mine. Affecting irritation, Ogden appeared actually stunned by the significance of the moment. Even Sofi, who'd developed the pose of boredom to a high art, was overawed at the prospect of taking her first steps outside Fraze.

As the creaky tonnage of the portcullis rose, there was a stir of excitement. A pale disc of sunshine slipped out from a smudge of dark cloud. Through the open entryway a soft breeze redolent of recent rain, moist earth and pine filled the stone antechamber in which we waited. With the portcullis finally up we stood in silence for a strangely protracted moment, staring at the wide, unobstructed path opening before us.

"All right," Toby said, clapping his hands. "Casket and pallbearers first. I want the young people two abreast and directly behind. Umberto and Wanda next, and I'll take up the rear."

"Where would you like us?" Colonel Porphyry asked.

"Just behind our group at the rear, if you please, Colonel."

Porphyry nodded, a slightly pained look on the man, I thought.

Uncle Toby quickly reviewed the matter of security. "I'd like the house guard to distribute themselves as follows: one in front, one in back, and a file of five on either side of the procession. I don't anticipate trouble, but if it comes I expect each and every one of you to do your part. Act responsibly. No panic. Stay together and, in the event of trouble, under no circumstances is anyone to break from the group and run off by himself. Is that understood?"

He gazed bleakly around, as though making his own private assessment of what to expect from each of us. "The burial grounds are about two miles from here. It's a stiff walk, mostly uphill. At this time of year the path shouldn't be too overgrown. But the casket is heavy and our progress will be slow. Once in the forest we must all stick close together. No stragglers. Keep a sharp eye out on either side of you. Be alert. Be vigilant. Any questions?"

He looked around as though defying anyone to speak. No one did. "Very well, then. Move out."

Five, ten minutes out from Fraze, I could barely describe the sense of strangeness I felt. No stone. No mortar. No iron or glass between myself and the sky. Our slow, winding procession toiled up a shallow hill. Mourners straggled along in the wet gorse. The pallbearers leaned forward, straining under the heft of the casket. You could hear their grunts and sighs as they labored up the shallow hill.

I am told the ancients considered the old Indian graveyard sacred ground. People buried there, the original inhabitants of our island believed, were not dead but merely in a state of suspended animation. Soon their souls would awake and they would be reborn to join their loved ones. Periodically, the aboriginals would exhume the remains of loved ones to revisit them on special occasions, even have picnics together, then bury them again.

The burial ground, for some reason, is feared and hated by the Woodsmen. Jones, however, was committed to the idea of being interred there, along with all of his kith and kin. Uncle Toby seemed determined, or possibly just intimidated enough by his older brother, even in death, to carry out those final instructions to a tee. All the way up there I couldn't help but wonder why.

The path we traveled was a narrow aisle carved out of the forest, lined on both sides by a wall of towering spruce. The way was weed choked and full of burrs that stuck to your trousers—but for the most part passable.

Roughly twenty minutes out, the hill steepened and Uncle

Toby called a rest. The pallbearers, visibly winded, set down their load. Madam Lobkova's face had gone beet red from the exertion. A covering of thistles stuck to her wide flowing skirts, while Signor Parelli, bristling with disapproval, scampered about, issuing orders in his high nasal voice.

Colonel Porphyry and his party waited in a small cluster at the rear. They smoked cigarettes and chatted, seeming to enjoy thoroughly the sunny break in the weather and the walk in the woods.

Just as we were about to resume, I thought I heard a sound off to my right. Nothing unusual. An unremarkable noise, not enough to make you even turn to look.

Then just at my side a dull thud sounded and a security guard, no more than a foot or so from me, suddenly toppled over. Slipping to the ground, he made no noise, only put a hand up to his forehead as though he were trying to recall something.

In the next moment all the forest was moving. There were screams and shouts. I could see nothing except a frantic blur of motion and shapes hurtling past.

Then I saw the first of them—short, barrel-chested, a long tangled beard and that funny pointed little hat that seemed so playful you wanted to laugh. What had always seemed so amusing on an individual basis became far less so when multiplied a hundred times. I watched with fascination the stumpy little piston arm rise and extend backward. An object, long and, I think, elastic, dangled from the hand behind him. The next I knew, something hit me from behind. I felt the air rush from my lungs and I went down.

"Get down. Get down."

Colonel Porphyry straddled my back, covering my head with his body. In that place where I'd just been standing, a boulder the size of a volleyball crashed into the earth, embedding itself halfway into the soft mud and squirting a line of muck across my trousers.

Suddenly they were all over, the air boiling with shouts and cries. Gunshots rang out. At one point, two of them came up so close to me, I could see the blank, colorless eyes that gave no hint of any human feeling behind them. Cut deep into the oversized heads, the eyes were gashes set unnaturally far apart. It was their gray, dead blankness that was so chilling.

At last I could see closely those long dangling objects they were carrying. They were slingshots. Not the harmless sort small boys use to bring down birds. These were large, fashioned out of

141

tough supple wood and strong with heavy thongs, probably made from the intestine of some animal. One group fired volley after volley of stones at us while another seemed intent on getting at the casket. They would run up and touch it, then dash away.

I became aware of Colonel Porphyry shouting behind me. His hoarse bellow was followed by a barrage of fire. From where I lay, sprawled on the ground, the whole forest appeared to tilt up and spin about me. Then, with that same unexpected suddenness with which they'd come, they left. The shouts and cries, the gunshots and crashing of figures receding through the forest all stopped at once. There was a moment of silence, tentative, expectant, as though everything in that vast wood, man and creature, was awaiting some crucial signal. Then all at once, as if on cue, the birds resumed their song and chatter.

It had all happened in less than a minute. The Woodsmen were gone, fled back into the forest. Several of the security guard, despite orders to the contrary, had panicked and run off. Another lay dead (the one I'd seen topple when the attack began). Colonel Porphyry was on his knees, administering first aid to a figure prone on his stomach, blood seeping from his mouth. One of those round, chunky boulders sat in the weeds nearby. Had it not been for Porphyry and his men, we would surely have all died. The so-called household security guards had proved themselves inept and untrustworthy. Not at all reassuring to a small community of people who now, it appeared, needed security more than ever.

Needless to say, there was no question of continuing on to the cemetery. Everything was in disarray. The casket lay on its side, part in the bush, part on the path, its lid open an inch or two. One of the pallbearers struggled to right it before it could open further. Several of us hurried forward to help him. Fortunately, none of the pallbearers had been injured.

Ragged and badly rattled, the procession reassembled. Shortly, we were once again on the path, straggling along in untidy retreat, fast as we could, back to the safety of the castle.

It would be hard to say how long the return took. Though it had taken only a mere twenty minutes or so to reach the place where we'd been attacked, the return seemed far longer, even though the way was mostly downhill and far less arduous.

When we'd started out that morning the household guard numbered twelve. Now they were eight. Three had run off during

142

the attack and one, gravely injured, had to be carried back in a makeshift litter. They walked along in two single files on either side of us, dispirited, rifles dragging, their former pose of bold, fearless protectors badly punctured.

The general mood of the outing had turned grim. There was little talk and a great deal of anxious backward glancing as we stumbled with our heavy burden and heavier hearts down the path, eager to get home.

The sun was now at a point directly overhead. The wind had dropped and suddenly it was quite warm. Uncle Toby appeared to be smothering in his formal blue funeral suit, now spattered with mud. Still, he made no concessions to the heat, unwilling to even loosen his tie.

But it was on the pallbearers that the heat took its heaviest toll. Straining under their load, they groaned and muttered amongst themselves. Gradually, I became aware of an odor I couldn't identify. I thought it might have something to do with the damp earth or rotting vegetation. It was sweetish but vaguely unpleasant. I paid little attention to it.

All the while we trudged on, the smell grew sharper. The pallbearers muttered more amongst themselves. It was then I realized that others were just as aware of the odor as I.

Stumbling along at my side, Cassie looked up at me, made a queasy face, and pressed her nose delicately between thumb and forefinger. Beautiful even in distress, Sofi strode on ahead, a lace handkerchief crushed to her mouth.

Approaching Fraze from the edge of the wood, the pace quickened. In our haste to get indoors, some of us had started to jog and were now tripping over one another. Slowed by her girth and tangled skirts, Madam Lobkova struggled to keep pace.

As we approached the castle, the big portcullis rose slowly with a great creaking and clanking of wood and chains. When we'd passed through it, actually jogging the last few yards or so, the casket bumping perilously on the shoulders of the pallbearers, the great gate came rumbling down behind us.

The pallbearers, panting and red-faced, put down their burden. In the confinement of the small space in which we now stood, the sharp, unpleasant odor had intensified.

Uncle Toby had the dark, scowling look of a man whose deepest wishes had been thwarted. Something had gone terribly wrong and now he meant to seek out those who were responsible. He barked something to the pallbearers. I believe he'd asked

143

them to carry the casket back up to the chapel. They were about to do so but Signor Parelli stayed them with a hand on the arm of the lead bearer, then whispered something into Uncle Toby's ear. There was a moment in which the two of them, heads together, conferred. Toby seemed quite upset when he motioned Colonel Porphyry to join them.

The conference continued with the three of them huddled together, talking in lowered voices. Parelli's head nodded emphatically as he made some point or other. Uncle Toby looked exasperated. Appearing to moderate between the two, Porphyry looked decidedly uncomfortable.

Toby finally yielded and redirected the pallbearers to carry the casket down to one of the innumerable little limestone grottoes beneath the castle.

At last we were dismissed, told to go back to our rooms. The outing had been a disaster. Everything that could possibly have gone wrong went wrong. There was a pressing need to get Jones into the ground before much longer. Though it would have been unseemly to speak of it, and surely no one dared to, the body had begun to decompose.

In the past when people had died at the castle, the custom was always to put them into the ground as quickly as possible and then without benefit of the embalmers' handiwork. But in Jones's case, this was scarcely feasible. Between torrential rains and the open hostility of the Woodsmen, who, for some reason, seemed determined to prevent his interment, such an undertaking was risky, if not downright dangerous.

We'd always known that the Woodsmen were unpredictable, that they represented a distinct threat. But, on the other hand, we'd never had an opportunity to see what form that threat could take. Now we'd seen it and it was something of an eye-opener.

Shortly after noon the sun we'd seen that morning disappeared. Where I last saw it, the sky had lowered and turned an ominous green. The thunderheads we thought had blown themselves out to sea had actually turned around and come snarling back with a vengeance. The sky darkened in the west and the wind was back up. Through the huge leaded panes in the conservatory, you could see the tops of trees lashing about at the bottom of the garden. Big drops of rain slanted down from the sky, making sharp, cracking sounds on the glass. Shortly, those drops began to beat a loud cannonade on the rooftops and by two that afternoon the sky had closed down so completely that outside it looked like late evening.

"I can't tell you how impressed I was."
  "Oh, come."
  "In all of that chaos to be able to conduct oneself with such . . ." Colonel Porphyry sat erect as he reached for the word. ". . . aplomb."
  "Really, Colonel. You go too far."
  "No, no, my dear madam. I assure you, I don't go far enough."
  Trying to look annoyed, Lobkova frowned. But her color was high and suddenly the room seemed warm and far too small for the likes of her.
  They were in her cozy, spacious apartment in the west wing. They sat in her library, which adjoined a small sitting room. Its large expanse of windows looked out over the black tarn beyond which lay the forest and a distant range of mountains.
  Like its principal occupant, the library was a study in excess. Too much furniture. Too much brocade. Too many knickknacks, every surface of exposed wood littered with curios of one form or another. Thick oriental carpets consumed every cubic foot of air and Madam Lobkova, seated on a long, low recamier, appeared to fill all of the space that was still unoccupied.
  Then, too, there was the bizarre element—the cabalistic signs, the ouija board and planchette on a well-worn card table beside the hearth, looking as though it had been in recent use. The bookshelves running floor to ceiling were crammed with titles revealing a marked interest in necromancy and the black arts. The crowning touch, dangling from a bracket above the mantle, was a shrunken head from some island in the Marquesas.
  "Downright heroic, I call it," the Colonel went on, warming to his subject. "I watched that little chap come right up to you and raise his arm. He had a hatchet. A hatchet, mind you. I feared—actually feared—for you. But I saw at once I had no reason to. None at all. You faced him right down. Didn't bat an eye." Porphyry laughed out loud and slapped his knee. "Poor little fellow didn't know what to make of you. No, ma'am. That he didn't."
  Madam Lobkova cared little for all of this gushing, and she suspected it was disingenuous. But, on the other hand, she didn't

exactly cut the Colonel short. "You're much too kind," she said coolly and looked away.

"No, no. I assure you. I wouldn't insult you with cheap flattery. This is genuine admiration from one who's seen his share of bravery in his time. You spoke to one of them, didn't you?" Porphyry remarked.

"Speak? I didn't speak at all. I shouted at him."

"Quite right. You shouted and he fled."

Porphyry, bolting from his chair, imitated the Woodsman trundling off on stumpy legs. That finally melted her and she yielded to a moment of embarrassed laughter.

"Well, I do speak the language, you know."

"So I've heard." Porphyry wiped his teary eyes. "What did you tell him?"

By then she had begun to glow a bit. In that moment, for all of her substantial girth, she managed to convey an impression of daintiness. She was actually quite pretty. She put the Colonel in mind of a certain kind of lapdog. A Pomeranian, perhaps, primped and curried. With her widow-peaked hairline, her lips painted into a vermillion bow, her face became a valentine.

"I said to him, 'Trug gron buj dodan.'" She rattled out the words in rapid fire.

"That sounds quite authentic," he said.

"It means, 'Little pig, get back to your hovel or I'll squash you.'"

Porphyry's eyes widened in astonishment. "Where did you learn to speak their tongue?"

"Directly from them. Many years ago. When negotiations were first going on here to lease the property."

"From the Woodsmen?"

"Yes, of course. One day Jones and Toby took me out to their camp. We went a number of times as details were being worked out. As I had a certain facility with languages, Jones asked me to accompany the group. Someone was needed as translator, you see, to serve as go-between for both parties. The Woodsman . . . an old devil by the name of Edwig . . . I wonder if he's still alive. . . ." Her voice trailed off as her mind drifted backward over the past. "He was very sharp. Sharp for one of them, anyway. Not quite so common, you understand. In any event, this Edwig fellow sensed my confusion and started me off with a number of hand gestures. Then, by pointing to certain objects about us, he would assign a vocal sound to each."

146

"I see." Porphyry nodded thoughtfully. "What do you suppose they were up to today? What could have provoked such an outburst?"

"We've had incidents like this before." Madam Lobkova grew solemn. "Never quite so violent."

The Colonel rose and slowly paced the room.

"Where did they come from?" she asked.

Porphyry dragged deeply on one of his cigarillos. "No one knows, really. Several hundred years back they lived on the mainland. They were despised by the general populace and welcome nowhere.

"As a matter of plain survival, they were forced to live by pillage and rapine. They were so feared by the people that eventually they had to be rounded up, forced out of the cities and towns where they'd wrought havoc, and ferried over here from the mainland. They came with their goats and little else, and over centuries of repeated inbreeding produced this race of fierce, dwarfish creatures." The Colonel stopped dead in his tracks and smiled to see Madam Lobkova staring keenly up at him. Then he continued. "They own the land you've built on. It was deeded to them in perpetuity by the government as an inducement to keep them from migrating back to the mainland. The arrangement, I take it, has been satisfactory?"

"Satisfactory, my dear Colonel, is putting the best face on a bad business. Mr. Jones tried on a number of occasions to buy the land outright. He offered them fortunes, but they always declined."

"Have you any idea why?"

Madam Lobkova raised her palms and shrugged. "No. They would only agree to lease, and I suspect that's because at some point they plan to repossess the land, along with the castle."

"Any idea why they should choose this day—the day of Mr. Jones's funeral—to act up?"

Up until that moment Madam Lobkova had been receptive to the Colonel's questions, amused at his cleverness, flattered by his mild flirtations. Now, suddenly, something leaped in her eyes, and she grew wary.

"You've been here a long time, haven't you, madam?"

"From the very beginning," she said, a slightly triumphant tremor in her voice.

"You know a great deal of the history of the house?"

"I know something of it. Certainly not all."

147

"Is there anything in this Covenant between Mr. Jones and the Woodsmen that might have provoked today's attack?"

She cocked an eyebrow at him. "Who told you about that?"

Porphyry appeared surprised. "The Covenant? It's mentioned often in the Foundation documents I've been poring over the last several days."

"Oh, yes, of course. It would be, wouldn't it?"

"Say, some breach of terms? Some default of payment? Something?"

"I'm afraid I can't be helpful on that."

"You've seen it though?"

"The Covenant? Certainly."

Something like displeasure crossed his face, then he laughed offhandedly. "What do you suppose are the chances of my getting a peek at it?"

The pencil-line brows arched upward.

"I'm a bit of an antiquarian, you see," he went on. "I have a passion for old documents and it may just prove helpful."

"I fail to see what light that particular document could shed on Mr. Jones's murder."

"Probably no light at all." Porphyry smiled. "But, then again, it just may reveal something. Some small detail that might push me further along, if you get my drift."

If she did, she felt no obligation to say so.

Porphyry's smile was playful, but the intent of his words had been far from that. "I've already spoken to the young people and a number of the staff. Mr. Toby and Signor Parelli are a bit harder to pin down. I fear somewhat intentionally," he added. "And if you don't mind my saying, it's been pretty much uphill all the way with you."

She made an odd face. "It's only that, to be perfectly frank, I'm no longer certain exactly what you're here for," she explained. "To discover Jones's murderers or to study the history of the castle."

"The fact of the one may just possibly be explained by the other. Why did you say 'murderers' just now? Do you believe there was more than one?"

Madam Lobkova herself seemed surprised by her use of the plural. "I suppose it's because so many people have already confessed to it. Do you believe there was only one murderer?"

"As of now I have no idea how many there were. But I do think it would be helpful if I might see this so-called Covenant."

Madam Lobkova pursed her lips, her voice growing more clipped. "In the case of that particular document, you would have to have Mr. Jones's approval and right now, as you may well imagine, he's in no frame of mind—"

Madam Lobkova rose abruptly and, with all of her considerable dignity, strode to the window.

Colonel Porphyry refused to be sidetracked. "Perhaps if I were to ask Mr. Tobias," he persisted gently.

"About the Covenant?" She shrugged. "Feel free. But I doubt you'll get much in the way of encouragement."

His shrug imitated hers. In the next moment he rose, bowed stiffly from the waist, and turned to go. Then, pausing, he turned, smiling at her over his shoulder. "You know what I think those people were after this morning?"

She gazed at him, waiting.

"Forgive my morbidity," he continued, "but I believe it was Mr. Jones's casket. Or, to be more precise, they were after Mr. Jones—his body, that is. I think you know that, too, and it was absolutely splendid the way you protected the casket. The way you put your body between it and them. You would have died before you let even one of them touch that casket. Isn't that so?"

Her jaw dropped and her ramrod posture appeared to sag. "You're a sly fellow, aren't you, Colonel?"

"Not half sly enough, I'm afraid, madam." He winked at her and was suddenly jovial. "Would you mind terribly if I were to call you Wanda?"

25

High on the upper story of the castle, in the big, sprawling north wing, was a series of four large rooms. They'd been effectively sealed off from the third-floor living quarters by means of a thick steel door. Each, in turn, was interconnected by a narrow passageway. It was here within these four rooms that one came upon laboratories and workshops crammed with state-of-the-art technology. The first of these consisted of rows and aisles of work units, each equipped with sinks and burners, scales, flasks, cylinders, vacuum jars, autoclaves and electron microscopes of the most advanced design.

The second room had all of its windows darkened by means of thick black drapes. This was to accommodate a variety of radiological equipment—X-ray machines, spectroscopes, gas chromatographs, tomography and magnetic imaging equipment for use in scanning.

The third room appeared to be set up for purposes of dissection. Here were rows of long steel tables with trenches to catch bodily fluids. Standing nearby was a variety of equipment for administering anesthesia as well as for resuscitation. Tall green cylinders of gas lined the walls, along with a tangle of oxygen hoses, incubators, cathode screens attached to heart monitors, telemetry radios, suction machines and various other instruments associated with life-support systems.

The fourth and final room was by far the largest. There were no windows here. The entire space from ceiling to floor had been turned into a dizzying grid of aisles and intersecting paths made up of steel cages. They were of various sizes, the smallest containing hamsters and mice, guinea pigs with a scattering of dogs and cats as well. The medium and jumbo cages occupying the center of the grid contained primates of varying sizes and species. Mostly these were rhesus monkeys, with a goodly number of chimps and baboons.

During the day, these four rooms hummed with activity. Men and women in stark white smocks moved back and forth with the solemnity of druidic priests engaged in some ancient cultish rite.

Where the animals were kept a heavy zoolike smell hung like a warm haze above the place. Must and straw, rotting food and waste matter were everywhere. Roof fans were kept going twenty-four hours a day to keep down the odors.

During the day, the noise from the room was frightful— chattering, ear-piercing shrieks, barking, the screams of agitated animals, the rattle and banging of food pans against the cage bars. The ceilings and floors were soundproofed to keep down the din. Between the noise and smell it was impossible to remain there for long.

But with dusk a curious quiet descended over the room, as the animals, one by one, settled down for the night. The only illumination came from a series of blue-colored electric night lights hanging from bare electric cords at evenly spaced locations across the ceiling.

It was in this room that Colonel Porphyry found himself shortly after one in the morning, at a time when all the castle was long asleep. The heavy steel doors leading into the suite of laboratories, he'd easily penetrated. He had a way with locks, the Colonel, even the most sophisticated. This particular lock, equipped with bolt-retracting gears, he found to be juvenile.

He'd been on the top floor for roughly three quarters of an hour. At that particular moment, he was investigating the fourth room, using a small pen flashlight to inspect the cages of sleeping animals. Some of them snored; some twitched; some wore grins frozen with fright; some of them—particularly the smaller creatures like the guinea pigs and mice—cowered in the corners of their cages, watching him out of stunned pink little eyes as the thin beam of light fell upon them.

In a far corner of the room, in an area screened off from the rest, the Colonel found what appeared to be a holding area. Here were animals that were either undergoing experimentation or recovering from the trauma of it. A number of monkeys lay strapped on surgical tables. Some wore blindfolds over their eyes; others had their entire heads bandaged. Some lay in restraining devices, some with cathodes inserted into their skulls at the base of the neck. Some of them had needles in their arms attached to plastic hoses, through which fluids dripped into their bloodstreams.

About him Porphyry could hear the wind howl and the rain batter the glass transoms in the ceiling. Over in the corner a big mandrill baboon, his head bandaged from recent surgery, flinched with each crack of thunder, appearing to count numbers on his nervous, twitching fingers.

Porphyry had no wish to remain there longer. Having come upon such a place in a medieval castle struck him as odd. But nothing seemed too out of the ordinary for an organization known for its range of wide, if not sometimes bizarre, scientific investigation. Still, one thing Porphyry had seen there in the fourth room had aroused his curiosity. A number of wood crates, newly arrived, had been stacked up near the entrance, the bills of lading and shipping manifests still pasted to many of them.

Clearly, live animals had been shipped in these crates. Porphyry found numerous indications in many of them to corroborate the fact. Each crate was addressed to a certain warehouse on Great Jones Street (curious coincidence), a small waterfront cul-de-sac on the mainland. The Colonel knew it well. It was on Great Jones Street that he usually bought unpackaged tea from a Chinese merchant.

Each manifest bore a stamp indicating that each crate shipment had originated in Geneva from an enterprise called the Humanus Institute, S.A. Each had been signed by a certain Dr. Felix Fabian.

The fourth room appeared to open onto a fifth, but entry to this chamber was barred by a locked door that even Porphyry, for all of his ingenuity, couldn't open. Exasperated, he put an ear against the door and listened for some time. But all he heard was a deathlike silence. At last he threw up his hands and, muttering, walked away.

A short time later, up on the battlements, Colonel Porphyry was making his final tour of inspection before retiring for the night.

"Anything up?" he asked the drenched figures assigned there.

Rain sluiced down off the wide brims of their rain hats. It poured onto their coat fronts and into their boots. They'd been standing there for the past four hours and looked thoroughly miserable.

"Nothing special, sir," one of them said.

"Except . . ." the one called Magnus added. "There is one other thing."

The Colonel cocked an eye at him.

"It's nothing we can see, sir," said Magnus.

"But we can hear it, sir," the second went on.

"Hear what?"

"A banging sound, sir. Hard to describe. It's fairly regular. Coming from the direction of the forest, down there."

Porphyry's eyes followed where the hand of the first man pointed. Indeed there was a sound, barely audible, above the keening of the wind. "Sounds like the ring of an ax to me. Someone chopping trees," he said.

"Yes, sir. Just what we were thinking."

For a moment they stood there, all three of them, staring at each other somewhat awkwardly while the wind whipped about their sodden rubber garments.

"Very well, then," Porphyry said. "Why don't you chaps go below, get yourselves a cup of something hot? I'll be fine up here until the next watch reports."

They required no further prodding. But as they rushed off, Porphyry called after them, "Oh, by the way, when you're down there, will you ask Lieutenant Englund to ring up home office? Have them run a check on a Dr. Fabian. First name Felix. Also, whatever they might come up with on a Humanus Institute in Geneva."

Alone on the tower, the Colonel walked along the battlements, leaned his elbow on them and stared down to the place where the chopping sounds appeared to come from.

So faint was the noise, if it hadn't been called to his

attention, he might well have missed it entirely. But having it pointed out to him, it now seemed to ring out over the treetops deafeningly. He strained his eyes in that direction. A wall of cold, wet fog had come rolling up over the sweeping lawns, dropping the visibility to virtually zero. The searchlights on the battlements could pierce the dark no more than a foot or two beyond the walls. At the point where visibility ended and the mists began, a spectral image born of fog and murk danced in midair.

Porphyry blinked and rubbed his sleepless eyes. Again he listened for the chopping sound, wishing it were just as illusory as the chimera swaying off in the mists. But no, the faint ringing noise was still there, barely audible over the gale, yet no less real. There was little doubt that what he'd been hearing was the sound of axes applied to trees. To what end, he had no way of knowing. The Colonel had always been an interesting mixture of realist and romantic. What he imagined now he put down to the romantic side of his personality, the side given to leaps of fancy. He was realist enough, however, to take that side of himself with a grain of salt, but not so much of a dolt as to discount the significance of his imaginings entirely.

The morning dawned with little sign that the storm would abate. Quite to the contrary, it had returned with renewed fury. The temperature had dropped during the night and an unseasonal hail had dusted the trees with a mantle of ice. The big conifers had been crystalized, some of them bent in half, their branches clicking like old bones as a rushing wind strummed them like a harp.

With that a deep, unsettling silence had settled over the forest. It was as though every living thing within it, spent from the ordeal of survival, lay back for a moment in breathless anticipation of what might come next.

After closing his eyes for an hour or so in bed, Colonel Porphyry rose and showered and shaved. Then, shortly after dawn, he was abroad and requesting an audience with Mr. Toby Jones. Informed that he was not available at the moment, the Colonel asked to see Signor Parelli and was told the same story.

It seemed that a crisis had arisen during the night and both were off trying to resolve it. They were in the castle but not immediately reachable. They were expected back later that morning.

Colonel Porphyry could only conclude that the crisis had something to do with the still unburied Mr. Jones and the uncomfortable fact that, unembalmed and after seventy-two hours, he had still not been laid decently to rest. What Tobias Jones had imagined would be merely a routine procedure had now snowballed into a major problem, not to say something of an embarrassment.

Coming down that morning for breakfast, the Colonel's highly sensitive nostrils twitched at the smell of something rank and putridly sweet. It had crept up the stairs to meet him and grew more pronounced as he descended. Others were apparently aware of it, too, for a small fan had been placed in the dining room and whirred discreetly from a corner.

After breakfast, which he took by himself, he was back up on the tower walk, prowling the battlements with a pair of field glasses.

"They still at it?" he asked a guard as he positioned himself between the sides of one of the embrasures and scanned the forest's edge.

"Afraid so, sir."

Far away over the frozen air, he could hear the faint ping of metal impacting on wood. "Enterprising little beggars, aren't they?"

"That they are, sir. And just as busy off to the other side of the castle as well."

Porphyry's field glasses lowered slowly and he turned to the guard. "What's that you say?"

Somewhat rattled, the guard repeated his report.

"When did you learn this?"

"Just this morning, sir. Mr. Morgan over on the opposite tower told me at breakfast."

The guard had more information to convey, but the Colonel was gone before he was able to do so. Minutes later, Porphyry was ascending the narrow stair that led up to the drum tower on the opposite side of the castle, taking the steps two at a time. At his sudden appearance, Mr. Morgan, one of his subalterns, whirled around in astonishment, his rifle cocked. "Oh, beg pardon, sir. You startled me."

For some reason, the fellow's words annoyed him and he was curt. "You've heard sounds from the forest on this side of the castle?"

"Yes, sir."

155

"Why the devil didn't you report it?"

"I did, sir . . . I mean, you'd already turned in for the night so I recorded it in the duty book."

"Oh . . ." Porphyry said, baffled and at once contrite. The man had done no wrong. He'd acted responsibly and done what was correct under the circumstances. The Colonel had no reason to be cross.

Rain drilled down on the copper roof, making an awful row. It sounded like the pounding of empty steel drums. The tower stones had turned slick and black. Large puddles of wind-driven water like sheets of tin slid back and forth over the stone floors.

Porphyry, muttering to himself, ploughed angrily through one of the puddles. The water rose over the vamp of his shoe, but he ignored it, slogging right through it and positioning himself on the wall, from where he stared gloomily out at the forest.

The cloud ceiling was quite low by then. Gobs of mist had impaled themselves on the soaring turrets. Torn in ribbons, they broke up and drifted off, quickly replaced by others. Still, it seemed to the Colonel, squinting into the fog, that he could make out the silhouette of something taking shape at the forest's edge. He watched it for some time, his jaw slack, not at all certain his eyes weren't playing tricks on him again.

The thing that he watched appeared to be floating just above the treeline, something not of nature, but man-made. Still, in that weird light, he couldn't be certain. He knew what he suspected but he hoped he was wrong.

"Why didn't you say something before?"

"I wanted to—"

"Why did no one tell me about this? Surely your uncle, or this Parelli fellow—"

"It's hard to explain."

"Try me, Mr. Jonathan. I think you'll find me all ears."

Colonel Porphyry, just back from the tower, turned to accept a cup of tea from the butler. Still attired in his rubber slicker, beaded with raindrops, he sat at the small desk in the windowless cubicle adjoining the library that had become his temporary office. The desk before him was stacked with three toppling mounds of files and documents waiting to be read.

"Where do I start?" Jonathan asked gloomily.

"You might start by telling me what you and your uncle and

156

brothers and sisters have so studiously avoided telling me for the past three days. Your brother—what's his name again?"

"Leander?"

"Leander. Right. Your brother Leander disappears twenty-four hours before the murder of your father—and you could see no connection?"

"It's not quite so easy as you make it sound," Jonathan snapped back.

"Kindly help me to understand, then," Porphyry said. "You want to tell me something? Am I right?"

Jonathan's eyes traveled upward and moved along the ceiling. The Colonel followed the progress of his gaze.

"You think someone is listening to us here?"

Again Jonathan nodded.

Porphyry rose and, taking Jonathan beneath the arm, the two of them strolled out through the library and down the hall, chatting in low voices like a pair of old chums out for a turn on the boulevard.

"I know it sounds crazy," Jonathan said, his eyes glued to the floor.

"You mean the fact that your brother vanished—just like that?"

"Just like that. Into thin air. During a performance of *The Tales of Hoffmann*. I'm sure it sounds absurd."

Colonel Porphyry shrugged. "Not all that absurd. Skillful magicians do it all the time. With pigeons, rabbits; I've even seen it done with grown people."

"I've seen that, too. This wasn't quite the same thing, though."

"You say your uncle is an adept magician."

"He is, but it makes no sense," Jonathan protested. "Why would he—"

"I don't know, but if we're looking for a simple mechanical explanation to your brother's disappearance, stage magic performed by a skillful magician would not be all that farfetched."

"You think Leander might still be alive?"

The Colonel gazed down into his palm at the brass button Jonathan had put there. "Until we have a body," he said consolingly, "I see no reason to assume otherwise."

Jonathan accepted the words of hope gratefully, but privately he placed little faith in them.

They strolled on through the gloomy corridors.

"It's most important your father be put decently into the ground," Porphyry said. "And soon."

Jonathan nodded grimly. "The whole lower floor reeks of it." The young man glanced uneasily at the Colonel, "What can I do to help?" he asked suddenly, his voice a plea.

"Start right now by telling me everything you know."

"Everything?" The word had the doomed sound of finality about it.

"Everything." Porphyry nodded. "For instance, what is everyone here so frightened about?"

Part 7

The Wood King

"... but do you imagine that anyone is so insane as to believe that the thing he feeds upon is a god?"

—Sir James G. Frazer, *The Golden Bough*

26

J.

Something's up. Can't explain now. Must go to Woodsmen's camp. Say nothing to anyone.

Please follow soonest. Will explain later. Please . . .

Cass

It was propped up on the bureau, wedged between a hairbrush and a bottle of cologne. It was her hand, all right, no mistaking that. The big, wavery, roly-poly letters of an adolescent with penmanship and personality still unformed.

The message couldn't have been more alarming. It had something to do with Leander. He was alive, perhaps, and had somehow gotten word to Cassie.

By then I didn't know if I was more alarmed about Leander or Cassie. Clearly, she'd managed to uncover something. Leander was with the Woodsmen. Knowing that he was alive was itself a relief. But it was also terrifying. But even more terrifying was the thought of Cassie alone by herself in those boundless, untracked woods with the goat people creeping all about, lurking out there in the dark.

Like the rest of us, Cassie's experience in the woods was virtually nil. She'd no notion in what direction the Woodsmen's camp lay or what sort of terrain she'd have to cross in order to reach there.

It had been three hours since I'd had Cassie's message and still I hadn't bestirred myself. Where was she now? Staggering about in the dark forest, unable to get her bearings; or possibly, there already in the clutches of the Woodsmen.

Outside, the rain showed signs of finally abating. Weather reports picked up on the radio were predicting a clearing trend and Uncle Toby was determined to mount another attempt to carry Jones up to the burial ground the next morning. Clearly something had to be done soon. The situation had become intolerable. Though people didn't speak of it, the smell had begun to reach into every corner of the place. Fans were kept going all day despite the fact that it was quite cool, even cold, inside the castle.

Upstairs in my room I kept reading Cassie's note over and over again. "Something's up. Can't explain now. . . . Follow soonest . . ." And then the words trailing off into that desperate *"Please."* I could almost hear the catch in her throat as she said it.

There was no sleeping that night. I had frightening visions of Leander and Cassie. I could see them in some dark place, crying out to me, their faces twisted by fright and pain. I saw, too, swarming all around them those oblong leathery faces with the thin lifeless gashes above the cheeks where eyes were supposed to be.

Sunrise was still a good six hours off. A great deal could happen in six hours to young people out in the woods—by themselves at night. Several times I imagined I heard cries outside my window, only to realize that it was just the keening of the wind, not the cries of my brother and sister.

Something odd occurred a short time later. I have no way of explaining it and no clear recollection of how it came about, except to say that at a certain point, much against my better judgment, I rose, got out of bed and dressed. I have no idea what had been going on in my mind or what I intended to do. Reaching the bottom of the drum tower, I found the small arched door through which I'd walked the day before still unlocked. A sliver of moon lay on its back in a clear dark sky. I took a deep breath and stooped beneath the low lintel of the door.

Setting out from Fraze that night, I had no idea where I was going. I merely surrendered to a force that appeared to be leading me. Call it conscience, or guilt, or whatever you like, that force had brought me this far and, no doubt, would ultimately bring me to a fate of its own choosing.

I moved briskly down the long sweep of lawn stretching out to the forest's edge. It was toward precisely the place where yesterday morning in the window of my room Cassie and I had watched the goat people gather. In another moment I'd reached the edge of the woods. Without once looking back, I slipped noise-lessly into the forest, drawn along like a twig on a coursing stream. Without needing to be told, I knew for a certainty I was bound straight for the Woodsmen's camp. Although it was pitch-dark, I was moving quite fast. Not running, but almost. I couldn't see a hand before my face and yet I never tripped or crashed into anything. The rain by then had pretty much stopped and I could hear the steady drip of water sifting down through the branches. Shortly, I was sopping wet.

That was a minor discomfort. All I could think of then was the two of them, Cassie and Leander. Were they all right? I had as yet no plan for rescuing them, no strategy, only the vague, pitifully simpleminded hope that once directly confronted with the problem, something would present itself. Yet, in the face of hundreds of hostile Woodsmen who clearly had other plans for my sister and brother, there seemed little that I, acting alone, could do to help them.

In total darkness you have no sense of climbing or descending. You have only the pressure in the back of your legs to give you some clue to your orientation. In this case, I had the sense that I was moving for the most part downhill.

Although there was scarcely any illumination from that slim sickle of moon, I knew for a certainty that the hill I was descending was growing progressively steeper. I had to dig my heels into the crumbling earth in order to keep myself from pitching headlong down the side of the mountain.

All the while I went a sharp wind kept soughing through the trees, bringing with it the fishy, brackish smell of water. From far off came a dull, roaring noise, not unlike the sound of distant thunder. Yet it wasn't thunder. I had no idea what it was—only that it was a somewhat unnerving sound and it came exactly from the direction of the place to which I was moving.

Another half hour of hard going, out of breath, legs and back aching, I finally saw lights up ahead and smelled smoke. The closer I got to the lights, the more pungent the smell grew. Shortly, I saw a clearing and then a blaze of illumination—huge bonfires surrounded by innumerable little orange squares. Those, I reasoned, were windows set within dwellings of some sort.

Standing there on the side of the slope, looking out over the encampment, I felt a sharp twinge of fear start to gnaw at that sense of resolve that had brought me this far. It occurred to me that there was still time to turn and flee, yet something riveted me there, looking out over the ring of fire that appeared to float within the inky darkness.

Crouching on all fours, I started to inch forward. Innumerable tiny black dots came into my line of vision, moving back and forth before my eyes. The scent of smoke I'd noticed before was now sharp and unpleasant. It made me think of burning hair. From time to time the bleats and panicky squeals of animals sounded, followed at once by an upward shower of sparks.

There was a great deal of activity all about the camp and, as I approached, my feet lagged and my resolution grew fainter. As I moved closer, a number of small animals came into view. They were tethered to trees nearby the fires and pulled and strained at their lashings. They appeared to be goats. Periodically, one or two would be dragged off by one of the Woodsmen using a sharp pike to prod them forward. Some went with great docility to the flames; others fought and kicked. It was then you'd hear the frantic bleating, followed almost at once by that shower of sparks shooting upward at the sky.

I still had no idea of the size or the layout of the compound, nor its number of inhabitants. But just from the lights and fires visible through the forest, I had an impression of something fairly extensive.

Nearer to the fires I was able to see through the tangle of leaves and dark branches a jumble of huts, densely packed, one beside the other. They were of varying sizes. Most were simple rectangles, some quite small, no more than sheds with lean-to roofs. Beyond them, looming in the background, were a number of long, darkish silhouettes. These were taller, oblong in shape

164

and far more imposing in size, designed, I imagined, for activities more formal than mere shelter.

From somewhere in the forest, off to the left of me, an owl hooted, followed by the light crack of a branch.

The next moment I was slithering along the soggy earth on elbows and knees, moving closer toward the fires. In my place of concealment, I felt reasonably secure, my intention being to lie there until daybreak, when I could see more clearly and get a better lay of the land.

I'd been lying flat on my stomach close to an hour, peering down at the camp through the narrow chinks of light coming through the branches. My legs were thrust out behind me; my arms were outstretched and slightly elevated at the elbows. Lying there, I felt a wistful longing for my bedroom at Fraze, my warm dry bed, my thick comforter.

What happened next happened so quickly that I can only provide the most sketchy of descriptions. One moment I was conscious; the next, I wasn't. I recall a sharp blow to the back of my neck, air bursting from my lungs, a ringing in the ears, then total darkness.

When I woke, I was lying on the bare floor of an evil-smelling place. It turned out to be a hut. I'd been stripped naked and my legs and arms were in irons.

The hut was unfurnished and it was dark except for the brilliant shaft of sunshine streaming through a single window. The window had no pane. It was open to the outside—large enough to permit air to circulate but too small to climb through.

I was aware of a constant jabber and caterwauling. A steady stream of footsteps tramped past the window, as if many people were nearby, engaged in some sort of noisy activity.

I'd been tethered to the wall by means of heavy chains at a point below the single window. If I stood up on my tiptoes I could just barely see out. The sight I saw there was enough to ice the blood.

I was in the center of a large encampment in the depths of a gloomy forest. Soaring evergreens of one kind or another encircled the place, blocking out most of the sunlight and creating an impression of perpetual twilight.

The hut in which I was imprisoned stood in the midst of a compound of many such huts, some larger, some smaller than the rest. Arranged in no special order or design, but merely scattered about like so much debris, these dwellings were

165

rudimentary. Mostly, they were raw plank with mud patched in as a sort of mortar to seal the holes that formed where the planks didn't join neatly.

Each hut had either three or four walls with one small window set high up, about six feet. A curious placement, I thought, for a people not much larger than half that height. The roofs were thatched with vines and rushes and had a shallow slope to them by which, I suppose, rain was intended to run off. But there were no gutters or leaders to facilitate that and so ditches of muddy water ran along the walls of many of the huts, causing large areas of damage where the wood below appeared to be rotting.

The three-walled huts were done in the style of lean-tos. These were the most primitive of dwellings, where, no doubt, the lowest order of Woodsmen resided.

If the Woodsmen were poor carpenters, they were outstanding breeders. The number of them outside my window at any given time was staggering. All of them seemed to be shouting at once in their high, yipping, staccato voices. They made a continual harsh humming sound like insects thriving in a hive.

The goats were no less prolific. Interspersed between the huts were large pens into which hundreds of the creatures had been jammed. Still hundreds more of them wandered freely up and down through the narrow lanes and byways of the compound, mingling freely with the crowds. Immense fires roared outside of every hut and were never permitted to go out. Each hour legions of scurrying dwarfs would come and stoke them with fresh wood. In addition, a number of iron forges belched large black puffs of smoke skyward.

What the forges were used for, I had no idea. I imagined they had something to do with the tempering of metals used to make the iron weapons and cooking implements which were everywhere in evidence. Even living in a period of technological wonders, the Woodsmen clung stubbornly to their Iron Age ways.

Earlier I'd thought hopefully that some sort of rescue party might come out from Fraze. But now, in the cold light of day, seeing the barricades and heavily armed fierce little people, I realized that all such hopes were nonsense. No rescue party from Fraze would have the numbers or the temerity to penetrate this place.

I don't know how long I lay there on my back, chained to the wall, watching the sun's transit through the upper right-hand corner of the window. When at last it appeared to stand directly overhead, the sun beat down on the thatched roof, heating up the hut to near suffocation.

Still, no one had bothered to come and check on me. There was no sign of food or water and no indication that any would be provided at some time in the immediate future. Nor was there any hint outside the hut of the presence of a guard whom I could summon in case of need. To all intents and purposes, I'd been left alone to fend for myself.

Several hours later that afternoon when the hut had become an airless furnace and the sun began to slant west, I was woken from a doze by a sharp cracking sound. The next thing I knew, the door of the hut burst open.

Still dazed from sleep, stiff from lying naked on the damp muddy floor, I blinked at the sight before me. Three fierce little ruffians barged into the hut. All jabbering and barking at once, they made directly for me. I started to scramble to my feet but tumbled over, tangled in my leg irons. They burst out laughing and immediately set about me with crude wooden paddles. They pummeled my bare limbs and when I tried to protect my head with my arms, they kicked me in the ribs with their heavy buskins. One of them tried to drive the tip of his boot into my groin. There was a great deal of sniggering and skipping about.

There was no clear reason I could see for the attack. Its sole intent was meanness for the sole pleasure of it and to drive home the point that I was theirs to do with as they pleased. By the time they'd left me, my skin was raw from the flaying and a nasty gash had been opened above my eye.

But if I thought this punishment unwarranted, what followed was utterly bizarre. About thirty minutes after the Woodsmen had left, the door opened again. Framed in the doorway stood a tiny figure. It wavered there for a moment or so, staring at me across the hut, then stepped in without a sound and closed the door.

In the half-light of the cabin I watched, transfixed, as the dwarflike figure moved slowly toward me. I can't say what there was about the motion and carriage of this particular Woodsman that was so markedly different from the others that had preceded him. All I know was that it was different—slower, rather sinuous and more regal.

The difference became fully apparent to me a moment later

167

when, through the encroaching shadows, I had my first clear view of the Woodsman's face and realized that he was a she.

I can't imagine why this came as such a shock. Yet here before me was, undoubtedly, a female of the species. Undoubtedly now seems too strong a word, since the creature standing silently there regarding me was virtually indistinguishable from her male counterparts. There were no obvious anatomical differences I could readily detect. The outer garments of this creature were exactly the same as those worn by the male. Like the male of the species, the facial skin was leathery and seamed with cracks, weathered and tough as old board. And like the male, the eyes were merely two long gashes chiseled deeply above the cheeks and set far apart on either side of the skull. The Woodswoman's stature was exactly the same as her male counterpart's, perhaps a bit less paunchy. The only concession this creature appeared to have made to her femininity was a scent she wore—so heavy and cloyingly sweet you had to turn your face from it.

She stood a short way off, staring down at me. Her mouth moved stiffly in a sort of reptilian way, a wide lipless hole. I stared back up at her, watching her, unable to speak.

Then, for the first time, I noticed that she carried a kettle in one hand with several large wood bowls in the other. Over one arm was draped several lengths of a rough drab fabric.

She continued to mumble sounds and make gestures intended to evoke some kind of response from me. I could only stare back at her blankly, until the mumbling grew louder and somewhat more threatening. Clearly, she was losing patience and, for a moment, I thought I was in for another drubbing. But, instead, she put down her kettle and bowls and knelt beside me.

It was then I had my full first blast of that suffocating scent. Reminiscent of patchouli, or extract of vanilla, yet a hundred times more intense, there was beneath the suffocating sweetness the smell of something rotting.

She withdrew from her arm the bolts of fabric and held one up before me. Then, making a series of harsh, guttural noises, she did a pantomime of someone washing her face.

Then I understood. She'd been sent here to bathe me. The kettle contained hot water and the bowls were vessels into which she would pour it. One of the bolts of fabric was for washing me, the other for toweling me off.

Given the condition of my body from the recent paddling,

the thought of warm water was not unwelcome, and when she started, I didn't resist. On the contrary, I helped by moving my body, lowering and raising it this way and that so as to simplify her task.

Her fingers were short and stubby, the skin just as leathery and unsightly as the facial skin. The hands were strong and, as they swept over my body, they didn't massage so much as they kneaded and, as rough as they appeared, their touch was not ungentle.

All the while she worked over me she seemed to come closer, making a low, murmuring sound as she did so. That overpoweringly sweet smell became more invasive so that I no longer even tried to turn my face from it, but merely succumbed.

Lying flat on my back I found her face quite close to mine. Her murmurs had become a soft, burbling sound. Since the features of these people are, for the most part, inexpressive, I could only guess that she was smiling. All the while her hands continued to roam up and down my limbs, at times lingering here and there in ways that might be viewed as provocative.

While I grew uneasy with this activity, I must admit I'd become increasingly aroused. My conception of sexual desire had been based on the commonly held belief that it began with visual allure and moved on from there. But the Woodswoman had quickly put the lie to that principle. In the next moment, her hand capped my crotch and squeezed hard.

It didn't hurt so much as it surprised me. The Woodswoman's hot cheek lay crushed against mine. It had the prickly feel of cactus and the smell was suffocating. The hand that clasped my crotch continued its slow, manipulative rhythm, all the while a low, hoarse, almost feral sound, not unlike a dog's growl, rose from deep within her throat.

Bound in irons, my freedom of motion was greatly limited. Yet I found myself squirming this way and that, not entirely certain whether it was pleasure or disgust I was feeling. If I had doubts regarding the meaning of my gyrations, however, she did not. That lizardlike mouth slowly opened and closed, and out of the corner of my eye I watched the darting flicks of her tongue shoot out over the lipless hole that was her mouth.

In the next moment she sat erect, quickly undoing the buttons of her leather jerkin. Beneath that she wore a kind of coarse cotton shift which, with no trace of modesty, she hoisted upward above her thick thighs. A pair of soft, shapeless dugs

169

spilled outward. Then, straddling me with her bare legs, she leaned forward so that her breasts drooped heavily across my face, giving off a vague smell of earth and mold.

She lay prone atop me, her breath warm and fitful. Her moaning had grown vaguely musical, a series of shivery trills that could have been either humming or giggling. Finally, she lowered her trousers about her hips. Her thighs and rump were enormous—entirely out of proportion to the rest of her body. The belly was a limp sac that sagged down over the dark, tangled shadow of hair just below.

She never removed her trousers, only dropped them. Then, still astride me, she lowered her squat, paunchy torso until the dark patch of hair made contact.

The initial touch was revolting. I squirmed to avoid it, but she pursued me with her hips until I'd been pinned against the wall. Before I could squirm again, I felt myself slipping inward and upward into the goat woman. It was cool inside her and extremely wet. The odor rising from within her was vaguely saline. As her hips began to move slowly, her voice caught in her throat, and then she made a gagging sound that continued throughout the next several minutes.

The motion of her hips gradually gathered momentum. Shortly they began to punch and stab at me, building to such searing heat, then peaking in the most exquisite prolonged orgasm I'd ever known.

As long as I kept my eyes shut, it was wonderful. I'd never thought that the activity man calls making love could deliver such an all-enveloping pleasure. With my sisters it had always been a mechanical thing, prophylactic, like brushing one's teeth. Pleasurable enough but, once done, quickly forgotten.

Now there was this. All the while it was going on, I kept my eyes shut tight and thought of Sofi. I thought of everything I'd ever wanted to do to Sofi, of every imaginable indignity I could inflict upon her to make up for all the clumsy, embarrassed attempts at love I'd made toward her which she'd rebuffed. And now, lying there on the dirt floor with the Woodswoman atop me, when the climax came, it tore through me like a hot needle—an ecstasy of such exquisite pain and joy there are scarcely words to describe it.

When my eyes opened again she was still sitting there astride me, looking down at me with that strangely reptilian smile flickering about her lipless mouth. With her softly squeak-

170

ing voice, she uttered a few words. Not words I could recognize, but more articulated sounds than the senseless burbles and moans that had come from her moments before. She repeated these sounds over and over again until at last, by simple inflection, they appeared to take on the sense of a question. But I had no idea at all what question was being asked.

"Ayub—dab-dabai-eni—be'ena," she seemed to say, and repeated it so often that I began to feel some urgency about replying. Still, I could neither answer her question nor ask any of my own.

At last she rose to her feet, tugging her trousers up and rebuttoning her jerkin. Then, watching me all the while, she poured more water from her kettle into one of the bowls and proceeded to wash me again. When she finished she dried me down. Her hands were quite gentle, at one point almost lulling me to sleep.

As bizarre as the experience had been, I felt relaxed—a relaxation so full and complete as to border strangely on a sort of peace. With the shadows of early dusk beginning to creep around the hut, the Woodswoman gathered me into her strong arms and rocked me gently, as though I were her infant.

I must have slept for some time, for when I woke again it was dark. The woman was still there and I still lay in her arms. Toward the end of my nap, it seemed to me I'd heard noises. They came from just outside the door. They were metallic sounds, mingled with the rattling of wood.

The woman had heard them, too, for she rose and went to the door. Her back to me, she knelt and appeared to pick up a number of objects that had been left at the doorstep while I slept. She returned, carrying various pots and pannikins of food which shortly she was portioning out to me on thin flat boards that served as dishes.

The first dish was a kind of wild cucumber marinated in a sharp, slightly bitter liquor. I hadn't eaten in well over twenty hours. I was famished and so I ate it, but its pungency made me gasp and brought tears to my eyes. This was followed by a mash of some sort of root. It, too, appeared to be laced with the same strong, bitter liquor as the cucumber.

Next came a meat course. It was potted, stringy and tough. The flavor was strange to me and I assumed it was one of the hapless goats I'd seen spitted and roasted live out near the pens the night before. Chunks of the stuff had been wrapped in little

171

tricorner pockets of sorrel. It was tasty enough, highly seasoned, although I didn't care to eat very much of it. Humming and chattering, fussing all about me, the Woodswoman served me dish after dish and poured me glasses of a beverage not unlike beer. She appeared to take great delight in all of this.

When I'd finished, she wiped my mouth with the same bolt of fabric she'd used to bathe me. She then cleared the dishes and set them outside the door. When she returned, she had with her a large package wrapped in a coarse brown paper and bound with thick cord. Making those breathy little burbling sounds, she undid the package, all the while watching to see what reaction, if any, I betrayed.

When at last the package fell open, I saw folded there in a neat square what appeared to be a white garment. On top of that several additional articles of clothing had been placed. It seemed I was to be dressed. And, indeed, that was the case. The white garment I spoke of turned out to be a kind of tunic which was donned by slipping it over one's head through a hole in the center of the material. Once on, it reached to well below the knee—clearly no hand-me-down from a Woodsman but cut expressly for me. It had sleeves of half length and was worn loose and unbelted around the middle.

With hands still chained, my arms remained imprisoned beneath the tunic. My legs were also still in irons, forcing the woman to stoop in order to fit my feet into a pair of coarse leather buskins, the soles of which were fashioned out of tree bark. These were then tied up the length of my calf with thongs made, I'm certain, from the intestine of goats.

At that point, the Woodswoman did something very odd. She made me kneel before her and lower my head, in the position of a supplicant. She then carefully placed on my brow a wreath of mistletoe into which sprigs of a yellowish leaf with waxy white berries had been braided.

After much fussing and primping, she at last signaled me to rise. When I'd staggered to my feet, she walked around me several times, eyeing me critically, making a number of last-minute adjustments.

It occurred to me that I was being prepared for something, yet I had no idea what. The wreath on my head was particularly unsettling. All I had wanted in coming here was to find Cassie and Leander and to get us all out again as quickly as possible. I had no illusions that this would be easy or that the Woodsmen would be at all cooperative along those lines. I still had no assurance that either Cassie or Leander were actually here and, if they were, I felt certain that the Woodsmen would see to it that they remained here. But for what reason they were being held, I had no idea.

My musings were interrupted by a loud knock at the door, followed by the noisy appearance of five Woodsmen bursting into the hut. They pranced around me, poking and prodding me with short wood canes sharpened to a lethal point. There was much gleeful shouting and grunting as they jabbed me this way and that. When I failed to respond quickly enough, they'd administer another quick jab with their canes.

All of this was accompanied by sniggering sounds that passed, I suppose, for laughter. They would have gone on doing this for hours had not the Woodswoman intervened on my behalf. Waving her arms and shouting, she appeared to berate them in their strange guttural tongue until at last they slouched off to sulk in the corners of the room.

The Woodswoman now stationed herself protectively in front of me and proceeded to bark commands at them. They scurried quickly about in response to her words. Her control over them was remarkable.

At last, when she'd arranged them about me in a kind of wedge formation, she came and stood behind me, well inside the wedge. Then, lifting the part of my tunic that trailed on the ground behind me, she barked another sharp command. Instantly, one of the Woodsmen opened the door and our party shuffled forward and out into the fiery sunset.

With dust gathering around the encampment, innumerable fires had begun to glow before the huts. Countless Woodsmen and their families milled about in the muddy lanes and potholed alleyways of the village. The twilight hummed with the steady din of their voices and the bleating of penned goats. Over all the scene hung the thick, choking smoke of animals roasted live in their skins. The narrow, dirty avenues throbbed with the fierce plinking of a sort of stringed instrument—a small, hand-held harp I'd never seen before.

No sooner had we stepped outside our hut into the lane then there was a loud outcry as hundreds of elfin figures surged toward us, shouting and thrusting each other aside to get closer.

I stood well within the wedge, frightened by the sheer noise and shivering in my tunic. I wore nothing beneath it and the

173

evening had already grown cool. An uproar of jeers and howls went up as we started to move. The noise had a distinctly unfriendly sound. Fists rose and arms waved. Cries rent the air. The sight of it was enough to curdle your blood.

We walked along a broad path lined on either side with huts all jammed cheek-by-jowl one atop the other. The way, littered with trash and mired with mud puddles, appeared to be a main thoroughfare. We followed it through the center of the village, then descended toward an open space in which large swaths of pale violet sky were visible through the trees.

No sooner did we pass them than the Woodsmen closed in formation behind us and, chanting, followed us down the hill toward the open space. At the bottom of the hill the path funneled outward onto the bank of a broad, swift river. Already, the first stars of evening had begun to flicker on its choppy surface, and a white crescent of moonlight rose shimmering like a wraith from beneath its gloomy depths.

In the rapidly failing light I could see a number of large dark silhouettes bobbing on the river's roiling current. Drawing closer, the silhouettes began to assume the shape of boats—boats about which I'd only read and seen in photographs. Low-keeled, graceless, bargelike things, they carried a high prow and, at a point roughly midship, a tall, oblong superstructure. Mostly, they resembled pictures of houseboats I'd seen in books and magazines, but larger and nowhere near as cozy and welcoming. Instead, something distinctly menacing hovered about these vessels with their black, upswept prows upon which birdlike and predatory creatures had been painted.

From the path we marched on I assumed it was toward the boats we were headed. But then, suddenly from behind, I felt a sharp tug at the train of my tunic, jerking me to the right as though I were a horse guided by reins. In the next moment, my Woodsmen escort executed a sharp flanking movement, sending me tripping and stumbling up the bank in my leg irons, toward a large soaring structure—surely the largest I'd yet seen in the encampment.

It was in the center of a thick grove of trees, brilliantly illuminated by what appeared to be hundreds of pitch pine torches stuck here and there all about it in the soft earth. The place had the look of something official—a council house or, possibly, a temple used for ceremonial functions. A soccer field in length, with two-story timbered walls and a gabled roof, the

174

structure, while not at all attractive, was impressive for its size alone.

Hundreds of the Woodsmen already thronged the large courtyard out front when we arrived. They milled about, pushing and jostling each other for a better position from which to view us. There was an air of garish festivity about it all, as though it were a holiday and they had come to witness some momentous event. Indeed, when they saw us approach, a great roar went up. Fists shot skyward and the hooting and jeers resumed. Several fights broke out as they scrambled over each other to get closer.

All the time we drew nearer, I'd been vaguely aware of the tall conifers surrounding the grove. Objects, dark and shapeless, appeared to be hung in their branches. Situated high up in the trees, these objects swayed slowly back and forth in a languid dreamy motion, propelled by a light breeze.

It wasn't until we'd actually entered the grove and begun our final approach to the building that I saw the true nature of these decorations. Goats, literally dozens of them, had been butchered into parts and trussed up high in the branches. Several had been hung whole, upside down, blood dripping from their muzzles and through huge wounds gaping in their throats. Goat heads had been mounted at the very tips of the trees. They leered down at us, their tongues lolling in their open mouths. To say that I was unnerved would be an understatement. Panic comes far closer to my state of mind.

Led between the steadily growing mob, the scene lit with hundreds of glowing torches, there seemed little doubt now as to the object of this frenzy. Something was about to happen, something not necessarily pleasant, and it was going to happen to me.

Indeed, as we climbed the stairs to the entrance of the building, the mob surged forward in an attempt to follow, while dozens of Woodsmen armed with pikes and clubs struggled to hold them off. Once inside the place, heavy oak doors closed soundlessly behind us and suddenly we were engulfed in darkness and silence.

My heart banged in my chest and my mouth went bone-dry, all the while my eyes strained to adjust to the dim light. The odor of incense and melting wax was oppressive. The solemn hush cast over the place strongly suggested a sanctuary or a place of worship.

We were standing in a large, bare anteroom, waiting for the

two Woodsmen there dressed in beaded ceremonial robes to lead us forward into the temple. When, at last, they took their places at the head of our formation, the overall effect must have been imposing. Lurching ahead, the Woodswoman tugged at the hem of my tunic and immediately our party shuffled forward into the dim light of the main assembly hall.

My first impression of the room we entered was that it was semicircular, although in that faint light I couldn't be certain. It was quite large, however, with high, soaring ceilings that converged above us to a dizzying point. Directly beneath that point stood an immense brazier, at least nine feet in diameter, upon which a bed of coals glowed fiery red. This appeared to be the room's sole illumination until I gradually became aware of innumerable tiny specks of light that glowed in the shadows around us. The odor of incense encountered in the anteroom was intensified here a hundredfold. There were no windows inside the structure and so the air was saturated with it. It burned your eyes and choked you when you breathed too deeply.

The source of this choking smog could be quickly traced to these countless specks of light. On closer inspection, they turned out to be tall, thin shafts fashioned from a kind of fungus, each nearly a foot long and rolled into cylinders. When ignited, they gave off a smell not unlike burning punk.

Moving forward toward the center of the room, our group formed a kind of processional, almost stately in its slow and orderly deliberation. As we passed the brazier, it glowed and hissed. The waves of heat radiating from it nearly flattened me. When we reached a point near the head of the room where we could go no farther, the procession shuffled to a halt.

In the next moment, a voice deep and resonant boomed out of the shadows. It spoke in what were clearly the guttural grunts and yippings of the Woodsmen's tongue. But this voice differed. It lacked the rapid-fire jabbering I'd come to associate with the language. There was, instead, a solemnity to the sound. The words, what there were of them, were articulated clearly in a slow, measured cadence that became almost incantatory.

On a level just beneath those lulling chants, I'd become aware of a strange buzzing sound. Undoubtedly, it had been going on all the while we were there but so faintly that it couldn't be heard above the hissing of the coals. Now, however, I realized it was intended as a kind of liturgical counterpoint to the

176

chanting. The nearest I can come to it would be that of a number of individuals all humming at one time.

Shortly the humming began to swell in volume until the sound of it filled the room. I could feel it vibrate in my stomach. Then, from behind the brazier stepped a figure attired in flowing white robes upon which a jumble of runic characters had been stenciled. Somewhat taller than the average, this was a Woodsman to be sure, but of a more noble caste. The impression of nobility was heightened by the long white flowing beard and the tall mitered hat. The robes he wore were opulent and the runic characters I'd seen on it were comprised primarily of a large upright figure in the shape of a cane. The impression of a priest or shaman of some sort was inescapable. That impression was heightened as the figure moved slowly toward us, hyssopping with a smoking censer, all the while continuing his deep, mesmerizing chant. Eyes closed, censer swinging slowly back and forth, he approached us, then passed between us without once acknowledging our presence there.

We stumbled after him, circling the entire inside perimeter of the temple. I say "temple" because by now the place had clearly identified itself as that. Not the sort of typical place of worship I'd seen in books; there was no trace of religious statuary, incons, priceless paintings or tapestries. This was quite another thing—primitive, crude, almost prehistoric. Here the only objects that adorned the walls were the hides of flayed animals and dried cobs of corn. The only icons were effigies carved from wood or fashioned out of corn husks. The art was limited to pictographic scenes scratched onto large rocks, stick figures engaged in some sort of mystical rite.

One of these rocks turned out to be an altar before which our party, including the white-robed priest, came to a halt. It was an immense, uncut boulder with a flat top. Painted on the face of it in bold white was that upright canelike figure I now realized I'd been seeing all throughout the camp. The sign appeared inside the huts and out, scratched on chimneys, stenciled on ceremonial dress and plastered over every available wall.

The top of the altar was flat. Several candles atop it hissed in the gloomy light, casting large shifting shadows all about the place. In front of the candles stood a chalice of some sort, fashioned out of stone.

Beyond the altar, I saw what appeared to be a dais. Raised

177

several feet above ground level, it was arranged in a way that followed the inside curvature of the building.

Gradually, my eyes were able to make out a number of figures seated at the dais—a dozen, perhaps, humped over and all attired in hooded robes. They were seated on long low benches at the foot of a tall, soaring object that loomed above them. At first I took it to be another boulder. But suddenly it was illuminated. A pair of flares or Bengal lights had been thrust in the earth on either side of it, then ignited.

What I saw before me then took my breath away. It was a huge straw figure seated on a throne of stone. At least fifteen feet tall and nearly half that in breadth, it soared above the temple. It had no face other than a noselike object fashioned out of a dried corn cob, and wore a hat looking much like the same sort of pointed Tyrolean worn by the Woodsmen. Though it had no eyes, the straw figure appeared to brood down upon us, its manner remote and uncaring. On its chest had been sewn a representation of the large upright cane.

The priest Woodsman now raised his voice and fell to his knees before the altar. Immediately, all those about me followed suit. Having no idea what was expected of me, I remained standing until I felt from behind me the heavy hand of the Woodswoman grip my shoulder and press downward. I dropped to my knees.

The priest then moved about to each kneeling figure, pressing something firmly on each forehead. I was the last. When he reached me, however, he didn't touch my head. Instead, he took me roughly under the arms and raised me to my feet. Even with his mitered hat he reached a point only slightly above my midsection. Without once looking at me, he turned, then moved in his slow, stately stride to the altar, signaling me to follow along behind him.

My heart thumping, my mind racing millions of miles ahead, I stumbled after him, trying to anticipate what would happen next.

When I reached the altar the priest motioned me to stop. I did, at which point he raised a stone chalice slightly above my head, once more proceeding to chant. Slowly, he led me past the dais, where a dozen or so small, hooded figures sat hunched over, a silent tribunal gazing down upon me. Because of the hoods I couldn't see their faces. But it was evident from their stature that they were Woodsmen. One of them, however, who sat at the very end of the dais, was not. Even robed and hooded, you could tell that this was a person of average, if not above-average height. He sat nearly two full heads above the others and though he was among them, he was decidedly not a part of them.

Not surprisingly, it was this figure who riveted my gaze. I was certain that I'd seen him before, but by then everything was happening so quickly that I'd given up trying to recall where. Moving past the dais, the priest chanted and swung his censer. I followed, heading toward the big straw figure astride his throne. When I reached there, the Woodsman priest motioned me to drop to my knees before it. I must have hesitated, because in the next moment he seized the back of my neck and forced me roughly down onto the damp earth.

When I raised my head again I was alone, kneeling before that tangle of vines and thistle that was the throne. Looming immense above it all, the big straw figure peered down at me, something cold and pitiless in his eyeless gaze. I stared back up at it, unable to avert my eyes. Any moment I expected him to raise one of his huge straw arms and crush me beneath it.

That didn't happen, of course. What did was far worse. I would have much preferred quick annihilation at the hands of a straw robot to the kind of nightmare I was about to be subjected to over the next six hours.

My thoughts were interrupted by a slight disturbance from somewhere just behind me. In the next instant, the tall, robed figure who'd sat at the end of the dais appeared. He was moving toward where I knelt before the straw man and pushing something before him. I watched with dumb fascination as the thing, apparently on wheels, swayed and rattled toward me.

While I watched, transfixed, it suddenly occurred to me where I'd seen the robed figure before. It was Cassie's monk, of course, on the night of the masked ball, the night of Jones's death. Though I'd only noticed him toward the end of the evening, when I'd had far too much to drink, I could never forget that robe and hood and the odd little shudder I felt on first seeing him.

Now this same hooded figure was approaching me from the shadows and I saw what it was he was pushing before him. It came rattling and swaying toward me on those same little wheels it had sat on in Uncle Toby's library the night of the magic show. That night Toby had been able to make it float in space, project a voice from beneath its carved lid and make the lid rise as if someone (Jones, we all thought) was inside it.

Whether or not this was the same casket or just a replica, I couldn't tell. All I knew was that the face struck on the lid in bronze was, without doubt, the same sleeping saintlike figure with the same lean ascetic features. The casket which, only two days before, we'd attempted to carry up to the old Indian burial grounds now came creaking to a halt before me.

The priest broke off his chanting. The humming ceased and a hush fell over the place. The hooded figure stood motionless above the casket. The only noise audible was the low, persistent hiss of coals simmering on the brazier.

Had I not known he was dead, indeed even seen him dead, I would have been certain this figure swathed in gloomy monk's robes beneath the hood was Jones. But even if he were alive, what conceivable purpose would have brought him to this dismal place?

All about me people had taken up various positions around the casket. They stood with lowered heads, mumbling to themselves what I took to be prayers. This couldn't possibly be the same casket I'd seen in Uncle Toby's magic show. How did it get here? Who carried it through the woods? When I last saw it, it contained the body of Jones. Surely Uncle Toby would never have surrendered it to the Woodsmen. Not willingly. Not without a fight. And yet, here it was. Surely there couldn't be two such uniquely fashioned coffins.

The priest had begun to address the assembly. His voice was sharp and curt, barking commands. Several Woodsmen had lowered the casket to the ground, then came forward at once, trundling toward me with their typical pitching, rolling gait.

One of them came around to my right side, took me by the arm and started to pull me toward the casket. I stumbled after him while the priest took up a position directly behind us. Just up ahead the robed figure stood motionless above the casket, awaiting us.

When we reached there the robed man turned, stooped slightly and proceeded to lift the heavy bronze lid. It made a squealing sound as the sleeping bronze face swung past and out of my line of vision.

I felt a sharp poke in my back as the priest prodded me forward until at last I stood above the box, peering down into its empty interior. Upholstered in dark purple satin, its interior was richly studded with silver and gold appointments. The bottom and sides of it were thickly cushioned. It had more of the look of a cozy bed than a box that one would sleep in for all eternity.

My mouth went dry as sand. My breath grew short and I was certain I was about to be sick. I knew what was coming next, although my mind could scarcely encompass it.

The priest's prodding finger poked my back again. He murmured something in my ear. I knew what he wanted me to do but I couldn't bring myself to do it. The prodding finger came again, this time more impatient. The hooded figure beside the coffin watched me, even as the circle of fierce little dwarfs coiled closer and more menacingly around me.

The situation was desperate. There was little I could do and I had no wish to prolong the horror a moment more. In the next moment I'd lifted a leg over the ledge of the casket and was stepping in. At the same time a number of hands reached forward as though to press me down into the silken interior. I waved them off and, to my surprise, they fell back away from me, a sudden hush of awe overcoming them. Determined to show no fear, I lay down inside the box and folded my hands above my chest.

As the robed man leaned forward to lower the lid, I had a quick impression of a nose just visible beneath the cowl of the hood. Then a dark curtain of velvet dropped slowly down from above until it came to rest at a point only several inches above my forehead.

No sooner had the lid closed than I could hear screws being tightened into place. The slow stately chanting of the priest resumed, accompanied by that low humming and the scrape of sandaled feet across the floor. I strained my ears listening to the various sounds recede and grow faint until at last there was total silence and I knew I was alone.

The worst of it was at first—the darkness and the silence, the suffocating confinement. Before, darkness for me had been, at most, the darkness of my bedroom when I went to sleep. But there had always been a certain degree of light that crept through the windows there. Even with blindness, I imagine, there is at least a faint grayness to give one a sense of light and some connection with the world outside. But here there was none. Here was a total absence of light—a blackness so complete you could touch it. It lay across you with a palpable weight like a dark cloth over your face. It took away from you your sense of body and made you short of breath.

And then the silence—so complete your ears rang. After a while, the silence actually grew louder so that I had to concentrate on not hearing it for fear it would drive me mad. At one point I began to shout and scream to deafen the awful sound of it.

I must have screamed and shouted for well over an hour. I pleaded for mercy, to be taken out. No one came. But I never seriously expected anyone would. I was convinced I'd been buried alive and left there to die.

I thought of the image of the sleeping bronze saint above me, his face just inches from mine. The idea of that horrified me and I started to kick and punch and flail at the crushing weight of the lid. It wouldn't budge. There wasn't a hint of give between the lid and the top of the casket to offer even the smallest hope that any such effort could succeed. Nor would anyone come to save me. On that score I had no illusions. I could only think of Uncle Toby heaving a great sigh of relief that I was no longer at Fraze and he'd be spared the inconvenience of having to remove me from there himself.

At last, I lay quiet in my coffin-bed, waiting, wondering how long it would take before my oxygen would give out and I would expire. Would it be painful? Would it be quick? Would I die of thirst before I died of suffocation? All such matters took on immense importance to me.

In that soundless, lightless, remorseless black, resignation overtook me and I grew peaceful at last. To distract myself, I thought about my life at the castle. On the face of things, it had been what most people would call privileged. Yet, in truth, Fraze, for all its splendor, had been more of a jail to me than a home or a way of life by which one might achieve some small measure of fulfillment.

It occurred to me, lying there in that moldy darkness, that what I'd wanted, yearned for from the time I was first capable of reason, was to get away from Fraze. To put it far behind me. Whatever the Woodsmen were, as odious and treacherous a people as they were, life amongst them was at least real. One knew what to expect from a Woodsman and, bad as that was, for that alone one was grateful.

The hot, airless confinement of my coffin suddenly didn't seem all that bad. I was tired. My limbs were heavy and cramped from long confinement. My narrow bed inside this stone box felt warm and secure. I was drifting gently off to sleep. Darkness and silence were enfolding me. Lack of oxygen had begun to take its toll. I would sleep forever, just like the image of the drowsing saint above me.

At last my eyes closed and I slept. When they opened again, I was immediately awake, my head throbbing, with no recollection of having slept, no sensation of time having passed. Yet, the inside of the casket was now quite cold. It had been uncomfortably warm when I'd dropped off to sleep. Time must have passed. Had I slept so deeply or was I now dead? Was this cold I felt the chill of death? Or was it merely the sensation of dying?

Lying there in total darkness, I'd become disoriented, no longer knowing up from down. I wasn't certain where my head was in relation to my feet. I no longer felt that I was a part of my body. I was dissociated from it.

I fully believed that I was dead or near dead until the moment when all the noise began. Just outside the temple I was conscious of excitement. There were shouts and cries and a great deal of running about. Suddenly voices sounded from inside the building, followed by the scuffle of approaching footsteps.

A great row had started up nearby the casket. I could hear Woodsmen barking at each other in that excitable jabber of theirs. Suddenly the casket shuddered as though a number of hands had taken hold of it at once. A jolt followed that nearly tipped the box, and I felt myself being hoisted up. Suddenly we were moving, bouncing and careening along with great haste, the din of shouting voices all about me.

Badly jostled inside the coffin, I slid from side to side. At one point I banged my arm against a part of the interior brass. I began to shout and pummeled the lid once with my fists, demanding to be let out.

My shouts made little impression on the Woodsmen. They continued to hurtle ahead at what felt like great speed, all the while the racket of their frantic jabber rending the air.

The headlong flight sent my shoulders and head sliding forward and backward. From the angle at which I lay, it was clear we were moving downhill. After several minutes of rough bouncing I felt the casket being lowered, none too gently, as it settled onto the earth. Amid a welter of grunts and shouting, I could hear screws turning and latches being sprung. A jet of cold air hit my neck as a seam of daylight flashed beneath the lid. A sharp crack shuddered the box somewhere in the vicinity of my head. A latch was thrown back and then hinges squealed as the lid rose.

In the next moment, groping hands seized me and jerked me to my feet. I nearly toppled as the sudden rush of blood roared back into my head. Three or four of the Woodsmen lunged at me to keep me from going over.

Blinded by sunshine, pinwheels of color spun before me, my eyes blinking and struggling to adjust to daylight. We were back once more on the bank of the river. All about me were Woodsmen, hundreds of them. They stood on the beach in a wide circle, viewing the casket with a watchful, expectant awe. Their numbers were staggering—more than any of us had imagined. Uncle Toby's annual census had pegged them at two or three hundred. What I saw before me appeared to be closer to a thousand.

Moments before, they'd been milling about, shouting and unruly. But the instant I'd been hauled up out of the casket, swaying and teetering unsteadily on my feet, a great silence descended on the scene. Then something remarkable occurred. They all faced me and fell on their knees, heads bent forward, touching the earth. The spectacle of that so startled me that I half turned, ready to flee.

The priest then rose before them, arms upheld to the sky. Some sort of prayer followed, during which time my eyes wandered to the nearby river. Not far offshore lay the small flotilla of dark stubby boats I'd seen the night before. Six, possibly seven, of them bobbed up and down in the choppy current.

I watched their slow, balky progress downstream and as I did, I caught sight of the straw man. He was directly behind me now, ten or twelve feet high, seated on his throne just as he had been the night before in the temple.

Undoubtedly, they'd moved him out into daylight for this occasion—whatever that was to be. There he was again, soaring above us on his throne, the eyeless face peering down at me incuriously. The attitude in which he sat, a slight tilt of the head and slouch of the shoulder, conveyed a sense of almost godlike indifference. In his right hand he carried a cane of witch hazel.

Sunrise prayers on the beach then over, our attention was drawn down to the water where the procession of boats from

184

upriver had slowly drawn abreast of the place where I now stood, upright and wobbly, still inside the casket.

Just then one of the boats, the lead one and the largest, spun slowly counterclockwise and pointed its fierce prow landward. The other six followed in turn but stayed back, slightly behind, permitting the lead boat to drift in first. At a certain point, perhaps twenty feet offshore, it dropped anchor, then pitched and rolled to a halt, causing a series of small whitecaps to slap noisily at its prow.

The other boats went through a similar maneuver, but continued to hold back from the first vessel, as though keeping a respectful distance. I watched as two large birch dugouts pushed off from the shore and slowly paddled their way out to the lead boat.

When the dugouts reached it, several Woodsmen emerged from the wheelhouse and scrambled down along the rail. Seizing the gunnels, they held them steady alongside the tossing boat. From where I stood I could hear their high, shrill cries drift in over the water.

Whatever was going on at that moment commanded the absolute attention of the hundreds gathered on the beach. They stood stone silent. Several more Woodsmen had come out on the deck of the lead boat. They'd emerged from a narrow door in the wheelhouse, and appeared to be struggling to maneuver a longish object through it.

With the sun in my eyes it was hard to make out what they were carrying. But at a certain point the boat turned slowly on its mooring and for a moment I had a clear view of the action from the side.

The boat's crew was out the door and now stood on deck holding between them an object that looked like a board. Taking the most elaborate care, they carried this object toward the rail where the two birch dugouts waited.

More chattering drifted in over the water. As the long boardlike object was lifted with utmost care over the rail, eager hands rose up from below to take hold of it and guide it down. It was then that I saw that it was not a board but a litter of some sort in which someone was being carried.

In a matter of moments the litter was secured to the stern of one of the dugouts even as it pitched from side to side on the heaving currents. A short time later, powerful stubby arms were paddling the dugout toward the beach, a thin rippling wake fanning out behind it. The second dugout followed close behind.

The instant the first dugout carrying the litter scraped up on the shore, dozens of eager hands seized the gunnels and hauled it up on the beach. The other dugout followed with a number of Woodsmen wading out hip-high into the stream to grab hold of it and tow it onto the beach. When it had been beached the high priest, along with several other robed dignitaries, stood beside it, conferring in hushed voices.

Shortly, as if on signal, a half dozen Woodsmen sprang forward from the crowd and lifted the litter off the dugout. As it was borne forward, a procession consisting of the high priest and a number of important-looking elders fell in behind it. In turn, a throng of Woodsmen closed in formation behind them. I still had no idea what they carried in the litter but as the procession passed through the crowd, a high keening sound rose amidst them. I'd never heard such a hair-raising ruckus before, but I was certain it was the sound of mourning.

The procession was now moving toward me. I recall the frantic scramble of my mind and trying to control my mounting sense of panic. I appeared to be the center of attention, and there was little doubt that all this activity had something to do with me. But how and in what way, I had no idea. This is a dream, I kept telling myself, saying it over and over again until it became an incantation. When I wake I'll be in my bed at Fraze, sprawling deliciously beneath the goosedown comforter, doing my wake-up yawn. Shortly Cassie will burst into my room. There would be Leander behind her and the two of them would trip over each other, laughing, shouting, desperate to reach me and tear the blankets off my bed, as they always did in happier times.

The procession coming up from the beach was now no more than a dozen or so feet away. When that space had narrowed to a mere two or three feet, the group shuddered to a halt before the priest.

The wind blew in hard off the river and, above its raucous gusts, the priest's voice rose in wailing chants. He turned and came toward me, the Woodsmen bearing the litter struggling along behind him. Then, all in a single motion, the procession veered sideways and the litter loomed large before my eyes.

What it contained should have been no surprise. And yet it was. But, seeing those strange little feet and the blackened toe sticking out inelegantly from beneath a soiled white covering of some sort told the full tale. Even in those sharp windy blasts, the

186

stench of mortification was overpowering. As the litter passed them, I watched the Woodsmen avert their faces. Staring down at it with dumb horror, something caught in my throat. I couldn't say for certain if it was a gag or a sob.

Another Woodsman, a pompous preening little fellow with a pigeon chest and a kind of wizard's steeple hat, suddenly pranced in barking several words at the sky. Instantly, a group of nearby Woodsmen rushed forward and I felt myself being lifted bodily over the rim of the casket, then set roughly down on the ground just beside it.

Almost simultaneously, another group had lifted Jones's body off the litter and set it down with the most solemn care in the place I had just vacated.

Once more the sound of priestly chants rose as the lid of the box was lowered and the screws firmly tightened.

How had it all come about? How had they come by that casket in the temple the night before? It was without doubt the same one that had sat in Uncle Toby's study, a prop for one of his more startling parlor tricks. It was no duplicate. And now here was not only the casket but the remains of Jones as well. How had that gotten here? Someone had to have given it to the Woodsmen. Or else it had to have been taken forcibly. How had that trick been managed? Had there been collusion at Fraze, or had there been a battle of catastrophic proportion? Feeling completely betrayed by those closest to me, I still feared for Fraze and the fate my family might have suffered there during the night. Were they all dead—Uncle Toby, Madam Lobkova, Signor Parelli, my sisters and brothers, Colonel Porphyry and the entire household staff? All gone now? It seemed inconceivable and yet only that could account for the presence of my father's remains in the possession of the Woodsmen.

These thoughts swept through my head in a matter of seconds, and then all at once I found myself looking down into the hard, chiseled features of the priest. His hands rose toward me. They carried the chalice that had been sitting on the altar. It was heavy and fashioned out of stone. Glancing down, I caught a glimpse of objects floating in a murky broth inside the bowl of it. I looked away, but my mind retained an image of things pink and shapeless.

Once more, the chalice rose until the priest held it above his head and slightly forward. Then the hand that held it slowly lowered and the chalice jerked jerked toward me, thrust beneath

187

my nose. Almost at once I had a whiff of something rank. I had no idea what it was but I was strongly disinclined to take it.

Again the chalice jerked at me while the old priest, spraying me with spittle, barked gruff sounds up into my face. His impatience grew with my increasing hesitation. Too frightened to anger him further, I took the chalice, holding it at arm's length in badly shaking hands.

I had a vague idea where this was leading and it was confirmed moments later when the priest thrust a fist to his mouth, pantomiming a gruff drinking gesture. He snarled a word at me. It sounded something like *sagri*. Then *bandik*. *Sagri bandik*. He shouted it over and over again until each shout felt like a blow to the head. The cup was now no more than an inch or so from my lips, so close I could feel the chill of the stone on my chin.

"*Sagri, sagri,*" the priest snarled once more while, out of the corner of my eye, I glimpsed the circle of fierce little people tighten and press hotly around me.

Again I peered down into that awful gruel swimming with what I now had little doubt were bits of viscera. As a child I recalled Madam Lobkova reading to us about the ancient Egyptian kings; how the priests cut organs from their bodies when they died, preserving them in canopic jars, bits of human tissue to serve as talismans against evil. Sometimes the organs were buried with the king. More commonly, they were ingested by the king's successor to insure that he would take on all the virtues of his predecessor. But those were barbaric pagan times and we were now living at the apex of civilization.

"*Sagri.*" The priest howled again and stamped his tiny buskined feet in growing irritation. From above, like a huge sentinel, the straw man peered down at me out of his eyeless face.

The crowds of Woodsmen encircling us shuffled restlessly. Infuriated, several other priests jabbered at me. I must have stared back at them blankly because the chief priest seized me by the elbow and tried to physically force the contents of the cup between my sealed lips. I wish they would have killed me then. It would have been easier than what followed.

"*Sagri bandik,*" the headman shrieked again. His feet kicked up clouds of dust from the earth like an angry bull on the verge of charging. Terrified, I clamped my eyes shut and bit down hard on the rim of the cup. The putrid bouquet from within filled my head and nearly made me swoon. I felt a bolus of something rise in my throat and fought it back down. Through nearly shut eyes I had an image of my wrist tilting. A bit of something in the cup grazed my lip. I felt the liquid, cool and viscous, slide over my tongue and down the back of my throat. It wouldn't stay down, however, and came back up, a retching, sour chyme streaming from the corners of my mouth.

When I sagged, a number of hands reached forward to catch me under the arms and jerk me back up on my feet. Once more the chalice was forced to my lips. By then I had little will left with which to resist. I closed my eyes, raised them heavenward and drank.

Chunks of tissue slid over my tongue. I didn't chew it. Not any of it. I simply hoped to get it down as quickly as possible and so I swallowed. Various bits of things dropped down my throat, and when I gagged and coughed a hot sour lava came bubbling back up, choking me, making me sputter and gasp. It was an act of will to take it back down.

When I'd drained the cup there were tears in my eyes. Were those tears the result of nearly choking to death? Were they tears of outrage? Or had they come with the knowledge that I'd been forced to eat the flesh of my father? If I was supposed to believe that in so doing I'd taken on the noblest virtues of Jones, I certainly didn't feel that way. I felt degraded and sick to death.

There was, for an eerily protracted moment, the most deathly silence. Then suddenly, as if by signal, hundreds of voices broke into tumultuous cheers. The high priest, who moments before had abused me, now fell on his knees and kissed the hem of my tunic. Next he removed the tunic, pulling it gently over my head so that I stood naked and trembling before the cheering mob. The hundreds of Woodsmen assembled there watched transfixed while I was costumed in rich robes of velvet and brocade. At last a crown of gold, encrusted with gems, was placed upon my head.

In the next moment a roar went up and a swarm of bodies rushed toward me. They crushed and trampled one another in an effort to get close enough to touch me. To my dying day I will forever see that tangle of hands—hands scaled with fungus rashes, open running sores, stubby, gnarled fingers straining toward me, and sometimes I still wake at night hearing those wild, primitive yawps—of joy and ferocious triumph—ringing in my ears.

189

27

I suppose you might call the event my coronation, for I'd certainly been anointed some kind of king. From that moment on, I no longer occupied the crude, unfurnished hut where I'd been imprisoned the day before. I'd been installed now in a far more impressive dwelling. Consisting of several high-ceilinged rooms, furnished with hand-wrought pine pieces, my new home was almost regal when compared to even the more elaborate Woodsman residences.

The moment I took occupancy my royal robes were stripped from me and I was bathed and rubbed with incense by my keeper, the Woodswoman. Throughout the ceremony she had never once left my side and, by now, she had grown almost unbearably proprietarial. When the ceremony was over, she'd stood between me and the surging mob, fending off well-wishers when they came too close and shrieking commands at the retinue of ten Woodsmen who'd been appointed my private guard. Through the noisy throng they led me back to my new residence. The Woodswoman wouldn't leave my side and, when I dropped off for an hour or so in the late afternoon, she sat in a corner of the room, silent and observing me. Once, pretending to sleep, I had a glimpse of her through half-closed eyes. Something in that alert possessive tension of her body made my blood run cold.

When darkness came she dressed me again. This time I found myself in robes fashioned from animal skins and lined with some indeterminate furs. They gave off an oily rancid smell and bore front and back a number of those mysterious canelike figures so visible everywhere throughout the camp.

With the crown of gold atop my head, I was led out into the blazing night with my thuggish retinue of bodyguards moving like juggernaughts before me. My overbearing lady keeper trailed perhaps a foot or two behind.

As we moved down the main avenue of the camp, the throngs parted, their roar of approval deafening. Up ahead I could see a large square where a number of banquet tables had been set with a raised dais placed at right angles to them. About that was a throne made of huge timbers tied with thongs of goat leather.

All the while we moved, our procession was accompanied by a band of elfin musicians piping pipes and banging timbrels. Woodsmen danced along beside us. They turned cartwheels, laughed and chanted and strew flowers in our path. It was here I first noted within that sprawling mob a number of Woodsmen, set apart and different from the typical Woodsmen. For one thing, they were of average to above-average height. I'd not noticed them before because they were a distinct minority. But clustered together and segregated in a roped-off area from the others, their physical difference became more evident.

Reaching the throne, I felt the sharp poke of the Woodswoman's finger at my back, directing me to climb up and take my place there. As I mounted, a number of priests and dignitaries on the dais rose at once. Facing me, they murmured several words in unison and bowed deeply. Only when I'd taken my place on the throne did the dignitaries on the dais resume their seats. That was the signal for hundreds of Woodsmen and their wives and yowling infants to race for places at the many long pine tables that had been set out.

Instantly, an army of servers streamed into the area. Food and drink were brought and laid out on the tables without much ceremony. Great frothing pitchers of ale, along with huge clay tureens of goat stew, were slammed down on the planks. Almost immediately the Woodsmen fell upon the food, fighting each other to ladle great slopping portions of it onto their plates.

When food was brought to me, it was presented with great obsequiousness by a half dozen or so drone servers. I noted that they were not permitted to serve me directly but had first to present their offerings to the Woodswoman, who made a great show of tasting each course before permitting it to come to me. A number of these dishes she turned back with a wave of her hand. For that, I was grateful. What finally reached me I could barely eat, so repulsive was it all.

The ale, which the Woodsmen call *Jum*, was sour and very strong. The taste of vinegar comes quickly to mind. Whatever it was, it was less objectionable than the food, even though a variety of what appeared to be insects and small foreign bodies floated on its surface.

Throughout dinner the musicians weaved their way up and down the aisles between each table, their pipes and timbrels banging with a throbbing repetition that soon grew hypnotic.

The banquet went on for hours. Toward the end of it, a great ball of fiery orange appeared to explode in the sky at the top of the avenue. A wild roar went up as the glow grew brighter and seemed to slowly approach us.

Shortly, a column of Woodsmen appeared at the head of the square. Yoked to an enormous wagonlike dray, they pulled it, lurching and swaying down the main avenue toward the dais. As it drew near I was able to make out in the roaring flames the outline of the straw man on his throne, now a shaft of fire nearly a dozen feet high.

As the wagon rattled toward us, a great shower of sparks like a million fiery meteors rocketed up out of the straw man's head into the evening sky. All the while he sat teetering on his throne, one arm outstretched like a drunk and dying god offering beneficence. By the time the wagon drew past us with a slow, plodding solemnity, most of the figure's outer shape had already been consumed in the flames. What remained was a mere sticklike skeleton that had served as a kind of armature beneath the straw.

Dozens of Woodsmen had joined hands and formed a circle in which they danced around the burning figure. It was a moment of great joy, and yet there was something ghastly about it. The waves of ovenlike heat from the flames were nearly suffocating. The Woodsmen, already far gone in their *Jum*, grew wilder and more raucous. Many pranced and tumbled up the muddy aisles. Some had removed their garments and, running naked alongside the wagon, flung them up to be consumed on the straw man's pyre. Others spit house dogs on pikes and pitched them squealing and barking up onto the flames. Those Woodsmen who had thrown off their clothing moments before now coupled freely on the ground and beneath the tables of the square.

It was barely controlled mayhem which grew worse as the night wore on. More food and drink were served. The music grew increasingly frenetic. Someone had led a muzzled bear out on a leash and then a half dozen or so Woodsmen prodded the poor beast with spears in an effort to make it perform.

I was sick to my stomach from the goat flesh and sour ale and sick to my heart from the spectacle of cruelty. I had no idea what it all meant, or, more to the point, what was intended for me. Attired in my absurd robes and crown, I had little doubt that something most assuredly was.

The worst of that night came at the very end. The most pathetic sight I saw was my little sister and brother. At first, I didn't recognize them, for they stood together in a knot of rough, unruly goat people lining the avenue to wave as I passed. Both small in stature and, dressed as they were in Woodsman garb, they barely stood out.

Something, I don't know what—perhaps a sudden movement—drew my eye in that direction, and there was Cassie. She stood slightly forward of the rest of them in the rutted, puddled roadway. A foot or two behind her stood Leander. It was much harder to recognize him, so completely had he been transformed into one of them. Dressed in goatskins and Tyrolean, he held his sister's hand and stared straight before him, at nothing in particular. He was docile and lifeless. Cassie appeared to be far more alert, pathetically protective of her brother, as though she and she alone was all that stood between him and all of the horrors so visible about us.

They seemed very much alone, the two of them, and for a moment, I had the curious notion that being King, I might simply walk over and take them with me. Then I saw the leashes. But *leash* is far too kind a word. Actually, it was just some lengths of frayed rope knotted around their necks. And then I saw the armed thugs at the other end of those ropes. I had all I could do to keep from breaking away from my guards and running to their aid.

Still not certain they recognized me in my kingly attire, I had confirmation of that when we passed and Cassie made a sudden movement toward me. Her frightened, desperate eyes sought to attract me. Immediately, her head snapped and the rope-leash dragged her back. The motion had somehow tugged Leander forward and I had this view, this never-to-be-forgotten memory of my little brother dressed in that grotesque costume.

He stood no more than five feet from me. By reaching out, I could have touched him. But when I tried, a sharp slap pushed my hands aside. It was one of the guards. So much for my kingly powers. In that brief instant, I had a view of my brother's eyes. They looked directly at me, blank with no expression. Nor did they convey any sign of recognition. Behind them lay a gray and awful void. And though the night was warm, a deadly chill crept up all about me.

There was one last thing—one final horror to crown the many horrors of that night. I was led back to the temple where I'd spent the night before, entombed in Jones's coffin. The huge casket was still there, and something told me that it now contained whatever was left of Jones's remains.

Along with my lady keeper, I was led to the altar where the high priest awaited us. And there, amid incantations and the suffocating smell of more incense, before a packed gallery of noisy and besotted goat people, a tiny ring of pleached vines was slipped on my index finger by the Woodswoman, and we were wed.

28

"I'm sure it was locked when I went to bed."

"Well, it's open now."

"No sign of the door having been forced. Who else has a key?"

"Mr. Jones has one. I hold the other." Signor Parelli produced the key for Porphyry to see.

"Is that the only other?"

"As far as I know."

"May I?" the Colonel asked.

"Of course."

Parelli handed him the key, whereupon Porphyry, stooping, inserted it gently into the lock. He flicked the bolt several times, listening to the solid reassuring thump as it shot home. Then he handed the key back to Parelli. "You're certain this hasn't been out of your possession for the past forty-eight hours?"

"Absolutely."

The Colonel turned to Toby Jones, who'd stood silently frowning for the past several minutes, observing the interrogation. "And you, Mr. Jones—your key?"

"Right here. On this chain."

He withdrew a long, clanking chain from a vast pocket inside his jacket. Fully two dozen keys on a ring glinted faintly in the dim light where they now stood. Uncle Toby opened his jacket to demonstrate how the chain had been locked by thin metal wires to his inside pocket. "The chain never leaves me. It's always attached to my person."

Colonel Porphyry tugged thoughtfully at his chin. They were standing in one of the low-ceilinged limestone grottoes beneath the castle. A number of such subterranean cells comprised the north end of the building. Here the cellars, unlike the updated central and southern sections, remained unfinished. Because of the unvarying chill of these grottoes, unaffected by outside temperatures, they served as ideal repositories for the storage of perishable goods. They also comprised the castle's considerable wine cellars.

The particular grotto in which they now stood had been used as a granary for wheat and corn. But most recently it had served as a temporary holding place for Jones's casket until it could be moved safely up to the old Indian burial grounds. That corner of the cell recently occupied by the casket was now empty. Where it had been, only a shroudlike sheet remained. Used to protect the container from the relentless drip of condensation, it lay now in a small, untidy clump off in a corner.

"I find it incomprehensible that a band of these Woodsmen fellows could have gotten themselves into the castle, found their way down here to this locked cell, opened it without benefit of a key and then made off with the casket. And all without once being observed by anyone." Colonel Porphyry's characteristically genial mien had gone a touch sour.

"That's the damned house guard for you." Signor Parelli scowled. "Not very reassuring, is it?"

"There'll be the devil to pay for this," Toby Jones muttered.

"To think, with all the extra precautions taken, and the so-called impregnability of the castle, these little riffraff could still get in and out with such ease—" The Colonel stared at the two men regarding him in the gray gloom of the grotto. "Unless, of course, they had accomplices inside the castle."

"Rubbish." Toby glowered. "You're not suggesting any of the . . ."

"Why not? Or the domestic staff; the laboratory personnel. I simply toss it out as a possibility."

196

"But—" Toby blustered. "All of these people were devoted to Jones. Why would they . . ."

"Why would several of Mr. Jones's own children all be so eager to confess to having murdered their father? Or at least having wanted to? Not exactly what most people would regard as filial devotion."

Toby reddened. "Preposterous. You surely don't believe—"

"I'm not sure what I believe, Mr. Jones." The Colonel smiled cordially. "I simply wonder why they would go to such lengths to concoct such a strange set of confessions. And then, too, I wonder what bearing all this has on the sudden disappearance of your niece and nephew from the castle."

The Colonel pondered the puzzle he himself had just posed, then merely shrugged and wandered forward into the grotto. His shoes made a hollow, clicking sound on the wet stone floor. Reaching the place where the shroud lay in its untidy little clump, he knelt down and hovered beside it a while. On his face was a look of the most perplexed sadness.

A short time later, they had all gathered up on the battlements.

"I don't think I've ever seen anything like that before." Toby Jones stared gloomily down at the strange derricklike structure that had been reared up there overnight. Signor Parelli hovered just behind him while below a half dozen of the Colonel's men armed with rifles fanned out over the grounds in a large half loop, searching for additional signs of the Woodsmen.

"Siege tower," Porphyry remarked offhandedly. "Sort of thing invading armies employed during the Middle Ages in order to breach fortress walls."

"Must be fifty feet tall."

"Closer to seventy-five, actually. There's another at the other side of the castle."

"Amazing," Toby murmured, caught between admiration and rage. "Who'd have thought they'd be so clever?"

Colonel Porphyry smiled at the crude ingenuity of the mechanism. "Its genius is its simplicity. No more than some hewn pine lashed together with a few thews of goatskin. You mount it as you do a ladder. Only with this, a goodly number of them could all be climbing at the same time."

"And that racket we kept hearing from the edge of the woods during the storm?"

"Our little friends hacking down trees to build the towers," the Colonel explained.

Signor Parelli inched forward to the wall's edge, clearly uncomfortable with the height. "How do you suppose they got it up here from the forest? Must be two hundred yards at least and uphill all the way."

"They set it on logs and rolled it." The Colonel pointed to a swath of flattened grass, perhaps twenty feet wide. "You can see the trail they blazed, dragging that contraption."

"And we all slept right through it." Toby Jones shook his head gloomily.

They stayed a while longer, then trudged back down the winding stairway through the tower and into the castle.

"No doubt you'll be wanting to put together a rescue party to go out to the encampment," Porphyry went on as they strode along one of the lower corridors. "Time is of the essence. The less we tarry, the greater our chances of finding the young man and the girl unharmed. As you know"—the Colonel's voice dropped discreetly—"these woodspeople can be a nasty lot. We don't know what's on their minds. I'll be happy to lead a strike force of my own people out there. I'll also need a number of yours for backup. . . ."

It was at that moment that it occurred to Porphyry he'd been running off at some length, and that Mr. Jones and Signor Parelli, trailing behind, had offered nothing by way of response.

Glancing back over his shoulder, his eye fell on Toby Jones and he knew at once something was wrong. "I imagine you'll be wanting to come along as well."

Toby Jones swept past him without a word. Parelli trailed close at his heels, leaving the Colonel to watch, dumbfounded, in their wake.

Porphyry lingered a moment, watching the place where both men had disappeared through a door. Then, eyes blinking, he followed quickly, catching up with them in the nearby conservatory. Without waiting to be invited, he swept in and closed the doors behind him.

Inside the high glassed enclosure the air was warm and moist as a sponge. Every available inch of space had been jam-packed with oversized botanical specimens, some of them soaring twenty feet up into the lofty skylights. The air smelled of soil and humus and green growth running riot. Reaching a tall,

198

thronelike rattan chair, Toby settled heavily into it. He signaled the Colonel to take a seat in the matched chair opposite him.

Signor Parelli bustled forward, assuming his guard dog pose at Toby's side, his darting eyes wary and charged with defiance.

"Now look," Toby Jones began somewhat brusquely, "you're concerned about my niece and nephews. That's all very good, and I am gratified. But that's not why you're here. You're here to discover what happened to my brother and who is responsible. That and only that."

Porphyry was speechless—but for only a moment. "I only recently learned that another nephew, one Leander by name, is also missing."

"That's true."

"He is your nephew, is he not?"

"He is."

"You do care for him, I presume?"

"Of course."

The Colonel could scarcely control the anger in his voice. "Then why did you go to such lengths to conceal this from me? I need help here. I don't need obstructions."

The wicker creaked beneath Toby Jones as he sat back in the chair with a great sigh. His handsome, dissolute features wore an expression of tired forbearance. "I know that what I'm about to say to you now will no doubt sound strange. Callous, perhaps even unfeeling. I have no plan at the present time to retrieve my niece or nephews from the Woodsmen's camp."

Something rose in Porphyry's throat and caught there.

"Please let me finish," Toby went on. "Before you say anything, I must remind you that those of us who live here at Fraze observe a set of values quite different from the outside."

"I'm aware of that."

"Are you?" Toby's smile seemed impertinent. "Then if you are, you also understand that more than anything, Fraze is a laboratory, a place where human behavior is studied and the species' potential is tested to its outermost limits."

The claims being made struck Porphyry as grandiose. And Mr. Jones, as he spoke, seemed to swell with self-importance. "What you see here is the core of an experimental program set up by my brother a half century ago, known by most educators and scientists of human behavior as the System."

"We have a rather complete file on it at headquarters," the

199

Colonel murmured. "Its principal tenets, I gather, are somewhat unorthodox."

"Unorthodox?" Toby Jones seemed startled, even offended. But then, taking a more conciliatory tack, he broke into laughter. "You're behind the times, Colonel. That's what they were saying ages ago. Now those same tenets are taken for granted."

"Yes, yes, I see," Porphyry said, beginning to show unmistakable signs of impatience. "But I still fail to understand what all of this has to do with abandoning these young people to the tender mercies of the Woodsmen."

"Abandoning?" Toby Jones seemed offended. "What makes you think they've been abandoned?"

"You're not telling me they're out there by design?"

"In a manner of speaking, yes. We do have an arrangement with the Woodsmen. An arrangement worked out by my brother in accordance with the tenets of the System."

"And is this so-called arrangement what is known as the Covenant?"

At the mention of the word, Mr. Jones's eyes blinked. "Any more, I'm not at liberty to say, except that my niece and nephews are in no danger."

The effect of the words caused a certain breathlessness in the Colonel. "But what earthly purpose . . . These people can be quite vicious."

"As I say, Colonel, you'll have to trust me when I say that my niece and nephews' presence out there is integral to our work. Therefore, when I tell you to put aside all thoughts of their rescue for the time being, I know wherefore I speak. Rather, concentrate your efforts on bringing to justice my brother's murderer. That's why you've been summoned here. The world demands an explanation. Bring to justice the killer of this extraordinary man. Leave Cassie and Leander and Jonathan to me."

Porphyry was silent for some time. During the course of Toby Jones's startling talk, he'd sat stiff and erect in his chair. When at last he spoke, his voice was low, somewhat quavery, as though he were struggling to contain his feelings. "I shall, of course, do what I've been called here to do, Mr. Jones. I'm as eager to bring your brother's murderer to book as you are."

"Splendid." Toby thumped his knee for emphasis. "Any questions you may have, any assistance you may need, go directly with your request to Signor Parelli. I trust Madam Lobkova has put the archives at your disposal."

"She's been most helpful."

"Whatever you want." He wagged a finger at Porphyry. "And if there's any fact or small detail that Parelli or Lobkova can't provide, come directly to me."

"In that case, I might start by asking you the age of Mr. Jones at the time of his death."

Toby Jones hadn't been prepared for such a swift response to his offer. The effect of it was to take a bit of the wind out of his sails. "Why . . . he was born in . . . let me see . . . in 1980. That would make him ninety, wouldn't it?"

Porphyry gazed at a point on the ceiling. "I did turn up a birth certificate for him in your family files with a date of March 21, 1980. But I must tell you that when I examined the file more closely, I had the distinct impression it had been tampered with."

"Tampered with?"

"The entry was fresh. It looked as though 1980 had been written over another date that had been recently eradicated."

All the while he spoke, Porphyry watched the range of expressions shifting on Toby Jones's face. "I took the liberty therefore of running my own check through headquarters on the mainland." The Colonel reached into his inside vest pocket and withdrew a crumpled cable. It trembled slightly in his hand as he unfolded it. "There is, indeed, a birth certificate on record in the courthouse of Baltimore County, Maryland—a record of an Orville Jones having been born to a Mr. Irvine and a Mrs. Kathryn Locke Jones. The date is March 1, 1980, and that, indeed, would put him at age ninety."

"That's correct," Toby nodded, somewhat miffed.

"However," Porphyry continued, scarcely looking up from the cable, "headquarters located another, earlier birth certificate for an Orville Jones for March 1, 1921, Baltimore, Maryland. Also the son of Irvine and Kathryn. That, you see, puts him closer to one hundred and fifty years of age—one hundred and forty-nine, to be exact." Porphyry peered up at Toby through his yellow-tinted lenses. "There's obviously some error here."

"Obviously. . . ." Toby chuckled, but there seemed little mirth to it.

"Jones is hardly an unusual name, but Orville is somewhat less common. And Baltimore, Maryland, with parents also called

Irvine and Kathryn—note the spelling. Very unusual—" Having expressed his puzzlement, the Colonel awaited clarification.

"As you say—it's a mistake."

"I would hope so. And I shall so notify our records bureau. One hundred and forty-nine years is hardly the typical three score and ten." Porphyry folded the cable back into a square and returned it to his vest pocket. When he looked up again, he was somewhat startled to find the eyes of both men riveted on the place where the cable had vanished. "If it isn't too personal a question, Mr. Jones, how old are you?"

"I'm four years younger than my brother."

"That would put you at eighty-six." Porphyry reared back in astonishment. "What a marvelous specimen for your age. I would have guessed no more than half that."

A long, uneasy silence followed as Toby Jones stared hard at the floor, a faint flush rising to his throat. "Well, I'm not eighty-six, as you can see," he said brusquely. "And yes, there is a mistake on those birth certificates."

"On both of them?"

"An error in transcription. But I'm afraid, once again, I'm not at liberty to discuss the nature of it, except to say that it was . . ."

"Intentional," Porphyry completed the thought for him.

Toby Jones sat back in his seat, some of his assertiveness wilting beneath the Colonel's gaze. "I told you, you wouldn't understand everything I've been trying to tell you here."

For some time after they'd left, Porphyry remained seated. The tall, thronelike wicker chair made him appear strangely diminutive and doll-like as he puffed smoke from his cigarillo into the moist, overheated conservatory air. Outside, the sun had burned off the mist from the treetops and, but for a dollop or two of stationary clouds dreaming above the castle towers, the sky was clear.

The Colonel reflected on all he'd seen and heard that morning—the siege towers and the predawn attack of the Woodsmen; the theft of the casket containing the body of Orville Jones; the disappearance, whether voluntary or forced, of three of his offspring, a fact in which Mr. Tobias Jones appeared to calmly acquiesce. And now, this awkward business of what appeared to be deliberate falsification of public records, for reasons Mr. Toby

Jones was unable or unwilling to disclose. "All right, I can accept that," Porphyry reasoned to himself. "But to what end?"

Much, the Colonel concluded, was going on here at Fraze, most of it unseen, going on at the cellar level. But a goodly part of the action appeared to be concentrated on the top story of the castle as well.

Having availed himself of the opportunity for a midnight stroll through the upper reaches of the house, he was now contemplating a tour of the lower depths. What he'd found on the topmost floor was hardly what one might expect to find in a twelfth-century European castle transported from Europe to the remote wilderness of North America. But on the other hand, in a medieval castle transformed into a modern-day scientific research center, what he'd seen up there was perfectly reasonable.

Porphyry reached back into his vest pocket and withdrew, along with the cable he'd just read aloud to Mr. Toby, several clippings that had been wired to him that morning from headquarters.

The first was a brief entry from the Columbia Encyclopedia:

WOODSMEN. Maritime Islands. Canada. Goatherds inhabiting the remote and largely unsettled interiors of Labrador and Newfoundland. A wild, fierce people. Dwarfish in stature. Indigenous inhabitants of the area first come upon by Monsigneur Thierry Duschene (1642—?), Missionary of Canada and northern provinces who described the first colony of Woodsmen as a pagan tribe of goatherds, possibly Celtic in origin, clinging to barbaric rites several thousand years old.

Attempting to missionize them, Monsigneur Duschene lived among the wild goatherds for several years. His weekly correspondence to the Archdiocese in Quebec continued until 1648, at which time it abruptly ceased, whereupon he was never heard from again.

WOODSMEN . . . euphemism for a low, primitive people with degenerate bloodlines. Slang expression meaning oafish, brutelike, criminal.

The next was a small clipping, frayed and yellowed with age, from the back pages of a local Canadian newspaper. It carried a deadline nearly twenty years old:

203

The article went on to tell how a handful of Canadian loggers, working in the interior of one of the unpopulated Maritime Islands, stumbled on what appeared to be an ancient Indian burial ground located in a peat bog. Each grave was marked with a shallow mound of stones upon which no writing appeared to identify the occupant of the grave.

Several of these graves were dug up, at which time the loggers found not far beneath the surface cadavers not in caskets but interred directly in the earth in their clothing. Forensic and odontological examination revealed that the cadavers were at least four to five hundred years old and, undoubtedly, the remains of a race of people small in stature—said to have inhabited the area at that time. Radiocarbon analysis of the clothing found on the cadavers corroborated the time frame suggested by the forensic evidence. Fiber tests of the clothing suggested that it was made from the hide of deer, or possibly goats. Buried unembalmed, no explanation was offered for the near-perfect state of preservation in which these bodies were found, but several researchers who examined the remains spec-ulated that the unusually high concentration of tannins found in the peat may have been responsible for the phenomenon.

Stapled to this clipping was another, shorter one. It was datelined the following day and, undoubtedly, was a follow-up. It reported that in addition to the human cadavers unearthed were those of a number of small primates, principally chimpan-zees and rhesus monkeys. Their presence in the bog posed an even deeper mystery, since none of these creatures is indigenous to the area. Nor could anyone offer an explanation for their being there.

The article went on to report that the primate graves ap-peared to be of relatively recent vintage and that tests conducted on the bones and dentition of the primate cadavers revealed the fact that many of them had exceeded their normal life expec-tancy by two to three times. Primatologists from nearby McGill University verified the credibility of the report but were at a loss to explain it.

The last clipping Porphyry had came from a small article contained in a box at the back of the Sunday *New York Times* financial pages. It was dated some forty years earlier and referred to a certain Dr. Felix Fabian, a Swiss-Italian geneticist, molecular biologist and member of the faculties of medicine at the Universities of Heidelberg, Tübingen and Uppsala. A long string of imposing titles and professional memberships followed his name. The article went on to report that Dr. Fabian was the director of a small biomedical laboratory in Geneva. The laboratory was one of a series of many operated by something called the Humanus Institute, S.A., described as an organization established and funded by a consortium of private philanthropies, all of which preferred, for unspecified reasons, to maintain strict anonymity. This was also the name Porphyry had seen affixed to dozens of manifolds and shipping crates stored in the laboratories of the upper story of the castle. The glimmer of something as yet vague and inchoate began to take uneasy shape in his mind.

"Dr. Fabian," the article concluded, "was known for his pioneering work in the field of gene splicing and recombinant DNA, particularly as it relates to human longevity."

When he'd completed the reading, Porphyry folded the clippings, then, holding them between index finger and forefinger, drummed them lightly on his knee. He mused for a time over his quarrel with Mr. Toby Jones and the events that had brought it about. It had much to do, of course, with the question of his missing niece and nephews. But, as Mr. Toby had been quick to point out to him in no uncertain terms, that wasn't why he was there. The subject at hand was Mr. Orville Jones, and how to bring to book those responsible for his death. The fate of Mr. Jones's children, as his brother had pointed out, was at this time a secondary issue.

Peculiar, to say the least, but if that's the way Mr. Toby wanted things, that was his affair. Porphyry was just as eager to snare Jones's murderer as anyone else. Knowing far more about the lifestyle of the Woodsmen than he'd care to divulge, Porphyry wouldn't have entrusted a dog to their tender mercies, let alone three inexperienced youths.

The Colonel gave a sly little laugh, then, folding the clippings and returning them to his pocket, he rose and, toddling slightly, walked toward the big glass conservatory doors.

A dozen feet or so outside the conservatory, Colonel Porphyry became aware of the soft tread of footsteps coming quietly up behind him. He turned in time to see the short, bulky figure of Madam Lobkova bearing down upon him.

"Colonel."

"Madam?"

Red in the face, breathing heavily, she came to a shuddering halt an inch or so before him. "What did he tell you?"

"Pardon?"

"Whatever it was, it was a lie."

"Madam, I . . ."

"Don't believe a thing Toby Jones says about his niece or nephews. He has good reason for wanting them out of the way. And that Parelli riffraff is even more treacherous. Mark my word—they're in there up to their eyeballs with those people."

"What people?"

"Never mind what people." She stamped her foot in a huff and, bearing down hard, she backed him down the corridor. He could feel waves of heat rising out of her clothing. "Cassie and the boys. What did he say? They're with the Woodsmen, aren't they?"

"That's almost certain."

She stifled a small cry. "I knew it. I knew it. And no doubt he told you that they were fine. Everything just as it should be. You were to do nothing about it. Am I right?"

"As a matter of fact . . ."

"I told you so. Did I not?" She turned and clapped a wad of crumpled tissue to her mouth.

Porphyry watched her dab fitfully at her chin. Her eyes, rimmed with kohl, had gone runny from tears. Gently, Porphyry pried the tissue from her hand and wiped the smeared eyes. "Really, this is all very unfortunate."

"I'm afraid you have no idea how unfortunate, Colonel."

"Quite right. I'm at a bit of a disadvantage here, madam. No one seems to want to tell me very much."

"I'll tell you. I'll tell you that these two men are ruthless. They'll stop at nothing. . . . Never mind what they've done to me."

"What have they done, exactly?"

"Oh, well." She rose and wandered off, wringing her hands.

"You really must be more frank with me, madam." Porphyry trailed after her. "Once before, I asked you to tell me about this so-called Covenant."

Mere mention of the word brought her up sharply. He could see fear in her eyes.

"I blame myself," she said after a moment. "I can't tell you how much I do."

"Yes, I can see that. But why? Tell me."

"Because I agreed. I acquiesced. Did I not? Well, not actually. But by saying nothing, I acquiesced, you see . . . well, that's not exactly true . . . I did protest. Perhaps not forcefully enough. But had I stood firm . . . Had I threatened . . ."

Porphyry captured her flailing hands, pressed them back down and held them gently. "My dear madam, I don't have the faintest idea what you're talking about."

A low, quavery wail rose from her chest.

"Tell me about Leander. He's the one I never met."

The wailing grew more distraught. "He disappeared the day before you arrived."

"Yes—Mr. Jonathan told me," Porphyry explained. "During a musicale of some sort, I take it?"

Her head nodded wearily. "And did he tell you the reason for the boy's disappearance?"

"He wasn't all that helpful. I don't think he knew, actually."

"Oh, he knows all right. Jonathan knows quite a bit. Don't let him fool you. He's just afraid. Well, who wouldn't be in this place?" She cleared her throat and stared uncomfortably around. "I'll tell you everything. About Leander. About Cassie and Jonathan. About us here at Fraze."

She made a short chopping motion with her hand. "But now you must promise to help. There's not much time. As for Leander, I don't think there's a chance anymore. As far as he's concerned, what's done is done. These two men here are bad. Very bad. When Jones was alive, we had some control over them. Now with him gone, there's no telling what they might do. And then . . ." Her voice trailed off.

Colonel Porphyry hung upon its fading ring, waiting for it to renew itself.

"Cornie—you'll have to know about Cornie, too." Her brow rose and a new edginess came over her. "Wait here. I'll be right back."

In the next instant she bolted up and fled down the corridor. She was back in a minute, standing there, staring down at him, her face redder than usual. She carried in her arms a thick stack of papers.

"Read this," she said, dropping them with a thud into his lap. "You don't have to read it all. Only the passages I've clipped."

"Is this the Covenant?"

"That will come later."

Porphyry frowned. "What is this, then?"

"You'll know soon enough, without my having to explain."
She wheeled sharply and marched off.

Porphyry stared down at the papers with a sinking feeling.
Another mountain of documents to digest. The sheer bulk
depressed him. A full five inches thick, the paper was yellow
and crumbling. Bits of it showered a scurf onto his trousers. They
gave off a musty, waterlogged smell.

With the sense of dread one feels on the verge of learning
something he has no wish to know, Porphyry lifted the top page.
There, written in a small, precise hand, were three words,
evidently the title of the document. The words floated up at him
from off the page, proclaiming itself something called The Fabian
Diaries.

Part 8

The Fabian Diaries

"Indy realized what this treachery was all about. 'That's what you've got these slaves digging for . . . these children . . . ' The anger started to churn within him."

—*Indiana Jones and the Temple of Doom*

29

May 12, 1951

To be perfectly frank, I didn't believe a word of it. Of course, I'd heard the name before, but I thought the fellow was an imposter. I figured it for a hoax, a not terribly funny practical joke. One of the richest men in the world summoning me to lunch in a letter so profuse with praise for my work, for me personally, as to cause me to blush. Me blush? Can you imagine? I've never been much for blushing—at anything—but this did beat all.

Why? For what earthly reason would a man of that lofty station want to have lunch with a penniless, obscure, though admittedly brilliant scientist? Why, with the exception of myself and a few others at the forefront of scientific inquiry, who even knows or, for that matter, cares a jot or a tittle about me or what I'm up to?

But lo. Now comes this legendary figure (that is, if he is who he claims he is), rich as Croesus, imploring me to break bread with him. Me, Felix Fabian, living in exiguous circumstances, in makeshift quarters situated behind a brewery on the unfashion-able side of the Lake of Geneva.

Working alone, barely able to pay bills, I'd had to dismiss my assistant while still struggling to continue my work. At wit's end and barely able to eke out an existence, I'm reduced to publish-ing monographs doomed to go unread in penurious, if perfectly respectable, journals. And now, as though fate had taken up my cause, this North American potentate presents himself to me as though I were some god, approaching with extreme diffidence—effusive, apologetic, genuflecting and forcing money on me in sums that can only be characterized as obscene.

Well, of course, he's mad. An imposter. You have only to look at him, a kind of Yankee bumpkin, his boots still stinking from the dungheap. At the designated time and place, I came upon him at an outdoor table of a modest estaminet in the Byere district. Not a particularly grand establishment for a billionaire. He told me he'd chosen it because it was out of the way and private and that he was certain he was being watched. My eyebrows went up at that and I'm sure he noticed. I'd carefully planned my own arrival for a fashionable twenty minutes late—late enough to proclaim one's independence and yet not so late as to get off on a bad foot, just in case the fellow was legitimate. He was sipping a *fino*. A small dish of olives, half devoured, lay in a bed of grayish pits before him. Crumbs dusted his lap from the wine biscuits he kept nibbling at like a rodent all throughout lunch.

I confess when I first met him I nearly laughed out loud. My instincts were all for offering apologies, pleading sudden illness, and making a quick getaway. Anyone would feel the same, seeing him. There's a good deal of the klutz about the man. Ill-fitting clothes, hands rough and unmanicured, table manners execrable. In all respects a true clod, except for the eyes, which struck me as shrewd and arresting. At times, even mesmerizing.

Otherwise, altogether average. Average height. Average weight. Thoroughly unprepossessing. You'd never notice him except, possibly, for the purple splotch across the forehead. Hemangioma in the shape of a perfect little cat's paw. At first I couldn't take my eyes off it. But after we'd talked a while, I confess he made me forget it completely.

He said he'd been reading about my work in several jour-nals. He mentioned two. I was moderately impressed. They're esoteric and not widely circulated, but top drawer. Then he asked what I'd been doing recently and I told him. I didn't intend to, but I did. I can't say exactly why. At heart I felt it was all just a waste of time. But I told him anyway. And then, too, I hadn't eaten so well in months. There was something so distressingly earnest about the fellow—all of that lachrymose twaddle about the outcast and disenfranchised, the needy of the world. Why bother me with that? I thought. What can I do about it? I know of no one quite so outcast and disenfranchised as myself.

And then out of the blue came those few questions about gerontology—a subject in which I have more than a passing interest. And suddenly he's talking to me about histocompatibility, bacterial E-coli transfusion, DNA repair. I nearly choked on an escargot. In no time I was beleaguered, overwhelmed by the barrage of questions, the sheer weight of information he had at his fingertips. Most of it, I knew. But there were parts of it, significant parts, I confess, I'd never heard of before.

I asked him about his schooling and whom he'd trained with.

"I've had no formal schooling," he said. "Unless you count an eighth grade education as formal schooling. And I trained with no one except, possibly, Archie Touhy, a neighbor in Baltimore and a garage mechanic. He was certainly a good teacher, but you couldn't call that formal training."

He spoke rapidly in a high, slightly stuttering voice, and all the while his eyes twinkled. I thought he was impertinent. I thought he was having a joke at my expense. I didn't believe him for a minute. All of that modesty. All that self-effacement. I have no use for it. It nauseates me. What need, I ask you, does a billionaire have for self-effacement, if indeed he was a billionaire. It requires a bit more than ordinary intelligence to make a billion dollars, and one far more than ordinary to want to give it away. And that's precisely what he was preposing to do. To give it to me. Not all of it, mind you. But a goodly moiety. A handsome chunk. I was not opposed to that at all. But I hemmed and hawed and looked flustered as a virgin being offered something improper.

"I'm a researcher," I said, almost apologetically. "What would I have to do for it?" I was certain he was going to suggest that I produce a cure for alopecia or a revolutionary corn plaster for bunions. Something deadly prosaic like that from which you can turn a quick dollar. That's all the Yanks care about anyway.

213

"I want you to continue to do exactly what you're doing now. What you've been doing for the past eight years."

"That's all?"

"That's it."

"You mean the work in helicity and super genes?"

"With an emphasis on the irradiation factor in DNA repair."

"And you'll pay for it?"

"Every plug nickel," he said in that slightly uncouth American way, as I watched a particle of beef waft from his lips onto the edge of his plate.

"For how long?" I asked, waiting for the other shoe to drop, waiting to be read the small print in the final clause.

"For as long as it takes," he says, all the while those eyes twinkled naughtily in his head. Frankly, I didn't know what to make of the man. I didn't know whether to slap his jaw or kiss his hand.

"You're a fraud, aren't you? An imposter? Not the Mr. Jones?"

He laughed heartily and ordered another bottle of wine.

"What exactly is your game?" I went on, surprised to hear myself reverting to crude Yankee coloquialisms.

"The same as yours," he says.

Aha. Now we begin to understand each other, I thought. "So money and fame is your game."

"Long life is my game, and you're welcome to most of my share of those other things you speak of." He said it all with a perfectly straight face, then drew a thick wad of papers from his inside pocket and lay it down before me on the table. I didn't have to look. I knew it was a contract. "Read that over tonight and we'll talk in the morning."

He called the waiter and paid the check, then rose to leave.

"How old are you?" I asked him, without knowing exactly why.

"How old do you think?"

I looked at the gray thinning hair and the spray of crow's feet at the outer corner of each eye. "Fiftyish, I should think. Fifty-two, fifty-three at the outside."

"I celebrate my thirtieth birthday next week," he said, and there were those damned eyes laughing at me again. I was certain he was lying and was about to say something sharp. And he deserved it. Who did he think he was kidding? Sly devil, thinking that all of his millions gave him the right to make sport

214

of people. But, instead, I merely laughed. I'm not sure why. Possibly it was because I finally caught on to the joke, or maybe it was simply that it occurred to me that this pleasantly demented fellow might actually be signing my paychecks for some time to come.

All in all, not a bad lunch. It had gone far better than I thought any business lunch had a right to. Escargot, *ris de veau*, a gorgeous bottle of Montrachet, freshly picked *frais* and a fat contract for dessert. Not bad. Not bad at all for a day's outing, except for the fact that I couldn't get away from a nagging sense that somehow I'd been duped.

May 13, 1951

He's a Mendelian, my little Lorenzo de' Medici. How endearing. How chicly unfashionable. He hews to the old line and doesn't even know that he hews to the old line. He thinks the old line is *the* line. Well, we shall see. We shall teach him a thing or two about pea pods, won't we?

July 9, 1951

I cashed his binder and the bank honored it. I confess, that surprised me. I'd been holding my breath.

I am in my new laboratories overlooking the lake, with the swans gliding up to the bank to take bread balls from the strollers. How does the line go—"Lake Leman lies by Chillon's walls; a thousand feet in depth below" and so forth and so on. The place is quite spiffy for all that. New equipment arriving every day. I don't know where to put it all. And labs all chockablock with state-of-the-art technology. Just me and four bright new assistants, all out of the Institute Technologique. And the little white mice. Three hundred of them now and three different strains and more to come. And Mr. Jones assures me that soon we'll have a primate lab, too. And to top it all off, out in the back is a garage with a bright new Daimler for my personal use. And to think—just a few months ago I was getting ready to go on the dole.

Things couldn't be more ideal. All the money and the resources I'll need and more if necessary. Whatever I want. "Just say the word," my Yankee yokel says. And believe me, I will. I've never been bashful in money matters. It's been my experience the

215

more brazen you are about the stuff, the more apt they are to give it to you.

The only hitch is all the secrecy. He's absolutely gaga for secrecy. And that sign out front—HUMANUS INSTITUTE, S.A. Suitably vague. I mean, for all that, we could be a dental supply house or making prosthetic shoes. I can see his point, I suppose, but I don't appreciate the endless precautions, the slinking about, making certain we're not being followed. I'm not even allowed to dictate raw lab data into a dictaphone. Everything has to be written by hand—my hand, because he doesn't trust the secretaries—and then put on fiche and the original copies destroyed. Every night the fiche are stored in a vault to which only he has the combination. I'm positively certain now the fellow's mad.

In the brief time we've been here, we've already had one or two faintly suspicious individuals poking around the place, asking questions in town. Pharmaceutical blokes. You can smell them a mile off. Ether. Argyrol. Asafoetida. Cheap chypre. They reek of it. Feh! One even had the cheek to march up to the door and ask if he could use the toilet. I directed him to a pissoir down the road.

For all of our many differences, however, I believe we are getting used to each other. He comes to my rooms sometimes at night. We sit and listen to the victrola—Chaliapin and Lola Montez records. He particularly enjoys my collection of erotica. We quarrel quite a bit over procedures and the direction the work will take, but he's wise enough not to impose his will and tough enough so that he can't be bullied. It's *his* money, after all, and he does have a remarkable amount of technical information at his fingertips. You can't fast-talk him. I know. I tried. Philosophically, I'd say he comes closest to a very capable biophysicist. What I bring to the table is the molecular side of things. Jones is a neophyte in that area. Smart enough to ask the right questions and modest enough to leave the theoretical side of things to me. I believe that eventually we'll work out an accommodation satisfactory to both of us. But in the end, I am positively certain I will prevail.

November 23, 1951

War in Asia. The yellow horde has swept across the 38th parallel and turns its covetous gaze on the subcontinent. Swit-

216

zerland is as tranquil as a tomb and about as mindless. The people awaken only to count money and sip chocolate. But I don't complain. The situation is ideal for research. Let the idiots blow their brains out. May fortune grant the war stay as far away from here as possible.

Jones, too, seems untouched by the war. Or is it simply detachment? He moves about freely, constrained by no sense of national identity, no patriotic braying, just conducting business as usual. He appears to have some sort of diplomatic visa and flies around in a private plane that is granted diplomatic immunity. Even the Bolshies seem reluctant to challenge him.

Humanus Institute, S.A., has expanded again. The third time in a half year. We've added a new wing to house the primates and the staff, including biologists, immunologists, biochemists, biophysicists, geneticists, and physicians with a special interest in gerontological medicine, plus lab workers and *dieners* to clean up after the mess we make at postmortems.

We have a mice population of close to a thousand now. Every conceivable kind. Black-and-white mice. Custom-made mice. Mice that are programmed to develop diabetes. Mice that are neurological defectives. Autoimmune mice. Obese mice. Leukemic mice. Show me a mouse—any mouse—and I will write its biography from conception to extinction. The key to this happy situation is the fact that our little fellows lack the immune function, which allows them to accept all kinds of transplanted tissues, even feathers. If we wished to grow mice with feathers, we could do so.

March 1, 1953

It's true. Jones is only thirty-two, even though he looks a very haggard fifty. Poor fellow's been chasing money too long. We had a birthday party for him today. Just back from the Asian subcontinent with a shipment of rhesus and Capuchin monkeys, he was touched that we knew it was his birthday and that we thought enough to make a fuss over it.

But for a man of a mere thirty-two, he looks as though life had barged right past him. You'd think he was the victim of one of those freakish abiotropic disorders. Progeria or some such thing, which sends you rocketing into senescence by the time you reach puberty. Here is this slight, wiry man, scarcely out of his youth, with a bullet-shaped head nearly innocent of hair.

217

What there is of it is silvery gray and swept forward in sad little wisps designed to cover the shortfall up front. And there's his voice, high and quavery, just like your old grandmama. And then, of course, the purple cat's paw on his forehead.

But his mind is not old. Not a bit of it. It's young and resilient and a little frightening, if I say so myself. It contains voluminous amounts and has a retentiveness that's awesome— even to me. He speaks rapidly and somewhat disconnectedly on subjects ranging from alpha to zed. His suit pockets are crammed with innumerable bits of paper, upon which he incessantly scribbles a variety of notes to himself—mostly facts or statistics. (Like most Americans, Mr. Jones has a touchingly naive awe of statistics with none of the cynicism for the charlatans who are paid handsomely to confect such figures for the special interests.)

These scraps of paper he carries about. All madness, you know. A typical scrap of paper might contain figures relating to the current crop yield of maize in Guatemala, rainfall figures for the southern Sahara, the combined monetary resources of the world's major bourses, the current exchange rate of zlotys on the open market. Or, it may simply be some bizarre fact he's come upon in the Chronicle of World Records (Jones's favorite book). He claims to have read it forty-three times and to have committed nearly ninety-three percent of it to memory. He boasts he's never read a novel. Maintains it's not worth the candle.

His pockets bulge with all such rubbish. They spill from him like a shower of confetti. Beneath his chair and in his wake lies a clear trail of litter. His movements are quick and incessant, even when at rest. I cannot bear all of his leaping about. I am exhausted simply watching him in repose. I can't describe it except to say that it's a sort of Brownian motion, although not quite that random.

Like most hyperkinetics, Jones is a compulsive talker. Most of the talk is serious, with periodic lapses into the sort of scatology one associates with pimply, giggling adolescents discussing matters of the *toilette* with one another. At such times he's apt to break into a cackle which frequently escalates into shrieks that rattle your teeth and set your hair on end.

On those rare occasions when Jones is here and not traveling, he's on the phone constantly. He reads reports, journals and dozens of newspapers far into the night. Several weeks ago, he had installed above the garage a wire service ticker tape. All day and all night long it ticks news softly into the gas-fumed shadows. With its red and green blinking eyes, it puts me in mind of some living, breathing creature that never sleeps, never asks for a thing, but just occupies a corner waiting to be fed.

April 27, 1953

There are three known methods of life extension: reduced caloric intake; hypothermia; and DNA repair.

The fact that people in famished lands forced to live on 300 calories a day tend to live longer and are less subject to disease than those living on 2,000 is a given. No one even bothers to dispute it. However, in a world where such things as *foie gras*, joints of beef, coulibiacs of salmon, pasties and various savories are so readily available, as an option the idea is unappealing, if not to say totally unacceptable.

I wonder how many realize that if normal body temperature were dropped from 98.6 degrees Fahrenheit a mere four degrees and maintained, the average life span of man would increase by one third; that is to say, to 105 years. By dropping it an additional three degrees, men would then live on an average 200 years. Women slightly more. However, there are certain drawbacks here, too. For one, at a body temperature of Fahrenheit 88, it would be hard to maintain consciousness. You'd be torpid, constantly cold, and subject to strokes. As an option, therefore, in achieving longevity, one would have to classify hypothermia as distinctly impracticable.

Of all three options, there's only one that is acceptable and that is DNA repair. And that is the route Jones and I have chosen to take. Most researchers in gerontology today, that is, the sane ones, believe that aging takes place in the human body when human cells are unable to regenerate themselves. The key, then, to retarding aging, it would seem, would be to find a substance or a technique that would promote replication or repair of cells. This, it turns out, is polymerase.

Jones was one of the first on to DNA although I must say that I posited the possibility of it a good ten years before him. Granted, he had isolated something in a test tube, but he didn't know that what he was dealing with was DNA. Geneticists were aware of it but had no idea of its makeup. High-power electron microscopes with the capacity of 2,000-plus magnification had scarcely been conceived of, little less invented. No one knew much about DNA until recently, except myself and possibly a few mad Germans at Tübingen, and Jones hadn't the foggiest notion of what polymerase was. Nevertheless, he was working, and rather successfully, with both.

As I understand it, this came about purely by accident. To the best of my knowledge, it goes something like this. While running a series of tests for an industrial client, Jones had unknowingly synthesized a substance which, in addition to all of the typical polymerase properties, had the mysterious ability to regenerate human cells—cells that had been almost, if not wholly, destroyed.

One afternoon, while distilling a highly volatile fluid, a fire broke out. It nearly leveled the Jones experimental research station, which at that time was located at a place called Bethesda in the state of Maryland. At the height of the fire, while Jones was scrambling to save vital notes on his work, a glass alembic brimming over with nearly a gallon of the residue that accumulated during the final stages of the process, burst from the heat of the fire, splashing him with a milky liquid. Attempting to extinguish the fire, Jones sustained first-degree burns over nearly one half of his body.

The fact that such extensive and seemingly disfiguring burns caused so little permanent damage to skin that appeared to have been charred to a crisp puzzled his physicians. But as nonscientists the doctors seemed little inclined to pursue the implications of this, preferring instead to concentrate on controlling infection and saving the life of their patient.

Jones, however, was no quite so ready as were his physicians to dismiss what was literally the "saving of his skin." For him, the accident which might reasonably have been expected to disable him for life became the launch pad for a wholly new line of scientific inquiry.

In the months following, Jones abandoned virtually everything he'd been working on up until that moment to strike out onto a wholly new path of research—something that was at that time a total unknown—an infant science known as microbiology. The upshot of these investigations was to result in the discovery of what he calls TRX5. Forgive me, but I find that name so endearingly typical of the boy-detective mentality of the man and his passion for deep, dark mystery. I shall call it, therefore, an elixir, even though I recognize that the term smacks of the fraudulent. It is not. Take the word of one with firsthand experience.

But for now, suffice to say, TRX5 was, with only minor variations, the substance that Jones had synthesized in the summer of 1946 and was now convinced had wide medical application. This was to be seen later, most dramatically in the areas of Parkinson's and Alzheimer's diseases, spinal trauma, and the treatment of burns heretofore considered to be fatal. Most significantly, however, in ways unclear to anyone, this compound was able to work marvels in the spontaneous regeneration of human cell tissue. The implications for all of the above were enormous, but as regards the latter, they were positively stunning.

More about that later. While still recovering from his burns, all of Jones's creative energies went into the development and refinement of the so-called miracle Elixir TRX5.

Working in tandem with teams of researchers and specialists, all recruited from a foundation he himself formed for the purpose, after a dozen years of exhaustive experimental work carried on in deepest, darkest Jonesian secrecy in every corner of the globe, Jones's figures finally demonstrated that he was in possession of a substance that not only retarded aging but could regenerate human cells. In short, he was able to restore youthful resilience to organs and vascular tissue already considered to be far past their prime.

Mind you, there was no question of immortality. No tinge of the vulgarly miraculous. Jones is a practical man and a scientist with low tolerance for the comic strip excesses of science fiction. What was envisioned here was not life ever after, but more to the point perhaps, a doubling of the normal life span of humans from 72 years to, say, approximately 150. This was determined to be a realistic goal reachable within the decade just beyond.

As it turns out, the serum he had synthesized in that little workshop laboratory in Bethesda was superoxide dismutase, an enzyme that occurs naturally in the body. It's an antioxidant which slows the process of oxidation in the body, retards the production of destructive superoxide radicals and, in so doing, extends the life of human cells. Quite beautiful and classic in its utter simplicity.

Without truly understanding the magnitude of his accomplishment—synthesizing a human enzyme outside of the body—he knew, nevertheless, that he was on to something big. He had

221

in his possession an extraordinary tool. What he still lacked was a methodology for its clinical application. Was it not kismet that he should come to me, Felix Fabian, at precisely that time? The rest, as they say, is history.

August 31, 1954

He calls me from Ulan Bator, from Paramaribo, from remote outposts in the Andes, from a leprosarium on the equator. Six—eight—ten times a day. How are my mice? How are the wee cowrin' sleekit beasties? What are the day's scores? The rats are nearly at thirty-six weeks. A record. A record. The next day he calls from Madras with a million questions. He wants to know what the temperature is in the laboratory. I must keep the windows sealed and the temperature at a constant forty degrees Celsius. I know all that. I don't need him to call me from Madras to tell me.

January 12, 1955

Most impressive, the new scores we're achieving. Fantastic. Absolutely fantastic. Mean life span in the treated rats is now at 31 months against 28.5 months in the controls, while the maximal survival figures are astonishing—twenty-six out of the twenty-eight treated animals are still alive. We've stopped aging dead in its tracks. Soon we move on to the chimps. After the chimps . . . well, we'll see.

September 22, 1955

You ask me about longevity. I tell you quite frankly it will be no boon to mankind. More likely a bane. A Malthusian nightmare. Populations swelling exponentially; a planet of rapidly dwindling resources with failing ability to renew itself. So we'll live fifty or sixty years more. Say, even a hundred. But what of the quality of life—living one atop the other, breeding like fruit flies and fighting over scraps of food, aswamp in each other's waste—refuse the earth can no longer absorb. All of this sound and fury about life extension—just a stalling action. Putting off the inevitable. Eventually it must come. The moment we dread more than anything else. The thread is cut. We are extinct. We

222

cease to exist. *Forever.* Terrifying word that, is it not? *Forever.* Can the mind encompass *forever?*

So what am I doing here in the longevity game? It can't be won. Every gain we make here is a blow to the quality of life for mankind. The answer is simple. I'm here because the problem intrigues me even though there are no answers. In solving that one problem, I create a dozen more. But those are not my problems. I leave such matters to engineers, agronomists, sociologists—people of that ilk. If you're looking for boons to mankind, go speak with theologians or miracle hucksters. They abound in this age of quacks and frauds all masquerading as experts and visionaries. Better yet, speak to Jones. He's in the boon business. A molecular biologist has no such interests. All he sees are the cells. Cells and cells and more cells. The mystery of one cell dividing into another. Beautiful, gorgeous, mysterious, inexorable mitotic division. *Semper mitosis. Mitosis ad infinitum.* That's all you need know, my pretties.

December 24, 1961

Christmas. And what a present. Have located antigens at one small segment of chromosome six that correspond to chromosome seventeen of the mouse—in this particular case, congenic mice of the 057 black background—all identical as two peas in a pod. Suddenly, a dozen new doors have opened.

This is the stuff of a Nobel laureate, if I've ever seen it. Sweet vengeance for all the years of scorn and neglect from my sniggering contemporaries. Three quarters of the good old boys at Tübingen would slit their wrists to be sitting where I'm sitting today. And I can't say a word about it. Not a blessed word. I'm bursting to boast my head off to the world but Jones won't hear of it. Is it modesty, or merely that obsession for secrecy? I tend to think the latter but, even so, it's pathological. I grant you, there's some justification. The pharmo-boys are thick as flies around town and Jones says it's because of us. How flattering. They're a bit more subtle nowadays; more diabolical, perhaps. A bit harder to spot. But my sense of smell is still right on the mark.

But how do they know about us? It's certainly not the staff. None of them know enough about the big picture to be of any use to them. Yet, regardless of what precautions we take, word gets about. Anticipation of a big kill, I suppose. You've nailed down an adrenocorticoid or an interferon and the frenzy begins.

223

They're foaming at the mouth. Anything for a chance to get in on it. Driven by their masters, they come with steamer trunks of tax-free cash. They've approached me, of course. But my own master's larder is far larger than theirs and his bounty comes with fewer strings. I don't flatter myself on that score either. His generosity is not out of love for me, mind you. Nor has he any wish to make me a wealthy man—which, incidentally, he has already. Far beyond my fondest dreams. He's a very astute businessman, if I say so myself. He sees a good thing in me and I certainly see the same in him. We are fiddle and bow, ball and racket. A perfect match. What happy stroke of fate our paths should cross. So let the Nobel committee and the pharmo-boys and all their gold medals and negotiable paper go and stuff it. For the time being, anyway.

Jones is flying in tomorrow from Antofagasta for the holidays. We shall have a Christmas tree and a goose and three kinds of wine, including a Veuve Cliquot la Grand Dame 1923, carried out of France at great expense. It is sickening to think of the vandal hordes of tourists there, swilling up all of that gorgeous grape. Pearls before swine.

It has snowed. The lake has frozen and the treetops running down to it shimmer like spun sugar draped across the spangled water. For the first time in all the years I've known him, I'm looking forward to seeing Jones. It has taken time, but I believe we have just begun to understand each other. Not like each other, mind you. That, I can assure you, will never happen.

October 14, 1962

People ask me what I think of Jones. I tell them straight out. After twelve years of association with the man, I can honestly say I don't know what I think of him. Enigma, enigma, enigma. One of those Chinese boxes that keep opening into ever-smaller boxes. Very slippery. You may as well try and pick up mercury with your fingers.

In those early days I thought he was mad. And, of course, I still think he is. But if it is madness, it's of a most intriguing sort. Jones is not an ideologue with a sinister agenda. Nor is he one of those foaming-at-the-mouth anarchists all hot to blow the world apart over some mysterious grievance festering for years inside him. He'd rather heal the world. He's a scientist who also happens to be a romantic idealist. Full of that tiresome American

224

optimism without the brains or good grace to take no for an answer. He truly believes in the perfectibility of man—not through teaching, mind you, as a theologian would, but through chemistry. Better living through chemistry, as the motto goes. And he's determined to prove it.

Did I just say he's a scientist? Well, he's not. Not exactly. Not in the pure sense of the word. Actually, he's a magician-scientist. Like the old alchemists transmuting base metals into gold. He's as comfortable with the rational empiricism of modern science as he is with the magic and witchcraft of alchemy. And, like the old alchemists, he too seeks the elixir of perpetual youth.

If you think what I say inconsistent, think back on Newton. He was not out simply to learn about nature but to discover the activity of God in nature. If you ask me, it's lunacy, but both Newton and Jones were big enough to embrace the alchemical notion of a God present in the divine spirit of all things.

The first time I caught on to this in Jones was just about a year after we'd begun our long association. One day he breezed unannounced into the laboratory on one of those innumerable flying stops of his. He looked at the mice and some of the monkeys, checked data charts, and then wandered back with me into the office. I was talking to him about ordering a new, rather pricey computer from the States. We were swamped with test results and fresh statistics of all sorts. We needed some way to store information. We needed to build a data base.

All the while I spoke, making my pitch, Jones was looking through an electron microscope. He had some paramecia on a slide paddling through a droplet of water; thousands of them undulating cilia, dividing macronucleii.

He kept nodding his head and muttering to himself. I thought he was listening to me while amusing himself watching the paramecia. After a while I said, "Orville, what do you think?"

He didn't respond, so I asked again. "Orville, what do you say? Can I buy the computer?"

He looked up at me, and through me. I don't believe he saw me. It was as though I wasn't there. And then I saw that there were tears in his eyes.

June 14, 1963

It works. Gadzooks. We've seen it in the rats and now we've seen it in the chimps. No doubt about it. It works. Particularly in the old bucks in whom the signs of senescence are already clearly apparent. Jones is beside himself. Thrilled. He goes about here cooing like a gravid pigeon. Already he's ordered a battery of new tests, as well as four additional shipments of chimps and rhesus monkeys for corroboration. I pleaded with the stubborn fool to publish, at least in a preliminary way, our findings so as to stake out our claim in the territory, before the pharmo-boys steal it for themselves and grab all the glory. He remains unperturbed at the prospect and absolutely adamant.

I freely admit that the idea of excising the pituitary, then supplementing replaceable hormones in the creatures' water bowls was his entirely. Well, not entirely. I was actually the first to introduce the notion of surgical excision, even if my hunch about the hypothalamus was wrong. But not entirely. From the earliest anatomists and physiologists on up, the hypothalamus was always referred to as the "brain clock," as if the key to human aging resided there. It was a given. No one bothered to even question it. So, what more obvious place to start?

But, by God, the rejuvenation in these old buck chimps is fantastic—increased immune function, more youthful collagen, and the fresh growth of fur, far younger fur—absolutely astonishing. The creatures literally bounce around their cages, whereas a mere three weeks ago, they sat listless and torpid in a corner, picking their noses, manipulating their genitals, just waiting for their food pans.

Jones posits the theory that these astounding changes are due to the removal of a yet-unidentified pituitary hormone from the bloodstream. For the nonce we're calling it DECO, an acronym for decreasing oxygen consumption. This hormone, he believes, begins to do its dirty work on the cells' ability to repair DNA at about age twenty-one. Its specific action appears to inhibit the role of thyroid hormones from reaching their target cells. He's determined to go all out now to identify this mysterious hormone with an eye toward "engineering" it synthetically in the laboratory.

In the meantime, I push ahead on my delivery system. If, indeed, we are this close to the super-gene and the mystery hormone, there will have to be a way of getting it to the cell tissue without being too invasive. Transfusion may just be the answer. How ironic if it turned out to be something that simple. A dose of super-genes cultured in E-coli solution, then trans-

226

fused directly into the bloodstream and presto. Wonder of wonders. *Mirabile dictu.*

Jones was glowing that night after dinner. Early the next day he was flying to Kuala Lumpur and wanted a full night's sleep under his belt. I could see that he was still vibrating from the day's findings, and so I convinced him to take a snifter of chartreuse on the terrace, just to take the edge off before turning in.

Shortly, his cheeks were flaming. Instead of sedating him, the liqueur had loosened his tongue to the point where he was rattling on about where we were going from here.

"Soon mice and chimps won't be enough," I said. "You may as well face it, Orville. The next step will have to be humans."

He didn't answer but merely stared off into the twilight.

"Yes, I know," he said rather wistfully.

"All well and good then. Where do you expect these human subjects to come from? Will they be jailbirds awaiting execution? People in the final throes of terminal illness?"

"That's all we'd need." Jones laughed ruefully. "We'd be on the front pages of every newspaper and magazine the next morning. Cranks and civil libertarians picketing our doorstep."

"Then just where do you expect to find individuals willing to have their pituitaries plucked from the base of their brains who can also be depended upon to keep their mouths shut?"

He looked at me for a strangely protracted moment, something sly in his eyes. I tell you, it gave me a chill. I didn't know if it was the chartreuse or the excitement of the day. With his bald head and the wisps of hair swept forward on his scalp like a musical scroll, and the premature wattle quivering beneath his chin, he didn't look like any Jones I'd ever seen before.

His eyes glinted impishly. "Can't you guess?" he said.

June 15, 1963

We were broken into last night. Chimps and mice, most of them gone. At least those that matter. How they knew those that had been transfused and those that were controls is beyond me. Unless they've gotten to someone on the inside. People in the farmhouse across the road said they saw a van here late at night, lights on and backed up to one of the loading ramps. They thought it was just making a delivery. At two o'clock in the morning? A delivery? I tell you, it's a good thing the Swiss stayed out of the war. Leave them to cheese and cuckoo clocks, I say.

I called Jones. Luckily he wasn't far. Just Berlin, and grab-bing the first flight back. Before he did, however, he called the embassy here and had the airport and highways shut down. Imagine—one man having that much money and sheer brass to be able to shut down Geneva.

We finally caught up with the animals at the airport. They were in a holding area, crated into a shipment of ball bearings bound for Ottawa. No air, no water provided for an eight-hour transatlantic flight. The swine. How did they expect them to survive? And they would've gotten away with it scot-free, too, if it hadn't been for an enterprising monkey who began banging on the inside of his crate with a toy rattle.

When we got them back to the lab half of them were dead, but what's left is still enough for us to proceed with the tests. And, thank heavens, they didn't fall into the wrong hands. We gave them all extra water and a heaping supper that night. In no time they were good as new.

We know who's responsible, of course. It was marked for us right there on the manifold. The Prefect was livid. A sentimental soul, just speaking of the poor devils brought tears to his eyes. He implored us to bring charges. We had the buggers dead to rights. But Jones refused. The publicity, you see. Messy business. Jones would surely be called to testify. It would mean going public on matters we're not yet prepared to disclose. So we thanked the Prefect profusely and passed on his suggestion.

But make no mistake. They know now, these pharmo-swine. They know we're on to them. I imagine several of their boards of directors have spent a sleepless night or two since the episode. No better than Mafiosi. Their techniques are not much different. It will be some time before they try something like that again. They know that if they do, the next time we might not be so charitable.

But, mark my words, they'll try again. A bungled theft won't stop them for long. They grow increasingly desperate. They've stopped offering money. Offering Jones money is like offering salt to the Nubians. And all the while their people keep right on publishing papers in the journals. It delights me to see how far off the mark they are. We're light-years beyond them and the dangerous thing about that is they know it. And it drives them mad. As much as I hate to say it, Jones is right. We must be careful.

Still, I wonder. What's Jones's game? Why, I keep asking

228

myself, would he go to all of this trouble, spend all of this time and money to develop a procedure that could increase the average life span of man by some seventy-five to one hundred years if he didn't mean to profit by it? He, the emperor of mucilage, the da Vinci of the zip-lock bag, surely understands the sweetness of profit. And what, I ask you, in the end, is the difference between mucilage and an additional hundred years of life? None whatsoever. It's all product, is it not? But still, what a product a hundred years more of life is! Who would not pay his last penny to lay hands on it? Beg, borrow or steal, if need be, or do worse, for that matter, to secure a supply. It has what, I suppose, the marketing gurus call a "captive audience." With a hundred additional years to sell, you really have their full attention.

The pharmo-boys know this and Jones does, too. And how he loves to make them squirm. Occasionally, the sly devil lets drop that when his procedure is perfected, he intends to present it to the world free, offer it up gratis for the taking. It is his crafty way of driving up the ante, making the pharmo-boys squirm all the more. Believe me, all of that altruistic twaddle of his doesn't fool me a bit. When the time comes, Jones will fill his coffers with the same piggish glee as all the rest of them. And even if he were serious, they would never permit it to happen. Eventually, they'll get to Jones—either with money—great heapings, unimaginably vulgar gobs of it—or failing that, less pleasant means. They'll come, like the other night, and forcibly take it. The other night was merely a gentle warning. Either way, Jones won't be able to resist. Soon the pressure and the stakes will just be too high.

And when that day comes, frankly, I won't be disappointed. By now my holdings in Humanus Institute, S.A., have mushroomed to a dizzying sum. When the pharmo-swine are in the driver's seat, my shares will soar even higher. Split, split. And split again. Classic mitosis. Beautiful. The business of the world is business. Leave it to a Yankee clod to mint such folksy wisdom. When word of the serum gets out, even Jones won't be able to hold the dam back any longer.

July 9, 1964

Astonishing. Simply astonishing. And in less than a year's time. I'm almost afraid to look at him, so unsettling I find it. And

229

yet, I can't say why. It's miraculous, and if it's true, the implications are mind-boggling. And yet, I find it so unpleasant. Unholy, almost. What an odd word. But that's the only way I can describe it. The man seated before me last year at this time is scarcely recognizable as the same man who sat before me today. That man, the other Jones, was bald, sallow, rheumy-eyed and drooping—a man not much over forty rocketing headlong into codgerdom. This Jones—today's model—has skin firm and unwrinkled, the skin of a twenty-year-old. His scalp has regrown nearly a full head of hair. And not gray, mind you—a dark, lustrous chestnut, like that of a twenty-year-old. He looks like the young Keats. There's a spring to his gait. He fairly glows with vitality. He goes about like some sort of generator on wheels. You can feel the heat of the man as he rushes past. The only thing of him that remains of the past to tell me that this is the same man I lunched with thirteen years ago in that café in Byere is the little purple cat's paw stamped across his forehead.

And all of this from the plucking of a pituitary from its infundibulum. The way you pluck a cherry, I imagine. And just as easy, although we didn't know that then. To be sure, we'd established the fact that upper-order primates appear to do quite well without the gland, provided you supplement their diets with appropriate hormones. But the effect on man was at that time *terra incognita* and, as far as we knew, risky. Still, that didn't deter Jones. He had his mind set on it and, by God, nothing was going to stop him.

And then the choice of old Herzenstubbe as his surgeon. Not too many people I know, at least those of them who are *compos mentis*, would have permitted Herzenstubbe to lay one of his palsied hands on them. And here we are asking this old warhorse to perform a highly experimental, virtually unknown, surgical procedure—an old man still using surgical techniques he'd learned as a student fifty years ago. Positively antediluvian. It was bizarre. And yet you couldn't dissuade Jones. He would hear none of it. His passion for secrecy, you see. A neurosurgeon of any renown would have prompted unwanted publicity, by virtue of his merely having operated on the second richest man in the world. The media maggots would have swarmed all over it in a minute, not to mention the fact that surgeons, when presented an opportunity to proclaim their genius, are seldom given to attacks of modesty. The journals would have been out and the story all over the day after. So, of course, Jones opted for Herzenstubbe—with all of the risks that implied.

The day following the surgery we flushed his blood and transfused him with hemoglobins popping with SODs. He was up on his feet three days after and off to Xiang to have a look at some rare lemurs living isolated in a colony in the mountains and said to be congenic. One male with a harem of lemur wives is supposed to have sired several hundred offspring. Astonishing rate of histocompatibility. And all because of the isolation, and the curious absence of other male lemurs in the area. Here is a case of voluntary segregation combined with strict inbreeding to achieve a histocompatible purity within the offspring in the pack. This congenic purity increases with successive generations. I don't believe I've ever heard of anything like this.

Jones seems very excited. He rushed off this morning, his luggage stuffed with spansules of hormones, megadoses of vitamins and carefully measured ampules of SODs, all of which he promises to take daily.

If all of this about the lemurs proves to be true, it's momentous. But I am leery of what these Chinamen tell me. As a rule, Orientals are full of amiability and incorrect data. Computations on an abacus, while colorful, are distinctly limited. If the China chaps are right, however, then I can virtually guarantee Jones's next move and, I must say, it frightens even me.

September 9, 1971

Ever since Jones's return from Xiang he cannot stop talking about the lemurs. Not talking about them, exactly—thinking about them. For a garrulous fellow, he now often lapses into silences in which he appears to be millions of miles away. I know where, too—in the Kiangsu range above the East China Sea.

I know what he's thinking, of course. You don't have to be clairvoyant. Congenic mice. Congenic lemurs. Why not congenic humans? A race of men genetically engineered to eliminate undesirable traits and replicated for only what is best in mankind. How? Superhelicity. Supergenes. Excise chronic illness in the coils and in their place encode life extension. How? Retard tissue oxidation. Reduce production of free radicals. How? Photoreactivation and addition of tissue extracts containing dismutase. Look what it's done for Jones. Since his surgery we monitor his histology on a regular basis. The amount of DNA replacement in the tissue of a man that age is staggering. Simply unheard of. Comparable to that of a pink-cheeked postpubescent youth, and bless me if he doesn't have the semen production to match it. We did a sperm count the other night. Two-hundred and sixty million per milliliter. More like a boy of sixteen than an old codger of his age. *Fantastiche!*

That brings me to the latest wrinkle. Jones at fifty-two has suddenly discovered the frail sex. And with a vengeance. I used to think of him as one of those happily contented asexuals. Like a monk given over to nothing more problematic than a bit of harmless self-abuse at night before bed. Not so. Or at least that's what he was before SODs. He's that no longer. We are now dealing with a satyr. In a youth, this sort of thing is perfectly acceptable. In a man of fifty-two, it's unseemly.

But you see, he doesn't look fifty-two. That's the problem. Twenty years ago he looked fifty-two. Today he looks thirty. Thirty-two, thirty-three at the outside. Far from being offended at his outlandish advances, the ladies appear to relish them. I confess I'm a bit rattled by all of this sudden attention. Women suddenly strolling past our front door (they never did before), languid and dreamy, carrying nosegays and sprays of baby's breath, staring up at the windows. Finding reasons to linger. We have on the staff here a few demented younger males who believe all the fuss is for them. What a sorry thing is human vanity.

It is for our newborn baby boy they come. The SODs' prince. He exudes something that gets their dander up. Like the civet gland of a cat, the musk of semen hangs thick as haze above the laboratory when Jones is about. He's always stalking some new prey, and the ladies are just as edgy as he is, like cats in estrus.

"I'm going back to Xiang," he announced to me the other night as we sat on our little stone-flagged veranda behind the laboratory, smoking Monte Cristos after dinner.

"Why?" I asked, knowing full well why.

"To have another look."

"And if you indeed confirm what you saw there the first time?"

An odd little smile flashed at his lips.

"Exactly." I nodded. "I thought that's what was on your mind."

232

"It's feasible."

"I don't doubt it. All you need is one perfectly engineered prototype."

"A genetic template," he said.

I nodded, knowing precisely where this was headed. "And that is you, of course."

The smile that had merely flickered before now flowered. "Why not?"

"And the distaff partner?"

"Partners," he corrected.

"You mean to have more than one?"

"Absolutely. Imperative for our purposes."

"Selected how? Histological compatibility, I suppose."

"Correct. Just like the lemurs." He nodded. "A hair sample. A few fingernail parings. Perhaps a few light tissue scrapings. Very simple."

"And lo, you have a congenic match."

"As close to one as is possible in this sort of lottery. With odds running several billion to one, we're bound to come up with a clinker here and there."

"How inconvenient."

"Not at all. We'll find something to do with them." He pursed his lips. "Don't tell me you haven't thought of this, too?"

"It's the next logical step," I conceded. "But I confess, I thought of it as years off."

"I did, too. But that was before Xiang."

"It will be complicated, you know."

"It will, but I'm confident you'll work it all out."

"Me?" Flabbergasted, I started to laugh. "There are, I'm sure, innumerable women who, for a price—"

"The women are the least of it," he said, looking affronted by the suggestion. "I don't intend to stint. I assure you, it will be well worth their while. What's nine months of mild discomfort against a handsome trust fund in perpetuity?"

"Very neat," I agreed. "And you personally will select all these potential breeders—"

"As I go about. Traveling here and there. Attending to my various interests." He cocked a brow at me. "Don't look so disapproving, Felix."

He virtually never calls me Felix. Only Doctor, or Herr Professor. The sudden informality made me wary. "I'm not in the least disapproving."

"Tissue matching can be done anywhere."

"Providing you have a reliable laboratory, experienced technicians," I said. "I'm not worried about that. It's the logistics I'm thinking of."

"A bit cumbersome, perhaps. It will take some follow-up. Some tracking."

"Bookkeeping is more to the point. We'll have to keep records—where you've been, with whom, and how long ago."

He nodded. "We'll have to know when to return and pick up the package, so to speak."

"You'll need a legal staff, too. People to draw up agreements. Things must be absolutely ironclad. . . ."

"Surely you don't think there'd be any trouble along those lines?"

"You don't know." I found my voice growing a bit snappish. "What's to prevent one of these hired breeders coming out of the woodwork a few years down the line, claiming you've kidnapped her child and demanding satisfaction?"

"We'll leave that part to the lawyers," Jones said, rubbing his hands together distractedly.

"And the offspring? How many would you say we'd need?"

"That I leave to you, Felix. (There's that damn Felix again). You're the project leader."

"For the initial sample, as many as we can get, I'd say. Later on, we can be more selective. But for now, to build up the sort of data base we'll need, we'll require constant monitoring of human specimens for years to come." I had a sudden desire to laugh, and I think he did, too. The conversation was so bizarre, and yet deadly serious.

"What would you call a fair statistical sample?" he asked.

"We won't know until we see how many histocompatible matches you're able to come up with."

"A hundred a year? Two hundred?"

I couldn't believe he was serious. "You flatter yourself, Orville. Dismutase or not, you're still a man of fifty-some years."

Jones spread his arms, expanded his chest and unleashed one of those hair-raising American cowboy shrieks. "The way I feel right now, I'd guarantee one for each day of the year."

By then we were both roaring, but I could see this was a good bit more than a joke to him. He fully intended to sire his own personal line of human laboratory mice.

"Have you thought about what you will do with them?" I

asked. "You know, they'll have to be raised in total isolation . . . in a hermetically sealed environment."

"Of course."

"Germ-free space. Everything monitored. No contact with the outside. Daily readings. Urine. Serology. Cytology. Transfusions. The works. . . ."

He was irritated that I'd even bothered to mention what was so blatantly obvious. "Don't forget the mind, Felix. If these are going to be my offspring, I intend to see that they be extraordinary."

"Isn't that the purpose of the exercise?" I agreed.

"I have some very definite ideas about schooling. Some people may find them unorthodox, but if I'm to go to all the trouble of siring a race, it's got to be a damned sight better than the mutants we've got running loose 'round the world today."

Never unduly squeamish when it came to the ethical vagaries of scientific inquiry, even I felt this thing was a bit rank. I wondered if he was aware of how this might be viewed by others—I mean the sort of Dr. Frankenstein dimension to it all. I thought to myself, Jones sees this. Of course he does. Just as clearly as I do.

"You know," I said, "we're not equipped to handle something of this scale here. We don't have the space, the technology. And certainly not the isolation. . . ."

"Don't worry about isolation," he said. "I have just the place." And that odd little smile flashed again. And then he told me about this castle he'd purchased in the Loire, then had dismantled and shipped stone by stone in crates across the Atlantic. That was in the late forties, when he was a boy millionaire. Chateau de Fraze, he called it, although it was clearly larger than any chateau one's likely to see. Hundreds of rooms on hundreds upon hundreds of acres in the northern wilds. Room to raise hundreds of offspring, generation after generation. Room for laboratories. Room for staff and technicians, domestic personnel. Several times he'd spoken of a brother to me, only sketchily. Now he appeared eager to go into greater detail. Tobias was his name. His junior by several years. Brother Tobias, it seems, is in charge there—a sort of steward-cum-administrator. They run several philanthropic foundations out of the place. All of the Jones far-flung humanitarian enterprises are headquartered there. Of this place, de Fraze, he'd never once spoken to me. Typical Jones, I would say—the mania for secrecy. Now, suddenly, he was brimming over with information. In the past he'd spent little time there. Now, he assured me, he intended to spend much more.

It was to this castle, a hundred miles from the stress and pollution of the nearest cities, that he would bring his offspring; raise and educate them free of all outside bacterial, as well as cultural, contamination.

All of this talk about siring hundreds of offspring, about moving a castle stone by stone across the ocean, sounded megalomaniacal to me. But he was perfectly serious. I thought he'd be squeamish. Rant on for hours about cruelty to animals and such. Wax sentimental in the American way. But no—not a bit of it. He was not at all perturbed at the prospect of using his own offspring as laboratory subjects. Far from it. It was, for him, a source of pride that they would participate in his grand design. Moreover, he intended to give his little "white mice" the most privileged upbringing to be had on this planet. What he really had in mind, though he didn't know it, was a world that would become increasingly Joneslike; made over in the Jones image with the full advantages that implied. Moreover, these Jones offspring of his came with the extra bonus of a life span seventy-five to one hundred years beyond the average. Intellectually and physically superior in every way. They were *sui generis*—a breed unto themselves, these organically grown vegetables of Farmer Jones.

Then to my horror it finally occurred to this dim brain of mine that these hundreds of offspring Jones intended to spawn each year were merely the first step of a long-range scheme he had in mind for transforming mankind. He, Jones—Patriarch Jones—would personally take it upon himself to lift man out of the evolutionary mire in which he was presently stuck and haul him up to the next higher rung of the ladder.

Further, I realized that this scheme was no recent epiphany that had come over him in the past twenty-four hours or so. It had been simmering in his head for the better part of three decades, all part of a many-faceted master plan conducted on several fronts that was only just now all coming to a head.

After all, hadn't he purchased this de Fraze place long before there was a Humanus corporation, long before there was any talk of "congenic mice"? And, as a matter of fact, long before there was a me?

236

In the next instant he fixed me with his riveting gaze. "How old are you now, Felix?"

"The same as you. Fifty-two. You know that as well as I."

"But you look it. I don't." He laughed out loud, thinking what he'd said was very funny. I didn't find it so.

"What exactly are you getting at?" I asked.

"I'm looking a long way down the road. You and I have worked well together over the years. I'd like that to continue. But a man above fifty working long hours over problems that require the most exacting concentration . . ."

I felt myself beginning to fume like old rags. "Fifty-two is hardly antiquated. Say what you mean, Orville."

"I think," he said, pulling out his watch fob and staring at the big antique dial, "that it's time for you to pay a call on old Herzenstubbe."

October 9, 1972

I must say, Jones has taken to his patriarchal duties like a duck to water. He goes about spawning with near-missionary zeal. I wonder, did Abraham behave like this?

He rarely comes to Geneva now, so busy is he on the siring trail. The phone scarcely rings anymore with him on the other end battering me with a fusillade of questions, or oblique insinuations suggesting I've been derelict in my duties. How I miss that. Where are the good old days of persiflage and charming character assassination I've come to so depend upon? Nowadays I'd almost welcome a pleasant little tongue-lashing. If only you'd call, Orville. I have much to tell you.

But you can't reach the man anymore. For the most part, he's incommunicado. Off around the world, broadcasting his seed. Not like Onan in the ground, mind you, but in dozens of hired mature egg-layers all too eager to bear one of his progeny for the free ride that comes afterward in the form of quarterly dividends and clippable coupons.

But, my God, how the man has succeeded. Far beyond my wildest dreams. At last count our computer printout registered 198 successful impregnations since the project got under way a little over a year ago. Of these, 148 were carried to full term; 12 were lost to miscarriage and 2 to Sudden Infant Death Syndrome. The rest were misfires. On an annual basis, this works out to just a shade over forty percent, assuming he has intercourse once a

237

day. Two scores for every five shots. Forty percent success rate. Not bad for a codger of fifty-two, when you consider the sperm replenishment problems entailed in daily coitus. But, of course, Jones is not satisfied. He sees it all as some kind of soccer match. He's determined to bring his score up to at least fifty percent by next Christmas. Though I grant you, the man is something of a visionary, unfortunately he still has many of the instincts of an accountant.

November 17, 1972

We're now down to 1,100 calories a day, heading for 900. Jones appears to thrive on it. The rest of us are famished. We go about with our tongues hanging out, and cold all the time. The damned hypothermal drugs. Now approaching winter, I feel as though I'm encased in a block of ice, not to mention the fact that I'm drowsy all day. We take caffeine tablets to counteract that.

I have taken to stealing downstairs into the cupboard in the dark of night. But damn if the old fox hasn't changed all the pantry locks. I'm sure he doesn't starve himself when he's off on these junkets. Does he deny himself at the table of the Dalai Lama or the Sultan of Abu Dabi? I think not. Then why should it matter to him if I choose to squander two months or so of my life span on a wedge of *saucisson*? Why does he feel he can preside over my destiny, over all of our destinies, like a father? Why is it I feel I cannot cadge a morsel of food without incurring pangs of guilt, without his somehow knowing of my infractions, knowing all of my pathetic little sins?

January 9, 1973

A month or so ago he was back here on one of those increasingly rare visits of his. I made an unfortunately snide remark. Something about our seldom seeing him now that he was a full-time working patriarch. The temperature in the room must have dropped forty degrees. He grew livid, called me things I don't care to repeat. I have since mended my teasing ways, at least where Jones is concerned. I am no fool. But I do miss a certain give-and-take we used to have. Ever since he's donned this saintly mantle, the old boy has lost his sense of humor. He's deadly serious. All pumped up with dismutase and lofty ideals, he no longer sees things for what they are. Instead, he goes about martyring himself over the spread-eagled form of one compliant breeder after the next. Not enjoying a moment of it, he says. It's all fearfully hard work, the Lord's work, you see. He'd have you believe this. And all with a straight face.

Well, that's the way it is with great spiritual figures like Jones. I've never encountered a saint that wasn't a bit ramish. After all, what kind of a saint can you be if your loins aren't on fire twenty-four hours a day, all the while you go about whining over the weakness of the flesh as you eagerly succumb to its demands? What was it that Augustine chap said—"Pray I be good, oh Lord, but not just yet."

And this is my lot now, what I must contend with. He's certainly no longer of any use to me in the laboratory. I've had to hire two new people just to replace him on the conceptual side.

I'm not grousing, mind you, but it does irk me. I'm still every bit as serious as he once was about the importance of our work. There's a Nobel in this for me if we succeed and damned if I'll permit the old satyr to make me the laughingstock of Tübingen. Just once I'd like to grab him by the withers and shake him and tell him straight out—"Have a little honesty, for God's sake. Admit you're enjoying it, if only just a bit." Then I'd tell him that this notion of his about re-creating man in a finer, nobler mold is utter rubbish. The life-extension angle is perfectly feasible and I think it's well within our grasp. But transforming into gods mere men who are, morally speaking, still walking on all fours strikes me as ludicrous. I'd like to tell him this, but I won't.

November 16, 1974

It took him nearly a quarter century before he could bring himself to mention to me so much as a word about the "little folks." He chose tonight to do so. The question is why? Jones does nothing without some specific purpose in mind. *Kleine teufelen*, he calls them in his execrable German, thinking it pleases me to hear my adoptive tongue mauled by some unlettered provincial bumpkin. Imagine—the language of Goethe and Heine sodomized by this Yankee klutz. Then, a moment later, almost in the same breath, he tells me that he didn't acquire this enormous tract of land in the northern wilds out of a mere love of scenery. Not a bit of it. Behind this purchase was a nomadic band of goatherds who also happen to be dwarfs—a kind of freakish strain, like the dinosaur, doomed to extinction but intent on wreaking havoc before it achieved that. Woodsmen, I think he calls them. From what I get out of him, they're an aboriginal people living at the Iron Age stage of development, inbreeding amongst themselves for eons. Thieves and freebooters, all given over to pillage and rapine. You can imagine the spawn of such a union. In three or four generations you had a race of Yahoos. Four-foot Piltdown men of resolutely subsubstandard intelligence. Mouth breathers. Ground feeders. Bipedal shufflers.

And this is where and with whom Jones has chosen to set up shop. Why? I keep asking myself, even as he's describing it to me. But I know why. Intellectually, that is, I know the textbook explanation. My problem is my inability to understand it. What it comes down to is that nearly thirty years ago Jones had found himself a tribe of dwarfs, sociopathic homunculi so vicious they had to be separated from the general populace. Of course, they appealed deeply to his crusading sensibilities—the answer to his deepest prayers. They were to become a human laboratory in which to conduct experiments in a brand of eugenics that was perfectly all right for its time, practiced by well-intentioned nitwits, several of whom were my own benighted colleagues. But for today this sort of thing is outdated and thoroughly discredited. What respectable researcher, I ask you, gives the time of day to eugenics anymore? You might as well be talking voodoo.

I tried to explain this to him tonight. He would have none of it. He's convinced that with his advanced techniques of selective breeding he can raise these misshapen, misbegotten creatures out of the ordure into which they have so eagerly sunk. He believes he can transform them into gods and make the world a better place for men to foul.

"No, no, Felix. You don't understand," he says to me.

"I don't understand?" The trouble is I understand only too well. He calls this science. I call it hubris. I call it an abomination. I call it filthy and unnatural and unholy. Me. This is me talking. I, who never placed any limits on scientific inquiry. My unrestricted right to go wherever my curiosity takes me, that was my credo. Jones has taught me otherwise. Can it be? This Yankee peddler, this pious crook, has made an honest man of Felix Fabian.

His own children, mind you. That's the part I find so monstrous. To voluntarily turn over each year to these ferocious little trolls a contingent of perfectly bred congenically sparkling little Joneses. And this on the outside chance that by crossbreeding he can gradually remake this mongrel race of Yahoos. Monstrous. Utterly monstrous. And they call him "Master" and do obeisances to him, these little folk. They fashion icons and images of him out of wood and straw. He took me there once during one of those rare forced visits he insists I make periodically to North America to oversee the project. The squalor and the stench of the place—I will never forget it. And all about the encampment these figures scrawled on everything. So abased are these little sociopaths that even the so-called superior grade have not been able to manage the relatively slight demands of writing the English alphabet. No matter how they try, J, his initial, still comes out upside down.

But they don't realize that, these foul-smelling little people. They see it as an enormous leap forward. They believe that because of him they can write. And they worship him for it. Pathetic, I call it.

Before Jones appeared on the scene, the average life span of a Woodsman was approximately thirty-some years. Now, after transfusing these hybrid creatures with megadoses of SODs and free radical inhibitors, the average life span of the trolls has jumped to 42.5 years. And this also in individuals where treatment was initiated quite late in life. Is it any wonder that they worship him? They're dim, these Woodsmen, but not so dim they can't realize the boon Jones has bestowed upon them. Like any other normal human being they want—crave—immortality and they believe Jones can give it to them. Almighty god that he is, he's already added 12.5 years to their lives and promises them more, ever so much more in the future. All they must do for their part is to be compliant, willing whenever called upon to serve as white mice in Jones's magic laboratory of life.

March 1, 1981

Jones's birthday. We had the usual party. A small collation. Myself, people from the staff. I even had a few of the neighbors in. He's sixty, but looks half that. Remarkable physical and intellectual vitality. Sleeps well, enjoys superb digestion. Could eat concrete if he were so inclined and it didn't exceed 900 calories. Nor is he plagued with any of the typical annoyances afflicting men at that age—urological, gastrointestinal, and so forth. He has all of his teeth. His skin is innocent of wrinkles or unsightly sebaceous keriosis. And, of course, he continues to enjoy that astounding sexual potency.

I, too, have had my pituitary excised by Herzenstubbe (who incidentally died last year at the not inconsiderable age of ninety-two), and have been on regular hormonal supplements and polymerase therapy ever since. There's no doubt I'm stronger and more vital. I'm never sick. My concentration is a source of amazement to me. Each day at breakfast I read my *Sweissischer Zeitung*, turning first to the obituaries, and read with a quiet glow of satisfaction that another of my classmates at Tübingen has gone to his reward. The faces I see pictured there are, for the most part, sere and hoary, like dead leaves that have clung too long to the wintry boughs. It gives me, as I say, a certain pleasure. Of course, I have none of Jones's gargantuan sexual appetites and I am more than a bit grateful for that. It must be a terrible distraction, not to mention enervating.

We shared a cognac before bed. Full of birthday champagne and feeling a bit bold, I asked him if he ever felt badly about his children. I mean, the uses to which they are put and their ultimate fate. A sad, somewhat ambiguous smile crossed his features. He shrugged and cast his eyes ruefully around the room.

"If I allowed myself to acknowledge even a fraction of the sorrow I feel for them, I'd go down into the cellar and hang myself from the highest lathe. If there's a God somewhere above, I know I shall never be forgiven. I do what I must do."

All very touching. The old faker. "I do what I must do." Has he no shame? I never had much use for my parents. I scarcely recall who they were. Feckless drudges, both of them. But at least I knew they were there and not about to sell me off to Yahoos and pederasts in the dubious name of progress. God pity the poor child raised up in the tenets of Mr. Orville Jones's System.

I thought he was about to get up and retire for the evening. Instead he reached for the cognac bottle and splashed another four ounces into his snifter. When he spoke this time his speech was slurred and his eyes unfocused. In nearly forty years of our association, I'd never seen him in such a way. He wasn't drunk, but he was certainly tipsy. Of all his offspring, he confided to me *sotto voce* (slightly over six hundred by latest count), only one had given him that daily constant sorrow that comes closest to the true sensation of parenthood. And that one, he tells me, that most beloved of all children, is a noncongenic defective. Is that not a paradox in one who has made a religion of perfection? Yet this is the one in whom he sees the closest affinity to himself. Right down to the purple disfiguration on his face. It is this one, Jones said, his voice husky with alcohol and fatigue, that if he were to dwell too long upon the matter would reduce him to tears. He had never spoken so openly to me of any child of his before.

March 26, 1984

The latest count from computer printouts: 1,512. Phenomenal. They range between three months and 10.3 years of age. They're housed in twelve separate compounds strung out around the globe—the most remote and isolated parts of the world. Places like the sub-Sahara and the polar caps. We now have colonies in the Hindu Kush, the frozen fastnesses of the Himalayas, the Canadian Maritime. Accommodations quite *luxe*. Every imaginable convenience. State-of-the-art stuff. No concessions to the harshness of the environment. Jones is eager to acquire more such communities, all replicating the same work we do at Fraze. He anticipates our breeder population will go over 4,000 by the end of the decade. By then our first generation will be crossbreeding amongst themselves. Phenomenal. Only a few years ago I would have called such projections madness. Now I find them frighteningly plausible. The old ram has boosted his impregnation rate to slightly over seventy-four percent. Our infant mortality rate is now below two percent. Still he's not satisfied.

I don't know what drives him so—dismutase or masculine hubris. Old billy goat cock stuff. He wouldn't be the first such individual to fall in love with the image of himself as the progenitor of a whole new race. Read the Koran, the Bible, the Bhagavad-Gita. Heady stuff, that "Our Father" business. Although I must say, happily, nothing of the sort has happened to me. I've been on the same regimen for years and still feel not the slightest inclination to replicate myself. While the mysteries of birth continue to fascinate me, I find the mechanics of the process a bit messy. And frankly, bringing an innocent infant into this world strikes me as a truly nasty act.

July 4, 1984

American Independence Day. Jones has hung tricolored bunting all around the laboratory, making it virtually impossible to get up the aisles without entangling yourself in yards of the stuff. Totally uncharacteristic of him, he now sings jingoistic songs and waxes patriotic. He sets off firecrackers in the yard. Boys will be boys, ay? I suppose we must be grateful this sort of thing happens only once a year.

More disquieting episodes of the sort we've been having over the past year. Only now their incidence is more frequent. I lay it all to that Nepalese primatologist we were rash enough to take on several years back. Shifty, furtive fellow. I didn't like his eyes the first glimpse I had of them. I warned Jones about him but he is more trusting than I. If any of the staff was going to defect, I knew this was going to be the one. The pharmo-swine caught up with him while he was home on vacation. They got him drunk, bought him dinner and a whore in Katmandu, then stuffed wads of money in his pockets. He never reported back to work. Fortunately, he didn't know all that much. Just thought he did. But he does have a general idea of what we've been up to here.

It was naive, I suppose, thinking we were going to get away with this forever. Scot-free. No problems. We know the other pharmos are all paying fortunes for information from anyone with even the most slender connection to us. Just as they have their spies, we have ours. That's how we know we're light-years beyond them. Beyond them in helicity, free radical interference, photoreactivation, DNA replacement. We've already doubled the life span of laboratory rats and are well on our way to doing the same with rhesus monkeys. Our human subjects at Fraze, though still too young for us to be able to report anything conclusive, are making phenomenal strides. We know that just from the tissue studies. The trouble is our competitors know it too, and it drives them mad.

And how the old boy loves to taunt them. Every now and then he'll lift the veil of secrecy an inch or so, permitting some small but tantalizing item to leak out onto the pages of some notably disreputable rag. Last week the old devil floated an item about an anonymous billionaire philanthropist who'd cracked the genetic code to life extension and planned, in the near future, to hand over all his data for producing the serum, along with his facilities, to the World Health Organization. There was one proviso, however—that the serum be manufactured exclusively by a single producer of his own choosing and distributed free to all comers on a worldwide basis. They didn't name Jones in the story, which had been wedged in between an item on a teenage cinema idol and a British earl who liked to dress up like his mother. They didn't have to. Anyone in this line of work knew precisely who was being discussed. And anyone knowing Jones knew that it was he who had perversely planted the story in a common scandal sheet. Pure Jonesian mischief.

Several days later we were told by a paid informant that a drug titan, on reading the report, went into coronary arrest; another at a dinner party in Osaka strangled on a piece of Kobe beef when informed of this by another guest. A day later several bourses shut down early when trading became frenzied.

In the days that followed, we had a number of curious "queries" regarding the serum. Most of these inquirers described themselves as representatives of various "humanitarian," "non-profit" and "church-affiliated" groups, interested in sharing the costs of research and development of the serum. All they asked in return was the right to "recoup" their investment and share in some "modest way," etc., etc. By now, of course, we know the drill. These were the pharmo-swine. You could smell it a mile off. And so we told them they'd been the victims of a cruel hoax. We had no such serum.

Yesterday a consortium of Arabs and Japanese, with a sprinkling of West Germans (none other need apply), approached us with numbers that sounded more suited to a description of light-years between celestial bodies than to any sort of mere financial arrangement. This offer, too, was met with shrugs and blank stares. Poor benighted devils. They don't know what to make of us.

By this time the "humanitarian" impulses of the drug titans had turned a bit murderous. Putting aside all artifice, several of them baldly offered us billions of dollars and every conceivable blandishment while at the same time making frantic efforts to shanghai a number of our top staff.

Jones giggles with glee. He's delighted to taunt their naked greed. He roars with delight as their PR flacks crank out the standard rubbish about commitment to a better world, the preservation and renewal of the earth's resources, a healthier mankind, and so forth and so on. We all know the drill.

I, quite frankly, am a bit frightened. I don't know what these people are capable of. They're a rough crowd, when they've a mind to be, and right now they've a mind to be. He's humiliated them. If we were any other research group, they could handle it.

245

They'd all get together around a large table at some posh watering hole in the American Rockies and amicably arrange amongst themselves some cozy little procedure for sharing rights and artificially manipulating prices at the market level while eliminating all possible outside competition.

But they can't do this with Jones, you see. Jones is an anomaly with which they've had no prior experience. First of all, Humanus is a private corporation. They couldn't leverage us out even if they wanted to. Then, Jones is, or claims to be, uninterested in profit of any sort. How do you negotiate with that? He's quite possibly insane. How do you stop him before he literally gives away the whole ball of wax? I still don't believe he's serious about this, but if he is, he hasn't yet bargained on me. It's just a ploy to drive the pharmo-boys to frenzy. All the better then to bargain with. I'm sure this is the old faker's game. But just on the outside chance he's serious, and sometimes I half believe he is, I have my own game ready to put into play.

August 23, 1984

Just as I feared. The game gets rougher. Last week the consortium thugs finally grew bold enough to make a direct attack on me personally. Three apes in double-breasted suits, all friendly leers and smelling of cheap cologne, showed up on our front step. They said their car had broken down and wondered if they could use our phone to call a garage. They were told to wait at the door while the security guard, a trusting but doddering old retainer, came tripping back into the lab to ask my permission. By that time, the question was academic. The three plug-uglies were inside the door, muscling their way into the laboratory and waving machine pistols. They tossed a sack over my head. The security guard promptly fainted and if it hadn't been for my assistant, Frau Hubsch, who saw what was happening and had the presence of mind to slam the lab door shut, locking them in, then calling the police, I'm not at all sure where I'd be today.

If the intention was merely to frighten, it succeeded admirably. I called Jones, who flew home at once from Delhi. He laughed as I recounted the episode. I failed to grasp the humor but I could see he was also concerned. Concerned enough to go out the very next day and hire his own band of thugs to patrol the grounds. Their mission is to dog my tracks and make a general nuisance of themselves. Nuisance though they are, I'm not at all

246

unhappy to see them posted at every door, automatic rifles conspicuously displayed. I think we all understand now the sort of risk the project runs if I were indeed to be spirited out of here, held captive and possibly even tortured until I provided the consortium with the data they want.

They're a nasty-looking lot—those bully boys Jones has conscripted. Just as soon kill you as look at you. Not at all the sort you like to have skulking about the house but that, I suppose, is the cost of doing business in the eternity game. We call them the Iron Guard. They fancy things like camouflage fatigues and have target practice at five each morning. The neighbors, all decent law-abiding folk, are too frightened to complain. The Guard is led by a soldier of fortune—a mercenary by the name of Boggs who was deported from the U.S. for activities even that "fully open" society declines to discuss. "Best ask no questions," Jones says. "The man's precisely what we need."

And, of course, he's right. Since Boggs and the Iron Guard have come to live with us, we've had only one further disturbance. Another kidnapping attempt, not of me this time, but of one of the resident pathologists. It, too, failed but the poor fellow was badly shaken by the incident and took the first plane out that night. Our lads caught up with the kidnappers at the border and gave them such a drubbing that I think the pharmo-boys have finally gotten the message. At least they've been silent for some time. That doesn't mean that we can relax our vigilance. This crowd is not the sort to stop at a few ruptured spleens. What they can't and won't tolerate, however, is the jolt of bad publicity which might well ensue from blatantly bad behavior. It's bad for this image they like to project of themselves as enlightened humanists working selflessly and tirelessly to improve mankind's lot. Sometimes I think they actually believe it. At least, they're able to say it right off with a straight face.

I often ask myself why I haven't succumbed to them a long time ago. It would be so much easier. The cases of Remy, the beribboned boxes of fine old Havanas, the elegant whores (I suppose I might even learn to appreciate that), and, of course, the manila portfolios brimming over with all manner of negotiable paper. Why don't I just take? I ask myself. And with both hands. Well, for one thing, what Jones offers me here tends to make the bribers' offers look derisory by comparison. For another, one is never quite sure what to expect from Jones. In nearly four decades of association with the man, if I've learned one thing, it is to take nothing regarding him for granted. Had I actually caved in and gone with the pharmo-boys, it would not surprise me in the least to find myself late one night trussed up in the bottom of a boat, accompanied by several associates of Mr. Boggs, being rowed out to the middle of the Lake of Geneva, tied to a sandbag and dumped unceremoniously overboard.

No. I'll be strong—for the time being, that is—and keep a sharp eye out. I'll do what's right. And for once doing what's right will also be profitable. It's so seldom that equation works out.

April 12, 2070

He's on his way back to North America today. Thank heavens. The annual pilgrimage in which he plays out the farce of fatherhood, holds audiences in the dark with terrified, gullible offspring, rations out to each a pittance of paternal affection, then designates one of them for dispatch to the trolls. The annual tithe of human flesh. What a relief to have him gone. Now perhaps the place can get back to normal and regular work may proceed.

Again he asked me to go with him. Again I refused. Imagine. Me there? He must be mad. I'm a scientist, I told him. Not a matchmaker or a ponce. Let one of the house staff oversee matching tissues to prospective mates. I'll go there no more, thank you. I've done my time in that godforsaken place. To think I'd give up all this—even for a few days—my laboratories, my incubators, my autoclave, my boulevards and favorite haunts— for that . . . that swamp in the North American outback he chooses to call home. How quaint. And to have for company that unctuous brother and the degenerate Corsican, and with those horrific goat men always slouching about the premises. I tell you, the fellow's mad. The older I grow the less is my patience with these chronic do-gooders, forever wringing their hands and whining about injustice. All this rubbish about redressing inequity, revamping the social order. What nonsense. Only people like Jones with the vantage point of a dozen billions in the bank can afford to spout such rubbish. Imagine. Redistributing wealth. What a quaint notion. That all died eighty years ago, and for good reason. And good riddance. These goody-two-shoes. All of this prattle. Talk, talk, talk. Don't they realize? Man is a mercantile creature. Debits and credits. Acquisitions and mergers. That's what a man understands. What he lives for. Profit goes before all. Even before sex and food. Gold is the overarching drive. If you have the latter, the other two will follow in short order. A fellow can never get enough of the stuff. If he has one coin, he wants two, and if he has two, he must have five. There isn't enough gold in the world to satisfy any one man. Once he's had a whiff of the stuff, there's nothing he won't do to get more. That is his story pure and simple.

Except Jones, that is. I must confess when I first met him so many years ago I got him wrong. I took him for all the others. No different. No better than he should be. Doubtless, he was like that at the start, too, when it all began to come his way, when the coffers filled up and filled again and began to spill out over the sides, and it occurred to him how easy it was. But then he grew bored and deemed the daily pursuit of gold beneath his dignity. And that's when it occurred to him that he could use gold—not to store up for himself—but to give away. And he liked that infinitely more. It was his way of taking on the wardrobe of divinity.

Just imagine his asking me to go out there again. The gall of the man. It's not as if he needs me there. He's got a dozen top-flight clinicians on the spot—in the castle and in the compound—to run the tests and read the findings. I'll have none of it. There's too much coming to a head here now. And, frankly, I have no stomach for the game. The last time, God forgive me, I actually found myself making the mistake of becoming attached to one or two of the youngsters.

On the other hand, the data coming out of there recently, if it's true, is important. Unfortunately, however, I don't know if I can trust the brother to report figures accurately. He's a crafty one. It wouldn't surprise me one bit to learn that the pharmo-crowd has reached him. That he jiggers figures to whip up their frenzy even more. As for the Corsican, that's another matter entirely. He, I'm certain, has been compromised. I know that ilk quite well. They can be had for a few sous. Jones knows it, too, but he's either too squeamish or too sentimental to act. He's known Parelli since he was a boy. Virtually raised him.

I fear the whole thing is getting to be a bit much for Jones. He no longer has the same zest. Just watching him lately, I begin to sense the weight of years upon him. Nearly 148 now, he doesn't look more than a third of that. And in relatively good health, I should judge. But lately he's had his small complaints. Digestion, for one. Sleeplessness, for another. Minor things. But still, that's so unlike him. When he does sleep, he's troubled with dreams. "What sort of dreams, Orville?" I ask him. "Bad ones," he says, and refuses to discuss the matter further. But clearly, it unsettles him. A paradox, is it not? A man of science given to portents and auguries in dreams. Soon he may take up casting sheep's innards. As far as we've come, we're still not all that removed from the primal clay. I pray when my time draws near that I won't succumb to the solace of such twaddle. This, I think, is the case with Jones. He senses his time is short, though I can't, for heaven's sake, see why. He looks perfectly fit. Takes his SODs regularly. Transfused once a week. Maintains a strict daily regimen of 900 calories and a body temperature that never rises above 91.3. Despite all this, I have the nagging sense that something in him has changed. Something is different—a pastiness to the skin, a certain sag to the shoulders, a lagging gait, a slightly unfocused gaze. I can't quite put my finger on it, but he feels it too. Perhaps that's why he was so anxious to get away this time. Almost as though he felt he might never make the trip again.

I haven't told him yet. That man, the priest chap who seems to dog my heels as I do my marketing in town—he's shown up again. It's happened three or four times now. At first I thought it was coincidence. I don't anymore. He's quite brazen about it, too. Almost as though he wanted me to see him. I don't believe for one minute he's a priest. Something in his step. A bit too zippy for that crowd. And the way he opens his purse to pay for his purchases. All that fanfare. There's just a mite too much of this world about him to suit me.

The other day at the costermonger's in the Rue Guise across the way from the bridge on the Quai de Lausanne, while I was bent over a bin of white asparagus, he came right up and stood beside me, fingering through the vegetables, poking them rudely. The stench of asafoetida was choking. Today when I go to the market, I shall take two or three of the Iron Guard blokes along with me.

Before bed, I must remember to write another of those horrid little missives. That's another task I shall put a stop to. In fact, I'll tell him the moment he gets back. Why I permit him to impose upon me to do his dirty work, I don't know.

Ah, well, but there I go again.

Dear Leander,

Today we visited the great open air bazaar in the market-place at Dar Es Salaam. Tomorrow we take the ferry to Zanzibar to tour the leprosarium facility at Kisha. This should be excellent preparation for . . .

It was close to dawn when Porphyry laid aside the final page of Dr. Fabian's diary. Already the first pale streaks of dawn feathered the leaded panes about his head. He'd been reading all night and his eyes were red and bleary like those of one who'd stared too long into the roar of a blast furnace.

A deep hush hung above the house. Still no sign of people stirring, and though the room was toasty from the last remnants of a fire glowing on the hearth, Porphyry felt cold. There was a distinct, unsettling chill in his feet and hands for which he was at a loss to account.

He had been at it, the reading, sitting in that one chair beside the window, for the better part of six hours. Curiously, however, the time had whizzed past in a flash. It seemed to him only moments ago that he'd sat down with the mountainous stack of papers Madam Lobkova had handed him, her clips attached to selected entries for his special attention.

He sat quite still in the chair now, the stack of excerpts on his lap, staring off at some vacant point in the room, things moving there that only he could see. He felt suddenly tired. His mind was blank although he felt an odd tension in his limbs as if his body were privy to things his mind was just about to learn. He raised his hand, extending it in midair before him. He was not at all surprised to see that it was trembling.

His attention was diverted by a sound. A dull thud, it appeared to come from directly overhead and sounded like a shoe or as though some heavy object had dropped on the uncarpeted floor. That was followed by the high, thin, unmistakable wail of a young child; no doubt an infant, although to the best of his knowledge, he was aware of having seen no infant in the house. It was a forlorn sound, like a bleat of some stricken creature lost and wandering in the cold.

He couldn't say why but the sound brought him quickly to his feet. In the next instant, he was out the library door, streaking down the chilly corridors, the tails of his robe flying wildly behind him.

251

Part 9

The Block House

"And suddenly, in a trampled space,
I came upon a ghastly group."

—H. G. Wells, *The Island of Dr. Moreau*

30

My Woodswoman bride's name is Zann; at least that's what I've been taught to call her. She stood before me one day thumping her chest, shouting *Zann, Zann*, in that awful voice of theirs that sounds like something coughed up from the back of the throat.

"John," I said, mimicking her motion with my thumb. "John. John."

In this fashion, we learned to exchange bits and pieces of our respective vocabularies. Pronunciation is just as much a problem for her as it is for me. For instance, I've learned to recognize my own name when she addresses me as *Zon*. In her tongue the word comes out as a harsh gulp.

Similarly, I now know that the five monosyllables Ng, Jn, Nb, Gq and Rbn have something to do with food and eating. But all of the efforts I've expended trying to pronounce the words are futile. Even so, she appears to understand me when I say them.

Zann is with me twenty-four hours a day, as is my coterie, or guard. They number ten. We all live together in the large, sprawling thatch hut which is damp and smells vaguely of mold. There is no running water. There are no toilets. No facilities for cooking indoors. Washing, cooking, bathing, going to the bathroom are all done out of doors in large communal areas specially demarked for each specific function. Insects dart freely through the paneless squares that function as windows. The most troublesome of these by far is a large flying roach with the disconcerting habit of catapulting fifteen feet through the air and landing on your face or lap. When it rains, they come in droves. Ogden would find this paradise.

The hut has three large rooms. Zann and I occupy one and the guards occupy the other two. We all eat together, rise and go to bed at the same hour. As to matters of personal privacy, quite simply, there is none, even regarding activities at the most basic level.

As a king you would think I'd enjoy a certain degree of privilege. Nothing could be further from the truth. Kingship amongst the Woodsmen carries with it no governing authority. It's an entirely ceremonial office, its powers only symbolic. If I wished for one reason or another to order the guard out of my house, I couldn't. If I wished to take a stroll alone through the encampment, I couldn't. Even going to the bathroom is done under the watchful gaze of two or three of my coterie.

There's no hope of my ever escaping this place. Living under constant surveillance as I do makes such a prospect all but impossible. And though I am King, I have come to fear my subjects. They're capable of great cruelty. Even upon each other they wreak the most brutish acts. Cruelty is so innate a part of their character they scarcely notice it when it occurs. Were I to attempt to escape from this place, I have no doubt things would go very hard for me.

There's no question now, Zann is my wife. From that first night in the council house when we exchanged crude wedding bands fashioned out of pleached vines, she has been constantly at my side. Watchful, wary, proprietarial, she gives me not a moment to myself. The female of this species is as promiscuous as the male and my bride grows particularly aggressive when other Woodswomen are about.

Aside from keeping potential suitors away from me, Zann bathes me each morning, lays out my dress for the day and cooks all of my food.

Our sex life is active. Daily and often strangely violent, it is also fiercely passionate. Woodsmen view sexual activity as primary to their existence. They go at it virtually any time of the night or day. They will do it in the open in public places, and without bothering to disrobe. Their children do it from the moment they pass puberty. In that respect, they are much like us.

In those first sexual encounters with Zann, I was struck, even troubled, by how deeply I could respond to a love object as physically repellent as this creature. Even daily repetition hasn't blunted the intensity of the sensation, which I've come to look forward to as a child looks forward to candy.

Though I'm Zann's husband and her King, she nonetheless has total authority over the house. This is not because I'm her prisoner, which I am. It is because this is the custom of the Woodsmen. They are a matriarchal people. The men—the ordinary men, not the priestly or royal castes—are used for work that's little above the level of beasts of burden. They carry and build; they farm and dig; they slaughter and butcher. The women tend to do most of the managerial work.

From what I can see, there's no schooling, as such, amongst the Woodsmen. Children are free to do as they choose. What they choose is mostly wild, ungoverned rampaging. No effort is made to get them to comply with any of the codes of the clan. And make no mistake, there are codes, however subtle or nearly invisible they are to the outside observer. Woodsmen are not anarchic, although at first glance they may appear so. They go and come together; they carry out certain tasks as a group; they distribute resources fairly amongst each other and have shared goals. There is little tolerance for solitary activity or behavior intended to express one's individuality.

Nothing of what they do appears to be learned through formal education. Woodsmen children, as far as I can see, learn by imitation of their elders. But there is never direct instruction. Learning, they believe, occurs through passive assimilation—a kind of natural osmosis. Nor is there a set time in which it is expected that an adolescent should make the transition to adulthood. When it happens, it will happen, they believe, and from what I have been able to observe, this is largely the case. At a certain moment, which differs from one individual to the next, Woodsmen children put aside childish things and take their place, no matter how lowly or brutish that may be, within the tribal society.

My days here are all a blur; one seems to run into the other with mind-numbing tedium. Everything is planned. Nothing occurs capriciously. There is a deadly regularity about each day that almost erases one's sense of time.

Not since that awful night, the night when I was made King, have I seen Cassie or Leander. If they're in the encampment, I don't know where. I've walked all through the village with Zann and my guard, and I have yet to see any further trace of them.

At first I used to occupy the dullest moments of the day imagining Uncle Toby at Fraze, mounting a massive attack to storm the camp and free us. I have now come to see what a vain, foolish hope that is. I've given up scanning the horizon for them, or listening late at night for some telltale sound indicating that they're marching on the camp, coming to our rescue. That's clearly not about to happen.

Indeed, the very fact that we are still here after all this time, with virtually no sign that help is on the way, is evidence enough of my uncle's indifference to our plight. But why should that surprise me? In that regard, he's no different from Jones. In fact, he is the new Jones. The fact that we are here now, held as prisoners with no sign of protest from Fraze, appears increasingly to be the result of some accommodation made long ago between my father and these people. To what end, I do not know. But soon, I'm certain, I shall learn. Whatever it may be, it can't bode well for us. All I hope is that when it comes, it will be merciful and swift.

Part of my daily routine as a king is to dress up in kingly robes and promenade through the filthy grounds with Zann holding up my train in the rear. My retinue surrounds me with clubs to discourage my subjects from running up and trying to touch me. I have no doubt the clubs would be for me, were I to attempt an escape.

Several days ago as we went about our morning walk, I noted that we deviated from our usual course. This time our way took us on a path leading out of the immediate environs of the camp and northward upriver.

The path meandered for a mile or so through the woods. All the while we walked, Zann kept pointing to a variety of objects— trees, rocks, flowers, birds—at the same time in that ceaseless sputter of yawps and grunts, the Woodsmen's word for each.

As we trudged through a sun-dappled grove of spruce doing our word drill, it occurred to me that for the last quarter of a mile or so I'd been hearing the sound of shouts and cries coming at us

258

over some distance. They rang out through the woods and grew louder as we approached.

Shortly, we broke out of the woods and into a sunlit clearing. There, rising like a mirage before us, was something I couldn't at first grasp, so incongruous was its appearance there in the middle of that forest. To the best of my recollection, it was a long, low, single-story structure built entirely out of concrete blocks, a material one doesn't readily associate with the Woodsmen. It was windowless and surrounded entirely by another material just as alien to this culture—a fence of barbed wire, nearly ten feet in height, and topped off with a curtain of razor-sharp accordion wire canted inward. The structure, squat and graceless, sprawling several hundred feet or so, was grimly stark. The barbed wire was the final touch. The overall impression was of something punitive and menacing—possibly a penal institution of some sort.

Within this wire confinement, however, I saw the source of the noises I'd been hearing in the forest. Two dozen or so people were running about in that space, shrieking and kicking at a round object fashioned out of vines that had been rolled up like a ball.

Divided into opposing sides and punting the ball from one to the other, they appeared to be playing some sort of game—a crude version of soccer, it looked to me.

As I approached the fence, Zann followed close behind, all the while keeping up a steady stream of clipped grunts, as she tried to explain to me what I was seeing.

Of what she said, I understood little. But what I saw behind those closely strung lines of wire was quite unsettling. I'm not talking about the game, which seemed harmless enough. What I refer to here are the players.

They were attired in typical Woodsmen dress—jerkins of linsey-woolsey, knickers, buskins. They even wore those odd little Tyrolean hats that came to a point and gave them the appearance of elves. In all respects, they looked like ordinary Woodsmen, but not exactly. To be more precise, they looked like Woodsmen, but some had negroid features; others had features of distinctly oriental cast. Some were dark-skinned, others blond and as fair as new snow. Moreover, they were not dwarfs. I recalled that on my first night in the encampment, the night of the banquet, I had seen Woodsmen of average stature but, at the time, thought nothing of it. Now these I saw before me were not only average, but above average in height. Some might even be described as tall. I'm a shade above six feet; several of these "soccer" players stood nearly as tall. None of them had the typical stunted, potbellied profile of a Woodsman.

As they ran shrieking after the vine ball, kicking it and waving and shouting at one another, I was able to catch a word or two of what they said. Clearly, the language was Woodsmenese. *Jik*, I heard, which is their word for *ball*. *Ul*, meaning *me*, was shouted repeatedly. Each time a score was made, it was followed by a fierce, joyous cry which sounded something like *Neno*.

I turned to Zann for help. "Neno? Neno?"

"Neno," she said, and held up one finger. I took this to mean that *Neno* in Woodsmenese meant *one*. Within the context of a game, it most surely indicated that one point had been scored.

When the players broke for a time-out, they all came flocking over to the fence where we stood. Then, on closer inspection, I had my second shock. The individuals milling about before me were not Woodsmen at all. To be sure, they spoke Woodsmenese. Many had certain features of the Woodsmen—the slit eyes, the high cheeks, the cracked, leathery complexion. But most, with their medium-to-tall stature, wide eyes, fair skin and straight even features, looked to me very much like ordinary people, the sort I've seen and lived with all of my life. Though age is hard to determine in individual Woodsmen, within a group you can readily see the wide range of age among them. Some were quite young, children actually; others looked more my age and older.

My appearance there caused great excitement. I imagined they knew me to be their King, and crowded up against the fence in order to get closer to me. Several of them thrust their hands between the barbed wires, cutting and shredding their wrists just for a chance to touch me. One of them was particularly persistent. Clamoring in Woodsmenese, he waved his blood-streaked palm in my face, beseeching me to touch him.

Something in me responded to this simple, open display of affection. The fact, too, that he was penned up like one of the Woodsmen's doomed goats, behind this cruel wire, touched me deeply. I walked over to where he stood amid a crowd of others, all with their hands stuck through the wires, waving frantically at me. Reaching him, I raised my hand, placed my palm against his and held his bloodied hand firmly.

He was exactly my height and, when we stood face to face,

I found myself peering into a pair of large green eyes. I mention this to make a point. Green eyes are virtually unheard of among Woodsmen. If you're quick enough to catch a glimpse of those eyes beneath their thick, hooded lids, you'd note that they're gray, almost the color of dirty rocks. These eyes I found myself staring into were of the deepest, most intense green I'd ever seen. The green of chalcedony, of Polynesian seas that I had seen in picture magazines. These were not dead and cold like Woodsmen's eyes. They danced and laughed and were keenly intelligent.

I couldn't say why, but I felt certain I'd looked into those eyes before. I knew them and felt they knew me. Even dressed as he was in Woodsmen's garb, I knew this was no Woodsman. Not with his height and perfectly straight features. The few faint links, if any, to the Woodsmen physiognomy were a pair of strikingly high cheeks and earlobes that were fleshy and unnaturally drooping—almost, but not quite, the double earlobe of the goat people.

By then, they'd grown frantic in their efforts to get near me. Oddly enough, I felt no threat from them, but rather affection and a curious sense of kinship. In the next moment the guards drove them back and away from the fence. They didn't quarrel or try to resist. Instead, they made a high yipping sound, clapped their hands childishly at me and scurried back to their game.

For some time I stood there, watching them, aware of Zann's eyes watching me. I couldn't imagine who they were and where they'd come from. I turned to Zann, as though she might help me. But, of course, she had no way of telling me, nor did I have the language to ask her all I wanted to know.

Instead, she grew very quiet. The flesh against her cheek had tautened and stretched back along the line of her jaw. For some reason, she began to nod. At first I thought she was nodding at me. But then I realized she didn't even see me. The narrow slitted eyes were pointed elsewhere. When I followed the line of her gaze, I saw at once what she was looking at.

Across the playing field, between the tangle of leaping, shuttling figures of the players, I saw quite clearly two small figures, made all the smaller by the distance between us, at least two hundred yards.

Except for the white-smocked figure hovering possessively nearby, they stood alone at the corner of the building, as though huddling for shelter against the wind. They weren't watching the

261

game, but appeared instead to be apart and alienated from the others. There was something oddly touching about the way they held each other's hands, and like the players, they too were dressed as Woodsmen.

They didn't see me and I didn't call to them, although every bone in me ached to shout and wave my hands and run to them. But the stern, vigilant figure in the white smock, watching my every move, tended to discourage that. He looked not at all unlike one of the laboratory staff at the castle.

Ever since that day I was obsessed with the idea of returning to the strange, windowless building behind the barbed wire. But Zann was not inclined to permit that. She knew I had seen Cassie and Leander that morning. Indeed, I believed that's precisely why she'd brought me there. She knew I wanted to see them again. Had she intended to bring us together? Or had it been just to taunt me? Could she be so cruel?

I couldn't get them out of my mind—Leander's dead eyes and the sight of my little sister collared like a dog, a length of rough cord tied around her neck with the ring of raw red skin circling her throat where the rope cut her cruelly. Nor could I escape the feeling that something quite horrible was happening to them. Rather than help or protection, the figure in the white smock hovering about them seemed to suggest something more sinister. Could he indeed have come from the castle? If so, what possible reason had he for being there?

All I knew was that I must get to them. If I could get free for an hour or so—but that was impossible. I was never left alone. Not for a minute. Either Zann or the guard was constantly with me. And usually both.

Several times since then, as we started on our morning promenade, I tried, as subtly as I could, to lead my captors back in the direction of the compound. But always, just as we reached that narrow, winding path through the woods, running along the river, Zann would turn us around. Despite all my pleas and protests, she held firm.

There had to be some reason for her wanting to keep us apart. Why, I wondered, had they been isolated out there behind barbed wire, so far away from the main camp, in a building without windows? And if the occupants of the compound were indeed Woodsmen, why were they so strangely untypical, with their near-normal physiques and appearance? Something was

262

going on behind those concrete walls, and I had to know what it was. When I permitted my imagination to range freely, I thought surely I'd go mad.

For the time being, all I could do was wait and watch for my chance.

My chance came the next night. It came in the form of a fire. I was woken from sleep by the sound of shouts and the clatter of feet pounding past outside. When I rose and went to the window, the sky outside toward the east had turned a vivid orange. The fire appeared to be located somewhere at the center of the camp, but even from where I stood, I could smell burning wood and hear its low, steady roar carried on the breeze. The heat of it was like a heavy hand pressed hard against my face.

I looked around for Zann, but she wasn't there. I ran into the adjoining rooms, looking for the guards. They too were gone. The house was empty and the heavy wood door in the outer hall stood open, swinging on its hinges, bumping lightly back and forth against the door frame, each bump producing a low, hollow thud as it did so.

What happened next happened quickly and when the opportunity presented itself, I never hesitated.

In one of the rooms where the guards slept, I found precisely what I needed. Woodsmen's clothing. Mounds of it—jerkins, knickers, buskins. It was all there, tossed in a pile, a foul-smelling, undifferentiated heap of rags, just where the guards must have left them when they retired for the night. At the first cries and shouts they no doubt fled the place, heading for the fire where they'd be of help.

The clothing left behind was, of course, too small for me. But that didn't stop me. All I needed for the moment was cover, rough disguise. I crammed my arms and legs into whatever came first to hand. Anything sufficient to get me through the camp and up to the compound without calling too much attention to myself. Once there, the object would be to grab Cassie and Leander and get out as fast as I could. Where we'd go from there, I had no idea. My instinct was to make a break for the sea and then, hopefully, the mainland. In the darkness and all the confusion of the fire, the one thing I resolved we would never do was return to Fraze.

Outside, the night had a scorched smell, acrid and bitter, like that of burning rags. From the moment I hit the air I could

263

feel the heat from the blaze licking at my bare arms and legs. The sound of it was a low, crackling roar; something living, like a large, angry creature off in the forest feeding. Up ahead, great plumes of sparks showered upward out of the tips of trees, splintering into billions of fragments against the star-blown sky.

I'd already lingered far too long around the encampment. Zann and the guards could be returning at any moment. Spinning sharply on my heels, I plunged into the night.

I'd been to the compound once and had a vague sense of where it lay. But I was by no means certain. Darkness and the forest would complicate things further. In addition, once I reached it (if I did at all), there was no guarantee I could get through the fence and into the compound.

My way took me first in the direction of the river and from there north. I scrambled along over a rocky path, branches slapping at my flailing arms, pine boughs lashing my face. I clambered up hills and, at one point, pitched headlong down the other side, barking my shin so that I had to hobble. The buskins, too small for my feet, hurt. They kept slipping off, yet I was grateful for whatever protection they gave.

Reaching the riverbank, I glanced over my shoulder. The sky above the encampment had turned a lurid red. In the distance I could see the humped silhouettes of the black-hulled ships, sitting low in the water, their fearsome birdlike prows bobbing on the current. The water all about them, reflecting the flames, seemed lit with fiery streamers wriggling like serpents from out of its murky depths.

In the next moment I was charging up a narrow path, hedged in by trees, making my way toward the compound. From that point it went quickly. In no time, I'd reached the open meadow. The air there was cooler and the roar from the fire a low, whispering hum. Only the red glare in the sky, like a stain of spilled paint, remained to indicate that something quite out of the ordinary was going on.

The compound itself was quiet. Unnaturally so, I thought, given all of the excitement going on in the camp. Doubtless, the people inside were unaware of the fire. Out of earshot of the shouting and all the hullabaloo, they were sleeping right through it.

The next problem was the fence. Surely, if the Woodsmen had gone to the trouble of enclosing the place with barbed wire, they had good reason—to keep intruders out, as well as captives inside. In either case, one would naturally expect posted guards.

I ran around the fence's perimeter two times before I found a gate into the compound. This, too, like the door of my cabin, stood open. There was no one about, only a tiny sentry box where a guard was intended to sit. Inside the box, I found plates of unfinished food and a cup of Jum tipped over, spilling out onto a chair cushion, as though whoever had been posted there had left in haste, heading, no doubt, for the fire in the village.

The block house stood in total darkness, a low, squat, somber silhouette against the night sky. It occurred to me I hadn't once given a thought to what might await me once I got inside. I'd thought only of Cassie and Leander. I hadn't bothered to consider the peril and risk entailed in reaching them.

The door of the entryway was solid steel plate. Another surprise. Like concrete and barbed wire, steel wasn't a building material one associated with the Woodsmen. As a civilization, they're thousands of years behind that. The questions kept coming up: Where did these alien materials come from? Who built this compound?

The door itself was big and heavy—well over eight feet in height. My heart sank just looking at the sheer mass of it. There was no doorknob or handle, only a flat steel surface studded with iron hinges and thick ugly grommets that gave the thing a cruel daunting appearance. Where a doorknob would ordinarily be, however, there was a keyhole, but no sign of a key anywhere about.

I leaned hard against the door. I could feel its massive weight almost heave back against me in defiance. Just as I'd expected, it was locked.

My eyes swept around the door—the jamb, the lintel, all about the frame—searching for the sign of a ring or hook from which a key might be dangling. There wasn't any. Again, I leaned against the door, this time jamming my hip up hard against it, trying to budge it by sheer force. I couldn't. If anything, the door pushed back harder.

I recalled the little sentry box by the gate. That seemed a logical place to keep a key if you wanted it near at hand. An excited Woodsman sentry, in his haste to get to the fire, might well have run off, leaving it behind.

I scrambled back to the gate, conscious that time was fleeting, that guards could return at any moment. Reaching the sentry box, I rummaged frantically through two drawers before I saw a large, rusty key. It dangled from a ring almost in front of my nose. Whether or not it was the key to the front door of the block house, I had no idea. I learned soon enough, moments later, when I thrust it into the keyhole and turned hard. Nothing happened. I could barely budge it. I stood there, frantically twisting and jiggling the key this way and that. There was no give at all. I fumed and kept jamming the key in and out of the hole.

About to abandon the cause and flee for my life, I felt a tiny shudder in my finger, rather like a weak current of electricity. It ran the length of the key and up into my desperately fumbling hand. In the next moment, I felt the key serrations engage the pin tumblers. There was a click and suddenly a thin, vertical chink of light shot up the length of the door where it had slipped open a crack. Warily, almost timidly, I pushed with a short jab of my finger and watched in amazement as the door swung slowly back.

There's something strange about finding yourself in a place where everyone is asleep except you. Call it eerie, unearthly. Whatever. It's like being cut off from all life, as though you were the last living creature on earth.

Save for the hiss of a slowly dwindling fire in a large brazier, an unnerving stillness gripped the place, a stillness so total it made your ears ring. It conveyed an odd air of expectancy, as though all life hung suspended there, waiting for something momentous to occur.

The interior of the block house was as much a surprise to me as its exterior had been several days before. It bore no relation to anything a Woodsman might build, let alone even conceive. It was so far beyond the level of technology available to this culture as to make its presence there incomprehensible. How did it get here? I wondered again. It wasn't a question I was eager to pursue.

Entering the front door, I found myself in a small circular chamber. A hub, you might call it. Off of this hub, like the spokes of a wheel, ran four long corridors in four different directions. Each corridor was lined with doors, all of which stood open to the lighted hallways. There were no furnishings in the hallways and no carpets. The halls, stark and spotlessly clean, gave an impression of something clinical, utterly bleak. Naked light bulbs, set at regularly spaced intervals, illuminated them. That, too, struck me as odd. There was no electricity in the Woodsmen's camp, nor had I seen any sign of overhead wires leading into the block house. There had to be a generator somewhere about, just as we had at the castle.

There must have been hundreds of open doors. Behind one, I was certain, I would find Cassie or Leander, perhaps both, if I was lucky. But I had no idea where to start. By now the fire in the camp would be extinguished and the guards already tramping back through the forest. I didn't care to imagine what sort of reaction my disappearance would have on Zann and my personal attendants.

My search, starting at a jog, quickly accelerated into a panicky dash from door to door. As time wore on, the magnitude of the task became increasingly apparent. My method was to race down one side of a corridor and back up the other. Poking my head into each room as I went, I hoped to catch a glimpse of Cassie or Leander. The job was not as straightforward as it may sound. All of the rooms were dark. There were no windows. Each room was identical; each furnished in precisely the same fashion—a bed, a chair, a dresser, and no more.

Despite the meager illumination, it wasn't all that hard to get a decent look at the occupants of the rooms. Luckily, all of the beds had been situated close to the open doors in such a way that the light from the hall fell directly across the faces of the sleepers, an arrangement, no doubt, designed to simplify the task of the guards as they went about the business of nightly bed checks.

Each bed contained two occupants. They were of two distinct groups. The first was of the group I'd seen out on the soccer field several days before—not Woodsmen, yet bearing many of their physical traits. The second group, however, comprised genuine Woodsmen, each partnered with one of the quasi-Woodsmen. They slept in identical olive drab nightshirts and all were on their backs, faces pointed to the ceiling, absolutely unmoving.

There was something strangely disquieting about them. There were none of the typical sounds of sleep; no snores, no moans or sighs, they scarcely seemed to breathe. It was a sleep far deeper than any I was accustomed to. Not even the racket of my footsteps clattering up and down corridors, or my barging into their half-lighted cubicles, seemed to stir them. Their sleep looked like that of eternity, as though they'd been asleep millions of years and would continue so for many millions more. Actu-

267

ally, what I saw before me was more like a drugged slumber than anything else.

I nudged several of the sleepers to see if I could wake them. When I touched one, I shuddered. His skin was damp—clammy cold to the touch. For a moment it crossed my mind they were all dead. But they weren't. Their chests rose and fell in serene, untroubled breaths, yet try as I might, I could wake not one of them.

I'd been at the job more than fifteen minutes and in that time had seen no trace of Cassie or Leander. Worse yet, I'd been less than systematic in my search. I'd dashed from one corridor to the next, scarcely noting those in which I'd been or those to which I was going. Nor did the fact that all four corridors were identical in appearance help matters any. I was no longer sure which I'd searched and which I hadn't.

I was near frenzy. While good sense urged that I be gone from there, something else kept me tearing up and down those bare corridors. Finally, confused and out of breath, I slumped against a wall and tried to rethink my situation.

It was then I heard the footsteps, though they didn't sound like footsteps at first. It was more a whooshing sound like something being dragged across the floor. The noise didn't appear to come from the corridor I was in, but from one of the adjacent corridors. Each moment the steps grew louder, it became apparent they were approaching me.

The first thing that came to mind was that it was a guard making his rounds, or possibly the person in the white smock I'd seen outside several days before. The only reassuring thing was the fact that the footsteps I heard were clearly those of a single individual.

My mind whirled while my eyes searched for places to hide. There were no such places in the corridor; the only possibility was in one of the cubicles. I had no idea if there were closets inside, but if worse came to worst, I could always slip under a bed until the danger passed.

The nearest cubicle was possibly thirty feet up from where I stood. It meant heading in precisely the same direction from which the footsteps came. Before I could rethink my situation, a shadowy shape rounded the corner. The figure was still some distance off, at the head of the corridor. My mouth suddenly dry, I watched it shuffle to a halt, then wait there regarding me. We stood that way, peering back and forth, trying to make one another out in the dim light.

As the figure resumed its approach, it took on a more clearly defined shape. It was only when I saw the white smock that I knew at once what was to follow. Like a creature stunned before the headlights of an onrushing car, I watched it emerge from the shadows, teetering toward me with a slow, crablike motion.

The figure kept shuffling toward me, its pace slurred by what looked like a lame foot. Within twenty feet of me, it was still too dark to make out the features. I watched in amazement as its arm rose, beckoning me. Mine flew up in response, possibly intended as a greeting, but more likely a protective gesture.

My head was spinning and small flecks danced before my eyes. In the next moment, the white-smocked figure shook his head and stepped slowly out of the shadows.

"Mr. Jonathan"—a familiar face wavered slightly before my unfocused eyes—"I was beginning to think you'd never come."

31

"Sorry. Did I startle you?"

"A bit." I laughed with a rush of relief. Porphyry did too, aware at the same time of my eyes swarming over his flowing smock.

"Oh yes." He smiled and tugged at its lapels. "Not to worry. Just a disguise."

"I hope so. There's a fellow right here in this compound who dresses the same way."

"I know. I ran into him a short while back." Porphyry looked down a bit sheepishly at the robe. "He was good enough to provide me with this." Looking at my Woodsman's garb, the Colonel smiled slyly. "I see you're in disguise too."

He noticed another question start from my lips, and cut me off sharply. "I'll be delighted to explain everything later, but for now, we'd best get moving. My fire must be pretty much out by now, and our little friends should be back any time now."

"Your fire?"

"A slight diversion." He winked and took me by the arm. "To draw the little folk away from here so I could pop in for a look around. Meanwhile, we'd best get your brother and sister out of this place."

"I don't know where they are," I mumbled, crestfallen.

"I do. Follow me, please." He pulled the smock around his shoulders and ploughed off down the corridor.

I stumbled along at his heels. He, no doubt, had injured his foot at some point, because he was limping. Oddly, it didn't appear to slow him much.

Two or three turns later we arrived at a doorway situated at the intersection of two corridors. A retractable steel gate spanned the door jambs and had been padlocked.

Peering through the diamond-shaped interstices, I had a clear view of Cassie's blond head propped on a pillow. Beside her, partially covered by a sheet, lay the gross, misshapen form of a Woodsman asleep, his chiseled, hirsute features inches from Cassie's cheek. Even in deepest sleep, she appeared to cringe from that awful embrace.

I stared through the gate, at a loss.

"It's a breeding pen," Porphyry whispered gravely. "They're locked in." He plucked a small, wrenchlike device from under his robes and, with several deft rotations of the wrist, the lock's shackle popped with a light click out of the cylinder. The gate sagged, causing it to squeal open of its own volition. In the next moment, we were inside.

In that dim illumination, her face looked waxen. Above the bed hovered the rank smell of a goat pen. Cassie lay entangled in the hairy clasp of the Woodsman.

Bowing slightly above the bed, in an almost formal manner, Porphyry deftly disengaged the powerful simian arms from Cassie. The Woodsman never stirred. The Colonel then took a step backward and nodded to me.

Heart pounding, I scooped her up, carrying her like a sheaf of wheat bundled to my chest. Her skin was cold and clammy to the touch, like the feel of marble in the dead of winter. A soft moan rose from her lips but she, like the Woodsman, didn't wake.

"Drugged," Porphyry said, catching the worry in my eye. "It will wear off soon enough. Now for Mr. Leander."

We were out in the corridor again, doubling back on the route from which we'd just come. It was awkward, running and carrying Cassie. But she was strangely light. In the brief time she'd been among the Woodsmen, she'd dropped pounds and I

271

could feel the pitiful twiglike bones of her arms beneath the burlap nightshirt.

"This way," the Colonel puffed, his limp now quite pronounced.

"Your foot . . ."

"Twisted it, running up from the river. Nothing at all. A bit swollen. Sprained, perhaps. To the right here now. Watch your step."

He lumbered down another corridor. With Cassie bouncing on my shoulder, I struggled to keep up. This time he stopped at a room at the end of a corridor. Just as before, the door was open with a padlocked expansion gate spread across it. Porphyry's wrench was out in a trice. I watched his wrist snap once and then saw the gate yawn open.

"Wait here," he whispered. "I'll be right out."

Bracing Cassie against my shoulder, I peered into the tiny cubicle. Colonel Porphyry was bent over the bed, arms outspread and struggling to lift something. There was a shudder. The mattress creaked. I heard a startled outcry, quickly smothered. Then the Colonel was erect again, turning toward me, the limp, drugged form of a sleeper cradled in his arms. Slightly stooped, he moved toward me, and beyond his shoulder I glimpsed the outline of a Woodsman (no doubt a female) sprawled limp as a rag doll, half on, half off the bed.

"I'm afraid that one woke," Porphyry muttered, emerging from the room. And then I had my second glance at Leander. There wasn't much of him to see. The Colonel had bundled him in a blanket in such a way that only the top of his head and barely a half of his face showed. The hair was tow and blond, the unmistakable unruly mop I knew so well. The half of the face I was able to see, with its pallid, choirboy innocence, was that of my beloved brother Leander.

My heart soared. I can't describe the sense of relief. But that was not to last long. The look I caught in Porphyry's eyes as he turned to me had the impact of a fist closing over my heart. With Leander trussed on his shoulder, he put a finger to his lips, discouraging any questions.

"We'd better leave now," he said, his voice quiet and tense.

We got out not a moment too soon.

Fleeing the compound, we could hear the baying of Woodsmen and the racket of their footsteps thrashing toward us through the forest.

Just as we slipped into the stand of spruce on our right, the Woodsmen burst from the woods off to the left. They made no attempt to conceal their movements, but bellowed and yipped like crazed animals. The noises they made were hair-raising. Scarcely human, they bristled with anger, although at that moment they couldn't have known that two of their prize captives had been spirited out of the compound.

I followed behind Porphyry, who, despite his injured foot, moved swiftly and seemed completely familiar with the night forest. Leander is possibly thirty to forty pounds heavier than Cassie, but that didn't seem to deter the Colonel one bit. He loped along on his lame foot, Leander slung over his shoulder as though he were a sack of flour.

I, for my part, stumbled and lurched along behind, trying to keep up, all the while shifting Cassie back and forth to relieve my aching arms. Several times she moved, but still didn't awake. After ten minutes of steady going, I was winded and lagging badly behind. Porphyry sensed this and at one point came thrashing back. He peered anxiously at me through the dark.

"Are you all right?"

"I think so."

"Perhaps we might stop a moment." He lay Leander beneath a towering beech whose weeping branches drooped down to embrace him. I followed at once, placing Cassie down beside him.

Both Porphyry and I sat on the damp earth, our backs propped against the trunk of the tree, not talking, waiting for our gasps to subside.

"Where are we going?" I finally asked.

"To the river. Just a mile or so up ahead."

We sat a bit longer, peering into the impenetrable dark as though trying to read the mysteries to be seen out there. Suddenly, I felt the Colonel stiffen beside me. "Hear anything?"

"I thought I had, but I wasn't sure."

"It's them." He rose at once, hoisting Leander back onto his shoulder. "They're coming." Even in that darkness I could sense his urgency. "Best get moving."

Once more, limp, drugged sleepers slung across our shoulders, we were on our feet, crashing through the forest. With its burrs and pine needles and branches that reached out almost malevolently to swat you, the forest fought us every inch of the way. By then there was little doubt that the Woodsmen had discovered their captives were gone and were hot on our trail.

The last half mile was the worst—mostly uphill and the way barred by heavy thickets that lashed out and snagged our clothing. My legs were leaden, my lungs bursting.

Several times I wanted to cry out to Porphyry that I couldn't go on, but he had his own hands full. Not far behind us, across a rapidly narrowing distance, came the coarse barks and shouts of the pursuing goat men.

All the while I plodded forward, thoughts of Jones, my father, kept flashing through my head. Who was he really and what relationship had he to these subhuman creatures? Why were Cassie, Leander and I all here at this time? What part did we play in this strange scheme of his? The mystery of him deepened.

Crashing sounds jarred me from these thoughts. The turmoil of motion and the blur of dark shapes hurtled past me in the forest. If we'd had any lead time fleeing the compound, the Woodsmen had already taken every inch of it back. They were around us now, seemingly everywhere, their howls and blood-curdling shrieks rending the night air. At times they came so close we nearly collided. I had no idea where Porphyry was. Like me, he was groping his way toward the river but, by now, much farther ahead, having left Cassie and me to our own devices. As blind as I was in this pitch-black forest, I kept reassuring myself that the Woodsmen were just as blind.

You can't know the resilience of the human constitution until you've had an opportunity to test it for yourself. At that point, mine had been sorely tested, stretched to its limits. I have no idea what kept me moving. My legs and back had become one continuous column of pain. The skin beneath my tunic was drenched in sweat. The contact of the cool night air on it had chilled me to the bone. The Woodsman's buskins I'd worn going up to the compound I'd lost somewhere in the mud of the forest floor. I was moving in bare feet, sorely punished by rocks and prickly undergrowth. I'd long since passed the point where I could feel much sensation. It was a blessing of sorts, since I couldn't feel the sticky trickle of warm blood seeping between my toes.

At a certain point when it seemed the muscles would work no more, they began to quiver uncontrollably. Why they didn't simply give out, why I didn't crumple beneath my load, I have no idea.

In order to rest my shoulders and back, I kept shifting Cassie from one side to the other in my arms. The net result was that my neck bore the brunt of the extra weight I carried. And still, amazingly, throughout all the excitement, Cassie didn't wake, so deeply was she drugged. Only the occasional faint moan rising from her lips assured me she was still alive.

Staggering up a shallow hill, I saw through eyes stinging with sweat a clearing up ahead. Lurching toward it, I could feel the press of that awful banshee wailing bearing down hard on me.

"Up here. Up here." Shouts rang out from a point fifty feet ahead. "This way," it came again. It was Porphyry's voice.

Shifting Cassie's limp form to my other shoulder, I plunged toward the voice. With the last burst of energy I could muster, I broke out of the woods into a clearing that hung on a shallow knoll above the river. Ahead, I saw the dark outline of the Colonel, the tails of his white smock whipping all about his knees. He was waving frantically at me.

"Over here. Over here."

I didn't realize it (by then I was too far gone), but when I'd staggered out of the forest into the clearing, three or four Woodsmen had bolted out behind me, just within grabbing distance.

I heard Porphyry shout something at me but he was shouting into the wind and the words came at me muffled and distant. Later, he would explain that he was trying to direct me out of the line of fire between his revolver and the pursuing Woodsmen.

There was a sudden flash of blue light, followed by three sharp reports. I heard what sounded like a groan behind me, then several dull thuds.

I never looked back. The next I knew my bare bleeding feet were ankle-high in the icy river water. The shock of the cold felt numbingly good. Then I was beside a small skiff. Several of Porphyry's men held it steady as strong hands inside the skiff lifted Cassie from my shoulder and into the boat. Even as I struggled to clamber aboard, the skiff was sliding backward into the swift current of midstream. Several times we nearly swamped. A pair of oarsmen leaning to the creaking locks tried to steady the boat while strong hands grabbed me by the collar

275

and dragged me, headfirst and kicking, over the gunnels until I was flopping like a hooked fish in the bottom of the boat.

Twenty feet off to the right I could just make out another skiff going through the identical motions. It pushed off from the shore as a deadly hail of rocks and debris arched out from the bank behind it. Bouncing over the choppy surface, I became aware of a wide dark stain spreading across the riverbank, pouring down the beach toward the water. It was a mob of angry Woodsmen. The night air rang with their cries. But they were too late. By then, both skiffs had bobbed and bounced their way out into the safety of midstream.

Thirty or so feet off, I made out Porphyry's silhouette in the prow of the other skiff. His arm and hand were extended downstream as if to direct us. Up ahead where the encampment lay, a pale orange smear washed the evening sky, marking the place where only an hour before the fire had raged. Off to the east the first gray streaks of dawn had begun to rake the sky.

Huddled in the bottom of the boat, I cradled Cassie in my arms, trying to warm her shivering body with whatever pitiful body heat I had left to share. As we watched the dark humped outline of forest slide past on either side of us, everyone in the boat grew strangely silent.

Off to the left, dozens of tiny lights, like a swarm of fireflies, flashed through the trees. They were the torches of Woodsmen chasing us downstream, their fierce cries reaching out to us across the water.

"Where are we going?" I shouted to one of the oarsmen, trying to make myself heard over the buffeting wind. The man's arm flung out in the direction of a point directly ahead and opposite the Woodsmen's camp. From where I sat, it looked as though he was pointing downstream, straight at a place where the river narrowed. Within that area a small armada of the Woodsmen's ships had drawn up in a circle, anchored there and awaiting us.

As reckless as it seemed, that's precisely where the oarsmen were headed. A glance over at Porphyry's boat showed them to be on the same course, flying over the water at great speed. We were both moving cross-current, so that the chop, banging and slapping at the keel, rang out like cannonshot. You could feel the faint concussions in your stomach.

Colonel Porphyry's boat inched slowly forward and over-took us. Actually, we appeared to deliberately hold up so as to give him the lead. When he was about fifty feet ahead of us, we fell in behind and, to my amazement, began to follow him in. He was heading directly into the Woodsmen's flotilla, drawn up now in a tight menacing half circle.

Drawing closer, I could see lights swaying on the pitching boats and elfin figures darting about the decks. A number of skiffs had pushed off from the bank and were already bobbing like small fowl in the water, awaiting us. From shore came a steady caterwaul. There was about it a mournful sound. But as the skiffs drew closer, the sound took on a more ominous note, like the baying of hounds closing on a wounded stag. If I live to be a thousand years old, I shall always hear those inhuman cries rending the night.

There was a sudden movement behind me. Glancing back, I had a glimpse of one of Porphyry's men, the one who'd dragged me aboard. He was seated in the stern, a large-caliber semiautomatic rifle cradled in his arms, erect and still as a figure struck in stone. He stared impassively out at the scene unfolding there before us.

"We're not going into that," I cried to him over my shoulder. Silent, he gazed back at me and slowly nodded yes. Then one of the skiffs carrying three or four Woodsmen veered sharply and made a pass at us. Instantly, the rifle shot to his shoulder and a fiery stream of tracer bullets spat from the muzzle.

Screams followed. Through a swirl of gun smoke, I watched two dwarfish figures in the approaching boat stagger to their feet and tumble into the icy current. That was enough to give the other skiffs pause. They hung back, regrouping, as if to rethink their strategy.

Up ahead in Porphyry's boat there was more rifle fire. The noise had finally roused Cassie from her drugged sleep. She moaned, still unable to wake herself fully. Unmindful of where she was, her drowsy, unfocused eyes fixed on me.

With the next burst of gunfire, she cringed and reality flooded her bewildered eyes.

"It's okay, Cassandra." I held her face against my shoulder as though protecting her from the awful shouts.

Nearby, another skiff bobbed past us, unmanned. The water about it appeared to be teeming with dark figures, thrashing about, shouting for help.

The Woodsmen were, fortunately, not very good swimmers. When one of them reached our boat, his hands came up and seized the gunnels in an effort to save himself. They were soundly smacked with the butt of a rifle. There was an anguished yelp and I watched his grip slide from the boat as we pulled forward and past, leaving the floundering figure in our wake.

Up ahead Porphyry's skiff had reached one of the longboats and, to my amazement, had drawn alongside it. What came at once to mind was treachery, betrayal. Porphyry was surrendering us to the Woodsmen.

Shortly someone appeared on the deck of the longboat. Dazed, unspeaking, I watched that person drop a rope down to Porphyry's skiff. Someone there caught it and proceeded to tie it up alongside the scuppers.

"What's going on?" I cried out to no one in particular. Indeed, more Woodsmen's skiffs and longboats had moved into the area, gliding off their anchors, edging menacingly toward us.

"What is it, Johnnie?" Cassie's half-choked whisper buzzed at my ear. "What are they doing?"

It was sheer joy to hear her voice. "It's nothing, Cass. Nothing to worry about." I tried to reassure her, all the while convinced there was much to worry about.

A number of people were scurrying about on the deck of the longboat. Porphyry stood in the prow of the skiff, shouting up at them, brandishing a semiautomatic rifle. Then, dumbstruck, I watched something white drop from the deck of the boat, unfurling like a carpet along its sides.

It was a rope ladder. Sure, eager hands in the skiff caught its ends and fastened it hard to the longboat. In the next instant, someone had grabbed the ladder and was scrambling up it.

The air about us was thick with shrieks and cries and the crack of rifle fire. Fortunately, the Woodsmen had no rifles. But what they did have, in some ways, seemed more formidable. Launched by means of primitive catapults from the decks of their longboats, great fireballs made of foliage soaked in pitch pine were lobbed over the water at us. Were one to land on us, within moments we'd go up in a fiery blaze.

Three more skiffs suddenly broke formation and came bucketing toward us in a phalanx over the foamy chop. They were greeted by a volley of fire from the decks of Porphyry's boat. It was then I realized these were not Woodsmen up on the deck but the Colonel's own people, there to assist us.

Still in the prow of his skiff, barking commands from below, Porphyry raised the muzzle of his rifle. Dazed, I watched a bright rope of orange spurt from its barrel out over the water. There were more screams, followed by the sound of slapping water and boats overturning. Huge fireballs fell from the sky, sputtering and sizzling as they dropped into the water, sending jets of steam up all about us. The air was scorched with the smell of cordite and gun smoke. Figures thrashed about us in the water and a pair of overturned skiffs, keels belly-up, looking like huge lily pads, drifted serenely past on the surface.

A volley of fire from the deck of the longboat thundered overhead, giving cover to Porphyry's party as the last of them scrambled up the ladder, then clambered over the rail and onto the bigger boat.

It had taken two men, one working from the skiff and one from above, to hoist Leander's limp, drugged body up on the longboat. Only when that had been managed did Porphyry himself climb the ladder and board.

That, it seems, was the signal for us to come ahead. With a lurch, our skiff came hard about and, fairly flying over the water, made a beeline for the longboat. We could hear the shouts of people on deck, urging us on, followed by the bloodcurdling shouts of the Woodsmen behind us, venting their rage.

It was only then that I realized the Woodsmen's skiffs had retreated. The great din of shouting we'd heard from the woods shortly before had mysteriously stopped while an ominous quiet rushed in to replace it.

Drawing parallel to the longboat, our skiff rose on a swell, dipped into a trough, then with a deep hollow thump, banged its nose hard up against the side of the longboat.

Once more the rope ladder dropped from somewhere above and dangled over the scuppers. We tied its frayed ends to a loop in the skiff and boarding operations resumed.

"Send the child up first," Colonel Porphyry shouted from above. In the pale gray of dawn I could see a row of dark heads lining the rail, peering down at us, all barking instructions at once.

One of Porphyry's men came halfway down the ladder while one of our oarsmen lifted Cassie and gently raised her to the fellow clinging to the ladder. Encircling her waist with one arm, he began to climb, all the while assisted by hands both above and below them.

I came next to last. When I threw my leg over the rail, Porphyry was there to haul me over onto the deck. Even before I could get my footing, I was almost knocked back down by Madam Lobkova, smothering me in the great crush of her breasts.

"Dear boy." She buried her face in my neck and wept as I'd never seen her weep. "I thought . . . I thought . . ."

"Yes, I know." I patted her back the way you soothe a distraught child.

"I thought we'd never see you again."

"I'm fine," I said, still patting her idiotically. "Just fine. Where's Uncle Toby?"

The mere mention of the name sobered her. Something clouded her eyes.

Cassie was now wide awake. She made a series of small, whimpering noises. Madam Lobkova knelt beside her and gathered her into her arms. "My poor child." She wept unashamedly. "My poor beautiful baby."

"Best get going." The Colonel's stern voice brought us back to reality. "They're quiet now, but we haven't seen the last of them." He turned abruptly, mounted the ladder to the fly bridge and disappeared inside the wheelhouse.

The Woodsmen's longboats were intended to be sailed. There were no auxiliary engines aboard, and surprisingly little sheet for vessels of that size. They had a shallow draft with an unnaturally tall wheelhouse so that the boats had poor stability and were cumbersome to navigate once under way.

The wind at that moment was fairly high and the current swift and choppy. A mist curled slowly off the surface of the water, which made a slapping sound as it dashed against our prow. Several of Porphyry's men had unfurled the sail and were tugging at the sheets. In a matter of moments, a large area of canvas was creaking up the mast, snapping and luffing as it caught the wind.

At the helm in the wheelhouse, the vague outline of a figure stood. In that dim light I couldn't make out who it was. Another figure stood beside him. That I knew to be Colonel Porphyry, not only because I'd seen him enter the wheelhouse, but because I could see his smocked outline moving behind the glass.

With a great groan and much creaking, the prow came around into the wind. I had a glimpse of it from the side—the raging red eye, the powerful jaw, the row of big sharp teeth painted there to resemble some wild mythic bird.

In the next moment there was a shudder. The deck seemed

to rise underfoot as sails billowed and made a sighing sound and we were at last under way. A cheer went up—a bit prematurely, as it turned out.

"Where's Leander?" I asked.

"Forward."

I turned to see one of Porphyry's men standing just behind me.

"Below decks. In one of the cabins," he added, then gave me one of those telling looks that ices the blood in your veins. I looked around for Madam Lobkova but she was gone.

"I want to see him," I said.

"It's not a good idea," the man said, his voice mingling sternness and compassion. "There'll be time later." Just as he'd said it, there was a great poof, as if all of the air in the immediate vicinity had been sucked instantly out of the atmosphere. I felt my ears close and saw the sky light up all around us. The light was so intense I had to turn away. My eyes went dark for a moment or two after.

"Jesus," someone muttered, and a figure dashed past me. Another had fallen facefirst on deck. Several others were scrambling up from below. Looking up toward the windscreens of the wheelhouse, I had a glimpse of the two figures there, flattened against the glass. One was gesturing wildly in the direction of some point at my back.

When I turned to look, my legs nearly buckled. The whole river up ahead, from bank to bank, appeared to be on fire while all the time this great, hulking, unwieldy craft of ours went bucketing directly for it.

The next thing I knew Colonel Porphyry was out on the little fly bridge, waving his arms, shouting down to us. We couldn't make out a word above the roar of the flames. He kept pointing at them, then at us, then to a hatch leading down into the hold. Evidently, he wanted us to clear the deck. That could only mean one thing. Instead of going forward and around the fire (impossible, since it straddled the full width of the river), or back upriver (suicidal, since the full armada of Woodsmen was now in pursuit directly behind us), Porphyry had opted to take us straight through.

Along with six others who'd been on deck with me, I tumbled through the open hatchway down a steel ladder. Below were several cabins, a galley and a kind of crude salon in which another four or five had already gathered and now waited apprehensively. Off in a corner, Cassie, cradled in Madam Lobkova's arms, sat wide-eyed and terrified.

One of the men there I recognized at once. It was Porphyry's chief deputy, the man they called Magnus, a big, comforting presence who took charge easily and dispensed orders with a minimum of fanfare. The remaining two or three I had also seen at Fraze. Two of them stood guard over a pair of Woodsmen, part of the crew that had been captured when Porphyry's men had commandeered the boat. They were now trussed up with rope, squatting sullenly on their haunches in a corner.

Kneeling at Madam Lobkova's side, I stroked Cassie's cheek with the back of my hand, mumbling encouragement with little conviction. Only a short time before, her skin had been icy to the touch. Now it was fiery hot. Her body was rigid and she was too frightened to speak.

I shot Madam Lobkova a searching glance. Reading my eyes, she put a finger to her lips, silencing me before I could speak. Without saying it, I formed the name Leander with my lips. My heart plummeted as she shook her head slowly from side to side.

The place in which we waited was confined. There was no air and it smelled rank, just like the stench of the goat pens at the encampment. Those of us standing about had all we could do to keep our footing. With the wind at its back, our ship lunged along at a goodly clip, banging us up against the salon walls with each rise and dip of the ripsaw current.

Amid all the confusion, I glanced up at Porphyry at the top of the hatchway. He peered down at us as though mildly surprised to find us there. He'd removed the smock, revealing the shoulders of his dark suit dusted with ash.

"'Fraid it's going to get a bit bumpy from here on," he called out.

"Don't worry about us, Colonel," Madam Lobkova piped up. "We're all hunky-dory."

"Splendid—and the two little fellows?"

"None too happy." Madam dabbed beads of sweat from her brow and gazed crossly at the two captive Woodsmen. "We're keeping an eye on them for you."

Porphyry's eyes twinkled. Then he was gone.

As the boat lurched and bounded on its unruly dash toward the flames, it was to the scupper portholes we then rushed. Typical of Woodsmen handicraft, the portholes were just that— holes. They contained no glass. And even before we reached the

282

fire, the difference between air pressure in the cabin and outside sucked gusts of superheated air in upon us. The effect of that was to drive us all back from the portholes and up against the opposite wall.

The noise inside the cabin was deafening. From above came a series of loud cracking sounds. Magnus said it was the nails popping on the blistering deck.

"It'll be a miracle if we don't go up like tinder," one of Porphyry's men said. Cassie, her head buried in Madam Lobkova's chest, began to cry.

"We're going through," someone shouted.

The two Woodsmen were beside themselves. Several times they tried to scramble to their feet, charging at the walls in their panic, only to be forced back down by the guards.

In the next moment, tongues of searing flames were licking through the paneless portholes, spiking the cabin temperature dangerously upward. The force of the heat took my breath away. More nails popped and the deck planks, close to ignition, shrieked as they parted overhead, showering live ash down on us as they did so. With a fatalistic shrug, I resigned myself to being cooked alive.

"Lord God, have mercy," someone beside me murmured wide-eyed over and over again, like an incantation.

The din rose to truly hellish levels, then gradually subsided as the wild tossing motion of the boat glided to a strange stop. Looking out, I saw that we were in the very midst of the fire, yet in an eerie kind of calm, like the eye of a storm. Suddenly it grew very quiet.

I recall looking across at Magnus. He was staring up at the ceiling, a look of alert expectation on his face. Madam Lobkova was looking upward too, as if awaiting something momentous. The pose was contagious. Shortly, we were all staring straight up, even the Woodsmen, who'd stopped their jabbering and, like the rest of us, appeared to be waiting. It was the only time I was to feel something approaching a common bond with them.

The fire in the place where we had stopped seemed hotter and more intense. The cabin itself had reached temperatures that were scarcely bearable. A frightening thought had begun to take shape in my mind. Had the wind suddenly died? Were we becalmed in the midst of an inferno? Had our sails caught fire and burned, leaving us immobilized and at the mercy of the flames? If so, how long would it take for the boat itself, which

283

was all wood, to catch fire, to incinerate us and send us all to a watery grave at the bottom of the river? I had no doubt we were going to die. But whether in flames or at the bottom of the river became my major preoccupation.

While I pondered this, a head appeared at the top of the hatchway. Through the smoke and dust I was able to make out Colonel Porphyry. He was waving at us and shouting into the hold. "Come up. Come up."

We needed no second invitation. An unruly mob, we all rushed the ladder at once, scrambling up it, each on the heel of the other. Magnus had swept Cassie up in his arms. Meanwhile, Madam Lobkova and I had gone back for Leander. We tried several doors before finding him unconscious on a cot in one of the cabins. It may well have been my overwrought imagination but, dressed as he was in Woodsman's attire, he had to my horror taken on, in some inexplicable way, many of their physical characteristics.

"Take him," Wanda said, coughing and pushing smoke from her face with flailing arms.

I tossed a blanket over his head and arms to protect him from the flames, then gathered him up. He felt leaden and cold to the touch. In the next moment we were stumbling through the smoke-filled stateroom toward the gangway and ladder.

My first breath on deck hadn't come a moment too soon. Even though the air was scorched, there was less smoke and the temperature was far more tolerable.

It was a strange sight—everyone there lined up at the rail, staring at the fire. We were directly in the center of it and, yes, I'd been right. Our mainsail had burned completely and now hung in tatters, raining exploding sparks down on us.

While the wind had indeed dropped, it hadn't died completely. But without canvas we were at a loss to take advantage of whatever there was of it.

The fire itself was a wall forty to fifty feet deep and stretching the width of the river. We were stuck roughly at the center of it. It was clear now how the Woodsmen had made that wall. The river at this point was somewhat narrower than farther up where we'd commandeered the boat. Relying heavily on logging for building material and fuel, the Woodsmen used this particularly narrow bottleneck in the river as an area for storage of cut timber. When full, as it was now, it formed literally a bridge, stretching from one bank of the river to the other. What they'd done with their huge supply of pitch was to saturate the logs, then ignite them.

As formidable a barricade as this was, we might still have been able to bull our way through to the other side had we canvas enough. Without it, we were without power—lost. There was no going back, either. Behind us, looming like dark, humped shapes on the water, was a vast armada of Woodsmen's boats. Everything they had capable of floating had gathered out on the river, poised to attack the moment we attempted a retreat. As matters stood, there was little we could do one way or the other but wait helplessly and watch the flames slowly engulf us.

Glancing up, I was startled to see Colonel Porphyry back out on the fly bridge. He was smoking one of his Egyptian cigarettes and gazing cooly at that implacable circle of fire that seemed to be tightening its grip on us by the second.

I couldn't help but admire him. He appeared to be looking not at the fire but at the logs drifting past our prow, many of them making a big booming sound as they caromed off the keel. Then I realized he wasn't merely out sightseeing, but was computing the forward motion of our boat in relation to the speed of the logs drifting past us. When I grasped what he was up to, I saw that we weren't quite as dead in the water as I'd thought. The current carried us. There was forward motion, not a great deal of it, but nonetheless enough so that the invisible presence in the wheelhouse could keep us on course.

This impression was confirmed when I looked up once more at what was left of the mainsail. It was by then mostly ashes and sparkling tatters, but those were fluttering freely behind us now, like blazing pennants. A short time ago when I'd first looked, those same tatters drooped limp against the smoldering mast. Now risen to a point where they flapped at an angle of approximately thirty degrees between themselves and the mast, they served as telltales and seemed to suggest a freshening wind.

Staring up at Porphyry on the fly bridge, I nudged Magnus beside me. "What's he up to?"

"Waiting for the wind."

I stared sickly at the flames licking and crackling all about us. "What if it doesn't come?"

"We'll abandon the ship, get back in the skiffs and pull for the shore."

"And do what?"

Magnus looked at me, mystified. "We'll walk back to Fraze."

He said it as though it was the most obvious thing in the world.

"But it won't come to that," he went on cheerily. "We're at a funny point here on the river. The land forms a kind of depression. Those hills you see off to the left there serve as a breakwall. If we can just inch past this point, we'll soon have plenty of wind."

"But all of our sail is gone." I tried to sound calm and reasonable. "And besides, at the rate we're presently going, by the time we break out of this hole, we'll all be carbonized."

I was about to go railing on when I realized that Magnus was no longer listening to me. He was watching the top of the mast where what was left of the mainsail had started to flap a bit.

Porphyry had seen it, too. He was rapping on the glass of the wheelhouse, pointing out to the helmsman the tatters stirring fitfully about in the topmast.

There was a shudder. The boat groaned and dipped, then slid sidewards with a grating sound, not unlike something very large teetering over the edge of a cliff. Those of us on deck were tossed in the direction of the dip. The Woodsmen yowled and Cassie sent up a long terrified shriek.

The next thing I knew the boat appeared to rear back and pull free, like a man tugging his foot out of mud. It was gliding over water, the mainsail tatters lashing the mast and streaming out behind us, almost parallel to the deck. We hadn't sail enough for easy navigability, but clearly we were heading in the right direction.

The right direction was a solid wall of flames, some of them thirty feet in height, soaring skyward. From where I stood, I could see little in the way of a possible opening in that wall to the free water just beyond.

Porphyry was up on the fly bridge again. Framed as he was by a background of fire and burning water, he looked like some Old Testament figure painted on stained glass.

"Everyone to the stern of the boat," the Colonel shouted through cupped hands. "Get down as low as you can."

"Where are we going?" someone shouted up at him.

He pointed ahead at the wall of crackling flames. "Through it," he said, and ducked back into the wheelhouse.

Not pausing long enough to consider the consequences of such an action, Magnus grabbed Cassie, the guards hauled the two Woodsmen to their feet, I gathered Leander up into my arms and, with Madam Lobkova clinging to the seat of my pants, we all scrambled aft.

There was no way you could get right down on the deck. It was blistering hot. Evidently, we had a raging fire in the hold. Smoke was pouring out of the hatch and open portholes. The boat, virtually unmanageable without sail, continued to flop and flounder like a hurt bird, drawn irresistibly toward that last fiery barricade.

Though we'd been instructed to keep our heads down, I couldn't resist a final look about. If this was going to be the last time I'd see the world, I wanted to see it for what it was. The last thing I recall before entering the inferno was the sight of a patch of blue, serenely indifferent sky, in which a flock of geese in wedge formation streaked north across a pale white crescent of early morning moon.

Without further warning, we slipped into a channel of fast-running water that swept up directly into the heart of the flames. No more than, possibly, eight or ten feet across, the current hadn't been visible several minutes ago when we'd last looked for such an opening. But above in the wheelhouse they'd spied it and made directly for it. As we entered, it appeared to open even wider as if to accept us.

The heat took your breath away. It was searing. When you dared to breathe, it felt as though molten lava was pouring down your throat. By then the mast, merely smoldering before, had caught fire in earnest, blue-tipped flames streaking up its length. Three quarters of the way up, the mast suddenly leaned over and cracked, sending up a shower of fiery cinders as it descended with a slow, almost studied, grace. It slammed onto the deck with a thud, part of it still clinging by a sliver to the shattered base.

It occurred to me that flesh surely had a lower kindling point than heavy timber. If the deck and masts caught fire, shortly we would too. Just when I thought it must be impossible to endure another second of this heat, a pail of cold, life-giving water doused my body. I recall nothing before or since that time so completely satisfying.

Looking up, I saw Magnus shoot past me. He carried a bucket with a long rope which he dipped over the rail, hauling it up the next moment with a gush of water sluicing over its sides. When he dashed past me, I saw that his hair was on fire. Having dumped a bucket over Cassie and Madam Lobkova clinging

287

together, he dashed back to the rail, hauled up another bucket and doused his own head.

There was a moment when the boat appeared to hesitate. It looked like some drunken outcast thing that had lost its way and stood baffled and turning, trying to regain its course.

Had we remained there a second longer, I have little doubt we would have all gone up like tinder. But mercifully we were moving again, nudging and inching our way through a fiery canyon. Great floating logs bonged off our hull, sending hollow claps thundering up at the cold, uncaring sky.

And then we were through.

From the time when we entered the flames on the encampment side of the river, to the moment when our prow slipped clear of them to the other side, it could not have been more than three or four minutes. But in that brief period I lived several lifetimes and had no doubt aged an eternity.

Suddenly, the air was cool. A fresh breeze had come up and the boat, a singed and battered wreck, smoke pouring from beneath its decks and out its scuppers, canted sideward. With a fresh gust of air, we limped into midstream and crept down the river.

Behind us, the Woodsmen's armada, baffled and furious, cringed on the other side of the flames. They'd been foiled by their too-clever trap and were too frightened to run their own fiery gauntlet to give chase.

The sense of relief was palpable. Everyone was up reeling forward toward the rail, shouting, cheering jubilantly, hurling taunts back at the stymied Woodsmen. Various parts of the boat still crackled and smoldered, but except for the sails and mainmast, the vessel appeared to be miraculously intact.

Crowding forward with the others, I carried Leander in my arms. Still he hadn't woken. Yet he wasn't dead. I could feel the rise and fall of his narrow ribs against my chest. I told myself that through some miracle he would live—must live. But his sleep was like no normal sleep. Not even like drugged sleep, this sleep of Leander's seemed very like the sleep of coma—a sleep in which the sleeper, while conscious, is unable to wake but is doomed to inhabit a gray, featureless place between the world of the living and that of the dead.

Colonel Porphyry was back out on the fly bridge, gazing back over his shoulder at the fiery swath we'd left in our wake.

A grateful cheer went up from all of us below. Startled, he gaped down at us as though we were mad, then suddenly broke into peals of howling laughter. He gave a mock benediction and hyssopped at us with his hand like a pontiff. Standing there with our singed brows and charred clothes, we roared with delight.

Porphyry ducked into the wheelhouse, then reappeared with someone in tow behind him. You couldn't see who it was for all the smoke still drifting about us. The Colonel stood slightly off to the side and behind the man, propelling him gently forward. At last, emerging from the smoke and rags of morning mist, dressed in a monk's robe, the invisible helmsman, my brother Cornie, stood above us, waving shyly from the fly bridge.

It wasn't so much Cornie's unexpected appearance at that moment that so overwhelmed me. After all, hadn't he always been the good older brother who'd turn up at difficult moments to bring peace among his constantly quarreling siblings? It was later, however, when he began to talk, to speak, to greet us in a gentle, reassuring voice—a voice we'd never heard before—he, whom we'd always believed to be mute and dumb, now chatting amongst us in quiet, thoughtful and cultivated speech—that I finally broke down.

Far from out of danger, our way had taken us over both water and land. The boat, smoldering at a number of key points, had begun to list dangerously. A mile or so downriver it caught fire in earnest. We started to take on water at an alarming rate. The Woodsmen, whose number had swelled to hundreds, had been following us on foot along the far bank. They pointed at us wildly and leaped about. Jeers and caterwauling wafted out to us over the water and made our hair stand on end.

I knew the Woodsmen to be vengeful, particularly with outsiders, and didn't doubt they would be unsparing with those they believed to have spirited off their newly anointed King. The fact that they intended to have their King back was not lost on me.

At the helm up in the wheelhouse, Cornie pointed the prow of our crippled ship toward the opposite shore. We were hobbling toward it at an exasperatingly slow pace, racing both the Woodsmen on land and the spreading flames on board.

The two skiffs we'd used to escape the Woodsmen's compound upriver were still tied along our scuppers. Still several hundred yards from the safety of the shore, Porphyry gave the order to untie them and prepare to abandon ship.

It was no small task getting down the rope ladder. Cassie, terrified and writhing, had to be carried. Leander was lifeless dead weight. Madam Lobkova, by herself dangling from a rope ladder above the water, presented a huge logistical problem in itself. The two captive Woodsmen were by then frothing with fright. They scratched and kicked as they were prodded down the ladder. Several times they tried to scurry back up over the rail, preferring the inferno of the ship to the watery death of the river. One of them sank his teeth into a guard's wrist. Enraged, the guard kicked him down the ladder into the frigid water. Unable to swim, the Woodsman panicked and flapped wildly about in the water, nearly drowning, before he could be dragged sputtering over the gunnels onto the floor of the skiff.

Dangerously overloaded, the two skiffs rode low in the water. We had several close shaves, bucking crosscurrents, paddling obliquely over swiftly moving water before our keels scraped noisily across the pebbly bottom and bumped up on to the shore.

I don't know what it was that made me turn, but glancing over my shoulder, I had a view of the boat completely engulfed in flames. The prow with its carved and painted demon face, the sharp teeth and glaring eyes, once the object of such fright, now seemed merely funny and harmless—the sort of thing one sees illustrated in children's fairy tales, depicting djinns and witches, ogres and monsters.

The sun was full up now. On the opposite shore, in the bright light of morning, we could see hundreds upon hundreds of tiny black dots massing. They looked like a swarm of angry bees. Bloodcurdling shrieks carried over the water to where we stood on the sandy beach and watched with quiet gravity.

No sooner had we arrived at Fraze three hours later than Porphyry tried to get a call through to the mainland. He returned shaken. It seemed the lines were down, cut, he was certain, by the Woodsmen.

Though he didn't say it, I could see that the Colonel was deeply troubled. The Woodsmen would waste little time before mounting a counterattack. They had to act before the authorities on the mainland, curious about our failure to report, or their inability to get through, dispatched assistance.

Uncle Toby and Parelli, we were told by a badly frightened house steward, had fled the castle, setting out on foot for the mainland, they said, to seek help. They had departed two days earlier, shortly after Porphyry had countermanded Uncle Toby's orders and put together a rescue party to go out to the Woodsmen's camp. Reluctant to wait around for the Colonel to return, then have to answer a lot of uncomfortable questions, they skipped. Most of the house staff and technical personnel followed suit, but not before stripping the larders of most of the available provisions.

The weather had been threatening, the badly shaken steward said, and severe storms were predicted for later in the day. That always made the trails bad and the possibility of landing a rescue force virtually nil. Far more problematic, if the river rose, the way would be hopelessly impassable and we would soon find ourselves at the mercy of an overwhelming force of Woodsmen hell-bent on revenge.

"Are my brother and sisters still here?" I asked the steward.

"Yes," he nodded, somewhat uneasily. "For some reason Mr. Toby refused to take them along."

Part 10

Flight

"Let's fly, and save our bacon."

—Rabelais, *Pantagruel*

32

"The arsenal," Porphyry said. He didn't actually say it so much as blurt it out like something suddenly come to mind.

"Beg pardon, sir?" the steward said.

"The armory. Guns," the Colonel barked at a vocal level just beneath a shout. He didn't wait for an answer but wheeled and swept off across the room in the direction of the main stairway. Several of us stood there for a moment mystified, then dashed off after him in hot pursuit.

Attempting to make a point, the steward pumped a hand fecklessly in the air, then thought better of it and came barreling after us.

The arsenal, the place where Uncle Toby stored guns and ammunition, was a cramped tiny cupboard off a corridor on the second floor of the castle. A thick oak door, so low you had to stoop to pass through it, marked the spot. To the best of my recollection, the door was always closed, a big rusty padlock bristling importantly on its hasps.

When we reached it the padlock was smashed and the door hung open from only a single hinge, the bottom one having been prized out, tearing away part of the lintel with it. Porphyry was already inside.

"We're a bit late," the Colonel said gloomily. "The place has been stripped."

Indeed it had. Jones, disapproving of guns, was not unmindful of their usefulness. He'd kept upwards of a hundred on hand with crates of ammunition. They were always under lock and key.

I stepped inside. Magnus and several other of the Colonel's people followed directly at my heels, their voices dropping to a whisper as though they'd entered a sanctuary.

The smell of linseed oil and stored powder hung like a haze above the place. Well-oiled and regularly maintained, the guns had always been stacked upright in peaked clusters joined at the stacking swivels. They were always ready to be used in the event of any emergency—which Jones seemed always to expect but never truly believed would come.

Every last rifle had been taken and the crates of ammunition sledgehammered open and emptied of their contents.

"Who do you suppose . . ." I started to say, then looked up, startled to see Ogden, still in pajamas, looking slightly dazed and shuffling toward us. On closer inspection, he appeared somewhat disoriented. Letitia followed just behind him. Guiding him with a hand at his elbow, her stricken eyes fell on me.

"It was the lab staff and some of the porters," she explained as though she thought she was going to be blamed for it. "As soon as they discovered that Uncle Toby and Parelli had fled, they just ransacked the place."

She made a soft weary sound, then leaned against the wall. Ogden had bruises—one on his cheek and a purple-greenish one above his eye. He looked as though he'd been knocked about quite a bit. With his sense of natural entitlement badly undermined, poor Ogden seemed a bit bewildered. But seeing me was a tonic for him. The moment our eyes met, a resurgence of venom shot the color right back into his cheeks.

"Ogden tried to stop them," Letitia went on.

"I could've too." He fumed and glowered at me. "If everyone hadn't run out on me."

Porphyry took a step toward him. "They banged you about a bit, I see."

"I know the ones involved," he snarled. "They won't get off easy. What about Cassie and Leander?"

296

"They're both back here now," I said.

"Why did you run out on us?" Ogden snapped, turning on Porphyry. "If you hadn't run—disobeyed orders"—he gaped ruefully at the shambles of the gun room—"none of this would have happened."

"And you would have never seen your brothers and sister again," the Colonel replied quietly, his patience and tolerance a rebuke in itself.

"Have they all gone?" I asked.

"Who in their right minds would stay?" Ogden shot back at me. "After Uncle Toby and Parelli pulled out, it was every man for himself. Sheer anarchy. The guns are just the half of it. They looted the place. Anything they could carry—paintings, jewelry, silver. And, of course, the food . . ." He turned a look of sheer hate on me. "I hold you fully responsible. If you hadn't—"

"That will do now." Porphyry took Ogden firmly beneath the arm and led him outside into the hallway.

It was clear by then that Ogden was not quite rational and was under great strain. Letitia told us later that after everyone had fled, he'd attempted to organize the few poor souls who'd stayed behind into a force to defend the castle from attack. But he had no guns and the handful of people remaining had paid little attention to his instructions. Shortly, the place was in chaos.

"Where's Miss Sofi?" Porphyry asked, looking about.

"Miss Sofi's right here," a voice wafted hollowly up the corridor.

The next thing we saw was Sofi descending a flight of stairs, striding out of the shadows. She wore a flowered print dress that appeared somewhat soiled, and her hair, usually impeccable, looked decidedly unkempt.

No doubt she saw the shock in our eyes—not necessarily for her strangely untidy appearance, but rather for the tiny infant in swaddling clothes she cradled in her arms. Her features cracked into an arch smile. She looked at Cassie, then at me. "Well, I see you're both back from your little outing. We were beginning to worry." She looked about at some of the others—Magnus's burned hair, Porphyry's tattered clothes, the last few remnants of my Woodsman's costume. "Looks like you've all had quite a little party for yourselves. Did I miss anything?"

She caught me staring at the infant, who'd begun to make soft little cooing sounds. "Don't just gape like that, Johnnie. Say hello to your little brother." She thrust the squalling infant at me and laughed when I reared back. "I don't believe he has a name yet or I'd introduce you."

"What are you talking about?" I snapped. "What do you mean, my brother?"

"I think I know what Miss Sofi's referring to," Porphyry said.

"I'll bet you do." Sofi nodded knowingly.

"Madam Lobkova had hoped to tell you all at a more suitable time," the Colonel explained, his manner almost contrite. "But since Miss Sofi has brought the matter so pointedly to our attention, perhaps we might all just have a look around upstairs."

The invitation had left most of us somewhat less than eager to accept. Not so Sofi. "By all means," she said, full of a strangely manic cheer. "Then after that," she rattled on, "if you'd all excuse me, I'd like to go to bed. I've been on my feet for the last forty-eight hours."

The first thing that struck you was the devastation. It confronted you the moment you stepped from the stairwell and grew worse as you moved along the corridor.

The salons and sitting rooms, once so magnificently furnished, had been stripped of anything light enough to carry— small antiques, bibelots. Priceless paintings had been torn from the walls, leaving craters of gouged-out plaster where they'd been prized from their fastenings.

Much of it was destruction of a wholly wanton sort, with no thought of profit in mind—beautiful objects smashed out of spite, simply because they were too large or heavy to carry off or, possibly, as a gesture of sheer hatred for the wealthy owners and everything they represented.

Sofi led the way through an intricate maze of winding intersecting corridors. We were in a part of the upper story I'd never seen before.

"Where is she taking us?" I asked the Colonel at one point.

"You'll see soon enough," he said, his eyes fixed grimly ahead. He appeared to know exactly where she was headed.

We finally came to a pair of white swinging doors. A red warning stripe had been painted diagonally across them. Off to the side was a sign. Printed in large bold type in several languages, it read:

NO ADMITTANCE WITHOUT AUTHORIZATION

Sofi turned and looked at us over her shoulder. "This gets a bit unpleasant from here on," she said, still smiling, but by then the smile had begun to pall. In the next moment she turned and swept open the doors. We tramped in after her.

The smell hit you with palpable force. It was like walking into a wall. It took your breath away. There was no mystery as to the source of it. Hundreds of cages of various sizes lined the walls from ceiling to floor. Each contained an animal of some sort—mice, cats, dogs, rabbits, but mostly primates of one kind or another. Some of these poor creatures were still alive. A goodly number had died, expired in their cages, sending up the awful fetor of death. Many hadn't been fed or watered for days.

Those still alive were weakened and dehydrated, clearly frightened. They'd lain in their mess unattended. Despite their feeble condition, it was amazing what a racket they sent up at our appearance. Barks, cries, shrieks rent the air, but surely the worst sound of all, the most unnerving, was that of a large parrot, its wings clipped, seated on its perch, squawking shrill locutions into the darkened room.

"When the others left," Sofi tried to explain, "there was only me and one or two others. We've been trying to care for them. But it's just too much."

I thought I heard the first sign of her voice cracking. The jaunty façade of uncaring was rapidly fading. "Even giving them water . . ." she went on, trying to regain her old breeziness.

Departing the holding area, we wheeled through more swinging doors and into other laboratories. I could still hear the howling and barking long after we'd left the place. The smell reached out after us like long, clinging tentacles, threatening to pull us back. It was in my clothing for days, and the fierce, aggrieved shrieking of that parrot I shall carry to my grave.

We walked a full ten minutes before reaching the nursery (Sofi's term for it). The place that fled past us in those brief minutes was as remote and alien to me as a distant star. No more than one floor above the place we'd lived all of our lives, a totally different world had existed and we'd never known a thing about it.

The devastation here was as bad, if not worse, than elsewhere in the castle. No room had been spared, each subjected to everything from simple looting to destruction of the most malicious sort.

At the head of a seemingly endless corridor, we entered

another pair of swinging doors. Unlike the room that housed the animal pens, not a sound could be heard from behind these doors. A small placard to the right of them identified the place as simply Ward A.

Our group, numbering seven or eight people, entered. Though it was daylight outside, drawn blinds had cast the place in partial shadows. My eyes adjusting to the light, I saw that we were in a large, high-ceilinged room, rectangular in shape. Two neat rows of cribs lined either wall.

The moment we'd entered, Sofi turned to us and pressed a finger to her lips, signaling us to be silent. Madam Lobkova went before us, moving from crib to crib, adjusting blankets and buntings, gently rocking the side rails of those in which she found a child restless and about to wake. She looked like no stranger to the place—more like one who'd been there before and had often carried out similar operations.

For all of the filth and disorder we'd seen throughout other parts of the castle, the condition of things in Ward A was letter-perfect. Scrubbed. Immaculate. Not a thing out of place.

We padded unspeaking down the aisle, pausing here and there to gaze in wonder at the tiny sleeping occupants. Pink, rosy faces peeked out from the buntings. Pudgy little hands, tiny, perfectly wrought fingers curled above the silken borders of the blankets. Suspended from wires above the cribs, mobiles of infinite variety—ducks, angels, schooners, and witches astride broomsticks—drifted in languid circles in the still, shadowy air. Such tranquility in the midst of such devastation.

Leaning close above each child, you could hear the quiet, even rhythm of its breathing. The smell that came to me was of oil and talcum and that peculiarly pure, sweet, untainted smell of infancy.

I glanced across at Sofi, fussing from one crib to the next. Porphyry was watching her, too. The Sofi I saw there was not like any Sofi I'd ever seen before. For one thing, she appeared to have aged in a matter of mere days. She was haggard and drawn. Her shoulders slumped and the outfit she wore looked as though she'd been sleeping in it. But there was about her then, in all of that bedraggled beauty (for she was certainly still beautiful), a nobility, a certain generosity and even humility I could not quite associate with her. My first inclination was uncharitable, of course. I thought it was an act—a part she'd decided to play in order to achieve some more cynical advantage. But no, it wasn't that at all. This was genuine. When I looked again at Porphyry, I could see that he was clearly as mystified as I was.

From up ahead came a soft cry. Sofi moved forward at once. I watched her lean down over one of the cribs and had a glimpse of tiny hands straining upward, reaching for her cheek and throat. She took a pink little hand and kissed its open, squirming fingers, soothing the child with whispered words.

In the next instant, a figure moved out of the shadows. We watched as a small, swarthy man with a drooping mustache slipped in beside Sofi. Stooping down, he lifted the crying infant and, swaying, rocked it back and forth in his arms.

His back was to me and then I heard the high sweet sound of a children's lullaby. It was as though it were coming to me over vast distances—over the spate of years. And though his voice was low and the words muffled, I knew the language he sang in to be Italian and that I'd heard that song sung many times before—not only night after night in my own bedroom one floor below, but as an infant to send me off to sleep.

Standing outside the ward when we'd completed our tour, I was still stunned. Ogden and Letitia didn't speak. They appeared shaken. Madam Lobkova chatted in a low, excited whisper with the Colonel. Standing off to the side by himself, Cornie seemed overcome.

"Who are they really?" I asked, coming up to him. "They're not what Sofi—"

"Yes, Johnnie." He nodded sadly. "They're your brothers and sisters."

I stood watching him, not quite able to truly grasp the meaning of those words. "Jones's children?"

"All of them." He nodded and stared straight ahead.

"And did I too once lie in one of those cribs?"

"Many years ago."

"How many?"

"Shortly you'll learn."

We'd spent the better part of the day quickly boarding up windows and the few possible points of entry to the castle, not an easy task when you think of the great sprawling breadth of the place, the endless nooks and crannies. Toward dusk we'd finished nailing up every entryway on the first story. Porphyry established a rotation system of guards, using his own men. He

301

had eight with him. We were seven, not counting Leander, who lay upstairs. Several times we tried to revive him but to no avail as he kept sinking into an ever-deepening sleep. We had made up his old room and I had gone up there almost every hour to check on him. His breathing was hoarse and rapid. A series of harsh rales came and went from him in fitful spasms.

Porphyry's men, dispatched to stand guard on the battlements, rotated in four-hour spells. Each had only the weapons, mostly sidearms, he'd come to Fraze with. Ammunition was low, but the Woodsmen didn't know that.

We had dinner late that night. Actually, we shared what little was left behind in the larder—what couldn't be carried off on a hard trek over nearly a hundred grueling miles of forest.

It was plain but adequate fare, rice and tinned meat, sugared tea. There was plenty of wine (that being too heavy to carry), but no one seemed much in a mood to drink it.

No one had bothered to dress for dinner. We wore the same clothes we'd worn throughout the day, dusty and rumpled from our various chores, and sat at our usual places—all except Cornie. Colonel Porphyry had asked him to occupy the place at the head of the table formerly occupied by Uncle Toby. Madam Lobkova, next in seniority, sat at the other end. Toby and Parelli's settings had been pointedly removed.

What was surprising, however, was that the formal setting that had always represented Jones's place at table was now missing. The fact was not once mentioned throughout dinner nor did anyone so much as glance in the direction of that place, all of which tended to emphasize the fact that the single element that had loomed largest in our lives was now gone forever.

"They'll be back, of course," Porphyry remarked as we spooned up the last of our dessert—dried wafers and tinned plums in a sweetish syrup.

"How long can we hold out?" Madam Lobkova asked.

You could see the Colonel weighing in his mind the choice of being optimistic as opposed to being frank. He opted for a middle course. "Between twenty-four and thirty-six hours," he remarked abruptly.

The communal intake of breath was almost audible.

"I know that doesn't sound like much," he went on, "but that also depends on when, if ever, these little folk intend to mount their attack. I tend to think it will be sooner rather than later. They'll want to get here and do whatever it is they have to do before reinforcements arrive from the mainland—which, of course, they will," he added quickly.

"By now your people on the mainland are surely aware that our lines are cut," Letitia said, her voice quavery.

"No doubt, Miss Letitia," Porphyry assured her. "And checking equipment from their side, they'll quickly conclude that the disfunction is here. Finding that they're unable to reach us, they'll come right out and check for themselves. I don't doubt that for a minute."

"The question is," I said, "when?"

"That's what we're trying to ascertain now," Cornelius said.

"But surely," Letitia started, "once Uncle Toby and Parelli reach the mainland, they'll go straight to the authorities and advise them of our situation."

"That's precisely what they won't do, Lettie," Cornelius explained. "We're living testimony to their crimes. They'd prefer to see us perish here."

"They've stolen priceless documents from the Institute, as well, which they intend to sell for a fortune," Madam Lobkova added.

"And they'll get it," Porphyry said. "If those documents are what I think they are, they'll have their pick of takers."

"They are indeed," Madam Lobkova went on grimly. "That swine Parelli—he's in thick with those people."

Porphyry stirred restlessly. "Well, I don't intend to make things easy for them. Unfortunately, the breakdown in communication is working in their favor right now."

"What's the worst-case scenario?" Sofi asked. The question caught the Colonel off balance, but Cornelius leapt quickly into the breach.

"The worst-case scenario would be that the telephone lines remain down, that the weather takes a turn for the worse, making it impossible for anything to land here. However, even though that would delay reinforcements from coming out, it would also slow the Woodsmen. They're shrewd people, but they're not superhuman. I'm reasonably sure we're secure, and as the Colonel says, help is no doubt on the way."

"No doubt, Mr. Cornelius." Porphyry nodded gratefully.

A gloomy silence descended over the table. Dinner over, a sickening sensation had settled at the pit of my stomach. If the Woodsmen did actually come, I, more than anyone else, would have most to fear.

"If worse comes to worst . . ." Letitia looked at us uncertainly.

"I know what you're about to say," Madam Lobkova snapped. "Just put it out of your mind, Lettie."

Letitia seemed cowed, but Porphyry wasn't. He turned to her. "What was it you were about to say, Miss Lettie?"

She'd been thinking, of course, of the fortified room enclosed in cement block, deep in the cellars of Fraze.

"The cellar room . . ." she blurted out, watching Lobkova uneasily.

"By God"—Cornelius snapped his fingers—"I'd forgotten about that. We could hold out there for some time."

"I won't hear of it," Madam Lobkova sulked. "I simply won't hear of it."

Colonel Porphyry seemed perplexed. "What room? What's everyone talking about?"

All eyes turned to Porphyry as Cornelius began to explain.

Madam Lobkova insisted on spending the night with Cassie. The poor child had been fretful and weepy all day, still disoriented since the moment she'd woken from deep sleep to find herself in the middle of a river on a boat enveloped in flames. I had no way of knowing how much the horrors of her experiences amongst the goat people she recalled.

Madam Lobkova took her up to bed early, then refused to leave her side. One of the few remaining chambermaids made up a bed for her in Cassie's room and that was the last we saw of them that night. The rest of us lingered for a while over coffee.

Before retiring I joined Porphyry on his rounds. Like a good general, he made a point of seeing each of his men at his post. They were a stouthearted bunch. Most of them were exhausted from a day of harrowing events. I gathered from him that the majority of them hadn't slept for thirty hours. Neither had the Colonel, for that matter. Like any good leader, he didn't ask of his men things he himself was unprepared to give.

When Magnus came up to report, I noticed that his head was bandaged with some oily rags. He'd lost a good part of his hair in the fire on the boat and his scalp was badly burned. No doubt he was in pain but you couldn't detect a trace of that from his frank, open, cheerful face. Full of hope, he never once doubted the rightness of our cause or the success of its outcome.

I went up to make a final check on Leander before turning in.

If I'd been clinging to some slim hope of miraculous recovery, that was now all but gone. Over the past several hours his respiration had dropped, the raling gasps had passed. That was when he was still fighting. Now he merely lay still, accepting the inevitable. His skin was waxen. The struggle for life was over. The closest thing I'd ever had to a real brother was about to move off alone into the shadows of eternal night.

Exhausted, I returned to my room to be by myself. Several times during the night there was sporadic shooting from the drum towers. I'd woken from a fitful sleep to hear the gruff shouts of Porphyry's men and the tramp of their boots hurrying past my door. From outside my window the excitable chatter of Woodsmen could be heard.

Sometime about midnight it had started to rain again. It came heavily at first, then slaked off, only to come again with renewed force.

Lying there in bed, I thought of my brothers and sisters. They lay all about me in the clammy darkness, each in the solitude of his or her room, listening to the same frightening sounds and contemplating the bleak uncertainties of their future.

Where would it end? What was to become of us? I, for one, would find assimilation with the Woodsmen intolerable. I'd had a small taste of that already and, given a choice, I would most certainly opt for the spansules Jones had had the foresight to provide in the cellar room.

Far from showing signs of abating, the downpour outside had grown torrential. It had been going on for the past several hours, banging on the casements, gnashing at the eaves, virtually assuring that no helicopter would risk a landing on that slim, muddy strip, or that our telephone lines could be restored any time soon. I knew all this and I didn't need Colonel Porphyry to confirm it for me. We were hopelessly and completely alone.

"If you've come up here to laugh . . ."

I turned from gazing down at a tiny infant to see Sofi frowning behind me. She carried a bottle of formula in each hand and seemed slightly out of breath.

"I'm not laughing," I said.

She thrust me roughly aside and proceeded to strip the soiled bunting off a child. "What are you doing up here, anyway?"

"I came to look around."

305

"Well, now you've looked around."

Her voice bristled with hostility.

"They're my brothers and sisters, too," I said.

She never answered, but tugged off the soiled diaper and tossed it aside. Shortly, she was sponging the baby's bottom with warm soapy water. When she'd dried and powdered it, she finished off by pinning a fresh diaper onto the child.

"You did that well."

"I warn you, Jonathan." She glared. "I'm in no mood for jokes now."

You could tell she'd been up and running since early morning, her cheeks flared and slightly out of breath. Her hair hadn't been combed since the day before and she still wore the same dress. Despite all that, she looked pretty. Prettier, actually. Stress and frayed nerves became her.

To my offer of help, she would have preferred to tell me to go to hell. But she was tired and overworked and I could see she welcomed the offer of assistance. Her solution to the dilemma was to ignore me, so I merely fell into step beside her, snatching up several bottles of formula as I did so.

"I know what you're thinking," she said as we moved forward to the next crib. She stooped above a squalling little creature whose tiny fists rose up to fend off the intruder stripping off his bunting. "Whatever you're thinking about me, it's probably right. But just keep it to yourself—okay?"

"I wasn't thinking anything." (That's a lie. I surely was.)

"Good," she snapped, then gently inserted the rubber nipple of the bottle into the child's mouth. Instantly, the squealing subsided into a flurry of contented burbles. As Sofi held the bottle, her face wore an odd little smile, of which she was completely unaware.

"Why are you looking at me that way?" she snapped as she began rediapering the child.

"What way?"

"That idiotic expression on your face."

"I'm trying to remember you, that's all."

She glanced at me, vaguely annoyed. "You've only been gone a few days. Am I that forgettable?"

"No."

"Well—-what is it, then?"

"I'm trying to reconcile what I recall of you with what I see now."

She saw me staring at the infant with its splayed legs pedaling furiously in the air. She was daubing at its raw, chafed bottom with cotton swabs and baby oil when, suddenly, she stopped and looked up at me.

I had a sudden image of her in the conservatory on a snowy February morning so many years ago. She was jumping rope with Lettie and I recall thinking how annoyed I was at her without being old enough to understand that I was annoyed because I was so attracted to her. She was not too young to understand that, however. Even then she was hard as nails. She could tear the wings off a moth. It was that same morning I asked her to tell me what I looked like. In the absence of mirrors, I had no idea, and at that moment so many years ago, I was just silly and guileless enough to ask her. And that's when she laughed.

"Is there any need for us to still quarrel?" I now asked.

The question took her by surprise. Her body visibly relaxed.

"None at all," she mumbled, with safety pins stuck between her lips. "So, what was life like with the trolls? What did you see?"

"More of these." I gazed around at the drowsing infants. "Only older."

The swift motion of her hands working over the child paused and she glanced up at me. "I know. That Colonel fellow told me all about them. It seems incredible."

We moved on to the next crib.

"What did they look like," she asked, "our brothers and sisters?"

"Like us, but different."

"You mean like Woodsmen?"

"You can see traces of that in some. The hairiness and the leathery skin. Mostly, though, they look just about like anyone else. On a street in a large city, they'd go unnoticed."

"Except—" She gazed at me pointedly. "They have the same murderous traits as their Woodsmen forebears."

"Some do, I'm sure. Some don't. There were some I saw who seemed quite nice. They appear heartier than your typical Woodsmen, too. Bigger. Stronger. Longer lived. There's a man out there—their keeper, I believe. Probably one of the lab staff from upstairs. Runs this compound they all live in just like a clinic. Supervises their diets. Dialyzes them. Regulates their body temperature. Just like us. Ask Porphyry. He'll tell you about it."

We moved slowly through the high, stately rooms, making our way among the last remaining cribs.

For no apparent reason, she gave a funny little laugh. "How did you like being a king?"

"A breeder, you mean. That's all they really are."

"Did you like your mate?" She shot me a sly grin.

"I'll tell you all about her someday."

For a time we were both silent, then out of the blue, we burst into hoots and peals of healing laughter.

The noise brought the dark little gentleman I'd seen the night before (a ward assistant, I assumed) into the room to see what all the commotion was about. He seemed alarmed at first. Then, seeing us laughing, his large sad eyes twinkled.

He looked like nothing I'd ever seen around Fraze before. He put me in mind of an old Neapolitan organ grinder I came across long ago in a book of old prints—complete with battered derby and droopy handlebar mustaches. The derby had sat on his head, I recall, at a rakish angle and on his shoulder sat a monkey with a tiny pillbox hat and a chin strap. The old man cranked wheezy calliope music out of his ancient box while the monkey danced at the end of a frayed yellow rope, weaving in and out of the crowds, collecting coins in an old battered tin pot.

Laughable as the old organ grinder had seemed in that worn, faded print, there was something odd about him. Something vaguely sinister. He gave you an uneasy feeling.

"Where do you suppose Uncle Toby's gone?" Sofi asked while we gathered soiled diapers and sheets and tied them into a bundle.

"Probably halfway 'round the world by now, I should imagine."

"With his Corsican?"

"Given what each knows about Jones and the Institute and about each other, I should think they're going to have to stay pretty close from here on out," I replied. We smiled at the thought of that uneasy alliance. "I am a bit surprised though."

"That they skipped out?"

"No—that was to be expected. I'm surprised that Toby didn't take you."

Sofi made a face that had the look of irritation. "He asked me to go, but I said no."

She must have seen the doubt in my eyes and hurried on.

"Them." She indicated the infants with a quick sweep of her hand and gave me an infuriated little glance.

"He was just going to leave them here? To die?"

"Why not?" she said matter-of-factly. "No different from those poor animals out there in the lab cages. They meant nothing to him."

"So you decided to stay and take care of them?"

"Someone had to. Luckily, the old Italian gentleman decided to stay, too. Hand me that stack of dirty linen over there, will you?"

Just as we reached the swinging frosted-glass doors, I caught her by the arm and looked directly into her eyes. "What do I look like?"

She gave me a startled look.

"What do I look like?" I demanded sharply. "Tell me. How would you describe me?"

Her jaw dropped and she shrank a bit from me as though I were deranged. Then suddenly something like recognition dawned in her eyes.

"Oh, that." She laughed. "You do have an elephant's memory, Johnnie. That's eons ago."

"It was, but I assure you, I haven't forgotten it."

She laughed a moment longer, then suddenly grew serious. "I guess that hurt, didn't it?"

"You were always pretty good at that."

I could see her mind rushing backwards over the spate of years. "Yes, I guess I was."

She glanced up at me with a shrewd grin. "Oh, come on. It wasn't as traumatic as all that."

She must have seen something in my eyes and she broke off abruptly. "You are serious, aren't you? Here, let me see." She reached up suddenly and grabbed my chin between two fingers, then jerked my head from side to side. "Not bad, actually. Not exactly star quality, but it's a nice face. Open, and kind. Age has improved it a bit. Almost nice-looking, I'd say. There now, how's that?"

Just as we stepped out the door one of the babies started to cry. There was no need to go back because the old Italian gentleman had already reached the crib, lifted the child out and was rocking it in his arms.

As we trod silently, not speaking, down the empty corridor with its many doors opening onto room after room of shambles and devastation, I could hear the old Tuscan lullaby trailing after us through the darkening hallway, bringing to all of my lost little brothers and sisters the sweet, untroubled sleep of childhood.

"We are, therefore, I'm afraid, between a rock and a hard place."

We found ourselves gathered in Uncle Toby's study later that same afternoon. Colonel Porphyry's normally measured voice hurried on. He'd been speaking for the past several minutes, attempting to reassure us, while at the same time fully appraising us of a situation of the gravest danger.

"But that's only temporary, may I add. Once we get the lines repaired . . ."

"Did the Woodsmen cut them?" Letitia asked.

"Certainly looks that way," Cornie said.

"Then the break would have to be someplace nearby," Madam Lobkova reasoned aloud.

Porphyry struck a match to one of his pastel cigarillos. "Right now several of my people are out trying to locate the break." Seeing worry in our eyes, he breezed right on, seemingly untroubled. "I'll lay odds that at this very moment rescue parties are on the way."

"What about the others?" Letitia asked. "Those who fled."

"Still in the forest, no doubt," Cornie replied. "The coast is close to one hundred miles from here. There's little chance they could reach there before tomorrow."

"Traveling with all of that loot and at night won't be easy," I added. "And the weather doesn't make things any better."

"If the trails don't get them, the Woodsmen will," Ogden put in.

Porphyry looked as though he wanted to speak. But he didn't, falling instead into a troubled silence.

"And still we know nothing about Jones's murder." Sofi deftly changed the subject, then looked to Porphyry for clarification. He nodded, somewhat ambiguously.

"Let me understand . . ." Sofi continued, her breath coming faster. "You don't think my uncle or Signor Parelli . . ."

"Murdered your father?" Porphyry's manner was courtly. The talk of murder appeared to have roused him. "Not directly. But I should add that he and Signor Parelli were very much behind a plot of their own to kill Mr. Jones. The murderer, however, the one who actually killed your father, is seated at this moment among us, right here in this room."

No matter how we pressed him for specifics, he declined to go further.

Leander died that night. It was quiet and uneventful as those things go.

Shortly past midnight I was awakened by a dull jab. Opening my eyes, the first thing I saw was Madam Lobkova in a bulky flannel wrapper peering down at me, a stubby thick candle guttering in her fist.

"Come along," she said, "if you want to say good-bye to your brother."

When we reached there Cassie was already with him. She sat on a stool at the side of the bed, holding his hand and looking as though she'd been sitting there for some time. She didn't look up when we entered. Instead, her eyes were riveted on Leander's face. She sat forward on her stool, as though expecting some sign, a turn of events, not necessarily for the better.

Cornie arrived soon after, to be followed by Lettie, then Sofi sweeping in, still knotting the belt of her robe.

Clearly irritated at having been awakened, Ogden strode in, full of bluster. I watched the color drain from his face as he had his first glimpse of Leander lying there, close to death.

It was hard to reconcile the image of this cold, inert object lying waxen and still beneath a flimsy coverlet with the vital, funny, generous person I'd known in life as my brother Leander. The awful raling noises that had wracked his frail body only hours before had passed. Gone was the fretful look that had lined his youthful features and spoke volumes of the horrors he had recently endured. The face I saw now framed within the shallow hollow of a pillow seemed peaceful and untroubled. He was like someone who'd labored long and hard up a hill, then sunk happily beneath the shade of a tree for a bit of well-earned rest.

Sofi had played out her usual role of brash heartlessness as best she could. But when Leander, with a faint sigh, turned slightly on his side and passed over, her pose finally crumbled.

Only Cassie, the youngest of us, appeared not to have noticed his passing. She continued to sit beside him, holding his hand. Staring down at the waxen, masklike face, she seemed to be waiting there for him to awaken. She had no doubt that he would—if not now, then surely a short time later.

When it was at last unmistakably clear that Leander was gone, Madam Lobkova came forward, shuffling out of the shadows, and knelt beside his bed. It seemed to me she prayed. This was the position I'd been told people in grief assume in order to approach their gods. I'd never seen anyone pray before. None of us had ever known the comfort of a god and we possessed only the most primitive notion of what that entailed. Prayer was not encouraged at Fraze and the sight now of one of our own masters engaged in that activity came as something of a shock. Whatever god Wanda was approaching, I had no way of knowing. But, nonetheless, she prayed and wept freely. In ways I can't explain, I envied her her grief, for when she'd finished and rose again unsteadily to her feet, she seemed done with it.

In all the years since Leander's death, I have still not done with it. I am still grieving. I have still not found a way to exorcise my sorrow.

Porphyry had remained outside the room during this time. Given his sense of Old World decorum, he maintained a respectful distance from an event I'm certain he imagined belonged only to the immediate family.

He was waiting in the hall when we regathered there and stood shuffling awkwardly. There was about him an air of quiet concern, almost an urgency. When he spoke to us it was in a whisper. After offering his regrets, he asked whether any of us had heard noises outside our windows that night. Had we seen any sign of torchlights about the grounds? During the period immediately following dinner when we dispersed to our bedrooms, had anyone experienced anything out of the ordinary?

"What exactly are you trying to say?" Ogden demanded.

Porphyry hesitated. "I have no wish to alarm," he went on, his quiet manner showing signs of strain. "Nor do I wish to mislead you. Some of my people up on the battlements have reported seeing figures. What they describe as dark shapes moving into position 'round the castle walls. Of course, it's hard to see in the darkness and fog, and certainly imagination plays a part here."

Letitia whimpered softly.

"We've deliberately withheld our fire to conserve ammunition," Porphyry hurried on. "However, the moment any one of them attempts to enter the castle, we'll blast away."

He watched us to see how the force of his words had registered.

"And the phone lines?" I asked, a little hopelessly.

312

"Still down," Porphyry replied. "But we've managed to locate the place where they've been cut. Unfortunately, a large force of Woodsmen have been left there to make certain no one repairs them. My men just barely made it back here by creeping through their lines."

We buried Leander in the cellar of the castle. Surrounded as we were by Woodsmen, there was no question of carrying him up to the old peat bog which had served as Indian holy ground for centuries and the Jones family cemetery for as long as I can remember. Now, for poor Leander, it seemed that would not be possible. And as for Jones's mortal remains, we would probably never know his final resting place.

Magnus, that man of wide and constantly surprising skills, fashioned a casket for Leander out of planks of old cedar. They had lain in the cellar for years as a ready source of fuel at a time before the central heating had been installed.

I helped Madam Lobkova prepare Leander for interment. We sponged his frail emaciated limbs, then oiled his skin with a pine-scented balm of some sort. Wrapping him in shrouds, we lay him in the casket. Empty, it appeared to be far too small. But once we placed him inside, he fit perfectly. When we'd closed the lid and could no longer see him, the impression you had was that it was the coffin of a young and rather small child.

When the casket was at last ready, we carried it down into the cellar. It was all strange and yet oddly familiar, as though we'd done this countless times.

Digging a shallow grave in the grayish powdery earth, we then lowered the casket into it by means of ropes. Afterward, we stood about in a tight, nervous little circle, pawing the ground with our feet as Porphyry read a brief homily from a Bible he carried in his own kit.

The sermon was taken from one of the four gospels, which I gather a devout but ever-diminishing number of small cults on the mainland still read. It had something to do with the special affection in which the divinity held small children and the awful fate to be visited on those unwise enough to harm them.

We listened politely, albeit a bit bemused, until it was all over, none of us at all certain of what we'd heard or why.

Before we left the cellar, Porphyry asked to inspect the fortified "safe room." "Just," he said, "to get a lay of the land."

By late afternoon the sky darkened and the fog thickened. It leaned up hard against the glass windows and appeared to roll about and curl there like some soft, sinuous thing. The hope of a break in the weather seemed increasingly remote.

No longer did we go through the formality of sitting down to meals in the dining room. With the cooks gone and supplies dwindling, it was catch-as-catch-can. We ate in the kitchen, each at different hours, standing up and on the run. Each racing off to his or her appointed task.

Sofi we seldom saw. She spent all of her time attending the infants and the laboratory animals upstairs. Madam Lobkova divided her days between helping Sofi and caring for Cassie, who, since Leander's demise, had grown listless and apathetic.

Ogden and I took our turns with Porphyry's men on the towers. We familiarized ourselves with the use of firearms and stood watch through the day and night, listening for anything suspicious and hoping to hear a plane or helicopter circling overhead. But there was none. All you could hear was the occasional ring of the Woodsmen's axes and the dripping of rain from the trees in the nearby forest.

That night the castle grew cold. Without fuel, the furnace was no longer functioning and so we built a fire in Uncle Toby's library and gathered around it for whatever warmth and sense of security we might take from one another.

Sometime during those tedious wakeful hours, Madam Lobkova became nostalgic. She spoke of the past, of the Institute when there was still a bit of idealism to it all. Before the money got to be so big a thing.

"To Jones?" Lettie inquired.

"No, never." Madam Lobkova clucked her tongue. "To your uncle and Parelli. Never to Jones. Money was not his disease."

"You knew him well, Wanda, didn't you?" I asked.

"I used to think I did. Now I think, maybe, not so well at all." She shrugged. "Ask the Colonel. He's been rummaging through your father's papers for the past week. By now, he no doubt knows more about him than any of us."

"I'd be curious to hear what you've learned." Sofi turned toward him suddenly, an earnestness about her that startled me.

For a moment I thought he hadn't heard her. His eyes followed the motion of a shadow rushing past on the wall. When he looked up again, he seemed clearly uncomfortable. "Where

314

would you like me to start?" his voice croaked wearily. "I know pretty much the whole story by now," he went on. "I'll need some of you to fill in the missing pieces."

"In that case," Madam Lobkova said, cradling Cassie on her lap, "get right to it, and we'll see how we can help."

Porphyry brooded a moment. But if he had any reservations, he dispatched them quickly. "In that case, I'll start at the top."

It began with a lengthy recitation of biographical facts—dry, seemingly trivial data on a life, albeit a remarkable one, lived almost entirely in the shadows.

The Colonel made no attempt to dramatize his information. He merely recited it aloud in that quiet, take-it-or-leave-it manner so characteristic of the man.

Periodically, he'd stop dead in his tracks and peer off at some distant spot as though watching an odd little drama only he could see there. By the time he reached the point of Jones's experiments, the Humanus Institute and Dr. Fabian, his manner had become more clipped and guarded. From time to time, he'd pause long enough to light one of his cigarillos, inhale deeply, then hurry on.

"In order to carry on his work," the Colonel continued, "your father acquired a modest chemical firm, the Humanus Institute, one large enough to employ top people, but sufficiently small to go unnoticed by the giant pharmaceutical interests. At that point he felt keenly the need for a trained specialist with a proven track record in this mysterious, infant field of microbiology; also someone with the ability to organize and oversee a large, highly complex research program with developmental costs reaching upward into the billions. Those two skills came together in the person of a certain Doctor Fabian of Geneva, Switzerland."

"Fabian," I murmured, half to myself. "I've heard that name before."

"No doubt you've seen it on bills of lading or shipping crates around the castle," Porphyry replied. "Dr. Felix Fabian is a man of impressive credentials—a geneticist with a specific interest in the field of recombinant DNA growth hormone. He's also a physician with a specialization in geriatric medicine. In most regards, the perfect man for your father. There were, however, some unfortunate past associations—Fabian is a Romanian, born in Jassy, but identifies himself as Swiss. His real name is Fabiescu. As a young man, during the early years of the so-called

Good War, he was a member of the Iron Guard. Later, when the Wehrmacht overran the Balkans, Dr. Fabian's true talents were quickly recognized and he was sent off to the death camps to work on various medical research projects being conducted there. The research was in the field of genetics, and particularly in the area of life extension. Human subjects were required and many of the experiments we would call barbaric. Dr. Fabian to this day denies that any of it ever occurred and, with the assistance of the U.S. State Department and the British MI-5, he was able to have all of those records expunged.

"In his notes your father is quite clear on the subject. He loathed the man. And think what an odd combination they made—a humanitarian striking a purely pragmatic arrangement with a man most people characterized as a ruthless, amoral, utterly unrepentant monster, who also happened to be a genius. He was the foremost in the field and, for Mr. Jones, a means to an end. Your father struck a deal and never looked back.

"After the expenditure of several billion dollars and a dozen years of exhaustive laboratory and clinical testing, Mr. Jones and Dr. Fabian had assembled enough data to conclude that they were in possession of a substance and a procedure that did not merely regenerate human cells but could slow the process of aging to a crawl."

"But you said . . ." Letitia was flustered.

"Let him finish, child," Madam Lobkova chaffed. "He'll tell you in his own way and his own good time."

"We may not have that much time." Ogden spoke in a low voice, staring at the library windows, beyond which could be heard the distant but distinct ring of ax blades biting into wood.

"Go on," I said impatiently. "Let's hear the rest."

Porphyry squinted his eyes, gathering his thoughts, then resumed the tale. "As I was about to say, the goal of your father—an average life span of one hundred and fifty years—he hoped to achieve in this decade. They had already achieved doubling the life span of small rodents in the laboratory. They were well on their way to doing the same thing with chimpanzees and dogs. By means of computer projections, a life expectancy of two hundred years was conservatively estimated for humans in the decade just beyond.

"When Dr. Fabian informed your father one day that the work had gone as far as might reasonably be expected using only laboratory animals, a decision was made to upgrade the research

316

by including studies of the effects of TRX5 on human subjects. Dr. Fabian informed your father that this was a step that understandably involved risk. Your father never hesitated. He immediately volunteered himself as the first guinea pig. It no doubt took some courage, but the notion of self-exposure must have appealed greatly to a man of Mr. Jones's sense of personal mission.

"Your Uncle Tobias followed shortly after." Porphyry turned to his right. "You, Madam Lobkova, were next."

She nodded. "I took TRX5 for a number of years, then stopped."

"May I ask why you stopped?"

"Let's say for philosophical reasons"—Lobkova grew testy—"and leave it at that."

The Colonel couldn't resist a slight grin, then moved right on. "Signor Parelli was next to become a subject for the experiment, followed by Dr. Fabian himself, who, if you'll permit a bit of cynicism, waited long enough for clinical tests to guarantee that TRX5 taken over long periods posed no significant health threat.

"All of this occurred in the two or three decades following the Good War. With their need for laboratory animals on the wane and their need for human tissue greatly on the rise, it became all too clear to the Humanus research team that if work was to continue, it would be imperative to establish a constant and ready source of human test subjects."

"And that's where we came in," Sofi remarked, her voice nearly a whisper. "The guinea pigs."

Porphyry frowned. Clearly, her choice of words troubled him.

"I won't sit here and hear your father disparaged," Madam Lobkova fretted. "Much good came of his work. Future generations will benefit for years to come."

Porphyry cleared his throat. "I'm sure they will," he replied, but there was a note of ambiguity in his voice. "Be that as it may, however, the next job for Mr. Jones was to establish a steady flow of human subjects for purposes of experimentation."

"I'm not sure I care to hear any more of this." Letitia rose and started off into the shadows.

"I should think you'd want to, Lettie," Madam Lobkova called after her. "Liberties were taken with your body. You were never consulted. I should think you'd want to know."

"I want to know." I spoke quietly, fearing the grimness of the revelations to come. "This has something to do with what happened to Leander, too, doesn't it? And all of those others I saw penned up in that awful place out there with the Woodsmen."

"What others? What awful place?" Ogden turned on Porphyry. "What is he talking about?"

Madam Lobkova and the Colonel exchanged glances.

"Mr. Jonathan refers to the compound in the Woodsmen's camp," he explained. "It seems that many of those brothers and sisters you'd been told were chosen to join your father in his good works on the outside, in truth, never left here. After years of the most painstaking observation, they were sent out from Fraze directly to the Woodsmen's camp to go on to the next phase of the experiment."

There was an outcry. Lettie clapped her hands over her ears.

"This is outlandish," Ogden fumed. "Why should we believe any of it?"

"Because it's true," Cornie replied. "I can vouch for it. I was Father's liaison with the Woodsmen. I'm ashamed to even speak of the part I played in all of this, but I feel now I must."

We watched him, waiting for what would come next, almost afraid to hear it, and struggling to grasp the long-buried horrors now coming at us, one after the other in such a torrent.

I think I was the one who spoke first. "And the purpose of crossbreeding Jones's offspring and the Woodsmen . . ."

"Was simply to take a genetically debased stock and see to what degree it could be improved," the Colonel explained. "This had all begun, I should judge, around the 1970s . . . Help me with the chronology here, will you, Madam Lobkova?"

"The decade is essentially correct," Wanda replied. "Roughly a hundred years ago."

Porphyry nodded. "Mr. Jones at that time was a man physically and mentally at the height of his powers. Superior in every way. And since the project had to be carried out in absolute secrecy, it was decided that Mr. Jones himself would be the perfect choice to sire his own line of experimental animals."

He regretted the phrase the moment it leaped from his lips. But to his credit, the Colonel never once tried to retract or sweeten the words.

"Ideally, this would have suggested a common mother and father, producing a fairly common genetic pool. *Congenic*, I

318

believe, is the term used in Mr. Jones's log. The common father was easy enough. That was to be Mr. Jones, so long as he remained fertile and potent. But no single female, no matter how perfect a genetic match, could be expected to bear the large number of human subjects required to carry out such an enterprise over the great number of years needed to complete it. The only solution to the problem was to accept the principle of multiple mothers. . . ."

"But only within strictly limited variations of genetic makeup," Madam Lobkova pointed out. "The selection of prospective mothers was by no means random. It was the chromatic composition of each potential bearer that was the key. Most important would be the medical history. The medical records of each candidate would be searched for not only a history of family diseases down through the years but, particularly, for matters of longevity, deemed to be most critical."

Porphyry looked around at us sadly. "If you prefer, this can surely wait for another time."

"No," I said. "Go on. I want to hear it all."

"I do, too," Sofi said.

"What good is it for us to learn this now?" Letitia pleaded.

"The good is just that," Madam Lobkova said. "To know the truth. It's vital to know and to understand what was done to each of you."

"And this, this experiment," Sofi spoke the word as if it made a bad taste in her mouth, "project—whatever you call it. This, I take it, was the reason that all of us—my brothers and sisters and I—were encouraged to . . ."

"Correct." Porphyry nodded solemnly. "You were encouraged to cohabit. The reasons for that were twofold. Firstly, as you grew older, and more mature, this was thought to be an acceptable outlet for normal sexual desire. And secondly, as you know, your father and Dr. Fabian felt it crucial to their theories that their laboratory subjects be isolated from all forms of external contamination. Surely it would serve no useful purpose to produce a superior gene stock only to have it debased by one of inferior composition. The object was therefore insulation—environmental, cultural, sexual. That's why your father brought you to this remote place. That's why you live in a house—a castle, a fortress, if you please—with sealed windows. That's why you breathe filtered air and eat only foods produced here on the grounds. That's why all who come here to work—domestic staff, laboratory personnel—must undergo a lengthy period of quarantine before they're admitted to the castle. In all of this, I must add, your father was seeking only what he believed to be the very best for you."

"And so he fobs us off to the Woodsmen as breeding stock and test animals for his experiments," Ogden muttered bitterly.

Porphyry shook his head wearily. "That was the most objectionable part of it," he said. "And that's something each of you will have to come to terms with if you are to get on with your lives."

"But the Woodsmen . . ." Letitia's voice choked. "I still don't understand. Why those awful creatures?"

"Precisely," Porphyry remarked, "because of their awfulness. They were a debased people living in the most abject filth and squalor. A key fact to keep in mind is that they were short-lived. None of them, up until that point, survived much beyond thirty years. Your father had something they wanted, just as they had something he wanted. He offered them an opportunity to overcome many of their physical limitations, to achieve a better quality of life, and to live longer. What he asked in return was the right to use them as a kind of living, social laboratory for his experiments. Fertile ground in which to introduce his own genetically enhanced stock. In short, breeding rights.

"Your father hated that part of the Covenant. But Dr. Fabian convinced him that this last step was needed to confirm their data under conditions of the strictest control, and in this instance, Dr. Fabian prevailed.

"Your brother Cornelius was designated by your father as liaison between the camp and Fraze. He had the unhappy task of delivering the breeding stock to the camp each year and making certain they were not abused. Their only responsibility was to breed on almost a daily basis with the goat people. Then, at the conclusion of that year, they were judged to be contaminated by prolonged, intimate exposure to Woodsmen, forbidden to ever reenter Fraze, and therefore destroyed. Whereupon a new breeder was then designated from the castle and the cycle would begin anew."

"But why destroyed?" Sofi asked. "Couldn't they just be sent away?"

"It does seem extreme," Porphyry conceded. "But in the light of the Woodsmen's religion, it all fits together quite neatly.

The Woodsmen are animists of a sort. They see gods inhabiting everything. In trees. In rocks and rivers. For instance, they looked upon Mr. Jones as a kind of fertility deity. He was the bringer of a long and bountiful life. They worshipped huge straw effigies of him and struck his initials on every building and hut in the camp.

"As the offspring of Mr. Jones, your brothers and sisters were also believed to be deities. Within the Woodsmen's religion, these godlike breeders were referred to as 'Kings of the Wood' and looked upon as procreative gods. Within Woodsman lore, the typical life span of a Wood King is one year. Usually commencing on Whitsuntide, coinciding with Pentecost in the old Christian calendar, the King is born. Summoned forth by a Woodsman shaman from the land of the dead, the new king voyages to the land of the living in a vessel. Typically, this vessel takes the form of a casket. The birth of the new king occurs at the moment he steps from the casket. Part of the ceremony requires that he eat small bits of the vital organs of his predecessor—mostly the liver and heart, thereby taking on many of the best attributes of that king."

"So, that morning, they attacked us when we tried to carry Jones up to the old burial grounds—" Sofi's voice broke off.

"Precisely." The Colonel nodded. "Since they believed Mr. Jones to be their King, they felt they were entitled to his remains. More precisely, his vital organs. I'm sure Mr. Jonathan can tell us all a thing or two about that."

I was far too upset to reply but the expression on my face must have spoken volumes regarding my memory of the event.

The Colonel cast a wary glance at Madam Lobkova before continuing: "There was indeed a second and more practical reason for destroying the King after one year. From a strictly scientific point of view, it was crucial to observe directly the long-range effects of TRX5 on the vital organs of each subject in the experiment. Of particular interest was the vascular system, especially the coronary arteries. In addition, there were serology studies. Tissues had to be analyzed and cytologically typed. The postmortem examinations could only be carried out at the Humanus laboratories, where the most sophisticated state-of-the-art technology was available. Your brother Cornelius had the unhappy chore of collecting the remains from the compound to be sent on to Geneva."

You had to admire Porphyry for the calm, systematic manner in which he revealed the unpleasant details. It was orderly, concise, and yet remarkably tactful when you consider the circumstances under which they had to be presented.

"And all of those people Johnnie saw up there?" Letitia kneaded her hands.

"The ones penned up in the compound?" Porphyry asked.

"Exactly . . . I take it they're the by-products of the experiment?"

"Correct," Porphyry replied. "The offspring from countless unions between your brothers and sisters and the Woodsmen."

Ogden buried his face in his hands.

Porphyry watched him with a strange sadness, then hurried on. "What your brother Jonathan saw there were three generations of relentless inbreeding. All defective offspring were to be culled out and destroyed. What remains is primarily the new, improved race your father envisioned. These, in turn, were to be integrated into the general Woodsmen's community and then bred and crossbred over and over with the Woodsmen until, theoretically, in time, the desirable traits would all but eradicate the undesirable."

His voice trailed off and he looked at me. I could think of little to say. All I could think of were those blank, empty eyes behind the barbed wire.

"And what happens now?" Sofi asked, her voice nearly a whisper.

Porphyry glanced up at the ceiling and at the walls of books surrounding us, "You mean here? To us?"

She nodded, watching him fixedly.

"As of now," he went on, "the terms of the contract have been breached. Mr. Jonathan's being with us at this moment is a violation of the Covenant. The Woodsmen know he's here and now they've come to assert their right and reclaim their King. Mr. Jonathan is the next Jones."

The effect of those words was for me like the clap of doom. I recall the almost accusatory look of eyes turned toward me in the guttering firelight. I was the source of all present danger.

In the brief time I'd known him, Porphyry had always been a kind, tactful man. That last observation, however, despite the fact it was undoubtedly true, served to isolate me . . . to cut me off from the others. The chilling message in Ogden's eyes was all too clear. At that moment he was perfectly ready to turn me over to the Woodsmen in return for safe passage off the island. I couldn't say I blamed him.

My watch that evening ended at 12:45 A.M. I was hungry so I went to the kitchen. I found Porphyry there with several of his people, having a bowl of soup. He ate at a small table in his yellow slicker, his eyes ringed with red.

We chatted briefly and I asked him if there'd been a sign of anything hopeful.

He knew what I meant. "Not yet, but there ought to be something coming along any time now."

He said it in his usual chirpy manner, but this time I thought I detected a slightly more tentative note in his voice, as if he, too, was confused by the strange absence of any sign of help from the mainland.

I went directly to my room, undressed, and collapsed on my bed. Just as I was about to drift off, the quiet was suddenly shattered by a burst of gunfire and shouting. That was followed by a series of deep, resounding booms—a sound I couldn't really identify. They appeared to come from somewhere in the bowels of the building and vibrated upward through the timbers.

In the next moment I heard the heavy tread of boots pounding down the corridor past my door.

"Up. Everyone up."

The gunfire and shouting intensified. The loud booming sounds, which now sounded to me like wood impacting on wood, came at regular and frequent intervals. Only now they no longer seemed to come from one direction but two.

"Downstairs. Everyone downstairs."

I stuck my head out the door just as Cornie went flying past.

"What's up?" I shouted at his rapidly retreating figure.

"Downstairs. The Great Hall. We're all gathering there."

"What's all the noise?" I cried after him.

"The Woodsmen," he said. "They're about to break the door down." Then he disappeared at the end of the corridor.

Down below in the Great Hall, conditions were chaotic. Colonel Porphyry was issuing what rifles and short arms he had, allotting carefully measured handfuls of ammunition to those claiming to have sufficient familiarity with firearms to use them.

In the brief time since Cornie had passed my door, I'd managed to throw on a pair of pants, a shirt and a pair of boots, worn without the comfort of socks. Some of the others had not been so fortunate. They stumbled down, half-dressed in robes and pajamas, along with the odd bit of outerwear they'd managed to lay hands on before dashing.

All this time the noise of battering rams persisted. There was no doubt now that two were being used, one at each end of the castle. The noise was fearful and the boom from one appeared to answer the other with a fierce, exultant report, like that of cannon shot.

"We're going into the cellar now," Porphyry announced, his manner somewhat more abrupt than usual.

Madam Lobkova, swaddled in her outsized flannel robe, held Cassie firmly by the arm. Letitia stood just behind them, wringing her hands.

"How long will we be down there?" Sofi demanded.

"As long as it's necessary," Porphyry replied.

Sofi appeared dissatisfied with the answer. "I can't go . . . the children . . ."

Cornie and the Colonel exchanged glances. Porphyry attempted to soothe her. "We'll take as many as we can."

"I won't leave a single child behind. . . ."

Cornie started to protest.

"Not one." She stamped a foot.

"We don't have the room," he pleaded. "Or the rations."

"They can have my rations," Sofi said.

"And mine too," I put in.

At last Cornie and the Colonel relented. Porphyry sent several of his men along with us up to the nursery to start moving the children down into the cellar.

Throughout a ceaseless hail of gunfire and shouting, punctuated by the relentless booming of the battering rams, we clattered up and down the stairway, bundling squalling infants in our arms. Trip after trip had to be made. In the end we managed to take down all twelve along with their bassinets and other supplies. Still, Sofi refused to leave the ward and almost had to be dragged off. She only consented to go when the old Italian gentleman assured her that he would stay behind and care for the animals left alive in the laboratory. He had no intention of leaving them to the Woodsmen, he said. Nor was he afraid of what they might do to him. If the castle actually fell, and no help came, he thought he might be able to convince them to let him stay on as a kind of keeper. They might see use in this menagerie of creatures, many of which they'd never seen before.

With his broken English and a gentleness buttressed by a will of iron, he was altogether convincing. In the end Sofi, sobbing, permitted herself to be led away.

Just as we got downstairs into the cellars, Magnus and his people poured in through an intersecting tunnel. One of the great steel doors in the tower had finally given way, Magnus reported, and the Woodsmen were already streaming into the castle.

33

When we reached Jones's custom-built, heavily fortified cellar room (it was more a bunker, deep within the bowels of the castle), a number of Porphyry's men were already there. They'd been there since late afternoon, stacking cartons of flour, sugar, tinned meat and vegetables in neat rows along the walls. A great deal of these foodstuffs represented what had been left behind in the cupboards and pantries by those who'd fled several days before.

In addition, a goodly supply of freeze-dried food had been laid in long before, at Jones's direction, on the "remote chance" of just such an emergency as faced us now. Undoubtedly, Porphyry had anticipated this days before and had been quietly preparing for it.

To our relief, there was also a small additional cache of guns and ammunition—hardly enough to make a stand much beyond a few days, but enough, at least, to create an illusion of might in the eyes of the invaders.

Three small primus stoves had been provided, along with a supply of kerosene. One of the stoves was already lit, a kettle for tea whistling on its coils.

When at last all of the infants had been fed their formulas and settled in neat little rows in their bassinets, Porphyry counted our number. All told, there were something like twenty-nine of us, including Porphyry's people, the few remaining house staff, the infants, the two captive Woodsmen, and, of course, the immediate family. Finally, the big solid steel-reinforced doors were double-barred and sealed shut.

And so we came to the place where we were to make our final stand. In actual time we were not there long. Two or three days at most. But, locked behind those doors and waiting, the passage of time seemed interminable.

Jones, being the fastidious man he was, had built the cellar room to his own specifications. It was said to be impenetrable. For the time being, at least, we were safe. But another threat we faced was that of daily diminishing supplies. Of foodstuffs, we had enough to last approximately four to six days. If the bad weather persisted, however, and no reinforcements got through, we would be faced with some unpleasant choices. Though no one dared say it, everyone was quite aware that bad weather in these northern Maritime Islands at a certain time of the year could set in with a vengeance and last for weeks. Unhappily, this was that time of year.

As to water and sanitation, both were well provided in the form of a swift-moving underground stream. Several feet or so beneath the floor of the cellar room, it flowed from north to south, virtually at our feet. No doubt Jones had selected the site precisely for this stream. All the water we needed for drinking and cooking we scooped up with cedar buckets lowered by rope into the icy currents. Washing and other sanitary functions were carried out downstream. Foreseeing such problems, Jones had built into his subterranean lair narrow stone catwalks. Reaching out from the main salon, they wound their way along the main stream and several of its tributaries for great distances beneath the castle.

Where this stream came out, no one knew. The only thing that could be said for certain was that eventually it left the castle grounds and flowed out from a tunnel somewhere in the surrounding forest. Realization of that was reassuring as well as a bit off-putting. On the one hand, the water tunnel provided a constant source of fresh air as well as a route of escape; on the other, it was a bit disconcerting to think that the whereabouts of the tunnel opening might be known to the Woodsmen. If so, it could only be a matter of time before the goat people would enter from the outside and quickly overrun us.

A brief word regarding the physical look of the cellar room. The word *room* is misleading. It was actually a large, cavernous space hollowed out from a huge subterranean rock formation. A grotto, I suppose, comes most readily to mind. More or less circular in shape, it had a cambered ceiling that sat on natural arches. These in turn were supported by thick limestone piers. The place was all stone. In the absence of windows, you had that closed-in, claustrophobic feeling of a dungeon, although given the height and space of the area and the steady flow of fresh air, the overall effect was not overly oppressive.

Creature comfort, however, was not the room's principal aim. That was security, which it amply provided. If one looked for amenities, this was not the place to find them.

Sleeping arrangements were informal, if not to say slapdash. There was certainly no question of privacy. We all slept together on the floor in whatever place we happened to occupy when the feeling overtook us. Along with the supplies of food and firearms, Jones had wisely provided a number of pneumatic sleeping mats that had to be inflated by mouth. It was arduous work and took several hours. But, given the alternative, which was a stone floor that seemed to be in a state of perpetual sweat, we were grateful we had them.

The infants slept in the same bassinets in which they'd been carried down from the top story. Sofi, assisted by Letitia and Madam Lobkova, attended to their every need.

Cassie, increasingly morose, retreated further into herself. She would sit for hours, peering at the floor, her fingers fidgeting idly at a button on her blouse. What she was thinking about at such times is hard to say—most probably Leander, only deepening her sense of loss. When it came time to eat, she had to be spoon-fed like a child, a duty Madam Lobkova performed with almost jealous zeal.

It didn't take long for them to find us. Even Porphyry was surprised at how quickly the Woodsmen came around, once they'd taken possession of the castle. I think he'd counted on the remoteness of our hiding place and the intricate labyrinth of tunnels leading to it to keep us out of harm's way for a time. He may have reasoned that, not seeing us about, they'd simply conclude we'd gone, then go off quietly by themselves.

Sadly, that was not the case.

On that first day we huddled together in our stone bunker, listening to the Woodsmen moving about overhead. We could hear clearly the constant tramping of their buskined feet, their cries and yelps going on in a frightening din. We heard furniture being shattered and objects ripped from the walls. Madam Lobkova caught the gist of words pouring down through the masonry. Her impression was that the Woodsmen were convinced we were still about, concealed somewhere on the premises, and they were determined to flush us out. My name, Zon, figured frequently in their exchanges.

Eventually, their search took them deep into the catacombs of the cellars. As luck would have it, while they were prowling about in the vicinity of our hiding place, one of the infants began to cry. In no time, the cries swelled to shrieks. Holding the child in her arms, Sofi tried to stifle its squalling with her hand. It only made matters worse.

Their prowling came to an abrupt halt just outside the doors, followed by a great deal of breathing and hissing, whereby we knew we'd been discovered. One or two tentative pushes sounded against the reinforced steel. This went on periodically throughout the day, while we waited, crouched behind the big steel doors, our few guns and makeshift weapons at the ready. We took turns standing guard as the others slept.

As time went on nerves frayed. Tempers grew short and the infants cried more and more. At any moment we expected the first assaults on the steel-reinforced doors, wondering what methods they would employ toward that end.

On the second day, to buttress our spirits, we told stories, we played games, we acted roles from a variety of plays we'd performed on happier occasions. We exercised, too, albeit half-heartedly, but just as a means of dispelling anxiety and the troublesome thoughts that come of being confined in tight quarters for any length of time.

At a certain point (I couldn't be certain if it was day or night), the noise outside the doors ceased and it grew suddenly quiet. It was not a reassuring quiet, but a rather ominous one. It came so abruptly that it brought us up at once, all eyes peering intently in the same direction.

Nerves strained to the breaking, we waited to hear a sound,

329

some telltale sign of what was coming next. Still nothing came. Hours of boredom alternated with the sheer torture of imagining the horrors awaiting us.

The third morning came. We washed in the stream. We lit our primus stoves and ate our breakfast—what there was of it—cold cereal and tepid tea. Sofi and Madam Lobkova attended to the infants. Magnus and several of the others went off to explore upstream.

The rest of us sat about and waited. We talked of help coming and tried to keep ourselves busy. We told amusing stories and laughed. At one point, clear out of the blue, Letitia turned to Porphyry and asked: "How old am I?" There was a certain frantic boldness about the way she'd asked it—blurted it out, actually, as though she'd been considering the question for days but was too frightened to learn the answer.

Porphyry looked at her with what I thought was pity. "Of course, you'd have no way of knowing, would you? No birth dates. No calendars. Not even mirrors by which to see yourselves age. Your brother Cornelius, for instance," Porphyry put in, almost bluntly. "He's seventy-eight years old."

Letitia's jaw dropped. She laughed aloud, then quickly seemed to cringe as though about to be struck. "Seventy-eight? Cornelius? That's impossible."

"I've seen people of that age in pictures," I said. "Cornie looks nothing like that."

"But it's true," Cornie replied. "Colonel Porphyry was kind enough to show me the birth records in the file. There's no mistake. I *am* seventy-eight."

"And you, Miss Sofi," Porphyry's owlish eyes appeared large behind the tinted lenses. "You're sixty-nine years old. Born in the year 2001, and now on the brink of your eighth decade. Miss Letitia is sixty-six. Mr. Ogden, seventy-four."

A stunned quiet had settled over the place as he called out those startling numbers. Even the low ceaseless roar of the underground stream rushing past seemed suddenly muted.

"If any of you are curious about your birth dates," Porphyry went on, "I shall be happy to show you the Institute's records. Your uncle kept them quite well up-to-date."

Sofi started to protest, then laughed instead. "I don't believe any of this." But her laugh was nervous and lacked conviction. Sick at heart, I watched her scorn and defiance crumple before my eyes. She was so lovely at that moment. Just the way you'd imagine a girl of nineteen or twenty to look—creamy skin, full lustrous hair, firm muscles, not the hint of a wrinkle or blemish visible on her features. Then something odd happened. I had an image of her stooped and aged. But it was gone in an instant, the whole thing too sad to even comprehend.

"Where's Leander?" a voice piped up. It was Cassie, alert, erect, perched like a bird on the tips of her toes. She was barefoot in a white-flowered nightshirt, her hair done up in the pleached braids she always slept in at night. Porphyry approached and stood before her nodding his head with an absurd gallantry. "So, Miss Cassie. You are better, I see."

Cassie glared up at him. "Where's Leander?"

"Cassie, dear," Madam Lobkova reproached her gently, "you mustn't talk that way to the Colonel. He's trying to help."

"Don't lie to me," she snapped again. "You know where he is. I do, too."

Porphyry's brow arched. "Do you?"

"Of course, I know. I was with him, wasn't I?"

"Where is he, then?"

"With those filthy people. The goat people. They took him," she ranted on. "It's all Jones's fault." Mercifully, she had no recollection of her time spent with the Woodsmen or of Leander's fate among them. Some wonderful trick of the mind had blocked it out. Even though she'd been present at his bedside when he died, she had erased the sad episode completely from her memory.

A shudder appeared to ripple through her like a current of electricity and then she broke down sobbing. Madam Lobkova gathered her into her arms, looking like some old fresco of a Madonna cradling the infant against her bosom. And in that instant, Cassie indeed had the look of a child. But Cassie was no child. Based on the ages of Cornie and Sofi and the others that had just been revealed, I'd made a quick computation in my mind. Cassie could be no less than fifty-seven years of age. And if it was true that Cornelius was seventy-eight, I being the next oldest could be no less than seventy-six.

When I glanced up again, Sofi was up on her feet, wavering unsteadily. You had only to look at her to know her world had been shattered. It had, after all, been based on some gauzy notion of a timeless and imperishable youth. From years of watching old films and reading magazines from the mainland, she knew what seventy years looked like in mere mortal terms. Knowledge

331

that she was nearly that age, hardly middle-aged by Jonesian standards, had now drastically altered her perception of herself. "They call Jones a visionary," she said. "What exactly was his vision? I wonder if anyone here can tell me."

There was a long silence while we looked around waiting for someone to answer. Troubled as she was, Madam Lobkova made an effort to respond. "At first," she began to explain, "it was merely to make a long and healthful life possible for everyone, regardless of their station. Instead of threescore and ten, six score and twenty. Jones wanted to give that gift to the world. You see, all these things start out with such good intentions. But as more and more advances were made, I think he looked for something more grandiose."

"But why was that wrong?" Ogden cried out, his voice full of defiance. "If what you tell us is true, his vision strikes me as good. Even noble. To push the limits of human evolution. A longer, healthier life for mankind. To see how far we might go. How much a biologically degraded human might actually be improved. Was that so evil?"

"In theory, not at all. In practice, however . . ." Porphyry's voice trailed off. "It was only after your uncle and Signor Parelli, aided and abetted by large and powerful interests, got into the picture that the noble vision upon which the System was founded turned sour. In his logs I read how your father struggled to resist that. In the end, it cost him his life."

Part 11

Resolution

". . . and though the bride was one hundred years older than the
groom, nobody would have guessed."

—Andrew Lang collection, *Sleeping Beauty*

34

"... cost him his life."

The words glanced off the damp walls and hovered in the mist-hung air above us.

Only a few days before, Colonel Porphyry had let drop the fact that Jones's slayer sat among us in Uncle Toby's study. All of our attempts to extract more information from him had proved fruitless. In the time since then, the others seemed to have forgotten. As for me, however, once the Colonel had volunteered this knowledge, I never stopped thinking about it.

On the night of Jones's murder we had all, with the exception of Sofi and Ogden, confessed to having killed Jones, if not in actual fact, then at least to having strong desires to do so.

But confessions notwithstanding, Porphyry had appeared reluctant to give any of us much credence. That may well have been a pose. He was far too clever to tip his hand. Also, he had the gift of knowing how to wait.

But if the Colonel was skeptical regarding my confession, I at least had no doubt about the part I'd played in Jones's death. Whatever Porphyry may have thought, I knew that on that fateful night I'd held a pillow over Jones's face with the specific intention of killing him. Even if he was dead at the time, I hadn't realized it until after the act and so, to my way of thinking, I was no less guilty than the actual murderer. I know I didn't imagine that pillow. I did hold it over his face. I didn't dream it. It was a fact. It was real.

The sound of scurrying and the clatter of feet on the tunnel floor outside jarred me from those uneasy thoughts.

"What is it?" Sofi's voice dropped to a whisper.

We listened, straining forward toward the door, crouched in our places, awaiting the next sound. The stream rushed past, sending up a low, ceaseless roar. It made any careful monitoring of the sounds all but impossible. Magnus, standing by the door, stooped slightly, his ear pressed to the metal. He held one hand up in the air and one behind him, as though bidding us be silent.

The rest of us remained quiet, paralyzed, listening to each other's breathing, waiting for each new telltale sound. Across from me, Letitia cringed like some cornered creature. Beads of sweat glistened on Madam Lobkova's forehead. She'd drawn Cassie closer, nearly smothering her in her huge wool shawl.

At last the scurrying sounds broke off and went away, leaving in their wake a silence that was oddly even more unnerving. During that brief pause, I was suddenly more determined than ever to confront Porphyry.

"Well, if you don't believe I did it," I almost shouted, "then who did?"

"Who did what?" the Colonel asked, somewhat distractedly. "Oh, you mean about your father." He shrugged. "I don't know."

I can still recall the look of sheer dumb astonishment on everyone around me.

"But you said you knew," Sofi said, her cheeks flaring. "The other day you said you knew the killer."

"Did I?" Porphyry affected confusion. "It seemed to me that what I said was that the killer was sitting in the study among us. Not necessarily that I knew his . . . or her . . . identity."

His explanation left us speechless.

"That means," I shot back, "that Uncle Toby and Signor Parelli, not being present in the study with us the other day, may now be eliminated as suspects?"

"From a strictly legal position, that's true," Porphyry conceded. "But as a question of simple ethics, they're probably more guilty than anyone here."

Sofi flung her hands up in the air. "In other words, we're

right back where we started, aren't we? If it wasn't Toby or Umberto, then who did this nasty business?"

"I had some idea the first night I came here." The Colonel smiled sadly. "And despite the fact that several of you were so eager to confess to the crime, obviously you couldn't all have done it."

By that time, we all felt stretched to the breaking point.

I snapped, "If you know something, stop being so damned coy and tell us."

"Well, for one thing, I know it wasn't you, Mr. Jonathan. As much as you may wish otherwise," the Colonel gently countered. "At the time you claim to have been upstairs suffocating your father with a pillow, he was already dead." He consulted his notes. "You yourself have said as much and my forensic people have now confirmed that. Nor do I doubt the fact you saw your sister Cassandra drive a dart through your father's throat. That was roughly at two-ten A.M. But just as in your case, at that time Mr. Jones was already dead several hours."

"Well, then, dammit, at what hour *did* he die?" Ogden's voice choked with exasperation.

The Colonel lay on his back, his head propped against the wall. Steepling his fingers on his chest, he gazed ceilingward. "Let me see. The last person who claims to have seen Mr. Jones alive was Miss Cassie. That was at the masked ball. She says he came attired as a monk. He wore a robe with a hood pulled over his head."

"That's correct. I saw him too," I added hotly. "Cassie handed me a note during the ball. Something about 'The Monk,' or words to that effect. She was sure it was Jones."

"How could she be so certain?" Porphyry asked.

We looked at Cassie, asleep on Madam Lobkova's lap, far removed from any of the heated talk going on about her.

No one there seemed eager to answer the Colonel's question. He waited a moment, then continued. "Do any of you know what time Miss Cassie left the dance?"

"I can tell you," Letitia said. "It was eleven forty-five, or thereabouts. She said she was tired. Not feeling well. So I walked her up to her room."

"And then left her and came back to the ball?" Porphyry inquired.

"Yes."

"You came immediately from her room back downstairs?"

"Yes." Letitia sounded strangely breathy.

He paused, giving his point time to register, then hurried on. "According to Miss Cassie's account, she went up to your father's room on two separate occasions that night. The first time at roughly midnight. That would seem to jibe with Miss Letitia's account at eleven forty-five. The second time was at two-ten A.M., at which time she claims to have killed him."

Porphyry mused aloud. "Mr. Jonathan confirms both the time and the act. But as I've said, at the time Mr. Jonathan witnessed this from his place of concealment, Mr. Jones had already been dead five hours."

"Five hours?" Ogden gasped. "That would mean that Jones was murdered sometime around nine o'clock."

"Give or take a few minutes," the Colonel acknowledged.

Sofi had a wry, puzzled look on her face. "But that makes no sense at all. That was before the ball."

"The ball didn't begin until somewhere near ten," I added. "And Jones was seen at the ball."

"Not really." Porphyry smiled. "You only saw someone you thought was him. Someone got up in a monk's robes."

"But I dressed him in those robes." Madam Lobkova quivered with indignation. "He called me up to his room to help him with his costume."

"And the hour, madam?"

"Nine o'clock. I remember because—"

Her eyes widened and her jaw dropped as she realized the implication of her words. "Now wait . . . just one moment." Her mouth worked fitfully before any sound came.

"Then who was dressed up in his costume a short time later at the ball?" The Colonel asked.

Cornie, standing off to the side, suddenly stirred. When he spoke his voice seemed strangely sad. "That was me."

"You?" several of us cried out at once.

"Forgive me. I never meant to deceive you. I saw Jones early that evening, too. Right after Wanda left him, he called to see me. He told me he was feeling tired. He asked if I would stand in for him at the ball. He meant to get an early start in the morning and felt he needed a good night's sleep. Would I just slip on his costume, put in an appearance, so to speak, so that people would think he'd attended."

"And the costume you wore?" Porphyry asked.

338

"The monk's habit. He just slipped out of the costume and I put it on."

"Had you ever worn that costume before?" Porphyry asked.

"Often," Cornie acknowledged. "It was the robe Jones always wore when he visited the Woodsmen. They associated the monk's habit with him. When I went out to the camp, I wore it too. They naturally assumed I was his emissary and permitted me to approach."

"So that was you I saw there—that night in the camp . . . that night they almost buried me alive." I could barely control my anger.

"Yes, Johnnie. I'm afraid it was." Cornie's shoulders drooped. "I'd gone to the camp to see if I couldn't get Leander out. Once there, I learned that Cassie had somehow managed to slip away from the castle and was being held there, too. Then on top of that, you showed up, apparently coming after Cassie. You were two more than I'd bargained for."

Rapt, we listened as the tale of our long-predestined fates continued to unfold. Cornie's voice, quiet and oddly inexpressive, sounded disembodied in the high vacant grotto. At one point it seemed to come from somewhere above, as though he were speaking down to us from some great height.

"Leander was to be the next King of the Wood," he went on. "But he'd been badly traumatized by the move out there, unable to function adequately as a breeder. I think he was just too frightened. They thought Toby had fobbed off a defective king on them. The Woodsmen felt cheated. Then, Johnnie, you came along. You dropped in like something from heaven. An answer to the Woodsmen's prayers. Leander, like all defective breeders, was administered a lethal dose of sedatives and, immediately, was replaced by you as the next King of the Wood."

New noises sounded from outside the doors, noises we couldn't quite recognize. Several times we heard grunting, then scraping and bumping sounds, as though something heavy was being maneuvered into place. Several of the infants in their bassinets had woken, their moans and whimpering barely audible above the roar of the stream.

"Go on," I said to Cornie, disregarding the disturbances, eager to hear it all to the end. "Why did you deceive us all these years? Why did you play dumb?"

Cornie seemed truly distraught at the part he'd been forced to play in the deception. "The role of a mute. A simpleminded fool. You all grew up thinking that." He looked around at us woefully. "That was Jones's idea. Just a pose. Jones never trusted Uncle Toby or Parelli. . . ."

"With good reason," Madam Lobkova fumed.

"As time passed he grew more suspicious of them. When he first brought me to Fraze as a child, I was told to act as a mute and a fool. Because of that I could move freely between Toby and Parelli, and they would speak freely around me. With my special status, Jones granted me privileges not granted the rest of you, one of these being free run of the castle. Another being permission to leave the grounds at any time so that I might serve as liaison between the castle and the Woodsmen. I had to learn to act as a fool. The hardest part was learning never to speak."

Cornie paused, his eyes wandering to the guttering candle. "Those drawings I made . . . they were not very good."

"Not as art," Porphyry conceded. "But as information, they were revealing. If nothing else, they clearly showed one figure throttling another."

"And the one doing the throttling is dressed in a monk's habit," I added.

"Yes." Cornie nodded.

Porphyry tugged at his chin several times. "I take it that had something to do with your brother Leander."

Cornie gave a weary nod.

"You planned with Leander his escape, didn't you?" Porphyry continued. "That night of the ball you left open one of the tower doors. Then you unlocked his cell door and made yourself scarce."

Cornie could barely suppress his grief. "Right on all counts, Colonel. I had no intention of turning Leander over to the Woodsmen, as I had all the others. The plan was for Leander to flee the castle through the tower door. But a few hours later Jones was discovered dead in his bed. Naturally, I assumed Leander was responsible. At that point, he had more reason than anyone to do it."

"So you drew those little pictures of yourself in a monk's habit to deflect guilt from Leander," Porphyry said. "And to incriminate yourself."

Cornie nodded. "I could better withstand the consequences of that than poor Andy."

"And do you still believe that Leander killed your father?" Porphyry persisted.

340

Cornie seemed surprised by the question, as though the answer to it was so glaringly obvious. "Of course he killed him. He had the motive and the opportunity. And I'm responsible for having made it possible."

"Leander wouldn't have hurt a fly," Sofi shot back. "Little less drive a dart through someone's throat."

Ignoring her, Porphyry pressed Cornelius harder. "How do you think your father died?" he asked.

The question puzzled Cornie. "If the murder weapon, as you say, wasn't the dart, then I guess I don't know."

"It couldn't have been with a dart," I said. "It was Cassie who used the dart and Jones was dead by that time."

"Mr. Jones's windpipe was crushed," the Colonel remarked with uncharacteristic bluntness.

There was an uneasy silence as we tried to absorb the significance of that. Ogden was the first to speak, musing aloud to himself.

"Leander was a strong boy. Jones was quite frail. It's certainly possible he strangled him."

Porphyry shot him a shrewd grin. "No one said a word about strangulation. I merely said his windpipe was crushed. But you're quite right, Mr. Ogden. He was garroted."

"A rope." Letitia shuddered. "How awful."

"Nor did anyone say anything about a rope." Porphyry smiled again. "Something softer. Less abrasive." He turned back to Cornie. "You last saw your father when?"

"Shortly after nine that evening," Cornie replied.

"Approximately the time he died."

"When I left him, he was still alive."

"And it was just before then," the Colonel hurried on, "that you donned his costume and prepared to take his place at the masked ball?"

"Yes . . ." Cornie's voice was a dry rattle. "That's how it was."

"And you believe your brother Leander stole down from the tower, came to Mr. Jones's room shortly thereafter, and killed him?"

Cornie shifted his weight from one foot to the other. "If you say he died sometime between nine and ten, it would have to be that way. I saw Wanda leave the room shortly past nine. I entered just after. And when I left Jones was still alive."

"Then, after supposedly murdering his father," Porphyry's

341

eyes narrowed to slits, "Leander was to steal out the tower door and fly to freedom."

"That was the plan we worked out," Cornie confirmed. "Not to kill Jones, but to flee. Make a run for the mainland. Unfortunately, Leander was grabbed by the Woodsmen lurking just outside the tower door."

Porphyry's eyes closed as though he were visualizing the scene. "There was a struggle. We found all the signs of it. But what I don't understand is what brought the Woodsmen to the castle that night at the very hour Leander stepped out. Since they were there waiting for him, someone had to have informed them."

Ogden's back stiffened. He raised both hands as if fending off an attack. "If you're thinking it was me, you're dead wrong."

Staring hard at Ogden, Colonel Porphyry appeared unmoved. "I wasn't thinking anything of the sort, but I must say, of all your brothers and sisters, you had the best reason for wanting Leander out of the way."

Ogden stood there, making little puffing sounds with his lips.

Porphyry went on. "Going through Mr. Jones's papers, I came across the notes he took during his last interview with you."

Ogden breathed a bit harder.

"He told you that you'd been a disappointment . . ." The Colonel began to weave his way tactfully through the highly damaging report. "You were told that you could never hope to become your father's successor. You'd always taken it for granted that it was going to be you."

Ogden looked about at us in the gloomy light, half defiant, half appealing for understanding. "It should have been me. I'd worked harder than all the others." He flung a rude gesture out at the rest of us. "I did more . . . more than anyone. I upheld the principles of the System. None of them had the character to do the same." His eyes glowed with self-vindication. "And then the old fool told me he had someone else in mind to succeed him. Imagine. Just like that. As if all my efforts counted for nothing."

"And you thought that someone was your brother Leander?"

"I didn't think. I knew," Ogden shot back. "Jones had all but assured him of that at their last interview. Leander told me himself. It was unfair."

For a moment I was sure he was on the verge of tears. I

342

looked away, too embarrassed to watch. I noticed the others did too. But not Porphyry.

"When in reality," he went on doggedly, "what your brother Leander had been chosen for was just to be another sacrifice to the Woodsmen."

Ogden's shoulders sagged. He seemed suddenly very tired. "I didn't set out to kill my father. It's just not true. I only meant to talk with him. To present my side of the matter. I thought if I could just go up there and speak with him I could change his mind."

Porphyry's brow cocked. "Are you now saying, Mr. Ogden, that you too went upstairs that night?"

"Just to talk." Ogden's head bobbed on his shoulders. "Just to talk. That's all."

"And did you find his room?"

"No. I got upstairs, but never got beyond the stairwell."

"You're saying you lost your nerve?" the Colonel pressed harder.

Flushed with embarrassment, Ogden conceded the point with a weary shrug.

Porphyry consulted his note pad. "And when did all of this take place?"

"Twelve-thirty, or thereabouts."

"And when did you leave the stairwell?"

"About one A.M."

"It was closer to one-twenty," I said, and watched the Colonel's troubled gaze roll slowly around toward me.

"And how would you know, may I ask, Mr. Jonathan?"

"Because I was awake then and thinking about going upstairs too."

"He's a liar," Ogden shouted. "He's always been a liar. He has good cause to lie."

The Colonel appeared visibly annoyed by the outbreak.

"You may as well tell about the chloroform," I said to Ogden.

Again Porphyry's brow cocked. "Chloroform? Oh ho. You hadn't said anything about chloroform, Mr. Ogden."

Another silence followed as all eyes fell on Ogden.

"Go ahead, Oggie," Sofi prompted him, not unkindly. "You keep chloroform around."

"It's nothing . . . nothing at all." Ogden waved a dismissive hand. "And since, as you say, Jones was dead by the time I got up there, it really doesn't matter."

343

"True," the Colonel countered. "But it does say something about intent."

Ogden flung his hands up in exasperation. "All right. So I intended to use the chloroform. It crossed my mind. I'll admit it. Why not? I'm no different from any of these others. I also wanted to see an end to Jones. Why shouldn't I say it?"

"And this chloroform—" Porphyry persisted.

"I use chloroform to mount my specimens. I intended to saturate a handkerchief with it, then hold it over his face. Just for a few seconds. Just to scare him a bit."

He looked around at us, appealing. "Really . . . Honestly. That's all it was. He scared me, damn him." He laughed nervously. "I was so tired of being scared all the time."

Porphyry listened impassively.

"But I never reached his room," Ogden went on. "So what difference does it make anyway? I'm not guilty of anything."

"Nothing much," the Colonel muttered finally, and turned his back on him. "And you, Mr. Jonathan. That's when you appeared on the scene?"

"Right. One-twenty. When Ogden came back downstairs."

"But why didn't you say anything the other night in the library when we discussed all this?"

"Because I thought it was Ogden's place to speak, not mine."

"And now he's spoken."

I nodded uneasily.

"You saw him come down and you decided you'd better go up and have a look around for yourself?"

"I felt it was odd, his being there at that hour."

"As odd, at least, as your being out in the hallway at that same hour. But there was, of course, the ball that evening. You'd come in late, and a bit worse for the wine, if I may say." The Colonel's head fell sharply to the side so that he seemed to look at me from beneath his brows. "What did you find up there, may I ask?"

"I found Jones in his bed. I thought he was sleeping."

"And in that half hour between Mr. Ogden's departure and Miss Cassie's arrival . . ."

"I held the pillow over his face." I was shocked at how easily it fell from my lips.

"For how long did you hold the pillow in that position?" Porphyry asked. "Do you remember?"

344

Somewhere behind me Lettie had begun to weep, stifling her sobs in a wad of tissue.

"Somewhere between three to five minutes," I said.

"When did you realize he was already dead?"

"When it occurred to me he never struggled. I'd thought he was sleeping."

Once again, Porphyry's eyes dropped to his notes. "And it was at that point, a half hour later to be precise, that you heard your sister Cassie coming down the hallway. It was then you ducked into the big wardrobe outside your father's bedroom."

"Yes."

"And it was from that vantage point you saw Miss Cassie plunge the dart into Mr. Jones's throat?"

I gazed across at Cassie. Still asleep in Madam Lobkova's arms, she looked angelic, like an infant at her mother's breast. "Yes."

"And then she left?"

"Yes."

"You didn't linger much longer either?"

"I left immediately."

Porphyry's gaze wandered back to the doors where Magnus crouched, listening to the faint, ceaseless stirrings that came from just beyond. All about us was a tight sense of breathlessness, of people watching the door with one eye and Porphyry with the other. Only the Colonel seemed unfazed, vividly focused on the problem at hand. He turned back to Cornie.

"Mr. Cornelius, did it occur to you that you may have been indirectly responsible for the Woodsmen's discovering that your brother was going to make a break for freedom that night?"

Cornie frowned. He seemed dismayed at the suggestion. "I'm afraid I don't quite follow."

"Perfectly understandable," Porphyry hastened to agree. "But you did, in fact, engineer your brother's escape, and then made the unfortunate mistake of telling another person your plan for doing that."

Cornie's head swung slowly from side to side in silent denial. "I told no one."

"You had to. It's the only way word could have gotten out to the Woodsmen."

"I never," Cornie protested. "How could I tell anyone anything without revealing the fact that I could speak?"

A sly smile flickered at the edges of the Colonel's eyes. "You didn't have to speak. These spoke eloquently enough for you."

Porphyry extracted from inside his jacket three small white sheets of notepaper, then pushed them toward Cornie.

We surged around him, staring down at the three little sketches spread out on the ground before him. Executed in faint, wavering lines much like the one we'd seen several days before in the dining hall, the first depicted a small, boyish figure unlocking a dungeon door and stealing out. The next showed the same figure descending a stair, recognizable at once as the stone stair winding down from the tower dungeon. The third and last had the little stick figure slipping stealthily from the tower door to the outside. Each figure, in size and shape, without the aid of distinct features, managed to clearly suggest Leander.

Cornie gazed for a pained moment at the drawings. "Lettie," he murmured at last, his lips barely uttering the name.

"Where did you get those drawings?" A sharp, rasping voice sounded just behind me.

We all turned to face the speaker, but it was Porphyry who answered the question. "You must forgive me, Miss Letitia." He spoke in that quietly disarming voice he seemed able to summon whenever the occasion demanded. "I took the liberty of having your room searched."

Letitia had been standing perhaps a foot or two from me. Perhaps it was my imagination, but the person I was looking at then had become someone else entirely. She bore no resemblance to anyone I knew. Certainly not the sister I'd grown up with. It was eerie. More than that, it was frightening. Her carriage, rigid, erect as a shaft, every muscle in her body coiled, ready to spring.

"You had no right to search my room," she said.

Porphyry took the sudden force of her bearing head-on. "If it's of any consolation, Miss Letitia, I had *all* of your rooms searched. That's how I knew about these very revealing little sketches of Mr. Cornelius's. You asked him to draw them, didn't you?"

She didn't answer. She merely stood there, vibrating with rage.

"You can tell him, Lettie," Cornie spoke softly. "It's all right. She came to me the evening of that same day Leander vanished."

"Shut up, Cornie." Letitia's voice was a thin hiss.

"It's true, Lettie. There's no sense trying to hide it. He knows." Cornie turned back to the Colonel. "She came to me distraught. In tears about Leander." Cornie's voice trembled with the awful recollection. "She was in a terrible state. I wanted to reassure her. I wanted to tell her that it was going to be all right. That I had a plan to save Leander. But, of course, I wasn't free to speak then. I'd always sketched little pictures for her, for all of them when they were children. And so, just as in the past, I drew pictures of what I had in mind. If I'd known—suspected for one minute—that those little scribblings would cost Leander his life . . ." He glanced away as though he couldn't bear to face us anymore. "And so, after you'd seen those pictures, Lettie, you went and told Parelli, didn't you?"

"Shut up," Lettie lashed out, then quickly pulled back, taking a more conciliatory tack. "Not now, Cornie. Not here. We can work it out later."

"Keep going, Cornelius. Tell it all. Let it rip," I said.

"But we've all known this for ages," Ogden fairly whined. "Lettie and Parelli have been going at it for years."

I thought Letitia would tear his ears off, but instead she turned on Sofi. "You couldn't bear it, could you? Just for once . . . a man in the house who actually preferred me."

For the merest second, I was sure I saw the old mean glint flash in Sofi's eyes. But it passed quickly. What I saw there now instead was something verging on pity.

"Oh, Lettie, dear—you don't really believe . . ."

"He loved me," Letitia lashed back. "He told me that. Just the other day he said . . ." Her voice rang with a kind of vindication. "That's what he said. I swear it."

I could see what had happened. It was all so clear. Parelli had conscripted her. She'd become a spy for him. Sensing her hunger for love, he'd shrewdly acted the part of her lover. In return, she monitored all of our comings and goings, our fears, our hopes, reporting them back to him almost as soon as they'd been uttered. Then that night, eager to demonstrate her loyalty, she'd told him about the plan to free Leander, whereupon Parelli, determined to protect the terms of the Covenant, turned right around and told the Woodsmen. When Leander stepped out the tower door that evening, they were there, waiting for him.

"Then, I take it, the idea of disposing of Mr. Jones began with Parelli. Am I right about that, madam?" the Colonel asked.

Madam Lobkova's gray head nodded wearily. "The irony of it is that it was all so unnecessary."

"Unnecessary?"

"Killing him." She shook her head again and stared at the ground. "You see, he was dying. His physicians in Geneva had told him, just before he came here. It was only a matter of time. He'd lived nearly a hundred and fifty years. He could no longer rely on the dismutase, or the transfusions and hormones and whatnot. At that advanced age, the regimen simply ceases to have much effect; the body wears down, too worn to regenerate itself. That night of the masquerade he told me it could be any time. A few weeks at the most. He wanted to make things right. He was on the verge of signing all of his rights in TRX5 over to a philanthropic organization called the World Federation of Churches."

"To just give it away?" Porphyry asked. "Like that?"

"That's right."

Porphyry tugged at his chin. "All the more reason then why Parelli and Mr. Tobias had to act fast."

Madam Lobkova nodded. "They couldn't afford to let him leave Fraze this time. They had to get at him before he could do something . . . foolish."

"From outside came a new and wholly different sound, as if something heavy was being alternately rolled and dragged and scraped across the floor.

"Battering rams," Magnus hissed. "They're going to try to batter the doors down."

Magnus, a highly steady man, had begun to betray signs of unease. Without actually saying anything, his eyes and facial movements were clearly urging the Colonel to leave at once.

But Porphyry was in no hurry to go. He was like a dog clinging to a meaty bone. Now that he had it in his jaws, he was not quite ready to give it up. He turned back to Letitia.

"Tell me, Miss Letitia, did Signor Parelli at any time suggest to you that were your father out of the way, whatever obstacles lay between the two of you would quickly disappear?"

348

"Never. He would never." There was no timidity to her now. No indecisiveness. Nothing of the sad, shrinking, spinsterish lady we'd known all of our lives. At last, after years of mute obedience, Lettie had found her own voice and clearly seemed to enjoy using it. "He didn't care for my father and my father didn't care for him. That was no secret. And, of course, any kind of relationship between us, so long as Jones was alive, was out of the question. But, I can assure you, Umberto—Signor Parelli—never asked me to do anything. Least of all kill my father. That was my idea," she said defiantly. "Entirely."

It struck me that the pace of the Colonel's questions had quickened, as if he felt he were now racing the clock.

"If I may pursue this a moment more, Miss Letitia."

"All due respects, sir," Magnus interrupted. "Hadn't we better . . ."

Something flared in the Colonel's eyes and Magnus quickly backed off.

"Regarding your audience with Mr. Jones," Porphyry went on. "You said he spoke glowingly of your progress over the past year."

"He was lying," Lettie acknowledged. "He always flattered you. That was his peculiar treachery. He could praise you to your face one moment and, in the next, sign your death warrant. It was only a matter of time before he'd send me off to the Woodsmen."

"You don't know that for a fact," Porphyry chided.

"Of course I do. Parelli told me . . ."

The moment she'd said it, she knew she'd blundered. You could see in her face the panicky search for some way to retrieve the words.

"Ah." Porphyry leaned forward, about to pursue the question.

"Stop it. Leave her alone." Madam Lobkova rose suddenly, stumbling to her feet, moving her great girth swiftly to Lettie's side. "She had nothing to do with it. It was me. I did it. I went to his room."

Porphyry looked genuinely hurt. "But, madam, you just told me Mr. Jones called you there at nine o'clock to help with his costume."

"He did, but not to help with his costume."

Porphyry sighed. "You make it so difficult for me. This penchant you all seem to have for lying in order to protect each other."

349

"Of course I lied." Madam Lobkova glowered. "You think I could sit by any longer . . . knowing what I knew . . ."

"And that was?" Porphyry demanded.

"The fate of these children . . . my children." She waded forward as though she were about to strike him. "Well, don't look at me like that. They may as well have been mine. They never had a mother of their own. I came the closest to being that. I raised them. When they were sick, I nursed them. When they bruised themselves, I patched them up. I was as good as their mother. Year after year, I stood by mute, uncomplaining, helping them grow, only to see my babies snatched from me, told they were going off to some great honor, when, in fact, I knew they were going off to that horror awaiting them out there in the forest." She hurried on, her voice quavering with anger. "God forgive me. I'd looked away for so long. Always taking the long view, like Jones, that in pursuit of truth there was no room for sentiment. Nothing could be allowed to compromise the work of nearly a century."

She looked around at us, as though appealing for help. "I believed in the System more deeply than anyone. I believed from the beginning when the goals were clear and personal gain had not become the sole motivation. But by then Toby and Parelli and that vile creature Fabian had gotten their hands on things. . . ."

"Surely you're not saying they'd gotten control of Mr. Jones's empire?" Porphyry looked incredulous.

"No. Thank heavens, Jones still controlled that. One hundred percent. The plants. The laboratories. The Humanus Institute. The Foundation. A dozen accounts in as many banking institutions. And, of course, the formula. But of late he'd grown weary of all the quarreling. All the intrigue and duplicity. He was concerned about TRX5, who would succeed him as the head of the Foundation, and who would oversee the completion of his work. Clearly, he didn't trust his brother or Parelli to carry out his wishes. He had little faith in Fabian, whom he suspected had been compromised by the big interests. So, naturally, he chose Cornie, the closest of his children to him. Ogden, you were never even in the running." She looked at him with pity, then continued. "Jones was tired by then and afraid he could resist them no longer. He was ailing and simply too sick to continue fighting them off. That night, with me as witness, he signed the document willing all of his rights in TRX5 to the World Federation of Churches."

"And then he asked you to end his life for him," Porphyry said.

A tear slid down her cheek, then dangled absurdly from the cleft in her chin. She swept it aside as you would a fly and continued. "It was only a matter of days, a few weeks, perhaps, before nature would take its course, but in the end I agreed with Jones. We couldn't afford to wait. Toby and Parelli were bearing down hard. We concluded it had to be done at once. Jones requested only one thing. He hated violence and wanted it to appear that he'd died peacefully in his sleep— in his own bed, of natural causes. He wouldn't take a pill since that could be detected. He himself suggested strangulation with a soft cloth that would leave no ligature marks. The murder weapon was a red silk scarf. One of those scarves Toby uses in his magic shows." Her breathing came faster as her story unfolded.

"It was quite simple, actually. Like a baby being put to sleep. He slipped into his bed. I tied the scarf 'round his neck. He helped me knot it and then I pulled gently, gradually tightening it until he expired. He was quite peaceful throughout. He was at rest, knowing that his work of nearly twelve decades was going to the world, free to all who wanted it. It was his gift. I put him to sleep. He was ever so grateful."

"And when did this take place?" Porphyry inquired.

"Directly after Cornie left him."

"You waited up there?"

"Yes," she admitted wearily. "We arranged it together, Jones and I. That's why Cornie was sent away. Down to the ball. That was just a ploy to keep him from interfering. I waited in the room next door until he left."

Finished at last, she folded her hands across her ample chest and sighed with visible relief. Cassie woke at that moment and stared about questioningly.

Cornie had moved up beside Madam Lobkova and placed a hand on her shoulder. In turn, she placed her stubby hand atop his. There was great peace between them. Still gazing at Porphyry, relief showed in her eyes. "I still have the scarf if you need it for evidence."

The Colonel, grim up until then, nodded in his most engaging way. I have no idea what was going on in his mind at that moment.

351

During those last seconds I had an impression of Lettie nearby—not of Lettie herself, but rather a vague drifting shape moving ceaselessly in and out of focus. One moment it was there, the next it was gone, only to reappear at some other point in the area, a restless, pacing form.

I scarcely paid attention. I was too busy following Porphyry's line of questioning, trying to keep up with the endless zigs and zags.

Then there was that moment when Porphyry and Letitia came together. She'd stopped moving and he'd stopped talking. A strangely protracted moment followed, during which time I realized he was staring at her, or was it gaping, over a space of some twenty feet.

In the next moment, he lunged. There was a gasp as a wall of people fell away before his hurtling outstretched figure, nearly horizontal to the ground. The wall opened and there was Letitia on the stone floor, the Colonel fused to her, the two of them grappling and heaving. Porphyry's fingers were halfway down her throat.

I was aware of people rushing, pushing forward past me, and the harsh phlegmy sound of Letitia gagging. A moment later the Colonel, somewhat breathlessly, wobbled to his feet. He was wiping blood from his hands with a handkerchief where she'd bitten him. Between the thumb and index finger of his hand, he held what appeared to be a small blue-white spansule. It lay damp in his palm where he rolled it around and around in the dim light, leaving streaks of blood and a jagged blue trail of dye as it did so.

Letitia lay sprawled on the ground on her back, coughing and sputtering violently.

"You'd better let me have the rest of those tablets, Miss Letitia," Porphyry said, "before you really hurt yourself."

He moved to her side and in one swift, not ungentle, motion yanked her to her feet. "Come now," he said. "Let's be civil about this." He extended a waiting hand out before her.

She regarded his palm as though it were something unwholesome. For a moment I thought she was about to spit into it. But she didn't. Instead, she thrust a hand into her skirt pocket, rummaged about there a moment, then jerked out a small white box and nearly flung it into his outstretched palm.

"Thank you," he said, executing a quick, almost courtly bow.

The crisis past, Madam Lobkova rushed to Letitia. "Dear God, Lettie. That was foolish. What on earth possessed you—"

But her question was interrupted by a succession of earsplitting cracks at the door. They came in flurried bursts, three or four at a time. The noise alone was terrifying, but made all the more so as it rolled all about and down below us through those subterranean caverns.

Suddenly, all of the infants were yowling. Sofi was up at once, darting from one bassinet to the next. We were all on our feet, eyes riveted on the Colonel, waiting to follow his lead.

Three more sharp reports ricocheted off the doors, then continued without pause for a minute. By then, the din had become hellish.

There was another crack, this one louder than anything that had gone before. I think it was that last blow that finally jolted the Colonel into action.

"It appears," he said, almost wistfully, "that it's time for us to leave."

The crash of the battering ram that followed more than confirmed the wisdom of that decision.

When Porphyry spoke next, his voice was very calm. "May I ask each of you to pick up your mattress and carry it over to the edge of the stream. When you've done that, come back and gather your possessions. Take only what is necessary, light and portable. A few tins of food. Enough to last a few days."

He was about to go on but he was silenced by another fusillade of sharp cracks. When they stopped, he quickly resumed.

"What about water?" Ogden asked.

"There'll be plenty of water in the forest. Take something warm. Only one item. A jacket or a sweater. It will be cold out there when the sun goes down."

"What about the babies?" Sofi asked. She cradled one in her arms. The look of frightened anger on her face made her more beautiful than ever. "I won't leave without them."

"I had no intention of asking you to." The Colonel was peeved that she'd even suggested it. "Each of you will take a child on your pneumatics."

"I can manage two," Ogden offered.

"So can I," I quickly added.

Shortly, we were lifting squirming, squalling infants from the bassinets.

"Wrap them warmly," Porphyry called out above the pummeling noises at the doors. "We may be living outdoors for several days."

While we went about the business of bundling babies, Magnus and his men grouped in a wide semicircle fifty or so feet around us. They knelt, rifles at the ready, facing the straining doors, Magnus nervously glancing back to check our progress, almost willing us to be gone.

Despite the barely controlled sense of fright and pressure under which we worked, the entire loading process took just a little under a half hour.

Shortly, eighteen inflatables stood lined up at the stream's edge, a water caravan of food, odd bits of clothing, and whatever light additional oddments we had room for.

You had to give Jones credit. The inflatables were a stroke of genius. I had thought of them only as beds. Looking beyond that, he saw them as a means of escape in the event that should become necessary. Now, it was clearly necessary.

The last to be boarded were the infants. We carried them down to the water wrapped in their blankets and lashed them by means of our belts to the rubber eyeloops on the rafts.

The noise behind us was deafening. It actually hurt your head. There was no longer any pause between impacts so that the two rams working together produced the illusion of a single unbroken volley. The need to flee that noise was even greater than the need to get away from whatever unimaginable horrors the goat people might have in store for us.

Colonel Porphyry, unfazed by the din, busied himself checking the cargo lashings on each raft and making certain everything was secure.

At last, it seemed we were ready. It's hard to recall the excitement and confusion, the mixed emotions of those final moments at Fraze. Everything remains something of a blur in my memory. We were going. Leaving the only home we'd ever known (whatever shortcomings it may have had as a home), I felt strangely torn.

At a certain point, toward the very end, Magnus came down. Kneeling beside Porphyry, the sling of his rifle straining against his chest, he seemed to rattle off a barrage of final details. Staring at the ground, the Colonel gnawed at his lip, mostly nodding his approval.

The plan, as I understood it, was for us to set out directly.

354

Magnus and his people would remain briefly behind as a rear guard. Three or four rafts were kept back, separate from the main train, giving us some lead time before the Woodsmen demolished the doors and resumed the chase. Well before that, Magnus and his men were to make their break in the remaining rafts and meet us at a prearranged rendezvous outside the water tunnels.

I have no idea what words Magnus and the Colonel exchanged in those final moments. I'm reasonably certain it had something to do with timing and how much longer those so-called impregnable reinforced doors might reasonably be expected to hold the Woodsmen at bay.

Then Magnus was on his feet again, scurrying back to take his place within the crescent of riflemen. Porphyry moved down to the bank of the stream where we waited with our inflatables, bouncing and scraping at the shallow streambed. They had to be held in order to keep them from surging wildly out into the rushing current unattended.

The Colonel sensed our apprehension. He gathered us around him while the doors behind us thundered and the stream roared. With his stubby, slightly crooked finger, he pointed us downstream as if to say "That's the way."

"The tunnel," he shouted above the din, "runs for a mile. The stream fetches up in the forest to the south." His voice was lost in the general uproar. In the end it came down to reading his lips and catching a stray phrase here and there.

It was general knowledge that over the past several days he'd sent Magnus and a few of his people on exploratory trips through the tunnels. The object of such expeditions, we now understood, was to determine the navigability of the stream and to find the place where it came out in the forest. The key question looming large in our minds, of course, was if we knew the place, wouldn't the Woodsmen know it as well?

The Colonel could certainly read the question on our faces. I think at that point, with all of his failed promises of rescue parties and imminent reinforcements, he was grateful that no one pressed him for an answer.

"I'll see you all on the outside." He spread his arms and smiled. It was a comfort, that smile, just then—shy, bemused and oddly funny, given the situation.

Cassie, standing nearby, stared up at him in her shrewd, skeptical way. "But then where do we go?" she asked.

The sheer baldness of the question gave the poor fellow his

355

first laugh for some days. He couldn't resist a pat on the top of her head. "Into the world, Miss Cassie. Hold tight. You're about to be launched."

The words sound a bit inflated now, but at the time he spoke them, shouting at the top of his lungs to be heard, I recall experiencing a shock or jolt of something. Perhaps it was just adrenaline. After all, what did lie in store for us at the end of the tunnel? The world. It was out there awaiting us with all of its peril and risk. Woodsmen. Captivity. Enforced slavery. Possible death. Naturally, there was fear. But there was something else, too. Hope, I think it was. In all of my—what was it—nearly eighty years of life, I'd experienced many things. Hope was not one of them. Never before had I felt such a keen, pure, rapturous thing. The sense of being on the verge of something. Something new, momentous. I felt it rise from somewhere at the pit of my stomach, then well upward to where it lodged in my throat. It broke finally from my lips as something halfway between a shout and a laugh. Only Ogden, standing nearby ankle-deep in water, heard it. He'd been wrestling one of the inflatables to keep it from floating off and my sudden burst of laughter made him flinch. He glowered at me, which made me laugh all the harder.

Sofi laughed, too. I think she must have felt something of the same thing. Like me, she couldn't articulate it. All she could do was laugh.

Porphyry seemed baffled by our giddiness. He no doubt put it down to nerves or youthful foolishness. Although by then he must have surely recognized a certain irony in the fact that, appearances notwithstanding, we were hardly youths. In fact, all of us, including Cassie, were older than the Colonel himself, whom I'd reckoned to be roughly in his mid-fifties.

At last the moment for departure came. The rafts slid, dipped and half foundered as we struggled to board them without swamping them. The trick was to find the exact point in the raft where the distribution of weight between infants, cargo and ourselves produced maximum stability. It was no easy matter.

Finally, everything was secure. Eighteen rafts lined up at the stream's edge bobbed in the water, straining to break free.

"When you reach the end of the tunnel," Porphyry shouted through cupped hands, "you'll be in a lake. Pull your inflatables up on the bank and wait for the others. Under no circumstances are you to go off by yourselves. Stay together until we can reassemble."

A barrage of last-minute instructions had come to his mind, but at last even he realized the danger of delaying any longer.

Behind us, the hullabaloo of rams battering the doors was ungodly. The infants squalled, the stream roared. It was at that moment, just as the big steel doors seemed to groan and sag inward on their hinges, that Colonel Porphyry raised a stiff right arm, then brought it down with a swift, chopping motion, pointing us forward.

We were off.

Porphyry was in the lead raft. Improbably attired in his homburg and business suit, with almost laughable formality, he used his hands to paddle out to midstream. He had two infants with him and his mattress shimmied unsteadily. At one point, I held my breath, certain he was about to capsize even before we got under way.

When at last the current caught him, the mattress righted itself and turned into the stream with the slow, stately motion of a clock's dial. For a moment it appeared to tip sideways, then rose again like a breeching whale and lunged off into the roaring dark.

Cornelius followed with Sofi, then Ogden coming up behind. Given the events of a few moments before, there were grave misgivings about entrusting Lettie to a raft by herself. Madam Lobkova wouldn't hear of it, and so the two of them went catapulting off on a mattress that sat unnervingly low in the water. Needless to say, there was no room for infants on that raft.

I was to follow. My instructions, whispered hastily to me by Porphyry, were to stay as close behind them as I could, in the event Letitia "attempted something foolish." Cassie came with me, along with one infant.

The flight through the tunnel itself was fast. Though it was a journey of only a mile, it seemed over before it had begun and yet, as is said of drowning, my whole life seemed to pass before me during that period.

The physical experience of it is now just a blur. All I recall is that we bucketed through the dark tunnel at very great speed. The limestone walls on either side sped past and the ceiling was so low that you had to lie on your stomach with your head down,

357

at risk of skinning yourself badly. Cassie lay trembling under one arm with the infant whimpering softly under the other.

There was nothing to do. We were at the whim of the stream. Where we were going and how fast we got there was entirely up to the power of the water. We had only to hold tight to our rafts and our few possessions, and just go with it.

There was only one way to go and the tunnel was so narrow that the inflatables steered themselves. By merely stretching your arms, you could reach out and touch either wall of the tunnel and so keep the nose of the mattress pointing directly downstream. The tunnel was dark as pitch, so you couldn't see the raft in front of you or behind. Yet somehow you could feel them there, nearby, each occupant isolated in the dark, groping his or her way, waging a solitary battle against doubt and failing courage.

The water was not deep, possibly four feet at its deepest point, so you couldn't drown. It was very cold, however, fed by subterranean streams, and if you happened to tip in a current that swift, your chance of righting the mattress was slim. Moreover, prolonged exposure to waters of that temperature would be fatal. As for the infants, there was no chance they could survive a spill.

At one point it grew so dark you couldn't see the water, only the foam of it boiling beneath you as you heaved and shuttled your bumpy way along. The roar of it in your ears and head was harrowing. Lying on my belly with nothing but that slim band of rubber between myself and the stream, I could feel the current's immense power as if it were a part of me. We were no more than a sliver of something skimming perilously along atop it. There was no question of control. Once having committed yourself to it, there was no way of stopping, or going back. I merely lay there, holding tight, my arms spread-eagled over my two passengers, and praying that the stream would be kind to us.

Knowledge that there were inflatables not far ahead or behind us was hardly a comfort. To all intents and purposes, you were alone. You had only yourself from which to seek assurances and extort hope. Even Cassie and the tiny, squirming tot, only inches from me, seemed light-years away.

Then, suddenly, there was the pale arc of light up ahead. It glowed with an eerie luminosity, like dirty pewter. I'd never seen anything so startling, so otherworldly, before. And yet, on the face of it, it was nothing but a half-moon of grayish light to which we were rushing.

The spray of water fanning backward off our bows was an icy-cold shower, so exhilarating it made you want to shout. And I did shout, at the top of my lungs—a hoarse, savage, unending shriek. I was soaking wet and the roar of the water was in my head, all the while the frail slip of rubber that bore us along went bucketing toward the light.

The light was blinding. When it washed over me I felt its warmth at once. Violet discs danced before my eyes. Ahead of me I heard cries, shouts, splashing noises, shrieks and gruff voices barking commands. Still dazzled by the glare, I couldn't make head or tail of what was going on.

When my eyes finally adjusted, I saw that we had come out onto a fairly good-sized pond. The mattresses, all eighteen of them, had jammed up at the mouth of the tunnel, bouncing into and careening off of each other. Most of the mattresses still carried passengers; some had already managed to flounder up on shore. The infants squealed, full of healthy indignation for the bouncing about they'd taken.

Then I saw Porphyry. He was on the bank, standing alongside his beached inflatable, ankle-deep in water, soaking wet trousers rolled up to his knees. Amazingly, the homburg was still on his head, not so much as an inch askew. The suit and tie and white formal shirt were all still intact, but soaking wet.

Magnus's men were the last to emerge from the tunnel. Some in, some out of the rafts, dragging them up onto land, carrying their rifles above their heads. When they'd put their weapons safely down on the bank, they waded back into the pond to catch hold of the rafts still bobbing about and haul them up on the beach.

There was a general spirit of giddiness, as if this was some sort of day outing in the woods. A stranger coming upon us out there could never have guessed what we'd just come through or, for that matter, what still lay before us.

By then Porphyry was organizing, counting heads, making certain no one had been left behind in the tunnel. Sofi and Madam Lobkova attended the infants. Some of them were soaking wet from the ride and had to be changed into dry clothing. Now, with the absence of violent motion, many of them had begun to quiet down.

359

The danger was yet far from over. The forest here, though seemingly benign, like an Eden before the appearance of the serpent, could soon be crawling with Woodsmen.

The strong probability was that, by now, they'd suddenly broken down the doors and discovered what had happened. It would be no great mental feat to figure out where we'd gone. Superb trackers that they were, they knew every inch of the forest and would doubtless know the place where the stream under Fraze emptied out into the woods.

"We must leave at once." Porphyry spoke in urgent whispers. "They'll be out here in no time."

We tore at the ropes that had lashed our supplies to the mattresses, transferring them quickly to dry land. The babies had to be carried papoose-style on our backs and foodstuffs had to be bundled in our arms.

Amazingly, this was all accomplished with great dispatch, although the overwhelming impression I have of the moment is that of sheer chaos.

In short order we were all loaded up and ready to go. The plan was to head for the coast, roughly a seventy-mile trek west through deep, inhospitable woods. There would be rest periods, of course, but once under way, the going would be rough. Particularly if the Woodsmen were in pursuit.

And then, indeed, they were.

I was the first to spot one. He walked out of the woods as though out for a Sunday stroll. As casual as you please. The little feathered hat, the knickered trousers and puttees, the adz and hatchet clattering at his side, bumping along the earth, all gave the impression of a doll in some Tyrolean toy shop. If you didn't know the black hearts of these creatures and the bestiality of their ways, they'd seem almost endearing.

Then, suddenly, the face came into focus—the pointed chin and high cheeks, the pencil-line gashes where the eyes were meant to be, and the dark, leathery skin that made him look as though he were carved from wood.

Though he was perhaps thirty yards off, I could hear his high, startled cry when he spied us. He wheeled and bolted. Suddenly, the woods all about us exploded in a single, reverberating blast. The little figure stumbled, then went over in a heap. The man behind me who'd shot him darted forward. Reaching him, he stooped over him to make certain he was dead.

Colonel Porphyry waved his arms, signaling us to form a

360

tight line. The sense of relief we'd been feeling moments before was quickly over and then suddenly we were fleeing.

The single Woodsmen we'd seen was part of an advance party. We had no doubt there were others in the vicinity. Surely, they'd heard the shot and would rush to the place to investigate.

Knowing we were armed, the Woodsmen would be reluctant to approach. Still, they had no intention of letting us leave—especially not me—and would have no compunction about taking casualties in order to accomplish that end. They kept out of sight, but with typical perversity permitted us to hear them thrashing about in the brush, calling back and forth to one another, taunting us.

While we had started out in fairly good spirits, the mood of the march shortly turned grim. Clawing our way through the undergrowth, our loads grew heavier and the way through the forest more arduous.

There was no path as such. We had to make our own, hacking our way with sticks and rifle butts through a wall of nettles, burrs and pine needles that pierced clothing and lashed out at uncovered parts of the body. The mosquitoes and black flies were incessant and pitiless.

And, all the while, we could see the Woodsmen. You'd glimpse them shuttling noiselessly through the forest, not certain if you'd seen the white tail of a deer bobbing or a Woodsman making a pass around your flank. One thing of which there was no doubt, however: Each time they'd make a pass, they'd come a bit closer, growing bolder with each attempt.

The strain to keep up was great and the one who took the most punishment was Madam Lobkova. The sheer girth of her was a sure guarantee of failure. It was heartbreaking to see her stumble and go down, then flounder about, trying to heave herself back up on her feet.

Porphyry kept doubling back to help her. At one point she simply dropped to her knees with the slow, stately grace of a large ship sinking. We stopped and watched the Colonel kneel beside her. I could see his lips moving beneath the brim of his hat, encouraging her with kind words, all the while she shook her head despairingly from side to side. I knew she was asking to be left behind, but he had no intention of doing so. Instead, we waited while she rested and we watched as an ominous stillness descended over the encroaching forest.

Did Porphyry know where we were heading? Or where we were at that moment in relation to our destination? No one could say. He had no compass or maps. Clearly, he was relying entirely on instinct. No doubt his instinct for the vagaries of the criminal mind was keen, but there was no guarantee it was quite as keen at reading the numerous windings and shiftings of a treacherous forest.

The Woodsmen made their big move nearly an hour later. I'm not at all certain what finally triggered it. Possibly the fact that by then we might have been moving out of the area of forest thought to be their exclusive ground—a place in which they naturally felt most secure. No doubt they saw us beginning to flag, our ragged line straggling out farther and farther, our vigilance growing lax as we grew increasingly weary. Even Magnus's men, as dogged and indefatigable a pack of hounds as ever there was, were drooping badly.

When at last it came, it came swiftly, just like that time we'd tried to trek Jones's coffin up to the old Indian burial ground behind Fraze. Suddenly everything around us was in motion—a great din of shouts and gunfire, crashing sounds, boughs of saplings bending and whipping about, bodies hurtling through the underbrush. Big stone missiles, more than enough to crush a skull, catapulted from slings rained down from the sky.

Our guns blazed back, but at unseen targets. Unable to see the enemy, shortly we were in disarray and all seemed lost. One thing was in our favor, however—the attack occurred just as we broke out into a large clearing.

What greeted us there was the forlorn sight of a scruffy patch of open ground pitted with holes and strewn with rubble. A tough open place to make a last stand.

Porphyry had clearly hoped for some long-overdue miracle from the mainland. But entering that ragged little clearing I glimpsed his face. I have never looked into eyes so full of such a sense of crushing failure.

I'm certain he blamed himself for our predicament. He made no excuses. He never once complained about his colleagues on the mainland who'd bungled their part of the operation. Nor did he once seek to shift blame from himself to others.

As he saw it, he had promised too much and delivered too little. Even his mission at Fraze—to apprehend the murderer of the second wealthiest man in the world—seemed beside the point. What, after all, could he do now with the knowledge of

Madam Lobkova's guilt in Jones's death and all of our own indirect complicity in that regard. I think by then he knew we were more sinned against than sinning.

But if the good man was crushed, he was not defeated. Breaking out into the clearing, he startled us by beginning to bellow at the top of his lungs. Whether that was frustration or rage, I couldn't say. The sound that comes closest to it would be the cries of a stricken animal. If the dark night of the soul had a voice, it would sound something like that.

But there he was, in spite of everything, running toward the center of the clearing, flailing his arms and howling bansheelike at the top of his lungs. Attired as he was in his suit and tie, rumpled now beyond all redemption, the spectacle struck me as totally mystifying.

But it was also energizing. He'd meant us to follow him, and to that end he windmilled his arms above his head, unleashed an ungodly cry, and streaked for the center of the clearing like a man with his clothing on fire.

Utterly confused, we followed, mimicking his gyrations. The sudden uproar had precisely the effect he intended—that of momentarily stunning the Woodsmen. All motion lurched to a halt and in that instant I had a clear vision of the forest border encircling the clearing. It was studded with hundreds upon hundreds of tiny, dark forms. In their coarse brown waistcoats and knickers, they blended perfectly with the foliage, so that what I saw was not so much the individual figures as a single continuous shape. It was like a huge worm, coiling and uncoiling, threatening at any moment to close.

But still they didn't come. They stood poised at the edge of the forest, seemingly baffled by our shouts and lungings about. The howling of a dozen infants did little, I'm certain, to relieve their puzzlement.

There was no way of knowing how long the goat people would oblige us by delaying their charge. They could see we were exhausted and greatly outnumbered, and surely they suspected that our ammunition was close to giving out. But as long as our antics held them at bay, we were determined to keep up the melee.

Throughout the next several minutes the din rose steadily. We howled and thrashed about and raised an awful hullabaloo. Obviously, we couldn't keep it up much longer. It took energy to generate that much racket—energy we didn't have—and clearly the Woodsmen weren't going to be buffaloed indefinitely. They wanted, if they could, to take us alive. They'd come too far by then, and their King was too close for them to merely shrug and walk away. With a shudder I thought of Zann and what awaited me back at the encampment.

We stood bunched together in a tight little knot, our backs pressed against each other's, in this way keeping every inch of the clearing under surveillance. Once darkness fell, however, that tactic would be of little help.

Porphyry had instructed everyone carrying a weapon to hold fire to conserve ammunition. We were to shoot only in the event of a full-scale attack.

It was a standoff for some time. By then the sun was directly overhead, beating down unmercifully on the unshaded clearing. We'd grown weary of whooping and were flagging badly under full packs.

All the while we carried on in this fashion, we watched warily the big worm, coiling and uncoiling at the edge of the forest. You could almost gauge its restiveness by its unnatural silence.

Porphyry was just as restive. His keen gaze roamed nervously back and forth around the border. Periodically, he would glance up at the sky, which was cloudless and lacquered a bright hard blue. There was something in his frozen stance and the way his ears perked forward like a spooked stag. It was as though he were listening to that unearthly quiet and reading into it the most dire portents.

We stood grimly in our tight little knot, waiting for the rush which was now almost certain to come. Had the Woodsmen only guessed what pitiful little fight we had left in us, they would have launched their attack long ago.

Sofi, her back pressed hard up against mine, whispered to me over her shoulder: "Jonathan?"

"Yes."

"Are you there?"

"Of course I'm here. Where else would I be? What's up?"

"I'm sorry."

I gaped back at her over my shoulder. "For what?"

"For everything."

Uncertain what she meant, I was about to ask her, but just then a bloodcurdling shriek rent the warm, cricket-haunted air.

364

Suddenly, the worm encircling the clearing had begun to wriggle slowly forward.

"Rifles up," Porphyry's hoarse cry rose in response. "At the ready, Mr. Magnus. You will fire at the count of three."

The rifles went up accordingly but that ragged circle of elfin figures never wavered. They came on implacably, a wall of human sacrifice.

"One." Porphyry was just as implacable. "Two." His gaze fixed on the narrowing loop. "Three."

The first volley roared out. It was deafening. We watched figures topple and drop, only to be replaced by others quickly moving forward to fill the breach. Our guns, meanwhile, continued to blaze and Woodsmen continued to fall. The noise was horrific. Flocks of birds fled upwards out of the tree tops.

A large boulder came hurtling in. It made a dull, whirring sound as it pushed the air before it, then hit with a sickening thud cratering the mud around it. Someone—one of Magnus's men—sank to his knees beside me, tilted leftward, then fell, one cheek cushioned by the earth. The other, pointing to the sun, was raked with red. The eye facing the sun, the eye I could see, was open and staring straight ahead. Blood fountained from one ear.

Someone stopped to pick up the man's rifle, then slammed it into my hands. I started to fire it almost mechanically, not at anything in particular. Just straight ahead.

I felt its vibrations bang into my shoulder and the noise of it exploded in my head.

Then, it seemed to me that far away I heard another noise. It sounded like more guns, the same sort of dull concussive thud. But it was not exactly like the other guns. It was lower and had a growl. But unlike the guns which paused from time to time, this noise was steady and unbroken.

I looked at Porphyry and then at Cornie. They were gazing up at the sky. My eyes followed to where they pointed. At first I saw nothing. Still they pointed and began to shout. When I looked again, this time I saw a single black dot, a fleck of dust against the sky; then came another and behind them came two more.

Porphyry fired his gun straight overhead at the sky, trying to draw the attention of those black dots to our position. Several of the others fired their last rounds into the air as well. One of the dots—the one in the lead—veered, then canted left. It moved toward us, looming larger and larger. The others followed in a

365

wedge formation. You could hear the thud of big rotor blades pummeling the air as the helicopters dropped lower and began to circle the clearing. By then I could count at least nine or ten, but there may well have been more.

The Woodsmen had stopped their advance and were staring up at the sky. In the next moment, their ranks broke and they were streaming back into the forest in disarray. Their flight had started as an orderly retreat, but shortly, when one of the helicopters dipped down and hovered above us like a great dragonfly asleep on the wing, it became a full-scale route. From the cabin of the one hovering above us, a figure leaned out and pointed us back to the castle.

The other helicopters circling the clearing had by then started off in that direction as well. Great clouds of dust scudded up beneath them and small saplings lay over in the wake of their backdrafts.

We were on our feet, laughing and shouting, waving odds and ends of clothing up at them as we streamed through the woods back to the landing strip at Fraze.

Part 12

"Sleep is good, Death is better."

—Heinrich Heine

Epilogue

I live in a small fishing village now, on the mainland, up in the north. I live under an assumed name. So much notoriety attended our rescue and the inquiry that followed, so many versions of our story, mostly misinformed, appeared in the press and trashy periodicals, that Porphyry thought it best we change our identities, at least for the foreseeable future. To that end, the Colonel was more than happy to use his good offices to furnish us with birth certificates, passports and working papers— ordinary items to most folk; to us, things of wonder and mystery.

Thanks to the Colonel's enormous influence at the Ministry, a finding of death due to natural causes quickly put an end to the matter that, left to a jury, could well have become quite sticky for a number of us. In a sense, of course, it was true: Jones did die from having lived too long.

As the natural heirs to the fortune of the second richest man in the world, surprisingly little had been set aside in the way of financial provisions for our futures. Possibly because, in the scheme of things, my brothers and sisters and I had no future as that word is generally understood.

Having no special training, I work at a simple job. I am a

postal clerk. I have few friends. I come and go. Occasionally, I see my brothers and sisters though they live scattered all about, hundreds of miles from me. Despite the uniqueness of our shared situation, we still have little in common. The barriers between us are as great as ever, despite the fact that our upbringing in strict accordance with Jones's System was supposed to have eliminated all the known classic barriers between siblings.

Those first days on the mainland, when each of us wandered off to the place of his or her own choosing, we used to write to each other regularly, send gifts for holidays, speak on the phone. In our efforts to become "regular" folk—a real family, so to speak—each of us took a birth date and attempted to celebrate it together each year. The practice was doomed to die—not because we disliked seeing each other but because we simply had no idea what it meant to be together in the manner of a family.

Still, we keep up a show of this. We pretend to be interested in what's happening with one another. We keep in touch.

Letitia is married to a garage mechanic who, I suspect, abuses her. Sofi has joined a kind of sisterhood—not a formal religious order but a commune sort of thing, maintained by self-appointed lay nuns. She eats only fruits and vegetables and would love to have a child but is far too old for childbearing, though she looks no older than thirty. She's more beautiful than ever but it's a beauty that is far less flamboyant and far less assured than it used to be. I am told she goes about somewhat unkempt and takes every opportunity to repudiate whatever she was taught as a child.

Sometimes I'm tempted to see her, see if we can work things out. I don't mean marriage. Maybe simply some sort of accommodation by which we might stay together. But I don't know if she wants that. I don't know what she wants. Or what I want, for that matter.

Cassie lives with Madam Lobkova. This arrangement came about due to her insistence that Cassie (now sixty-two years of age) is still unable to look after herself. As things turned out, however, it's Cassie who looks after Madam Lobkova, swollen with dropsy and nearly blind from diabetes. She is, for all intents and purposes, permanently bedridden, and not expected to last another winter. But keep in mind, Madam Lobkova is by now well over a hundred years old herself.

Of all of us, Cornelius appears to have made the best adjustment to life on the mainland. For that, he has Porphyry to thank. Shortly after the Colonel established each of us here in a place of our own, he used his good offices with the local police to secure a position for Cornie. With Porphyry as his mentor, Cornie's rise was swift—so swift, in fact, that he now holds a rank of great responsibility. It didn't hurt matters that from early on Cornie himself demonstrated great reserves of physical courage as well as an uncanny acumen in matters of criminal investigation. No doubt Porphyry has taught him much and he is looked upon by his colleagues as the Colonel's protégé, his handpicked deputy, the one generally assumed to be the old man's successor.

Porphyry is somewhat more portly than when he first came to Fraze. Not quite bald yet, but what hair there still is has all gone cottony white. He combs it straight back so that furrows of pink scalp show between the intermittent strands. The eyes are still big and rheumy, as trusting as a spaniel puppy's. He has lost nothing of his great vitality and, though semiretired, won't hesitate to get out of a warm bed on a bitter winter's night to investigate some crime. He is especially drawn to those that are particularly heinous.

He seems to have taken a keen interest in the Jones clan. He writes letters to each of us and calls regularly. I'm sure he feels that, with the possible exception of Cornelius, we are an inept lot and would perish if left to our own devices. You might call it almost a paternal interest.

Once a year he comes to visit me. Invariably, he brings a bottle of good port, most of which he himself has consumed by the end of the evening, along with a good many of those pastel Egyptian cigarettes to which he remains devoted. Weeks after he's left, the draperies and upholstery still reek of latakia. The smell is not unpleasant and nowadays I find myself looking forward to those visits. We start a game of chess we invariably never finish. Neither of us has a penchant for winning, preferring instead to talk and drink.

We talk of many things, but mostly of Fraze, telling and retelling the parts each of us played in the story. With each retelling, the details change and our parts, particularly mine, grow more heroic—the way, I suppose, I would have preferred things to have turned out. Both he and I are aware of a tendency in me to edit out unpleasant truths about myself. But, with his unfailing tact, he has never challenged the veracity of any of my versions. He merely listens and nods and smiles.

On one of those visits, at the most crucial moment of our

chess match, he held his knight aloft in midair above the board and looked at me as though seeing me for the first time. "I find it so strange, Mr. Jonathan. I always thought of you as being like my son, had he lived. Only now does it occur to me that you're nearly thirty years older than me—old enough to be my father."

"And looking every day of it," I said after a moment, and we both roared merrily.

That's the way it is with the past. No matter how hard we try to hold on to it, it is constantly slithering off like an eel just as we're about to seize it. And with each successive attempt to recapture it, we manage to get further and further from the facts.

Last week I spent a few days with Ogden. Imagine, Ogden and me, together—taking afternoon tea in a sunlit parlor, strolling on the battery, exchanging slightly stiff pleasantries, sometimes laughing like old friends, trying to rediscover a camaraderie that had never really existed.

Ogden has aged dramatically in the last several years—far more conspicuously than I, although I can't imagine why. Off the regimen, we have all aged, but Ogden quicker and more so than the rest of us. He's gray and stooped, his memory is failing and he looks every inch his seventy-nine years. I'm certain he thinks the same of me. He's given up his passion for collecting insect specimens. The mere sight of a spider today or a small roach in his tiny pullman kitchen drives him into a towering fury. The human heart is indeed a mystery.

We talk of Jones, trying, in our bumbling way, to come to some firm idea of the man who was our father—who he was, what he did, what he finally meant to us. After the trial, when the events at Fraze came spectacularly to light, one half the world honored our father as a great humanitarian; the other half looked upon him as a self-aggrandizing, prurient old ogre who spawned flocks of offspring only to use them as human guinea pigs to further his harebrained scientific schemes. Huge, unseemly profit, they insist, was his sole motive. Surprising even myself, I now tend to take the more charitable view.

Despite all efforts by the World Federation of Churches and Philanthropies to prevent it, Uncle Toby and Parelli, along with batteries of lawyers and the huge consortium with which they entered into alliance have reaped astronomical profits from TRX5. The drug is counted a miracle, but to this day only the well-to-do can afford it; those who cannot must get on waiting lists to clinics and wait years before their number is called.

372

There is a huge black market that has sprung up around it. Unscrupulous operators have been putting up a completely bogus substance in vials with counterfeit labels and marketing it as the genuine article. Some, I'm told, have taken to stealing and killing for it. Already, several bitter patent suits are under way and a host of pharmaceutical giants have each come forward to proclaim that they are the true discoverers of dismutase.

But there are others who insist it's a hoax and scorn it. And, of course, there are the poor who cannot hope in this lifetime to know the benefits of TRX5. They must be content to live out their threescore and ten, then pass on, unnoticed.

Sometimes I, too, think it's all a hoax. They say Jones is not dead. There are constant reports of sightings in the newspapers; he's been seen here or there. Geneva, Delhi, Rome, but mostly in some remote outpost like Gabon or some such godforsaken place. Chasing down plague or famine. Ministering to the destitute. He's perfectly capable of that. Fooling them all. It's just the sort of thing he would delight in. Perhaps he is alive. Still on the regimen. Though I'm certain I saw his remains on a litter in the Woodsmen's village. I don't know what I believe anymore.

There's no end of Jones. You can't get shut of him, as much as you try. Just when you think you've heard the end of him, up he pops, someplace else. He won't let you be.

Uncle Toby and Parelli are seen much on the Continent. They live together, making lavish displays of their wealth. There are a half dozen residences around the world, one more sumptuous than the next. There are fleets of automobiles and princely entertainments. People who've had occasion to spend time in their company maintain that it's not a pleasant experience. For one thing, they loathe each other and make no effort to conceal the fact. They bicker incessantly, yet they must stick together in a kind of mutual defense treaty against the industry giants who are franchised to manufacture and distribute TRX5 but own no share in the patent. That fact, and that fact only, is what keeps the wolves at bay—fear that someday their franchise might not be renewed. Meanwhile, they must pay extortionate sums to the Humanus Institute and to their own lawyers for the privilege of playing in the longevity game.

Who does own the patent for dismutase? It's a fairly murky matter. I would have thought that Uncle Toby, as Jones's next of kin, had first claim. Not so, says Porphyry, who has reason to

373

know such things. The Colonel has sources in high places who maintain that Signor Parelli has recently wrested control of Uncle Toby's equity in the Institute and is in a life-and-death struggle with Dr. Fabian for ultimate control. Never a businessman or a shrewd contender, Toby tried at first to resist these powerful forces but, in the end, managed to get crushed between them. According to the Colonel, he's lapsed into a state of inanition. He still goes into his office every day and shuffles papers, but he's permitted to do little of any note. Some say he's begun to show all the classic signs of senescence. Why shouldn't he? He can be no less than 155, according to my calculations, though he looks perhaps one third of that.

For the most part, Uncle Toby's life has become an endless pursuit of pleasure. He squanders fortunes on frivolous things. He surrounds himself with lovers—pretty pets, both young girls and boys. Increasingly, he leaves the management of his affairs to Parelli and Dr. Fabian. Porphyry's sources report they are stealing him blind.

It's sad to think how far afield all this has gone since Jones first envisioned the idea of life extension as a practical reality and a boon to all mankind.

In the end, Ogden and I have concluded that we simply don't know who Jones was, and probably never will. Right up to his final days, our father preferred to remain a mystery—not only to the world, but especially to his children.

Jones, you must remember, did not create his children to be like everyone else. I think that my brothers and sisters are well aware that, when compared with the norm, we're odd. But we also know that we are the beginning of something else. Not necessarily something better, but something else. A new rung on the ladder. And that in itself implies hope that man may not yet have reached the evolutionary end of the road.

Whatever else one may choose to think, Jones has, at least, given us an opportunity to go further; to make the leap, regardless of the risk. It is commonplace now to hear him referred to as a dreamer. But that is not to suggest that he was such a fool as to believe he could stop time. He merely wished to slow things down a bit—to reduce the rate of mitotic division, to lessen the turmoil of blood vessels as they contract and expand, to slow the heartbeat as it ticks us on our way to oblivion. There's surely no mystery to this. Nothing sinister. All of it is mere mechanics. To

374

that simple end he succeeded. What long-range benefits have accrued to mankind, if any, remain to be seen.

There must be thousands of Jones offspring now, scattered about the globe—Jones progeny multiplied over and over again, many commingled with that brutal strain of people known as the Woodsmen. At the time of the inquiry, many of our brothers and sisters were released from their pens in the encampment and set free. Many well-intentioned people tried to adopt them, set up homes, integrate them into communities, mostly with sad, often tragic consequences.

I often dream of Fraze. I dream of going back there to see it just once again. Recently, a large magazine paid thousands of dollars to send a photographer there to take pictures. Sofi called me all the way from Manitoba to tell me about it. She'd seen the pictures. She said she couldn't recognize it. It looked to her like the remains of a huge anthill that had been plowed under. Deserted, mostly ruined, its outer walls were broken away so that you could see millions of tiny cells inside. They were crumbling and rubble-strewn and showed no sign of human habitation.

I told her I'd get the magazine at once and have a look for myself. But I never did. I simply didn't have the heart for it. Still, I'd go back myself to see it if it weren't for the Woodsmen. They're still there, though somewhat more closely watched by the government, since all the nasty disclosures at the time of the trial. And I'm certain they hold no fond wishes for their ex-King.

I wonder sometimes about Zann. I can't help it. Given even that brief time we were together. I wonder if there's a child. And if there is, what does it look like—one of them or one of us? Or, possibly, like one of those pitiful half-creatures in the compound—an unsatisfactory, misbegotten combination of both.

The child would be about five years of age now. The age of curiosity in children. I wonder if he or she ever asks Zann about their father—where he is and why he never comes. I wonder if, whatever the child is, it feels my absence and frets about it. I hope not. It isn't worth the toss.

Jones abhorred mediocrity. For my own child, I would be happy with mere normalcy. I have now seen myself in the mirror too often. Sofi was right. Just a bland, unremarkable face. I go unnoticed in a crowd and that's not bad.

Without the dismutase and hormone therapy, I'm beginning to age. The dimming sight, the vague aches, the occasional appearance of blood in the stool. The doctor laughs and pats me

375

on the back and assures me it's all perfectly normal at my time of life. None of that troubles me. I don't seem to mind the process at all. It feels comfortable and right. I look forward to long naps in the afternoon and slipping into bed shortly after dark. With drapes drawn against the night and weary from care, I await the hooded stranger. I look forward to his arrival. He is the dear old friend who comes to pluck us each from the hugger-mugger of the day and, with a few grains of sand, send us off to blissful sleep.

ACO-7742

11/23/93